MW01264173

POINTS

POINTS

A Novel by

David Barton

This book is a work of fiction. The names of persons and institutions or entities depicted in this book have been created by the author without reference to any actual person, institution or entity. Any resemblance between persons, institutions or entities depicted in this book and actual persons, institutions or entities is coincidental.

© 2005 by David Barton. All rights reserved.

No part of this book may be reproduced, stored in a retrieval system, or transmitted by any means, electronic, mechanical, photocopying, recording, or otherwise, without written permission from the author.

First published by AuthorHouse 05/23/05

ISBN: 1-4184-4077-9 (sc)

Library of Congress Control Number: 2003195194

This book is printed on acid free paper.

Printed in the United States of America
Bloomington, IN

Chapters 38, 39, and 40 contain the names of persons who have contributed to the scientific literature, and certain theories, observations and themes derived from these persons' scientific writings are woven into the fictional story. These authors are credited in the Author's Note of this book.

For my wife, children, and grandchildren — in the spirit of *Tikkun Olam*, the mandate that we strive to restore and heal the earth.

Do not allow thirst for profit, ambition for renown and admiration, to interfere with my profession, for these are the enemies of truth and of love for mankind and they can lead astray in the great task of attending to the welfare of Thy creatures.

— Physician's Prayer, attributed to Moses Maimonides, 12th century physician, rabbi, philosopher

ACKNOWLEDGEMENTS

I am indebted to the many people who have helped to shape the novel *POINTS.* To those persons who assisted me in trying to grasp the art and craft of fiction writing, I offer my sincere thanks. To the many friends who read the early versions of the manuscript and offered suggestions on form and story line, I am deeply grateful. I am also deeply indebted to those colleagues who assisted me with medical details. I especially wish to thank John Cummings who so artfully and skillfully produced the cover for the book.

My family and friends have lived with the writing and preparation of this manuscript for many years. I am very grateful for their devotion, support, and encouragement. I also wish to thank all of my patients who have contributed so much to my understanding of life's joys and sorrows. It is they who provide the impetus for me to strive to preserve the concept of attending to the 'other' in the context of a healing process.

To my wife, Lynn, who has tolerated and, at times, constructively encouraged or discouraged my intense investment in a multitude of projects through the years and who has offered so many helpful comments and suggestions about this manuscript along with her expert editorial skills, I give my enduring love and greatest appreciation.

Chapter 1

An unusually mild spring hurried the lilac shrubs to bloom abundantly on the grounds of the teaching hospital of Devan University Medical Center in Middleside, Pennsylvania, while inside the prestigious academic institution, seventeen patients with the same symptoms lay dying. All seventeen medical histories matched nearly perfectly. First, a single sore had erupted on each patient's skin, and then with uncanny speed, hundreds more had spread across the victim's body. Within hours after the first pustule's appearance, dozens of puffed blisters were bursting open, spilling their contents. The fragrance of the lilacs breezed through the air outside, while the future of medicine stood, like a cresting wave, on the edge of chaos.

Breaking the frenzied pace of their rounds, Dr. Tom Sullivan, Professor of Medicine, and Bob Kaplan, Chief Resident in Internal Medicine, stopped short just inside a hospital room door. In the bed, a man deliriously thrashed about. Between his restless bursts of movement, the man stared vacantly at the doctors, reached out toward them, and moaned garbled words. He shivered and shook the bed, causing the IV fluid container hanging on the rack above him to sway back and forth like the pendulum of a clock.

Tom studied the fluid seeping from the pustules covering the man's body as it trickled across his skin and dripped down on the sheets. Unlike any drainage Tom had ever seen, the oozing fluid glowed with a near phosphorescent purplish color.

Tom turned a pained face to Kaplan. "Fluids, antibiotics, pressors, antipyretics. We're doing everything I know to do."

Kaplan nodded silently in agreement.

In the hallway, the two physicians stripped off their masks, gloves and gowns and tossed them into a red container labeled, "DANGER — BIOLOGICAL WASTE." Then, at the sink, first one, then the other carefully scrubbed his hands with an amber antiseptic fluid.

"This isn't a textbook illness," the bewildered Kaplan commented, scrubbing carefully along his fingernails.

"Yes, the only certainty is that every one of these people is near death," Tom said to Kaplan. He predicted the probable futility of their medical interventions to himself, but he stopped short of speaking his thoughts out loud. His intuition had already built the case. He had sensed it immediately after seeing only a few of the patients. This illness likely would not be stopped with the usual efforts. And if usual efforts fail and the experienced physician has never encountered the disease before, he knew some kind of corner had likely been turned and the practice of medicine might never be the same again. Spare Kaplan that, he mused. A hopeful, inexperienced, young doctor might charge in uncharted directions and still make a difference.

Kaplan's brow furrowed. A half foot shorter than the tall, reddish-brown haired Sullivan, he stood gathering his thoughts, looking up at his mentor. Kaplan's black curly hair glistened with sweat. Beneath his armpits, perspiration soaked his green scrubs.

"Whatever the disease is," Tom said, "we need strict isolation procedures. See if Peter Hansen can get up here right away. Infection Control should be involved immediately."

Kaplan leaned across the counter at the nursing station and spoke. "Page Dr. Peter Hansen." His voice was shaky, but forceful. "Page Dr. Peter Hansen and page him stat."

Tom stared down the hallway. Up and down the halls, the nurses were fastening warning notices on the patients' doors. "BLOOD AND BODY FLUID CONTACT PRECAUTIONS — CONTA-GIOUS DISEASE," the red lettered signs said.

"Dr. Hansen is on his way," the nurse told them after Hansen had answered his page. "Said to tell you that he has an advisory bulletin from the Atlanta Infectious Disease Center in hand."

"Good, we can use all the help we can get," Tom said.

Seconds later, the telephone at the nursing station buzzed. A nurse picked up the phone, listened a moment, then held her hand over the receiver. "Admitting wants you to know Dr. Sullivan: six more patients in the emergency department, same history, same lesions," she said. "If this keeps up, we'll run out of beds."

"We'll put them somewhere," Tom said.

Soon, Peter Hansen stepped out of the elevator on the ward. Thank God for the microbe tracker, Tom thought when he saw him. Maybe he'll shed some light on this wild disease.

Three weeks before, Peter Hansen had arrived from the Centers for Disease Control in Atlanta to join the Devan Medical Center faculty as Chief of Infection Control. Skilled at picking up the trails and movements of contagious illnesses, he was known internationally as the Sherlock Holmes of infectious disease. Most recently, the short, stocky, African-American, silver wire-rimmed glasses wearing, CDC physician had gained his reputation for his brilliant studies of AIDS. His findings on the HIV virus alpha-2 protein antigens were pivotal in moving science a step closer to developing an effective vaccine to halt the spread of the disease.

"In eight hours, we've admitted seventeen patients with the same history and symptoms." Kaplan said, restating what Peter Hansen already knew too well. "And there are more on the way. They're all dying, sky high temperatures, irreversible septic shock…"

"We need time to get our bearings," Hansen said quietly.

Kaplan's speech was pressured. "The lesions; they have a peculiar, purplish glow," he said. "That has to mean something, doesn't it?"

"Yeah, it's weird stuff. I've just come from microbiology," Hansen said. "The pustules are filled with bacteria; the smears show cocci — bizarre cocci with unusually thick purplish cell membranes. They're unlike anything I've ever seen. Reproductive activity level is off the charts. Roaring intracellular metabolism makes them glow like fireflies. It's virulent Strep, but so far the exact type hasn't been identified." He held out the CDC report. "This came in minutes ago."

Tom took it from his hand and began to read. Hansen stood wide-eyed, shaking his head and stroking the fuzz of beard that covered his chin.

"Bacteria that moves like an out-of-control forest fire. Scary stuff," Tom said moments later, still reading on.

A string of red "URGENTS" ran across the top of the bulletin. The text followed:

> The Center for Infectious Disease is receiving reports from cities all over the country of occurrences of a febrile illness associated with pustular skin lesions. The majority of the patients are suffering from a febrile delirium. While it is too early to accurately assess the situation, the infectious process is rapidly leading to septicemia. A number of deaths have already been reported. Tallies received from some major cities are as follows:

> Seattle: 98 cases reported
> Chicago: 697 cases reported
> Boston: 423 cases reported
> New York: 727 cases reported…

The list ran on. Six hours of reporting and the total number of cases counted in the larger cities across the country was already in the thousands. Scattered occurrences were also being reported in the rural areas.

> Current diagnostic recommendations include blood for viral titres, blood cultures, and cell membrane analysis. Treatment supportive. Antibiotics, at discretion of treating facility. Reversibility has not yet been observed. USE ALL PRECAUTIONS: THE DISEASE IS CONSIDERED TO BE HIGHLY CONTAGIOUS.

Peter Hansen's eyes turned toward the floor. "This is a fierce one," he said. "The hospital will be packed in no time."

As Peter predicted, by the next morning the hospital rooms were filled to capacity and hallways held the overflow. In the crowded corridors, cots, mattresses, and pallets of sheets and pillows became

4

makeshift sickbeds. Physicians and other caregivers stepped through narrow, patient-lined paths.

Tom, Bob, and Peter began their rounds.

"Let's get going," Nancy Scott, the nurse practitioner said. She bounced through the narrow passages between patients reviewing charts and cataloging patients' needs. "This woman needs a blood culture," she said and flipped the chart of the newly-admitted patient back into the rack.

She checked her doubled gloves, stepped back, took a readied syringe from a nurse's hand, and then moved toward the patient. Kaplan tightened the tourniquet and held the patient's arm straight while Nancy poised the needle above the vein.

In the silent moment that followed, Kaplan blurted out a warning. "Careful, that blood is teaming with deadly killers. For God's sake, don't stick yourself. You could be infected in a split second."

Nancy flinched. She glared at Kaplan.

"Come on, Bob!" Tom snapped. "She already knows she's dealing with a deadly disease."

"Sorry," Bob said, standing back.

Nancy's hand trembled as she positioned the needle a second time over the bluish, round channel beneath the skin of the patient's elbow. "Steady now," she said. A smooth thrust and the needle's end was in the vein. The patient jerked reflexively.

Nancy loosened the tourniquet, withdrew the needle, and injected the blood into a culture tube. When the tube was filled with dark red blood, she handed it to the nurse. "The lab has checked all of the generations of antibiotics and they aren't touching these microbes," Kaplan said. "The bug is using a protective enzyme system to neutralize every drug we try."

Nancy Scott stepped off to the side, spoke briefly with a nurse, then returned to the group. "Nine more patients were admitted through the emergency room in the last hour," she told them.

"Death is crowding in on us," Tom observed.

"Yes, unquestionably, these are vicious little mobs of microbes," Hansen said. "And they may be swift and clever, but if we keep after them, we'll track down the little bastards and kill them off. They can't elude us forever."

Tom realized that the determined microbe sleuth spoke as if he were pursuing a band of murderers. Peter's confidence left little room for doubt. Hansen was convinced. Medicine would win out in the end.

Tom glanced down the crowded hallway. Unbelievable, he thought as he viewed the frenzied activity. The scene was surreal and immense, like a trite epidemic novel had come to life.

Chapter 2

Nancy Scott, twenty-nine, known in the hospital as "Scottie," had deep-set brown eyes and a short, boyish hair cut. Lean to the point of being hollow-cheeked, she had an attractive face and a playful sense of humor. She had become Tom's helper six years earlier, when she graduated from Devan as a nurse practitioner. He affectionately called her "The Wisp."

After rounds, Nancy walked up to Tom with a forced smile on her face and held out her arm for Tom to see.

"Should I be worried about this, Dr. Sullivan?" she asked in a child-like voice.

Tom glanced down quickly. On the top of Nancy's forearm, a half-inch, puffed, red spot, its center swollen with a drop of yellowish, blood tinged fluid, glared up at him.

He looked straight into her eyes. She already knew the answer.

"Have you been taking the prophylactic antibiotics?"

"Yes. Haven't missed a dose."

"Me too Nancy, but unfortunately that's no guarantee. There's no way to take care of these patients and not be exposed. We have to hope there's some kind of protection through cross immunity."

"I know," she said with a sigh.

"But we don't want to take any chances with this. Are you feeling alright?" He reached into his pocket, took out a pair of latex gloves, and put them on.

The look in Nancy's eyes grew worried. She glanced downward. "I'm no fool. I know it's not good, is it?"

"I'm too close to be objective about this disease. I want someone else's opinion. Let's go," he said. He took her by the arm and coaxed her along.

Minutes later, they were in Peter Hansen's office.

"Peter, take a look at this," Tom said. He pointed to Nancy's outstretched arm.

Hansen quickly put on gloves and moved her over to the window to catch the light. He studied the lesion, then looked up at Tom. His brow furrowed. "Admit her. Start IV antibiotics immediately," he said.

"I agree," Tom said, straining to maintain a more clinical tone in his voice.

Nancy Scott's face was becoming more flushed by the minute. She was starting to sweat. She was staggering and unsteady. Tom took her arm to support her.

"I'll be all right. Please don't worry," she said.

Fifteen minutes later she was in a room with intravenous antibiotics flowing into her vein. Tom stood at the bedside.

"We're going to take good care of you. You've been taking the oral antibiotics regularly and now we're giving you larger doses, intravenous push. This early, I think we have a good chance of heading the disease off at the pass."

"You know, I had a feeling my number was up."

"Come off it. You're going to be fine."

"Forget it, Dr. Sullivan. You're not very good at hiding your feelings. You're as worried as I am. I can read you like a book."

"Eat your food," he said, pointing to the untouched tray in front of her.

"I can't eat this hospital food. I need something more edible. Have to watch my weight you know." She smiled and Tom smiled back.

"Anything you want. The Wisp will have whatever she wants to eat. What will it be?"

"Cottage cheese and some fruit salad. Anything low cal."

Tom remembered when two years ago, he had walked in on her in a treatment room, her finger crammed down her throat to make herself vomit. Red faced, watery eyed, she had looked up at him pleadingly as if to ask him to guard the secret of her weight control.

"You need more sustenance than that. You're thin enough," Tom asserted.

"Cottage cheese and fruit salad! You said whatever I want. This could be my last supper."

He nodded his head. He left the hospital and soon returned with the food. Then he sat with her while she picked at it.

They talked lightly of the years of working together — patient situations, awkward moments, happier times, medical successes and medical failures.

"Remember Wallace Gill?" Tom asked.

"Old Wally and his roving hands. Who could forget," Nancy said.

"A ninety-plus-year-old man in love with his twenty-four-year-old nurse. He became a real bear when you said you wouldn't marry him."

Tom broke into uncontrollable laughter. Nancy laughed too, but when the laughter stopped there were tears in both of their eyes.

For a few, still moments, they were quiet, then she questioned him. "Were you really an Olympic athlete? We've never talked about it."

"Yep. Track scholarship at Devan College. Even have an old knee injury from a bad high jump."

"How macho can you get?"

"I was pretty macho," he said.

"So how did a good looking, competitive, tall guy with blue eyes, the wavy hair, and those chiseled features keep from being a surgeon?"

"Just luck, I guess," Tom said.

She smiled as she shivered and pulled her covers up to her chin.

Tom stayed with her for two hours.

"She seems to be feeling much better," the nurse told Tom when he stopped by Nancy's room the next morning before he made his rounds. He dropped in midday, and then returned to visit with her before he left for the evening. The nurses had placed a large vase of lilac cuttings from the medical center grounds in her room. Tom smelled the fragrance as soon as he entered.

"Pretty flowers," he said.

"Yeah, I love the lilacs. The smell is heavenly. I think it makes me feel better."

"Thank God we went ahead and got that mix of antibiotics in you early. Looks like it's working. You're much better."

"I can't get used to you hiding behind that isolation mask," she said. "It doesn't bother me when I have one on too, but when you're the only one wearing it, you seem so distant from me."

"I don't like it either. In fact, I don't like any of this."

"I'll be glad when I'm able to be on rounds with you again."

"Yes, we miss you." He took her hand with his gloved hand and squeezed it. "I'll be standing by, if you need anything. I'll call the floor in a couple of hours to check on you."

He called again from home to inquire about her later that evening.

"She's better," the night nurse said. "The sweating stopped, and her fever's down."

"Great," Tom said. "Call me if you need me."

He was wide-eyed at midnight, but must have fallen asleep soon after.

The phone on Tom's bedside table rang at 2:30 in the morning. He answered it on the first ring. It was Bob Kaplan.

"Dr. Sullivan?"

"What is it Bob?"

"It's Scottie."

"Yes, what's going on?"

"The news is not good, Dr. Sullivan. Scottie's septic. Her temperature has shot up to 106. She's shocky. Had two seizures. I think you'd better get on over here stat," he said.

"But she was better earlier this evening," Tom said lamely.

"Her condition worsened fast. Her fever spiked to 106, and she started convulsing. It took us a while to stop her. I called her family. They're on the way to the hospital. I believe she's going to die."

The truth hit Tom like lightning. No more denial. It was the typical course of the disease. Tom knew the trajectory well: with massive IV antibiotics early, patients sometimes looked as if they were improving, hopes were raised, and then the downhill plunge. But with Scottie he was sure it would be different. Illusive damned disease.

"I'm on my way. Is she talking to you?"

"No, she's in a delirium, completely disoriented, doesn't recognize me."

"I'm on my way."

Thirty minutes later, Tom arrived on the ward. Kaplan met him at the elevator.

"I'm sorry, I know how much you thought of her," Kaplan said, glancing downward.

Tom walked into her room as the nurses were removing the IV lines from her limp arm. Her motionless body was covered with the weeping sores. He rushed toward the bed. Standing at the bedside, his tall shadow crossed her body.

He thought he saw faint movements of her chest, but he knew that was impossible. Scottie was still and cold. The odor of disinfectant and the purulent smell from the sores on her body mixed with the sweet scent of the lilacs. Tom recognized the smell of death and realized he had not said goodbye.

"Why you, Scottie?" he asked, and shook his head.

Kaplan watched the scene from the doorway as the nurse gently pulled the sheet over Scottie's head.

Chapter 3

Late in the evening, after Nancy Scott's funeral, Tom lay quietly next to his wife.

"You did what you could," Katie said.

"It wasn't good enough. Scottie's dead."

"You did everything you could. No one knows what to do about this disease. It's out of control."

Katie Sullivan's reassurance was more than a wife's platitude. Herself a pediatrician, she struggled with the same frustrations as her husband. Children, like adults, were dying in huge numbers.

"I'll miss her," Tom said.

Katie wiped her eyes with a tissue. "It's okay to miss her. I'll miss her too. She was like a family member.

"What a great sense of humor she had," Tom said.

"Yeah, I loved it. Scottie was a real character."

For a few moments Tom was silent. Then he spoke. "I felt so helpless."

"You did what you could, but I know your standards. You should always be able to right all wrongs, jump every bar, do the impossible. Right?"

"You're a fine one to talk," he said as he pulled her closer.

Katie smiled. "It's good to have things in common," she said.

He gathered her into his arms, looked into her still misty green eyes, and stroked her long brown hair.

"This may not sound very courageous, but I've had it with trying to be heroic. The fact is I'm terrified of this disease," Tom said. I'm afraid of what could happen to us."

"That's completely understandable, Tom. This infection is very deadly."

"No, this fear feels different," he said. "There's no putting up any front. I can't fake it by acting brave. My denial is gone. This epidemic is catastrophic. In the three weeks it's been around, hundreds of thousands of people have already died. Thousands of health care workers are already gone. Nurses, physicians, techs. The health care system is collapsing. Everyone is totally depleted. The expense of taking care of these patients is overwhelming.

"I'm frightened for all of us, and I'm terrified about what could happen to medicine. This is far too much death to manage, and the truth is, underneath the appearance of my sure-handed doctoring, I'm as afraid of death as the next person."

"None of us is free of that fear," Katie observed.

"You know a lot, but you don't know everything about me. Once when I was an intern, a nurse called me to see a dying, breathless patient. The family asked for sedation for him, and I ordered it. When the nurse removed the needle from his arm, he took a deep breath and died. I wanted him to be more comfortable, but then I thought…maybe the sedation brought about his death. I've never forgotten that. It's absurd, but I had a sense of complicity in his death. Whatever the case, death had defeated me and I had a hell of a time pronouncing him dead. I kept going back to check, to be sure he wasn't breathing. Maybe he was still alive. I couldn't accept what had happened. Even now, it's never easy for me to pronounce someone dead. It's not good, a physician that can't accept death without becoming obsessive."

"It may be best for us not to be too accepting."

"Perhaps, but sometimes it feels like I'm walking on a tight rope without a net. The fear of death is only thinly layered over. Scottie's death has made me more aware and now I've lost some kind of balance. I'm doubting myself. Scottie's death was too close. Any one of us could be next. Katie, I hate it that Scottie died."

She pulled him next to her and held him tightly. "So much has happened in these three weeks," she said. "Our lives have been turned upside down by the epidemic and you're being too hard on yourself. We're all afraid of dying. That's why physicians spend so much time trying to struggle with death down to the wire. It's ourselves we're trying to save. Sometimes that's constructive, sometimes it's not."

"There has to be more to my being a doctor than that," Tom said.

"There is, and no one knows that better than you. And anyway, I love you, afraid of death or not."

"Thank God for that."

Once again, Katie's calm strength had reassured him.

Tom remembered when they first met. He was a resident in internal medicine and she, a fourth year medical student on her clinical rotation. When he walked by the nursing station after midnight, he found her examining a chart.

"This order is ridiculous. It's incorrect," she said, pointing to one of the senior staff physician's orders.

"I'll take care of it," the resident from New York told the woman raised in a small rural town in Oklahoma. "You know Dr. Browning's reputation. He gets irate and chews you out if you call him in the middle of the night. Incorrect order or not, let me take the heat."

"Thank you, but I believe I can take care of this myself, Dr. Sullivan. Dr. Browning needs to know that he too can make a mistake."

Tom's eyes widened when the attractive medical student dialed Browning's home number without a second thought.

"Dr. Browning, I hate to awaken you in the middle of the night, but your orders on Mr. Blake are incorrect," she said confidently to the half awake doctor. "He has already been on this antihypertensive med without adequate response."

"Thank you, Doctor Browning. I'll change that order right away," she said calmly.

"You're welcome, sir," she said. He had thanked her for her call.

She replaced the receiver and turned to look at Tom.

He rolled his eyes and sighed. "Brave woman," he said.

"Thank you, Dr. Sullivan," she said to him softly.

That night Tom had found Katie's midwestern self-confidence. Soon he came to know her soft, caring ways, and ten months later they were married.

Now, years later, there was another challenge — a killer epidemic.

Tom gave Katie an adoring look, then pulled her close to him again, and kissed her tenderly.

"When this is over, I want to start having babies. I want lots of them," she said.

"As many as you want," he responded.

"I love you; I really do," she said. "Sometimes, you're too concerned about being super strong, but you're a very caring human being and a very fine physician."

"Don't ever leave me," he said.

"Never," she replied, and they fell asleep in each other's arms.

Chapter 4

At 6:30 a.m., six weeks after the epidemic began, Tom pulled into the staff garage at Devan Hospital. Each day when he arrived, he found more empty parking places.

At least twenty of his Devan physician colleagues had died in the epidemic. Four days before, his medical school roommate, the vascular surgeon Gordon Grayson had developed the red sores on his arms and face. By evening they were all over his body. Twenty-four hours later the surgeon had died. Yesterday, Katie's pediatrician friend, Lil Williams took sick. Today he noted that her space was empty and added her to the list.

The death count across the country was already in the millions. Hundreds of thousands more were ill. Hospitals filled beyond capacity and as Tom had suspected all medical efforts had proved futile to stop the disease.

He pulled into the place marked, Tom Sullivan, M.D., Chief, Infectious Disease Section. Briefcase in hand, he walked toward the hospital. In front of the entrance to the hospital, the walkway Tom traveled split to ring a grassy circle. In the circle's center, on a chiseled granite base, surrounded by blooming lilac shrubs, stood a twelve feet tall bronze statue of the medical school's founder, Paul Devan. As if to challenge those in medicine who came after him, Devan's outstretched right arm pointed toward the heavens.

An inscription on a polished brass plaque bolted to the statue's granite base said:

PAUL DEVAN, M.D.
PHYSICIAN AND HEALER
1811 — 1888
INSPIRED BY THE DEVASTATING
DIPHTHERIA EPIDEMIC OF 1850,
THIS ESTEEMED PHYSICIAN
FOUNDED DEVAN MEDICAL SCHOOL.

Tom stopped briefly and pondered the inscription. He felt numbed by his own immersion in death. He asked himself how anyone could be inspired by the horrors of an epidemic? He gazed upward at the statue's Gallic countenance. Today, he was certain that the bronze likeness of Devan wore an unsettled look of gloom.

When Tom reached his office, the computer terminal on his desk was beeping loudly. On the monitor screen an urgent e-mail icon flashed. He entered his password, clicked on the bright red urgent icon, and viewed the message: "VICE CHANCELLOR CUNNINGHAM IS WAITING FOR YOU IN HIS OFFICE. WHEN YOU ARRIVE, REPORT IMMEDIATELY."

Minutes later, Tom entered the plush office of Raymond Cunningham, M.D., Devan's Vice Chancellor for Health Services. There, he found Devan's chief administrative physician sitting calmly behind his desk, his hands folded in front of him.

On the wall behind him, in the cluster of framed documents and pictures, hung a framed medical degree from Devan University School of Medicine. Alongside the diploma hung still another parchment, a Masters in Business Administration from a prestigious northeastern university.

Cunningham wore a full-body isolation outfit topped with a clear plastic globe helmet. Extending to his mid forearms, long latex gloves covered the mesh ends of his sleeves, effectively sealing him off from the air around him. He resembled a space traveler. Tom had thought that only the personnel who worked directly with the epidemic's dead and those who worked in the waste disposal dumps wore this much protective gear, but he gathered that Cunningham was determined to separate himself from the deadly disease microbes in the most complete way possible.

The air pump feeding filtered, germ-free air to the plastic bubble that covered his head made an intermittent hissing noise. As the administrator breathed, a film of cloudy condensation coated the plastic bubble near his mouth and nose.

Tom found the scene bizarre and surreal, not unlike the madness that characterized the epidemic itself. Then suddenly he took note of the man inside the plastic bubble. The man's full head of prematurely gray hair was as usual neatly combed and in place. His chin was slightly turned up in an air of superiority and he wore a frozen faint hint of a smile on his lips. Even inside the plastic bubble, he seemed smug and too sure of himself.

"Sit down, sit down," he told Tom. "I would shake your hand, but that would be a bit difficult under these circumstances."

Tom nodded in agreement and took a seat.

The Vice Chancellor leaned forward. "Let's skip the small talk. This is far too desperate a situation. Take a look at this," Cunningham said, handing Tom a small medicine vial filled with a fluid. "A special courier delivered this to me early this morning. I think this may be the answer."

Sullivan read the medicine bottle's label:

CELESTACARE HEALTH ENTERPRISES —
PHARMACEUTICAL DIVISION PRODUCT NUMBER 6027 —
LOT NUMBER 78
FOR EXPERIMENTAL USE ONLY

Tom held the vial up to the light coming in through the window. The fluid was clear and had a faint violet tint.

"You're holding the cure for the epidemic in your hands," Cunningham said. His voice was muffled by the protective dome covering his face.

Tom gave him a disbelieving look. "Impossible. Hundreds of drugs have already been tested. The bacteria resist every known antibiotic. A vaccine is at least six months away."

"Sullivan, you're like so many other doctors. You underestimate what capitalism and corporate driven research and development can do for science. Middleside's own corporate health care giant, CelestaCare Heath Enterprises, immediately placed its entire research division behind the efforts to develop an effective drug for this treatment resistant illness. And they came through. CelestaCare's top computer scientist, Laura Clark, designed this drug using her own molecular synthesis software. It's the first of a new class of drugs with a built-in DNA altering, enzyme-destroying tracking mechanism. The chemical uses what Dr. Clark calls a 'reverberating helix' to rearrange its own molecular structure and outsmart the bacteria's protective systems. The fact is, in their lab's two weeks of animal studies, the medicine was a complete success. I have the results here, in black and white," he said and tapped on the large notebook resting on his desk. "Admittedly, they're only animal studies, but CelestaCare has already secured government approval."

"Who is this Laura Clark?" Tom asked, trying to place the name. "I don't know her."

"She's a genius, an absolute genius. You name a direction in medical research and she's made a contribution."

Oddly enough, Tom found himself feeling competitive with Laura Clark. The top minds in the academic centers, including those in his own labs, had been unsuccessful in finding anything near a cure. Two weeks before, Tom had convened a conference of infectious disease specialists at Devan from all over the world. Three days of brainstorming and the group came up with nothing. Now the corporate world, rather than academia, had fielded the prize. He caught himself. What really was important was that a cure had been found.

"I'm terribly sorry that you didn't find a vaccine or an effective antibiotic protocol," Cunningham said. "But the fact is, your solid reputation in infectious diseases brought the drug to Devan anyway. CelestaCare wants our medical center to test the antibiotic in human subjects, and they want you to conduct the tests."

"Human trials already? This medicine may be lethal for human beings. It's one thing when people die in the epidemic, another when we kill them."

"That's true, but there comes a time when science can be too cautious. Of course we want a cure," he said. "But millions of people are dying. And there's another issue, one of the utmost importance." He smiled broadly for a few seconds, then made a dollar sign in the air with his index finger.

Before the sign, Tom had already guessed that the issue of utmost importance involved money. Cunningham was brought in a year before the epidemic began by the Devan Board of Trustees. Himself an honors Devan graduate as well as a recent *cum laude* graduate of a MBA program, his charge was to put the financially faltering medical center back into the black, to gather a bigger share of the market.

Cunningham continued, "Devan is faring badly under the weight of the epidemic. Like so many health care operations our medical center is on the brink of financial disaster. The Devan Health Maintenance Organization has depleted all of its assets. It's far into the red. But if we successfully test their drug, CelestaCare has graciously agreed to assist us with unlimited funding, perhaps even infuse a large amount of money in the form of buying a major share of our hospital. We do want to survive and we do want to be paid, don't we?"

"Of course," Tom said sarcastically. "Being paid is the bottom line, isn't it?"

"Let me remind you, Dr. Sullivan. I may not be on the front lines like you, but I am a physician also. I have an obligation to try to bring this epidemic to an end just as you do. We have no choice. With our current treatment methods, ninety-three percent of people infected die anyway. The health care force has been decimated. At yesterday's count, thousands of doctors, nurses and other health care workers across the country are dead or unable to work. In another few weeks there won't be anyone left to treat patients. Think about it. You may be turned off by the corporate world, but the truth is that they, not we, have come up with the cure."

As much as Tom disliked Cunningham's economic considerations, the administrator was correct. So far, even with the best of care, those infected usually died anyway didn't they? He thought of the empty parking garage, the deaths of his friends. Hundreds of health care professionals could be infected with the disease within the next few days. Katie could be among them. Even though the Vice Chancellor's reasoning was bound up with the dollar, he was right. If the drug were of any use at all, they needed to know. And Cunningham was an administrator. He was doing his best to keep Devan financially solvent.

"Can CelestaCare supply enough medicine for a valid study?" Tom asked.

With all of his talking, condensed moisture now coated the plastic dome over Cunningham's face, but Tom could still see his broad smile. "Of course, as much as you need. And CelestaCare is providing the medicine for the initial clinical trials totally free of charge. After that, they'll price the drug appropriately." He paused and rolled the vial filled with lilac fluid between his gloved hands. "By the way, they have named the drug Lilacicin."

"Lilacicin?" Tom repeated.

"Yes, for Paul Devan's lilacs. CelestaCare Enterprises wants to honor our founder and the name 'Lilacicin' will link the drug trials to Devan and to you, Dr. Sullivan. That's not bad press for both you and Devan. It's world-class marketing I would say."

"I'll do it," Tom said. "Tell CelestaCare I'll do it. I don't want the press, but I do want this epidemic to end."

As he walked back to his office, Tom recalled the vase of lilac blossoms in Scottie's room. He remembered the smell of the lilacs mixed with the smells of the hospital. His mind moved to Paul Devan's obsession with the lilacs. Every Devan Medical School graduate knew the story of the founder's lilacs. Traditionally, the Dean told the story each year at the medical school orientation for incoming students, and it was always retold at graduation.

When he landscaped, the medical school's founder, Devan, had planted lilac shrubs all around his hospital and grounds. The lilacs had become a botanic monument to the man. In the spring the fragrance of the lilacs perfumed the air. It was said that Devan believed that the scent of lilacs was the only fragrance that could cover the smell of death. No scientific evidence proved that this was true, but Devan had insisted that his observation was correct. In the spring, when the lilacs were blooming, he started the custom of having the hospital staff bring large sprays of the bountiful flowers into the hospital to decorate the rooms.

It was springtime now; the lilacs were blooming, and vases with bouquets of lilac blossoms were in almost every room of the hospital. The scent of the lilacs was everywhere, but the sweet odor did not begin to hide the smell of death. Tom had always thought the story to be sheer nonsense. Nothing could hide the smell of death.

Chapter 5

The reporters and commentators who came to Middleside, Pennsylvania to Devan University Medical Center for the media conference hurried toward the teaching building that housed Devan's historic circular amphitheater. Inside the building, the group assembled in the same walnut paneled amphitheater where Paul Devan had first convened his students over a century and a half ago. Now, in the classroom's presentation space, a woman who looked to be in her early thirties sat in a wheel chair before a group of men and women with recorders and notebooks. The woman smiled broadly at the video photographers clustered around her holding shoulder mounted cameras. At a podium behind a bank of microphones, Peter Hansen and Tom Sullivan stood ready to conduct a media conference about the miracle drug, Lilacicin.

"Let's get started," Tom said. "We want to thank Mrs. Emerson for being willing to speak to us about her miraculous recovery." He turned, faced the patient, and gave her a gentle smile. "How are you feeling, Mrs. Emerson?"

"Fine, Doctor, thanks to you and Lilacicin."

"The skin eruptions have all cleared?"

"Sure have. A few scattered ones are still healing, but it looks like the worst is over. And after being so near death, I'm getting well. Guess I'm one of the lucky ones."

"Yes, you are, and I'm very pleased that you're doing so well."

Tom turned and addressed the group crowded into the historical room. "Mrs. Emerson has shown a typical response to the new antibiotic, Lilacicin.   Within twenty-four hours after the initial injections, her temperature dropped to normal and her delirium cleared. After three days, the weeping sores on her skin begin to dry and heal.

"After a week, most patients receiving this drug can go home. This lady with you this morning, will be leaving the hospital later today, and I'm sure she will be happy to rejoin her family. Right, Mrs. Emerson?"

"Blessed. That's what I am — blessed," she said, looking up and smiling at Tom.

Tom continued, "We believe we have this epidemic under control. Dr. Laura Clark's 'miracle drug,' with its built-in resistance defeating system is as dramatic a breakthrough as penicillin was at mid-twentieth century," he said. "Now, we'll take questions."

A hand shot up near the front of the group.

"Yes?"

"How is it that Lilacicin got such rapid FDA approval?"   a reporter asked.

Tom looked toward Peter Hansen. "Dr. Hansen has expertise in the area of drug approval. Want to field this one, Peter?"

"I suppose it was a case of immediate need," Peter Hansen said. "Sometimes when there is an extremely urgent need for an untested drug, the drug is given provisional approval with limited clinical trials. It's similar to the approval category known as 'compassionate use.' Over a million deaths were already reported to the CDC, and because of the lethality of this bacterium and the disastrous proportions of its spread, Lilacicin was given immediate endorsement."

"Are you encountering side effects with the drug," another reporter asked.

"Very few," Tom said.   "Some headaches, some minor gastrointestinal upsets. There are minimal side effects with the drug, unless you consider poverty a side effect. Lilacicin is costly."

The audience snickered.

Tom continued, "It is a magnificently effective drug, but the price of Lilacicin has created some real problems."

Raymond Cunningham was sitting on the front row in front of the podium. Tom saw him wince. Sitting next to Cunningham was a tall slender man with a crew cut. The man wore a blue blazer with the CelestaCare logo on the coat pocket. In response to Tom's statement, the man had looked at Cunningham with his lips tightened and his brow furrowed.

Another hand. Tom nodded his recognition and the newsperson stood and spoke.

"As we all know, everyone hasn't been able to afford Lilacicin. Our understanding is that after the clinical trials, those people in CelestaCare's managed care plans got the drug for next to nothing. Everyone else soon came to know that one way or another they would pay an unbelievably steep price for the medication or go without the treatment," the reporter said.

"Yes, I know," Tom said. "Informed consent in many hospitals consisted of a signed acknowledgment of the cost of the drug. We knew nothing about this pricing arrangement when we agreed to test the drug."

The reporter continued, "Then you weren't told that CelestaCare's pharmaceutical division was going to price the drug to the non-CelestaCare insured at thousands of dollars for the four day course, payable on the front end? Wouldn't you suspect that was CelestaCare's way of intentionally trying to put its competition out of business?"

"I can't answer that," Tom replied. "I do know the drug works."

"How much do you think it costs CelestaCare to produce a course of Lilacicin?" the reporter asked Tom.

"I don't know," Tom answered. "But in response to the questions about pricing directed to their corporate headquarters, they've gone on record saying that their enormous research and development costs had to be factored in."

"One further question. When you say, 'We didn't know about the pricing of Lilacicin,' just who is 'we'?"

"I'm speaking of myself and Dr. Peter Hansen. We can't speak for Devan and CelestaCare."

Cunningham's eyes flashed anger.

"Who can?" a reporter in the back of the room yelled out. "People want to know what this is all about."

Tom shrugged his shoulders. The man in the blue blazer with the crew cut shifted forward on the bench. Tom watched as Cunningham held the man back.

A wave of whispers ran through the room.

"I have a question Dr. Sullivan," a reporter said.

"Yes, I'll take this one, then show the slides. You'll see how Lilacicin works."

"Is it true that the drug was named for the lilac shrubs planted all around the medical center grounds?"

"Sure is," Tom said. "And as many of you know, our founder Paul Devan had definite ideas about the lilac shrubs and their blooms. That's a story in itself, but we'll have to save that for another time. Now, let's see the slides."

Tom began to show projected slides demonstrating the action of the drug. He explained that the drug's internal rearrangement mechanism was designed to combat the bacteria's retaliatory enzymes. Lilacicin's built-in intelligence was able to overcome the resistance of the bacteria. The slides demonstrated its remarkable power. But as soon as the lights came up again, there were more questions fired at Hansen and Sullivan.

"What are the health care plans that can't afford the drug for their enrollees doing?" a reporter asked.

"Going out of business," one of the reporters in the audience blurted out.

Muted laughter rippled through the crowd.

"No, I mean what are they doing for their patients?"

"Using combinations of conventional antibiotics," Hansen said.

"Do they work?"

"No."

"Is that why people are leaving the other plans in droves and flocking to CelestaCare?"

"It certainly hasn't hurt CelestaCare's business," Tom said.

The reporter went on. "Yes, oddly enough CelestaCare, who previously made it impossible for anyone with any preexisting illnesses to get into its plans, has basically moved to a position of open enrollment to all comers. Even those victims of the epidemic with active infection can enroll and get Lilacicin at a reduced price."

Tom replied. "I don't work for CelestaCare, nor am I their representative and I'm sorry but I can't comment on that. However, I am very pleased that people like Mrs. Emerson are getting well."

The man who was sitting next to Raymond Cunningham shot to his feet. He was calm and composed. "Dr. Sullivan, I do work for CelestaCare and I can comment and answer their questions. I'm Ken Clark, CelestaCare Health Enterprises' Chief Operating Officer."

With a wave, Cunningham signaled to Tom to let Clark have the floor.

"Go ahead," Tom said.

Ken Clark stood tall and squarely faced the cameras. "As Dr. Sullivan has told you, CelestaCare did have significant research and development expenses. But let me make this clear. Our obligation was to those covered lives in our health care plans and to our shareholders. Certainly we had no obligation to our competition. It isn't our fault that all of the other companies had small print in their contracts that allowed them to rule Lilacicin an 'unreasonable expense' and pass the major part of their price of the drug on to their covered lives. And yes, we were in a position to give Lilacicin less expensively to the covered lives in our plans. It was our research that discovered the drug and our company that could produce it."

A reporter stood and waited patiently for Clark to finish. When he finally spoke, his voice trembled. "Mr. Clark, you're speaking about the lives of human beings. These so-called 'covered lives' are human beings…living, feeling, human beings."

Clark stood quietly for a moment, arms folded, his eyes gazing down toward the floor. The audience shifted in their chairs awaiting his response.

Ken Clark looked out at the audience. His voice softened and he continued. "Look, I understand your feelings. Of course they are human beings. These have been terribly difficult times. We had to give our managed care participants first shot at the drug. Production time itself was one of the limiting factors. Initially the high cost was part of the supply and demand equation. We did our best and now have reached a production level that will more than satisfy the needs of this catastrophe. I assure you that we have the same humanitarian interests as other health care companies."

Another reporter shot to his feet. "Supply and demand? We've learned that your company was able to produce Lilacicin by the ton."

"True, but purity and dose variation had to be fine tuned," Clark said.

"Double talk," one of the reporters yelled out.

Ray Cunningham stood, faced the audience and held up his palms to the group. "That's it for today. We're not here to bash CelestaCare Enterprises. After all, their drug will put an end to this epidemic; our hopes have been realized. And the profits generated by Lilacicin will be put to good use. As many of you know, with cutbacks in grants, our tuitions and endowment will not adequately support our teaching and care missions. You've seen the reports in the media. Ninety percent of the American health care facilities in this country have been wrecked financially by the epidemic and Devan Medical Center is unfortunately in that group. But yesterday afternoon the Devan University Board of Trustees met with CelestaCare Health Enterprises' Directors and we were able to complete a transaction whereby CelestaCare will purchase and run Devan Hospital. Now, with this gigantic infusion of funds and under CelestaCare ownership and operation, and in cooperation with our faculty, we will continue to serve the public as a model of the finest academic medical center in American health care."

Tom and Peter exchanged puzzled looks.

Cunningham continued. "Friends, the health care insurance industry has collapsed; the Medicare coffers have dwindled to nothing. One after another, hospitals are going so deeply into debt that recovery is impossible. Government intervention is expected soon. But regardless, Devan Medical Center will persist. And hand-in-hand with CelestaCare, we will survive into the future."

After the Lilacicin media conference, Bob and Tom left to make their rounds.

Bob Kaplan spoke, "Clark's explanation didn't make much sense. I understand that some loophole in the law allowed CelestaCare complete control of the distribution of Lilacicin even in a national emergency. But you would think that if nothing else, CelestaCare would have made some humanitarian concessions on the price."

"The truth, Bob, is that CelestaCare's concern is strictly a matter of the bottom line. With CelestaCare, profit reigns supreme. I may be a hero for doing the first clinical trials with Lilacicin, but I don't like being linked with CelestaCare's profit seeking."

"CelestaCare's interest may be in money, but still, you do have to give credit to the woman who discovered this drug," Kaplan said. "That was quite an act."

"You bet," Tom said, smiling at the man that walked beside him. "She must be dynamite in that lab."

Kaplan continued, "The word is that this Laura Clark has all kinds of new projects in the works. She's CelestaCare's secret weapon. They say she's Nobel Prize material."

"Katie tells me that Laura Clark's father was one of her attending physicians at Devan," Tom said. "She says he was a damned fine pediatrician and human being, and my wife's judgement of people is pretty good. He died a few weeks ago, one of the first physician victims of the epidemic."

"Wouldn't be surprised if his death didn't move Dr. Clark's work along," Bob said.

"Something did. No one else had a clue how to go about synthesizing the drug," Tom said, walking along at his usual brisk pace.

Chapter 6

Word of the happenings in Washington quickly spread through Devan hospital. Hurrying back to his office after rounds, Tom logged onto the Internet on his desktop computer to watch the news on the "All News Channel." He clicked on ANC just in time to see "LIVE FROM WASHINGTON D.C." appear as an overlay on the screen.

"They're about to land," the newswoman on camera said. In the background, the noise of helicopter blades grew louder, dust and debris stirred in the air, and soon a lilac-colored helicopter touched down on the heliport behind her.

The newswoman brimmed with excitement. "History in the making here in Washington! Can you imagine? Over two hundred thousand people, marching up Pennsylvania Avenue demanding a new kind of health care reform.

"The President addressed the marchers last night. To quote him, 'The Lilacicin debacle has made it clear. Health care delivery must change.' It was clear from his speech that the Health Care Task Force has come up with some new tricks, a new system, a way of lowering health care costs and tightening the controls."

The scene shifted from the reporter, and the camera panned the huge crowd of onlookers. Then the video came to rest on the granite edifice near the landing site and focused in on the shiny bronze "NATIONAL HEALTH AGENCY" plaque recently affixed to the building facade.

The reporter came back on screen. "He should be deplaning at any moment. Now the ramp is coming down. Yes, there he is: Dr.

Alexander Wade, the newly appointed Director of the National Health Agency, the President's man of the hour."

A loud cheer rose up from the crowd.

Tom leaned closer to the monitor screen for a closer view of the new director.

The man the crowd cheered for was trim, of medium height, and close to fifty. His bald head was rimmed by neatly edged graying black hair. A thin line of moustache curved down above his mouth. It was unclear what he was feeling; his face lacked expression. But whatever he was experiencing, his tight lips and piercing eyes gave hint of his intensity.

As soon as Wade cleared the downwash of the chopper blades, a rotund, red-faced man came forward to greet him. The man shook Wade's hand and placed his hand on Wade's shoulder.

Behind Wade, stood a stocky, broad-shouldered secret service agent. He plugged the earpiece of his two-way radio into his ear and eyed the crowd standing nearby.

The commentator continued, "Senator Ross Mandell of Colorado is welcoming Dr. Wade. Mandell is wearing a big, proud smile. This agency is his baby. He's the man who is credited with having the foresight to create the NHA to bring health care under stricter government control. He's the man who showed the public that the people running health care were more interested in profit than in lowering costs."

Mandell continued to shake Wade's hand, but the Director glanced across the Senator's shoulder toward the cheering crowd. Finally Wade pulled back from Mandell and victoriously raised his hands to greet the supporters. Mandell followed his example but Victor Brandt, the special agent who accompanied Wade, was soon between them gently edging Mandell off to the side.

Around the area, hundreds of protestors still marched and milled about, carrying posters proclaiming their discontent. Others, worn out from parading through the night, sat on the curbs sipping coffee. Awake through the night, weary children slept in their parents' arms.

A bearded young man shouted through a megaphone from atop a rickety platform. "Everyone deserves the best health care! Health care for all!" he yelled. The crowd cheered and took up the chant.

"Health care for all, health care for all, health care for all, health care for all."

Wade paused and listened to the chant. His eyes brightened. He smiled at Brandt, the six foot, four inch, two hundred and thirty pound agent, who had now successfully edged Mandell away from the new Director.

"They'll get what they want," Wade said, looking pensive.

Wade recalled his first trip to the Marshall building a year before. The President had convened still another Task Force in Washington to address the national dilemma. It seemed that almost everyone in control of health care was profit seeking.

Entrepreneurs made millions in every sector of the system. Quality of care was slipping dangerously; the public was catching on and growing weary of unfulfilled promises.

Once profits fell, the business interests would move on. Then what? There would be chaos. The entire health care system was a trembling house of cards.

The President asked that Wade be one of the fifteen experts to take part in the Task Force. Wade and the President shared the same small home town in Michigan, and the new director had practiced there since finishing his surgical training at Devan Hospital.

Prior to entering his specialty training in surgery, Wade had graduated at the top of his class from Devan University School of Medicine. He served now, as a member of his Alma Mater's Board of Trust.

Wade, a wealthy cardiovascular surgeon, had published a little known volume on health care policy a few years before the meeting, but he doubted that the President had ever read his book. In truth, he suspected that the President had appointed him to the health care study group as a token representative of the private practice community. But whatever the President's reasons, the surgeon who had vigilantly looked for a foothold in the political arena had gladly accepted the position that led to his rapid ascent.

The most erudite people in health care in the country had brought their knowledge to the conference tables only to be upstaged by the innovative insights of this little known practitioner. Wade eloquently expressed his view as to how the health care of the country might be reshaped.

When the experts' knowledge failed, Wade's "solution" grew more and more feasible, and became the most viable reality of the times. Now, a year later, in the wake of the epidemic, the President had appointed him to consolidate the health care "industry" under the power of the government. When he arrived to take his post as Director, the machinery to accomplish his assigned task was already in place.

Mandell inched his way back toward the Director's side and Wade greeted him with a near scowl. Wade studied Mandell's red face and rumpled suit.

Wade saw Mandell as a bumbling politician with little sense of strategy, one who accidentally stumbled into a politically advantageous situation and happened to have it work out for his own gain. Even so, he guessed that Mandell with his well established power base would likely be chosen as his party's next candidate for President.

"Alex," Mandell said. "The President must have had a damned good reason for selecting you. He handpicked you from hundreds."

"I plan to do what I can."

"The people are demanding change. They're desperate."

"Two million deaths will do that," Wade said.

"Look Wade," Mandell said, "succeed with this program and you can write your own ticket. This isn't just a medical problem; it's an important political matter too."

"Political? People are still dying. The epidemic has killed millions of people. For years, you politicians have been sitting on your duffs watching the health care system disintegrate, watching the whole damned thing crumble under the weight of profit taking."

"You're talking to the wrong person," Mandell said. "You know damned well that long before the Lilacicin debacle struck the nation's health care industry dead, I was working to give birth to the National Health Agency. I'm the man who brought health care under government scrutiny and control when the entrepreneurs were gouging the public."

Wade stared at Mandell with a stony look. He shook his head. "You just don't understand do you, Mandell. This agency isn't going to be a political showcase. The future of the country is at stake. I'll do whatever is necessary."

"Now look here, this Agency was my idea. You could at least acknowledge that. Whose side are you on anyway?"

"No one's."

"But you have some responsibility to us, to the government, to the President, you know."

Wade stopped and turned to face the other man. He stared square into Mandell's eyes. "Senator, I'm not here to give kudos to you or to anyone else. My responsibility is to the people. I'm not here to play your politics. There will never be another Lilacicin fiasco in this country. Each and every person in this country deserve the finest health care and they're going to get it!"

Wade and Mandell walked up the steps of the NHA building with special agent Victor Brandt a short distance behind. Wade glanced over his shoulder at the cheering crowd, then turned and smiled faintly at Mandell as he passed through the opened, polished brass doors.

Chapter 7

Inside the NHA building, at the door of a newly refurbished conference room, thirty of the country's top health care leaders stood in line to greet Director Alexander Wade. First in line was Sam Fisher, CelestaCare Enterprises' CEO. "I assure you that CelestaCare is behind your efforts one hundred percent," he said to the new director.

CelestaCare's Chief Operating Officer, Ken Clark, followed close behind Fisher. "Director Wade, we are indeed blessed to assist you with the work of reorganizing the country's health care services," he said.

"Blessed is a good way to see it, Clark."

Jeff Holt, Director of the National Informatics Center, came next. "The demographic data is all in the mainframe," Holt said.

Wade nodded his approval.

Alan Mulholland, the President's chief legal advisor, followed Holt.

"You're a regular Tom Jefferson, Mulholland," Wade said. "I understand you've done an outstanding job with the drafting of the Emergency Health Care Act. You laid the ground work for Congress to act as swiftly as they did."

"Health care is an inalienable right," the young lawyer said.

Others filed past. Bob Newall from BrilliaCare, and Will Thomas from ProvideItNow, the heads of two of the Nation's largest health insurers reached out to shake Wade's hand. Then came FantastaCare's CEO, Marilyn Schaffer. Tom Rabenshaw from

Healthforth International followed her. Then Brad Benson from CareSoMuch Managed Care greeted Wade. Finally, Sally Bennington-Smith, the Surgeon General and Rudolph Tyson, the President of the American Practitioners' Association wished Wade well in his endeavors.

Holt and Mulholland stepped back to watch the entourage pay their respects to the Director. A woman dressed in a lilac-colored outfit scurried between them and the receiving line, headed toward the cameraman.

"Who the hell is that?" Holt asked, studying the woman over his half glasses.

"That, Mr. Holt, is Carole Weeks, Wade's public relation director," Mulholland said.

"He stole her away from WasteTox International?"

"Yeah."

"Holy Shit," Holt said. "What a coup! That woman disarmed the whole state of Tennessee with her advertising campaign. She's the one who ran the program that got the voters to put the nuclear waste dump exactly where WasteTox wanted it. She could have gotten the public to turn the Grand Canyon into a giant garbage dump if she had set her mind to it."

Wade signaled to the group and the conference participants moved to take their seats. On the rising circular tiers, each participant sat behind a table in a tan, leather, swivel chair. In front of each person was a monitor. Already switched on, each monitor glowed with an image of the emblem of the National Health Agency — full blown lilac blossom plumes on a pale lilac shield overlaid by the letters NHA. The lilac plume motif and NHA overlay was repeated on the agency flag standing next to the podium in the front of the room.

The group waited expectantly while Wade spoke with Carole Weeks. The violet colored phosphorescence shining from the monitors in front of the conferees bizarrely colored their faces like pale, purple, Halloween masks. Two of the less notable health care executives near the back of the large room chatted nervously.

"I say the march was staged for effect. Someone damned sure wanted our current health care system to topple and it happened. The health care system that was is dead," one said.

"Who?" the other asked.

"I don't know. Government, Islamic extremists, Jews, Blacks, Wall Street — who the hell knows."

The two men swiveled around in their chairs, scanning the room.

"What do you know about this Wade character?" one asked.

"He's powerful as hell."

"Maybe he's behind the march."

"You're kidding."

"Maybe, maybe not."

"And the lilac stuff. What's with all this lilac stuff?"

"Wade has a strong attachment to Devan Medical Center in Middleside, Pennsylvania. It's his way of paying homage to Paul Devan, the founder of the medical school. Apparently this Devan guy was obsessed with lilacs and death."

"Odd combination."

"Yep."

Wade moved forward and tapped the lectern microphone with a brisk thump of his finger and a loud sound blasted from the speakers. "All right, let's get started," he said sharply. Instantly, the people in the room became still.

"Ladies and Gentlemen, I first want you to clearly understand the events that brought about this meeting. You are soon going to be watching a documentary produced by Ms. Carole Weeks. What you will see are highlights from network news stories of the past few weeks put together to graphically present the horrible realities of the epidemic and the dreadful truth about our health care system's inability to stay afloat."

The lights dimmed, the National Health Agency logo faded and a stirring musical segment from Strauss's *Death and Transfiguration* poured through the speakers. Suddenly, in neon green, the title "THE GREAT EPIDEMIC," vibrated menacingly on the monitor screens.

The title faded into magnified shots of the deadly epidemic causing microbes — undulating links of glowing purple spheres. A deep voiced narrator spoke:

"America's medical and legal investigative forces have yet to determine the source of the deadly infectious disease that has struck our country. Some thirty terrorist organizations have claimed credit for the spread of the infection, but we have no definitive answer as to exactly which group is the perpetrator. We do know, however, that the plague-like terror of the epidemic was the final straw in the collapse of America's health care system."

The purple microbes faded and gave way to scenes of patients with weeping ulcers all over their bodies. "It began like this...," the narrator said, as close-up views of sores, oozing with thick yellow fluid, flashed in view. One sickened member of the audience left the room.

Brief clips from the early days of the epidemic followed.

In the first, Robert Blanchard, M.D., Professor of Infectious Disease at Calford University, spoke knowledgeably about the cause and clinical course of the disease. "We are now certain. It is a bacterium — a previously unknown mutated strain that causes this rampant infectious disease process. It is highly contagious and spread by respiratory droplets. Those infected are likely to die. The killer bacteria rapidly produce a lethal chemical toxin that erodes the walls of blood vessels. Death comes from internal hemorrhage and shock."

"Baffling. Absolutely baffling," World renowned Devan Medical Center's epidemiologist Peter Hansen, M.D., reported as the map showing the case distribution flashed on the screens. "The lightning speed with which the disease has spread is phenomenal; the virulence of the microbe is astounding. I've tracked epidemics in New Zealand, I tracked them in Africa, I've tracked them in Russia. I can tell you that this distribution pattern makes no sense. The best I can say at this point is that the rapid spread must be related to wind currents."

Next came interviews of people on the street speculating about the responsibility for the disaster. Old, young, poor, rich, all had opinions. Their faces flashed with rage as they blamed extremist Islamic terrorists, other world powers, Blacks, Hispanics, Jews, Catholics, or homosexual activists. "Yeah, it's probably germ warfare; without question either the Jews or the Blacks are behind this. This ain't the work of Arabs," one shaved head young man wearing what looked to be a simulated Nazi uniform said.

"AIDS might have frightened the world," a bald young man with sunken eyes pointed out, "but it's not AIDS that will turn out to be the most threatening disease in centuries."

The documentary shifted to dozens of scenes depicting the epidemic's overwhelming effect on the health care system. The narrator groaned on. "Unable to manage the numbers, hospitals overflowed with patients. Therapeutic measures involved the use of the most expensive drugs and technology, but there was no relief. Serious supply shortages existed everywhere. As the resources of the medical industry became totally depleted, the giant health care corporations began to operate with a financial deficit. The disease was leaving a path of fiscal devastation in its wake. The health care 'House of Cards' was tumbling down."

Three weeks into the epidemic, Clarence Fletcher, HippocraCare Health Care's Chief of Finance spoke on camera. "We are only being reimbursed for ten percent of what we have to spend to take care of these patients. There's no way we can stay solvent."

Next, Professor Robert Keene, a famous biomedical sanitation expert, stood on camera outside Philadelphia near a huge fenced-off disposal dump. Both he and the newsman wore plastic suits with protective head domes. "The epidemic is generating millions of tons of dangerous biomedical waste," he told his interviewer. "We've had bulldozers gouge giant craters in the earth in rural areas outside every city in the country. In these pits, contaminated hospital gowns and bedclothes, bandages and syringes and the garbage of disease are burning day and night. Like smog, the stench from the waste hangs everywhere." On the screen, the viewers watched panoramic scenes of the burning dumps sending tall columns of smoke high up into the sky.

And then, the narrator became upbeat. "But when all hope was waning, a brilliant CelestaCare Enterprises scientist halted the bacteria's devastating march." In a scene filmed in the CelestaCare labs, Laura Clark, dressed in a white coat proudly held up a beaker of Lilacicin. "This woman saved the lives of millions," the narrator stated.

"To test its wonder drug, CelestaCare secured the expertise of the noted infectious disease expert, Doctor Thomas Sullivan, along with the resources of the famous Devan University School of Medicine in

Middleside, Pennsylvania. "Here," the narrator said, "you see Dr. Sullivan conversing with a recovering patient who, the day before, was on the threshold of death."

Next, a reporter interviewed Bob Newall of BrilliaCare on camera. In the NHA conference room Newall shifted nervously in his chair. "There is no way we can include Lilacicin in our formulary. CelestaCare's price is too steep and they won't negotiate. We will be bankrupt in twenty-four hours."

"Then you wouldn't be able to draw your ten million a year salary, right, Mr. Newall?" the reporter interviewing him said.

Newell's face turned cherry red. "Er, there's no reason I shouldn't be compensated for my work."

Finally, there were scenes of the march in Washington. A million angry, placard-carrying, shouting citizens marched down Pennsylvania Avenue toward the Capitol, demanding that changes be made in the health care system immediately.

In the last seconds of the video, a full, front view of Director Wade's stern face filled the screen. The picture soon faded, and seconds later, with the "Stars and Stripes Forever" playing in the background, the purple glow of the lilac plume reappeared on the monitor screens.

The lights came up and low whispers floated across the auditorium.

The Director came back to the podium and the room instantly grew still and quiet.

Chapter 8

Alexander Wade gripped the edge of the lectern. "Thank God, the epidemic is under control," he said. "Even so, there is still a national health care crisis and all across this great nation, the entire health care industry is toppling. You can be sure, however, that we have a plan."

Applause rang through the room. When it subsided, Wade continued.

"The President has authorized me to inform you that the government is prepared to provide whatever assistance is necessary to keep the health care industry afloat. However, to do so, we must be in a position to carefully monitor your utilization of funds. We want to help you survive as you develop new methods to deliver economically feasible care.

"We will need your help and cooperation, but the National Health Agency will be at the helm. Yesterday afternoon, Congress passed the National Health Care Recovery Act. As of midnight last night, a state of national emergency was declared. Each and every physician and health care worker, every hospital and health care facility in the country is now under the direct control of the President. The new law provides for the revocation of the credentials and licensure of any hospital, health care facility, or health care provider who fails to comply with our plan."

Will Thomas leaned closer to Bob Newall and whispered. "Surely this isn't constitutional?"

"Who the hell is going to argue it at this point? The country is devastated and so are we. So is every health care entity but

CelestaCare. The NHA will clamp any hothead who argues into a death grip."

"Shit…"

Wade was setting up his new order with the power of a fifty ton tank, rolling through a vanquished city. He continued to assert his command. "We have devised a unit system whereby each citizen will be allocated a specific number of health care units called 'points.' It is a simple plan, a universal health care plan that will continue to encourage the system of free enterprise and preserve the American way. The indigent and the uninsured will be covered. Every citizen will have the finest health care available.

"Health care facilities will provide the necessary services for individuals based on a point-for-service system. The government will reimburse the provider for points used. The government will determine the value of the point. To win one's share of the marketplace, the incentive will be to provide the best care for the lowest number of points. You must develop efficient new high quality care systems with minimal waste.

"Toward that end, we already have an exemplary effort in the wings. I have recently been informed that CelestaCare Enterprises will soon offer consumers a new form of inexpensive, high quality, automated care."

A number of the participants turned and looked toward Sam Fisher. He acknowledged their glances with a smile and a small wave of his hand.

"I would suggest that you would all do well to follow CelestaCare's example. Mobilize your research and development efforts, reduce your corporations' and the consumers' costs, and you will weather the storm.

"Now, ladies and gentlemen, I want you to see a key part of our new health care plan," he said, and motioned to one of his aides. She came forward, and on the podium, set a hand-held scanner gun like those used at check-out counters in stores. A cable reached from the device to a nearby computer terminal.

Wade held up a small, purple colored, plastic bracelet, then placed it around his left wrist. He held his wrist out and the aide used a tool, similar to pliers, to lock shut its clasp. In the silence of anticipation, the audience heard an audible click.

Wade pointed to the scanner. "This scanner uses a laser reading device to retrieve the information imprinted on the bracelet's data disk." He held up his left arm and pointed to the dime-sized disk fastened in the middle of the band encircling his wrist. "The equipment can read or change any information encoded on the disk. Let me demonstrate."

Wade pointed the scanning device toward his left wrist. A beam flashed across the disc of the bracelet. Immediately a read-out appeared on the screens. It said:

WADE, ALEXANDER, P.
SSN # 496-36-0951

Other identifying information followed: Wade's address, his occupation, an "in emergency notify" notation, and his religious preference. A brief summary of his medical history was outlined and drug allergies were listed: "Usual childhood illnesses; Appendectomy, Age 12; Allergic to Penicillin…" Further down the monitor screen, Wade's point data was given. It read simply:

TOTAL POINTS ISSUED: 10,000
POINTS UTILIZED: 000.00
POINTS REMAINING: 10,000

For the first time since he began, Wade smiled. "This, ladies and gentlemen is a glimpse of the points system. As you will learn, it will be the foundation of "PointCure," our new system of health care delivery and management. PointCure, my dear friends, is the government sponsored Universal Health Care Plan that the country has wanted for a long time. And you may be sure that Washington will be closely monitoring exactly how every single point is used."

Chapter 9

In his office at Devan Medical Center, Ray Cunningham gently tapped the fingertips of his hands against one another and leaned back in the leather chair, pondering how to begin his presentation to Tom Sullivan. He cleared his throat.

"It's difficult to believe that it's been six months since I called you in to ask that you conduct the clinical trials on Lilacicin. Now, Wade's points system is on the table and the fact is, Tom, I need your help again. I know how you feel about the corporate world's place in health care, but the truth is these people are able to financially back projects that we can't begin to fund. But they need us also. Academia has legitimacy and because of Lilacicin you're in a position that gives you tremendous clout and public appeal."

Sullivan was silent. Not exactly where he wanted to be, he thought and waited for Cunningham to continue.

"What credentials you have, Sullivan! An Olympic track hero, a doctor who takes excellent care of his patients, an outstanding teacher, and now the physician who conquered the epidemic. Whether you like it or not, you're Devan's poster physician."

"What is it you want, Dr. Cunningham?" Tom asked, moving the discussion along.

"CelestaCare Health now owns our hospital and over four hundred more around the country. They're buying up university medical center hospitals right and left and before long will be the dominant player in medical education. Now they have a new project, a top secret development, that will insure that everyone in the country gets the finest care."

"Dr. Cunningham, I'm a clinician, a teacher, and a researcher. I don't see myself as having any place in advancing CelestaCare's desire to own a bigger piece of the pie."

Cunningham leaned forward and spoke earnestly. "Let me explain, Tom. This is the future of American medicine we're talking about. You're Devan's top clinician. You're Devan's finest teacher. You've been the champion of every citizen's having the best in care. We can't let these people put in what amounts to machinery to care for patients without physicians overseeing what they're doing. With the point system in place, God knows how competitive things will get. Without people like you, patients will be treated like cattle. You have a responsibility here. We have to be damned sure that these new ventures are tempered with some sense of moral values."

"So, you're interested in my doing what, Dr. Cunningham?" Tom asked, growing more impatient. Suddenly, he questioned what Cunningham meant by "machinery." The word turned over in his mind. A metaphor, surely.

"You've seen yourself on television. Besides being a damned fine physician and the man that brought the country Lilacicin, you create a media image of a doctor that any PR agency would crave. You're tall, you look confident, and your shoulders slump just enough to make you look human." Cunningham smiled faintly, amused at his last observation. "Put you in a white coat, sling a stethoscope over your shoulders and you look like everyone wants their physician to look. Sullivan, with you on the side of this project, Devan and CelestaCare can win over the public with ease."

Tom shifted forward in his chair and glanced at his watch. "I have rounds to make, Dr. Cunningham."

"Yes, I know, but bear with me a moment. This CelestaCare research project will revolutionize medical care."

"Another Laura Clark project?"

"Of course, and while we're at it, let me tell you a bit about the Clarks. If you accept the position I have in mind, you'll be seeing a lot of them. Laura Clark's husband, Ken Clark, is one hell of a businessman, but he's as much concerned about delivering quality patient care as anyone I know.

45

"He may not be a physician, but he understands how the health care dollar flows, and I can assure you that he uses that wisdom in a humanitarian way. Of course, every man's odyssey is important and Clark is no exception. Clark's father was military and he twisted his arm until he went to West Point. But after a short stint in the service, he resigned his commission and decided to head toward a theology degree at Whitright Theological College. After a year or two at that, he reconsidered and decided that medical administration was his real calling. He went on to get his MBA in health management, then joined CelestaCare, and in no time worked his way up to the position of Chief Operating Officer of the corporation. The man grew up in a military family, so sometimes he comes across as rather gruff, but underneath it all he's a very fine man who is interested in the welfare of health care and humankind."

Tom ran his fingers through his hair, then rubbed the back of his neck to ease the dull ache of the tense muscles.

"His wife, Laura, comes from a medical family. She's unstoppable. Seems to feel the mandate of carrying on the family legacy in the form of furthering the health sciences. You might already know that her pediatrician father died in the epidemic. She's the warmer, engaging side of the Clark duo. Together, the Clarks make quite a pair. They're determined, dedicated, and intent on making real contributions to health care. And aside from both of them being very attractive people, I suspect their dedication is what attracted them to one another when they met at CelestaCare.

"One thing you have to bear in mind. Just because they work for CelestaCare, that doesn't mean that their only motivation is profit. Their intentions are good ones. Like you and I, these people are trying to improve patient care."

Tom glanced at the MD and MBA degrees framed on the wall behind Cunningham. His mind flashed back to the day he spoke with Cunningham when he wore his plastic bubble protection device. Today, the Vice Chancellor seemed less frantic and more interested in the future of medical care. Perhaps the protection device was no more than his human side, his fear of all that was happening. Perhaps his distrust of Cunningham and even CelestaCare was unfounded. But then he asked himself, were Cunningham's flattering words about him and his buildup of the Clarks all a part of some kind of sell?

Or was he sincere? The Vice-Chancellor had certainly been correct about Lilacicin and yet Tom had been suspicious that his motives were only monetary. But he was an academician, a medical center leader. Medical centers did require operating funds and the world of medicine had become more financially complex in recent years. The responsibilities of the Vice Chancellor were also more complex. Intent was not always as clear as it seemed. At least he should listen. He sat back in his chair. "Go on, Dr. Cunningham."

"When the project is set in motion, Middleside's 500 bed CelestaCare Hospital, Starr Memorial, will be its proving ground. Ken Clark will be overseeing the installation of the project and the take off himself. And here is where you come in. We need a medical director for Starr Memorial and we need one that can oversee the project to be certain that humanitarian care is built in. We'll need an outstanding teaching program at Starr for the medical students and residents. We'll need to emphasize the physician-consumer relationship. And here's the deal with CelestaCare. If the Starr Memorial installation takes off, Devan Hospital will get the next placement, and if the government feels the project is the way to go for the points system and underwrites it, the project will take off like a skyrocket."

"Okay, tell me about this new direction in health care," Tom said.

Cunningham smiled. "No, it's best that you see it for yourself. And when you do, you'll see where the future of medicine lies."

"Let me understand. I would have a teaching program and be in full charge of the clinical directions."

Cunningham thought a moment before speaking. "As you'll see this system has what might be called 'a mind of its own.' And since it's CelestaCare's project, it's only fair that they will have the last word on its utilization."

"Then it's still a form of managed care."

"Yes, of a sort Tom, but that's another reason why I want you at Starr. You've brought your own kind of power to health care negotiations. Your knowledge and forcefulness works to get what you want from the third party payers and the managed care people. I've seen you go up against innumerable denials of care and reverse the managed care company's decision. I've seen you negotiate contracts with these companies for the hospital. I don't think

CelestaCare or any other managed care company can push you around."

"If so, not for long, Dr. Cunningham." Tom said resolutely.

Chapter 10

The early morning drivers left their places in the bumper-to-bumper traffic, swerved across the lanes, and pulled over to the curb to let the emergency medical vehicle through. On the sidewalk, stunned pedestrians heard the siren's penetrating wail, eyed the flashing reds and yellows, and stopped stone-like in their tracks while the lilac-colored van roared by. The van's wheels squealed as it made a sharp turn around a corner on its way to answer the call.

Inside the vehicle, the driver glanced down at the sharply outlined multicolored map on the dash computer monitor. Two red coordinates intersected on the screen to mark the point of his destination.

Both the driver and his assistant wore lilac-colored jump suits with caps on their heads bearing the insignia of the National Health Agency above the visor. The same design, a bouquet of lilac plumes crossed by the letters NHA, was painted on the van's side.

The driver fixed the destination in his memory and then hit another switch. The map faded to a picture of the patient with his description underneath. The computer printer's mechanism hummed and spit out a printed strip:

Edwin Thomas Glass, 64-year-old male, Married, Caucasian, Protestant, CONGESTIVE HEART FAILURE (ICP code number 206789), CHRONIC OBSTRUCTIVE PULMO-NARY DISEASE (ICP code number 78409), Status: severe shortness of breath. Meds: Enalapril, Furosemide, Solostatin,

Ipratropium, and Albuterol inhaler. POINTS — 137 (one hundred, thirty-seven), MINIMUM ESTIMATE DIAGNOSTIC-THERAPEUTIC POINT REQUIREMENT 4600 — (four thousand, six hundred), POINT DEFICIT — 4463 (four thousand, four hundred, sixty-three).

The computer print-out stopped. The message on the screen faded and then another appeared:

POINT BRACELET READ
DISPOSITION: EXIT TO FOLLOW STAT PICKUP
FAMILY NOTIFICATION TO FOLLOW — END.

A large crowd had gathered, encircling the fallen man lying on the sidewalk. Heads turned as the crowd watched the ambulance screech to a halt at the curb. Among them, a small child stood, his eyes fixed in fascination on the emergency vehicle's blinking lights. He clung to his mother's skirt as they stood a few feet back from the victim. Next to the child, the victim's black, metal, curved-top lunch box had dropped and jarred open, spilling the apple, bag of chips and the sandwich it contained.

"Okay, get back, let them through," a policeman said, a whistle hanging out of his mouth as he parted the crowd to make a path for the emergency team.

The man's chest heaved forward and back. He made deep, hungry gasps to fill his lungs with air. Except for the lunging of his chest, his body was still, his eyes closed. Beside him, a policeman knelt still holding the pistol-like handle of the laser scanner he had used to read the disc on the bracelet on the man's left wrist.

Out came the stretcher from the back doors of the ambulance in the grasps of the two-man emergency health care team. Rushing through the crowd, they set it down next to the fallen man. The driver grabbed the man's wrist, took his pulse, and motioned to the crowd to stand further back.

Atop the stretcher was a polished steel canister. The assistant turned its valve and put an oxygen mask in place on the victim's face. The driver ripped the man's shirt open, slapped a series of electrodes on his chest and plugged the leads into a hand-held electrocardiogram device that he carried. He looked down, studying the jagged lines that pulsed from the machine's feed.

"Not much life left in this one. That's for sure," he said.

His assistant continued his ritual of readying injectables and setting up a portable respirator that might at any moment be required to treat the man. The crowd watched as the oxygen began to take effect. The man's breathing became less labored and quieter. His eyes blinked open for a moment and then closed again. He grunted and moaned as the two men carefully lifted him onto the stretcher.

The driver breathed a sign of relief. He lifted his cap and smoothed his hair.

"Now, Mr. Glass, you're in good hands," he said, as he retrieved a remote control device from his coat pocket and pointed it toward the van.

Seconds later, a recorded message blared from the speakers atop the ambulance as it might from a campaign car roaming the neighborhoods of a constituency. Slowly and dramatically, the deep, slightly muffled voice floated out across the crowd:

> You are watching the skilled, efficient, operation of Health Care Providers of the National Health Agency. Benefiting from the very latest in technology, another person is receiving the best health care available – PointCure. Thank you for any help you might have provided in this situation and thank you for your continued support of a health care system aimed at providing you, your family, and your neighbors with the very best health care possible.

When the message finished, it began again. The crowd began to disperse.

"Thank God for the NHA," a woman in the crowd said to the man standing next to her.

"Yes, the NHA is a blessing," the man next to her replied.

The driver and his assistant carried the ill man toward the open rear doors and guided the stretcher inside. The small crowd remaining in the street watched when the rear panels of the van came together as the lilac plume insignia of the National Health Agency.

51

Inside the lilac van, the driver quickly hung a fluid bag containing normal saline on a hook above the man's right shoulder. He patted the front of the man's elbow looking for a vein large enough to be a conduit for the IV. The patient grimaced as the needle penetrated his skin and reached into the bluish blood vessel.

"Load the solution," the driver said to his assistant pointing toward the small white cabinet behind the passenger's seat.

The assistant unlocked the cabinet, drew up a syringe of violet colored liquid from a vial labeled "EXIT SOLUTION", then held the calibrated barrel up to the light to check the dosage.

The man opened his eyes slowly and looked at the faces hovering above him. He struggled to speak but his dry lips would not form the words.

The two emergency health care technicians looked at the EKG monitor.

"His heart beat is getting more regular, the assistant said. "Can you believe it? He's coming around. Damn!" he said under his breath.

There was a few moments pause.

"Feeling better now, Mr. Glass?" the driver asked as he studied the electrocardiogram.

"Ye...es," the man said in a strained voice. He was gradually becoming more alert.

"Here, this should do the job," the driver said and handed the syringe to his assistant. "Go ahead. We have our orders. Give him the medicine. Intravenous push,"

The driver climbed through the van and slipped in behind the wheel. Then he turned and looked back toward the rear.

"How goes it with Mr. Glass?" he asked.

"Injection's done," the assistant replied.

The driver turned the ignition key, switched on the flashing lights, and crept slowly down the street. The recorded message began again.

"Whatya got now?" the driver asked after a few minutes.

"Flat-line," his assistant replied from the rear of the van.

"That's it; our job's finished," the driver said.

The assistant pulled a lilac-colored sheet over the man's head, shuffled forward, and climbed into the front seat. He lowered the dash computer keyboard and typed a short message.

Seconds later, across the city, a clerk named Joe Stark read the message on the monitor in front of him, jotted down some notes, picked up the phone and dialed.

Soon there was an answer. "Hello," a woman's voice said.

"Hello, is this Mrs. Glass?" Soft music played on the telephone behind his voice.

"Yes, who is this?" she asked, responding to the strangeness of the voice and the music in the background.

"It's Joe Stark, your National Health Agency Family Communication Specialist, Mrs. Glass. I'm so very sorry to have to tell you this…"

There was a brief pause.

"It's your husband. He took ill. He's dead, Mrs. Glass. He has exited this life. He collapsed over on fifth and seventy-sixth. But, the NHA ambulance was there immediately — in a flash."

"Good God! No!" the woman said. She began to sob.

The clerk continued. "They did everything they could. He made his exit in transit. You'll need to come to our Central Headquarters building to identify and claim the body." He paused for a moment. There was only low whimpering on the other end of the line. "Mrs. Glass, I know this is very painful and upsetting and I do wish we could have done more."

Her sobbing continued.

"His points were on the low side, Mrs. Glass, but rest assured, we did everything we were authorized to do." He waited briefly for her crying to subside.

"Now, what would you like done with the left-over 137 points, Mrs. Glass? We can transfer them to your own account or credit them to anyone you designate. You should be proud, Mrs. Glass; Mr. Glass exited with points remaining. That's good health care. And now he's cleared the way for someone else to live a healthy life. By the way, your family shows no point deficits so that you could, if you like, have a cash refund."

There was another pause.

"You need to be informed of the current point value. Let's see. Today the point is worth $4.70 base rate — that's four dollars and seventy cents a point. That comes to $643.90. Hey, look at this," he said with excitement when the next screen appeared before him. "You've got a premium. It looks like Mr. Glass designated himself an organ donor so the point is worth $4.80, and if you give us permission to do a postmortem exam right now, those points are worth $4.95 a piece. A total of $678.15. That's not too bad, is it Mrs. Glass?"

"I want to know exactly what happened," she said.

"Then you'll want a postmortem exam. Great! And we'll go ahead and have the point accumulation credited to you. Mrs. Glass, just go by your neighborhood PointCare Check Center and this will be taken care of in the usual efficient manner. They'll add the points to your bracelet. And you'll get the extras for the organs and the autopsy. If you would rather have cash, that's fine too. What a deal! And listen, The National Health Service has a bereavement gift especially for you. When you go to the PointCure Check-In Center be sure to pick up your plastic lilac bough and the spray can of lilac fragrance for your home. Oh, Mrs. Glass, I want to ask you to listen to this brief recording."

"I said what happened to my husb...?"

The tape began with an almost inaudible scratchy excerpt from Mozart's *Requiem*. Then, as the music faded, a woman's recorded voice came on to offer condolence from the National Health Agency:

The National Health Agency deeply regrets your loss. You needn't worry; you may be assured that everything possible was done to help your loved one at this time of medical crisis. We want you to know that your PointCure team stands ready to meet all your family's health needs. If there are any problems in your health transactions please feel free to call 1-800-NHA-HELP. We're standing by to answer your questions.

Chapter 11

Laura Clark herself called to arrange a time to show Tom the "project." As scheduled, she arrived at Devan Hospital at precisely 9:00 a.m., and Tom greeted her in his outer office.

She seemed taller than her pictures in the media — close to five seven or eight. Tom guessed she was in her mid-thirties. Her reddish blond hair was cut short and she wore a tailored, cream-colored dress with a wide belt clearly outlining her trim figure. Her large hazel eyes dominated her face and stood out against her fair, lightly freckled skin.

"I'm Dr. Laura Clark," she said officially when she held out her hand to shake his. Her words were distinctly pronounced and came out of perfectly shaped lips.

"Good morning," he said, shaking her hand. Her grip was strong, without apology, but her hands felt moist.

"Short notice, I know, but Dr. Cunningham wants you to see the automated system immediately. I understand that you'll be the physician in charge of getting this going in Middleside. Makes sense to have an academician do this; there's instruction for future physicians that needs to be done. And marketing can make good use of your being the person who did the trials with Lilacicin."

"Yes, it's sensational timing," Tom said.

"I'm not hearing sarcasm, am I Dr. Sullivan?"

"It's the truth, Dr. Clark. It is sensational timing."

"I'll drive. We can leave as soon as you're ready," she said.

Tom stood up straight. No small talk. So far, Laura Clark was all business.

"I'll get my coat," he said. He started to turn to walk back toward his office, but before he could, he found himself looking squarely at her face.

"We've met, haven't we?" he asked.

"I don't think so. Probably the pictures in the news. And some people think I look like Bara Thane, the writer. That's probably what's confusing you."

"I've never heard of Bara Thane," Tom said.

"Writes romance novels. I like them. The woman always gets her man."

For a few seconds the two of them looked at each other. Something made Tom uncomfortable about her gaze. She also appeared uneasy. She breathed in. Tom remained quiet and still. He crammed his stethoscope into the pocket of his white coat.

"You still use one of those? What about all the new ultrasound imaging techniques and PET scans?"

"Old fashion doctor," he said.

She looked at his wrinkled khaki chinos, then down at the running shoes he was wearing. She shook her head. "Not completely."

Her personal digital device beeped. She looked at it. "A reminder. They're expecting us at the system demonstration by ten," she said.

"Sure, let's go," he said with a slight shakiness in his voice.

Laura drove Tom to the CelestaCare Corporate labs in her new, white BMW sedan. Tom could smell the distinctive scent of the new car interior mixed with the delicate fragrance of the scientist's subtle perfume. Stopped at a red light on a corner, waiting for the traffic to move, Tom looked toward a crowded NHA PointCure Check-In Center. Patients sat on the curbs waiting for the long lines to move forward.

"The NHA didn't waste any time, did they? A house stood on that corner three months ago," Tom said. "Now it's a PointCure Check-In Center. Unbelievable!"

"Alexander Wade's a mover. Those buildings are modular. Built in Utah and shipped all over the country. They can have a center up and running in seventy-two hours. It's real efficiency, that's what it is," Laura commented.

His eyes fixed on the milling crowd. "I don't know. It's a bit like kudzu — something growing too fast. Sometimes things that grow too fast are malignant."

She glanced at him, a look of puzzlement on her face.

He continued, "People complained about waiting in doctors' offices. Point bracelets, computer interviews, efficient consumer management in neighborhood Check-In Centers are supposed to change all that. Waiting for doctors is supposed to become a thing of the past, but look at those lines."

"Yes, I'll have to take another look at the Check-In Center intake software programs. Our company has the contract for the PointCure software you know."

"Computers and the Internet can solve any problem, I suppose," Tom said.

"Not every problem. But with the Points system, people will get better care." She smoothed the back of her hair and pulled her visor down to block the sun.

Tom looked over at the person sitting next to him. She had put on her stylish tortoise shell sunglasses. In profile, he could see her high cheekbones and the slight angular shape of her face. Even with the angles and her assertive style, there was still a softness about her.

Her neck was thin. Her slender arms ran up to graceful hands that gripped the steering wheel tightly. On her left arm, her purple plastic points bracelet had slipped down to her mid forearm. Tom was quickly becoming aware. CelestaCare's "secret weapon" was a very stunning woman. A computer scientist? Bara Thane? Romance novels?

"Intake software, drug design, patient care systems. You do it all don't you?" he said.

"Before the epidemic, I was in charge of the computer software and the Internet research and development program at CelestaCare. I've worked on my automated care project for almost two years. After I designed the molecule for Lilacicin they've put me in charge of their entire Health Care Technology program. The job's a plum."

"How did you get into computers?"

"I really wanted to be a doctor." She pulled into the left lane and passed a car.

"A physician?"

"Yes."

"What kind?"

"I don't know, probably a pediatrician or something like that. My dad was a pediatrician. He would have liked for me to be a physician too. He died a few months ago — a victim of the epidemic."

"That's what I heard," Tom said.

She was silent.

"He practiced in this area, right?"

"Yes, in downtown Philadelphia. He was a good doctor. I loved him, mom loved him, kids loved him. Everybody loved him. Yes, I suspect we would have always been close if he had lived."

Tom noted Laura's eyes welling up with tears.

"I miss him," she said. "It has not been easy. Too many people died in that epidemic. Thank God, it's over." She took a deep breath and sighed.

"But I decided against it — being a doctor, I mean," she said. She wiped her eyes with her hand. "I made it as far as gross anatomy and then backed out. There was something about carving on human flesh that I didn't believe I could ever master. Dad wasn't too happy about it."

"You dropped out of medical school?"

"Yes, I knew a front row seat to watch disease and death take its toll wouldn't work for me. I needed to watch from the balcony. I had taken a couple of computer science courses in college. After the medical school fiasco, I got interested in how computer technology could be applied to medicine. I suspect my graduate degree in computer sciences and informatics from Cal Tech is as close as I'll ever get to being a 'Doctor.'"

"What about you? How did you decide to be a physician?"

"My mother's death when I was nine, probably my own fears of death, probably some attempt to play out my childhood fantasies of omnipotence, the desire to save lives, maybe to bring my mother back to life. I found out that medicine doesn't have that kind of magic, but I'm glad I went into it," he said, with a bit of self-conscious laughter. "I love taking care of patients. Don't like to see pain, but working closely with people gives life true depth. Everyone is unique if you look below the surface."

"Interesting, you seem to have it all worked out," she said.

"The other possibilities weren't as exciting. I ran track in high-school and college and even had an undergraduate scholarship here at Devan. I was pretty good, but it's tough to earn a living doing high jumps and running 400 meter races. Might have become a coach, but medicine won out."

"Then, you're *the* Tom Sullivan, the Olympic gold medal runner."

"Yes," he said, surprised that she would know this.

"You were more than just pretty good. You were spectacular. Track's a favorite sport of mine."

"It's nice that you remember my track career. Makes me feel good."

"I'm hopeful my work will be helpful to people," Laura continued. "Perhaps I'm motivated by some of the same kinds of desires as you. And to be honest, I suppose I'd like to bring my father back to life also."

"We all have our problems adjusting to being close to death in medicine. I had to use every coping strategy I knew to get through."

"Really, like what?" Laura asked.

"Making it into an intellectual game, distancing myself, a sense of humor."

"I'll bet you have a good sense of humor," Laura said.

"It comes through at times."

Laura smiled. "I wish I could have used my sense of humor more and stuck with medicine."

"Things happen for the best," Tom said.

"I hope so."

"But only when we make them turn out that way," Tom said, smiling at her.

She glanced over at him and smiled. "At the lab, you'll see how we are developing a new generation of patient care computer programs — programs that mesh with the points system to take better care of consumers. In the Automated Care System Development Plan, it's known as Phase I."

"Algorithms?"

59

"These go far beyond the old fashion decision-making programs. This software isn't developed at remote sites away from patients. It's based on data taken directly from actual patient care situations, distilled from the real thing. These diagnostic and treatment programs will be far more efficient and accurate than human beings can possibly be."

"Sounds like really fancy algorithms!"

"You're skeptical."

"It never hurts to be mildly skeptical."

"When people take care of people one on one, it's very expensive, you know. And doctors sometimes make disastrous mistakes. You're one of the first to see the project. It's been kept under wraps."

"Why all the secrecy?"

"Has to be. Competition for points in the marketplace. Our bracelets only give us so many points, you know. And we all want the very best product we can get for our point count. Everybody wants that. CelestaCare wants to provide the best for less."

"Yes, of course, with the least overhead. The company that can give the cheapest care makes the most profit. We all know CelestaCare isn't in this for fun. There's a reason to have people, rather than computers, taking care of people, you know."

Her eyes flashed. "I've heard that you have some strong feelings about CelestaCare because of the Lilacicin pricing. You're not cutting CelestaCare much slack."

Tom sat quietly, looking out the window.

Laura continued, "Well, you need to know. I didn't have anything to do with the price schedules. Business or not, as far as I'm concerned, there is still a place for science."

"Sure, there's nothing wrong with science. But science co-opted by entrepreneurs dealing in frenzied capitalism can spell greed."

Her face was flushed. "Perhaps," she said, "but do me a favor. Wait and see the project before you pass judgement."

"Why not?" he said.

Now there was tension. Why had he lost his temper? She had discovered Lilacicin and he had tested it. She was as concerned about being associated with the pricing of the drug as he. But then her new BMW was a few notches up from his Jeep Cherokee.

In the quiet, his eyes found the place where her ankles gave way to the graceful long lines of her legs. Where the clear white of her smooth skin disappeared beneath her skirt, he could see her figure clearly outlined by the taut skirt which was now pulled tightly around her hips. He felt a little guilty about looking her over.

He looked at her face, her reddish-blond hair, her large hazel eyes, her lightly freckled skin. Minutes before, there was the gentle ease and comfort of their almost personal exchange. Then a disagreement. Had he been too sharp with her? And why was he worried? What difference did it make?

The white BMW sped along and soon approached a circle of large new buildings. Neatly planted rows of hemlocks grew around the grounds, and the wide reflective expanses of the buildings' glass windows shimmered with the images of full white clouds that filled the morning sky.

"CELESTACARE HEALTH ENTERPRISES — CORPORATE HEADQUARTERS," the tall sign in front of the buildings said.

"Well, we're here," Laura said, her eyes meeting his.

He carefully looked across at her face for clues about her feelings. If he had been too harsh with her, she had already forgiven him. He was sure.

"The lab is just a short walk from here," she said.

"Lead the way, Laura. I'll follow. And I'm reserving judgment about your project — keeping an open mind."

"Sure Dr. Sullivan," she said, and threw him a broad smile. "Sure you are."

Chapter 12

An armed guard looked over the papers authorizing Tom's entry to the restricted area, then escorted Laura and Tom down a long hallway to a large set of sliding metal doors. "SECURITY-CLEARED PERSONNEL ONLY," the stenciled lilac-colored letters across the doors said.

"Security is tight," Laura told Tom. "Every health care company is racing to develop methods to cut points, but none is as far along as we."

The guard turned his key in a switch and the sliding doors opened. Inside, Tom eyed a brightly lit room the size of a gymnasium.

In the center of the room, separated by low partitions, a row of stainless steel hospital beds bearing patients stretched across the space. Crisscrossing computer cables ran in all directions forming spider web-like configurations on the floors around the beds. A dozen windowed stations circled the perimeter of the room. Inside each one, people were busy at work.

Tom saw a man walking toward them. "Here's Tim Austin, Chief Research Technician," Laura said. She introduced him to Tom. Tom registered the lilac color of Austin's lab coat, then realized that everyone in the lab wore coats of the same color.

"I have a demo consumer from Devan Hospital for your visitor," Tim said to Laura. "Gardner is his name. Severe, insulin dependent diabetes. He's had every known complication. He zeroed out his points a month ago. Fortunately, he was selected for the New Directions program. Now he's able to earn his way participating in research. Experimental care may not be his first choice, but he needs all the free points he can get."

Tom watched an aide push the patient toward one of the hospital beds in a wheel chair. The man was dressed in a paper-thin hospital gown. In the back, the tie was loose and the flimsy gown had slipped down over one shoulder exposing half his chest. His eyes were vacant and still.

Tim Austin walked over to him. "Thanks for coming over, Sam," Tim said. "It's gracious folks like you that are helping us develop our new health care programs."

Sam Gardner said nothing. He acknowledged Austin's syrupy greeting with a small circular wave of his hand.

An aide helped the man toward the bed. Nearly blind from the effect of diabetes on the retinas of his eyes, he stumbled, his arms outstretched, waving in front of him. The hospital gown slid further down his body, exposing his genitals and buttocks. He grabbed frantically for the gown to gather it around his private parts but the clothing slipped from his hand.

"For God's sake, man," Tim yelled at the patient. "Have a little modesty."

Tom frowned at Tim, and then rushed over to help the man cover himself. "It's not his fault," Tom said sharply to Tim. "He needs more help."

"He's a New Directions consumer. He's lucky to be getting any care," Tim said coolly.

Tom shot him an angry glare.

Once the subject was in bed, several technicians surrounded him and began to connect cables to various parts of his body. One by one they peeled the coverings from the adhesive backed microphones, probes, and electrodes, and fastened them in their proper locations on his skin.

"With those monitors, we can obtain a full range of diagnostic information," Laura said. "The consumer is being monitored for blood pressure, temperature, pulse, respiration, and blood oxygen saturation. There's an electrocardiogram, frontal electromyography, an electroencephalogram. We can hear virtually any sound his body makes. Put these on," she said, handing Tom a set of earphones.

Tom listened. He heard the sounds of Mr. Gardner's breathing come through the earphones. Laura touched the chest on the body diagram displayed on one of the monitor screens beside the patient's bed. Tom heard the "lub-dup, lub-dup, lub-dup" sound of the man's heart. When she touched the diagram over the abdominal area, the noisy growling of the man's intestines sounded in Tom's ears.

"Computerized analysis of these body sounds will give us useful diagnostic information," Laura said. "But we won't really need to be working this close to the consumer.

"We can work from over there," she continued, pointing toward one of the large glassed-in work stations. "Those are the Health Care Coordination and Control Centers. They're the nerve centers of the system. We'll go up and you can see what goes on inside."

Laura thanked Tim for his help and sent him on his way.

"Tim's a hard worker," she said.

"I think I'd use other words to describe him," Tom said.

"Excuse me?" Laura said.

"Nothing. Forget it."

Tom and Laura left the main floor of the laboratory, climbed the stairs and entered one of the glass windowed control centers. Tom glanced at the row of computer terminals that lined the desk inside. He counted at least ten monitor screens. A dozen workers busily adjusted switches and dials on the control decks.

The sounds of the equipment: the beeps, the buzzes, clicks, and humming tones generated a jumble of disconnected, loud, grating noises. Indicators flashed on and off. Colored bars of light rolled by on the monitor screens. Tom's eyes darted over the array of panels and screens.

"Hope this gets less confusing," Tom said.

"It will, trust me," Laura replied.

Soon, he saw the bars of color fade into columns of numbers showing the numerical measurements of the physiological activity in the patient's body. The workers took their places; the random sounds became more regular; the level of electronic activity became more serene. Then, the whirl of sensation died down to a monotonous machine-like drone. Tom took a deep breath, loosened his tie, rubbed his neck, and tried to relax.

Through the glass, Tom looked down toward the unattended patient in the bed in the center of the large room. Mr. Gardner seemed miles away. Wires, plastic tubes, and dozens of colored cables tracked their way to and from his body. An IV bottle, filled with a pale yellow fluid, hung at his bedside.

Mr. Gardner lay still, both arms outstretched. He was covered only by a strip of disheveled sheet pulled down below his waist and wrapped like a binding around one of his legs.

Displayed on six of the monitors inside the control station was a close-up of the man's face. He lay motionless staring straight ahead, wearing a frozen, frightened expression.

Tom looked through the glass out across the crowded room. A dozen people swarmed around the bed and not a single one was near the patient.

"Someone with him at the bedside might be reassuring to the patient," Tom said to Laura. "He's almost blind. If that were you or I we'd feel terrified out there all alone."

"Okay, I'll send someone to stay with him," Laura said. "Step out there on the floor and stay with Mr. Gardner during the procedure," she said to one of the nurses standing nearby. The nurse left the station and moved toward Mr. Gardner. Laura turned back to Tom. "Everyone in this station is giving him their full attention. Look at the readouts. We're monitoring data from over a hundred physiological and chemical markers. Don't you think that's reassuring to him?"

"I suspect it may be more reassuring to you than to him," Tom said.

She pointed toward Mr. Gardner. Tom watched through the glass. One of the nurse-technicians was fastening a small, clear, plastic cube packed full of colored, electronic chips to the inside of the patient's elbow with a velcro band.

"What's that?" he asked.

"My *piece de resistance*. That small plastic cube is a molecular screening analyzer. We place it over a vein or an artery; it projects electronic grids across the blood vessel. The grids are blocked off in small squares. They measure volume and count the molecules of the particular chemical or particle we want to measure. The counts enter the blood analyzer program and the final value is instantly calculated by the computer. Two-hundred blood counts and chemistries at your fingertips. All done in a split second: no contact with blood, no chemicals, no messy laboratory. Now, keep your eyes on Monitor 6."

After a few seconds, a long row of laboratory values rolled on the screen. She pressed a series of keys and a printer spit out a hard copy of the data. She tore off the printed sheet and handed it to Tom.

Tom scanned the printout. "This is amazing!" he said, reviewing the results.

"All this electronic equipment supports the heart of Phase I of our project. Over here," she said.

He followed Laura across the control room to another bank of monitors where a trio of people wearing lilac coats worked at keyboards.

"The physicians and nurses working here are experienced specialists in endocrinology," Laura explained. "They're doing what they would do for any patient with this illness at this specific phase of treatment. But there's an extraordinary product resulting from their care. Every detail about the patient and his treatment, monitored vital signs, lab values, diagnostic work, any treatment, responses — it's all being saved and sorted into data files."

Tom watched the monitor as each step of care moved by in sequence on the screen in front of him.

"These workers are constructing a segment of the software data base that will be the foundation of our automated system. Later, we'll convert this to software and be able to call up these diagnostic and treatment plans anytime we want them. They'll apply to any patient with the same or similar problem. Computer programs will make the subtle adjustments to fit the individual patient.

"This is only one 'event of care,' but before it's over we'll have software programs available for every disease — for every possible event in any illness, any injury. Any consumer with the same disease and complications as this consumer, any patient that matches this 'event of care' can be treated with this program.

"We're creating whole libraries of automatic programs containing hundreds of thousands of algorithms — decision trees, ready to instantly make diagnoses or dictate the most appropriate treatment directions. When we've installed the new system, patients will be connected to monitoring devices, readings made and the correct program placed in operation.

"There will be feedback programs in every installation. The feedback programs will be continually monitored for cost and outcome, and reconfigured to constantly increase expertise and efficiency over time. Everyone will get the best, most cost-effective, standardized managed care."

"Incredible," Tom said.

"We'll be installing forty of these units at Starr Memorial immediately. After that, the plan is to install them nationwide. Every CelestaCare Hospital in the country will have Phase I capability. And we've already begun work on Phase II. Look over there."

She pointed toward an area to the right of the control room where four patients lay on gurneys. On an IV rack above each, a fluid bottle hung, its yellow-green liquid dripping drop by drop into a plastic cylinder connected to plastic tubing. Tom's eyes followed the plastic tubing to its destination — a direct connection with the patient's blood circulation — a central venous line that disappeared beneath a small gauze bandage on the patients' necks.

"The central line will make the system even more foolproof," Laura explained. "It's an even more sophisticated way of monitoring the patient and providing treatment. There's no end to what can be done with these devices.

"With the new computer administrative programs and the reduced numbers of health care workers, we'll be able to cut the point cost down to practically nothing."

"And increase the profits for CelestaCare International?"

"Please Dr. Sullivan. I want the best for patients just like you do. Not only that, but we'll provide high quality, lower cost care for more consumers. If machines can do the same things as people and cost less, why not? There's nothing to be gained by keeping people doing what they don't need to do."

"It's impressive work, but I don't believe you can eliminate people from medical care."

Laura turned toward him. "If I had limited points, I'd want the best I could get for the least points, people or no people. The fact is, my programs will be able to do many of the same things physicians do, but at a lower cost."

Tom crossed his arms. "It's cookbook, generic, medical care, without the doctor-patient relationship."

"You'll see. There's nothing wrong with this kind of care. You need to get your feelings straight about the technology, Dr. Sullivan. Just look at this project as a scientist, a health scientist. But, I do understand. I suppose that whenever something comes along that replaces computers, I'll be a little threatened too."

Tom stared thoughtfully at the frenzied activity on the other side of the glass.

"I'll drop you by the hospital," Laura said when they were driving back to Devan. "That is unless you'd like to get lunch."

"No, I need to get back," Tom said.

"Well, on the way, you can educate me about something."

"I'll try."

"I know about Paul Devan's preoccupation with lilacs, and his plantings. I know about his obsession with death and the scent of lilac blossoms masking the smell of death. But now it seems that the entire health care world is obsessed with lilacs and the color lilac. The name for the antibiotic, Lilacicin; the color lilac as the official color of the National Health Agency; everything in health care is being colored lilac. And my husband is mad for the color. You saw the lab coats."

"Lilac is Devan's school color," Tom said. "Alexander Wade graduated first in his class from Devan Medical Center and now he's on The Board of Trust. He probably chose lilac as the NHA color because of some kind of dedication to his alma mater. I suspect Cunningham wanted your antibiotic linked to Devan Medical Center and requested that CelestaCare name the drug Lilacicin. It was probably part of the deal in agreeing to do the clinical trials."

"But why would my husband be so interested in the color?"

"What does he say?" Tom asked.

"Nothing, he just smiles and says he has great admiration for Devan's founder, Paul Devan. Great admiration is an understatement. Ken thinks Paul Devan walked on water."

"To tell you the truth, he has a lot of company," Tom said. "There are many Devan worshipers around. He founded the finest medical center in the country. And rather than being permanently undone by an epidemic, he found a way to channel his energies into something creative."

"Ken feels that Devan's own struggle with death during the diphtheria epidemic of 1850 resulted in his experiencing a kind of resurrection," Laura said. "He views Paul Devan's contributions as spiritual."

"Spiritual? I'm not sure I would go that far. But it's actually a very interesting story: a physician's struggle with death. And as we discussed on the way to your lab, we all do that in one way or another."

"Yes," she mused, "my husband is involved in the same struggle. His fascination with Paul Devan is just one part of his zeal to move health care in a more constructive direction. You mustn't let his driven style confuse you. Underneath it is a powerful motivation to improve health care and the well-being of humankind. That's what attracted me to him."

Back at Devan, the scenes and events of the morning came back to Tom as haunting images throughout the rest of the day: the lilac-colored lab coats, Mr. Gardner lying in the bed, isolated and alone, the frenzied pace of the workers in the control station, central lines placed in patient's necks to make the technology more efficient.

Why were his feelings about the lab so negative? Why couldn't he be more objective about CelestaCare's plan? And why did he have the feeling there was something dark, something still unknown, hidden in the project?

Perhaps Laura was correct. Perhaps he was threatened by the machines. Perhaps the thought of his own obsolescence was fueling his negative feelings. Regardless of what he thought or felt about the project, he was certain of one thing. Laura Clark was creating a cost effective, efficient, innovative approach to medical care.

And after all, that's what the country had asked for in health care; that's what the government desired, and that was what CelestaCare had directed Laura to design.

Chapter 13

At ten o'clock that evening, Tom finished his work. He scanned his parking card over the exit post and turned out of the Devan Medical Center parking lot toward home. Speeding along the interstate, he continued to ruminate about the tour of Laura's lab: more technology, more informatics, more generic care, less doctor-patient relationship, he thought. Where was this all going?

A giant billboard with a brightly colored painting of a crippled hand with swollen red knuckles towered over the road. It advertised the new arthritis clinic at Devan Medical Center. Further down the highway, another imposing billboard touted Middleside's CelestaCare Starr Memorial Hospital Emergency Services. A bright red star flashed on and off intermittently, illuminating the sign. "EMERGENCY CARE — GET IT FAST AT STARR," the sign said. Further down the interstate, still another mammoth lighted clock billboard displayed the virtue of the Infertility Clinic at Middleside Women's Hospital. An undulating neon sperm wound its way around the dial. Above the time piece, adorning the sign, was the admonition, "WATCH YOUR BIOLOGICAL CLOCK — IT'S TICKING AWAY." On still another sign, a simulated blue fluid poured back and forth between a pair of chemical beakers. "CHEMICAL IMBALANCE," the sign read. "That's why you're feeling depressed. ASK YOUR DOCTOR ABOUT NOMELANCHOL." Other signs flashed before him as he drove along: advertisements for eating disorder clinics, diabetes clinics, corneal laser surgery, skin care, the "best" in cardiac surgery, and cholesterol lowering agents.

Each sign promised the consumer huge savings on "points," and in lined off rectangles, like the Surgeon General's hazard warnings on cigarette packages, the familiar statement required by the government on all health-care advertisements appeared: "THE DIRECTOR OF THE NATIONAL HEALTH AGENCY SAYS: CONSERVE YOUR POINTS. USE THEM WISELY — THEY'RE AS VALUABLE AS YOUR LIFE."

Scoops, scoops, and more scoops. Arthritis, emergency care, infertility, eating disorders, heart surgery, you name it. Market whatever you need to capture a huge patient population in a profitable setting. Scoop up those patients.

Now I'll be a part of that, he thought. And Laura Clark's automated care may be the biggest scoop of them all.

Tom yawned, adjusted the dial on the radio, and turned the volume down on "Ticket To Ride," by the Beatles. A short time later, he exited the interstate and drove toward his street. Soon, he turned into the carport behind his home.

Taking his key from the door, he turned to see his wife waiting for him in the kitchen doorway. She was in a terry cloth robe with her long brown hair let down, falling on her shoulders. She walked over, gently squeezed his arm, and kissed him gently on his cheek.

"What a day," he said, putting down his briefcase.

"Oh?"

"Today was the day Laura Clark came to take me on a tour of her new automated care project. It was quite a show."

"Isn't she the one who's married to the CelestaCare executive, Ken Clark?"

"Right, do you know him?"

"He's the character Cunningham got to do the cost effectiveness studies on the Pediatric Critical Care Unit at Devan. He was at the hospital today, giving his seminar. He said a three-minute prayer before he gave his talk. It was a little strange for a presentation on cost control."

"I would think so. I'll be working for him. Great, huh?"

"You can deal with anybody, Dr. Sullivan. I have faith in you. So what is this new CelestaCare project they've got you working on now?"

"Laura Clark has developed a system to put care patterns on software. You name the disease or the medical situation, and they have the diagnostics, treatment plans and everything else on software. No more decisions by doctors or nurses, just machines."

Katie was pensive. She tilted her head. A quizzical look crossed her face.

"Laura Clark is super bright. These programs will be powerful tools," Tom said.

"Sounds like science fiction," Katie said.

"Some of her ideas could turn out to be useful."

"Sounds like she might have sold you on her ideas."

He shrugged his shoulders.

"What does she look like?" Katie asked.

"Who?"

"Laura Clark."

Tom made a face. "She looks like Laura Clark. You've seen her pictures."

"Yeah, but I mean in person."

"She's gorgeous, but so are you."

"I'm already jealous."

"You needn't be. But I'll have to say her work is impressive. It will probably make health care more affordable, but there's something ominous about it all. I think she felt she was showing me the light about technology."

"I'll show you the light," she said taking his hand and moving him toward the bedroom. "I've already had enough of CelestaCare and Laura Clark to last a lifetime. You can tell me about it tomorrow. I've waited up for you."

Minutes later, Tom was in bed.

Katie sat on the edge of the bed, brushing out her hair. She glanced at him out of the corners of her lively, green eyes. Tom watched her grooming herself and smelled the perfumed body lotion she had rubbed on her skin. Her adoring look pushed thoughts of the automated care units to the back of his mind.

"You've got no business working this late," she said in a whisper. She looked toward him admiringly, reached out and stroked his thick, wavy hair, then leaned forward and brushed her lips lightly across his forehead. Her lips were soft and he felt their moist path gently cross his skin.

He smiled and strained to kiss her as she pulled away. She turned off the light on the bedside table and got in bed sliding beneath the covers.

He pulled her closer to him.

"CelestaCare and Laura Clark only want your medical expertise and reputation. I want all of you," she said.

"You only want my body," he said.

"And your soul, I want all of you," she said, losing her words against his lips as she kissed him.

They moved closer together.

After a while, the two of them lay quietly.

"I'm glad I waited up for you," she said. "I think I can compete with Laura Clark."

"No doubt," he said.

The light from the bathroom shone in a narrow ribbon across the white sheet they lay under. Tom turned toward Katie and propped himself up on his elbow.

"What do you supposed Carl will think of all the new CelestaCare technology?" he asked.

"Damn, Sullivan. You can't get medicine off of your mind. First it's Laura Clark, CelestaCare's health care computer whiz, then Carl Hammerstone, Devan's Chief of Internal Medicine. I can deal with Laura Clark, but I'm not sure I can compete with Carl."

"I was just thinking how much I'll miss him after his retirement."

"Carl Hammerstone is no fan of CelestaCare Health Enterprises. He's the man who taught you that there's more to practicing medicine than technology. And he won't be happy about any kind of automated care."

"We may be entering another time in medicine."

"I think this Laura Clark has already made you a believer?"

"No, but medicine is changing. It has to."

"Yes, health care reform was an economic hoax," Katie said.

"Tomorrow's graduation exercises will be Cunningham's big moment," Tom said. "The first Devan Medical School class to graduate into the world of PointCure. We'll hear Carl's farewell speech, then a week later, we'll start installing automated care."

"Graduation starts at ten sharp," Katie said.

"Carl Hammerstone has been a powerful influence in my life," Tom said. "I'm terribly upset about his retirement."

"Yes," Katie said. "I know you'll miss him." She pulled up the covers. "A good night kiss would be nice."

He kissed her softly on the lips.

"Good night," he said. "I love you."

"I love you too," she said, then snuggled next to him.

Wide awake, he stared at the ceiling for at least a half an hour before he closed his eyes. Thoughts of Laura's busy lab and its frenzied activity would not let go.

Chapter 14

Along the route to Devan University, large signs with purple letters against a lilac background stood in front of each of the quickly erected PointCure Check-In Centers.

When the Sullivans stopped at an intersection, Katie read one out loud with a mocking voice:

DEAR CONSUMER:
FOR YOUR HEALTH AND WELL-BEING, HERE STANDS ANOTHER NHA POINTCURE CHECK-IN CENTER. STAY HEALTHY, BUT WHEN YOU NEED US, CHECK IN HERE.
ALEXANDER WADE, M.D., DIRECTOR,
NATIONAL HEALTH AGENCY

She folded her arms and breathed a sigh. "Well, I'll be damned," she said. "That NHA sure is terrific. And that Wade character is pure gold."

"The PointCure Check-in Centers all look exactly alike," Tom said, "like a generic lilac-colored version of a fast food restaurant."

"Generica, generica, God shed His Grace on thee," Katie sang loudly.

At Devan, Tom turned into the gates that marked the edge of the University. The car slowed to a crawl in the traffic that headed toward the graduation.

He steered the car along the oak lined street that paralleled the walkways near the finely manicured expanse of green lawn known as the "Green." How many times had he seen this scene: each spring amidst the blooming lilacs, graduates dressed in their caps and gowns marching across the Green to receive their degrees, proud parents and families of the graduates on the footpaths streaming toward the clearing to the graduation exercises, the youthful soon to be doctors sporting their traditional, green Doctor of Medicine satin hoods. This time, they were surely headed for a different kind of medicine than he had entered at his graduation years before.

Once parked, Katie and Tom made their way toward the Green. As they walked along, Tom heard a voice call out from behind him.

"Well, I'll be damned!" Carl Hammerstone said with his deep voice. "If it isn't CelestaCare's new chief physician. Off to cut the costs of medical care to the bone."

Tom self-consciously smiled, then studied Carl's face as he greeted Katie. Carl looked like one would imagine an aging doctor should look: full head of white hair, strong, sensitive kind face, wise, deep brown eyes. Carl put his arm around Katie's shoulder and gently pulled her close to him. Then Tom walked up and shook Carl's hand.

"CelestaCare people have never been up to any good and that won't change. I hope they don't eat you alive, son."

Tom stood tall. "I can handle them," Tom said.

"Damn, I hope so." Carl said.

Arriving at the Green, Carl left the couple and headed toward the podium. Tom watched as his mentor made his way through the crowd shaking hands with old friends.

Tom and Katie pardoned their way through the peopled passageway to two empty seats. They watched Carl take his place with the other gowned, academic dignitaries sitting in the folding chairs on the stage.

Tom's eye caught the full page advertisement for CelestaCare Health's new automated units on the back cover of the program. He skimmed the description of the planned installation of the automated patient care units at Starr Memorial Hospital. "Devan Medical Center will collaborate with CelestaCare to the fullest in the project," the copy said. "Add the best to the best and get the very best," the advertisement said.

He took a deep breath and thought of what Carl would say. "What a collaboration — Devan and CelestaCare were in bed together and the patients would get screwed."

Tom searched for Carl on the stage. Momentarily he lost him in the sea of black robes, green hoods, and tasseled mortar boards. Suddenly his head of white hair came in view.

His thoughts turned back to the time Carl Hammerstone called him to his office early in his second year of medical school. It was late in the afternoon and Tom sat quietly in front of the professor's desk.

"Your preceptors say you're slipping," the distinguished looking Chairman of the Department of Internal Medicine had said. "They tell me you seem preoccupied, worried, and maybe even depressed. You were close to the top of the class in your first year, but you've lost interest in what you're doing. Is something wrong?" Carl asked.

With embarrassment, Tom told him. "I've been raised to make it on my own, regardless. My father always told me, 'Sullivans take charge and work things out for themselves,' but my finances are becoming more and more of a problem. With the high tuition, living expenses and cost of supplies, the loans aren't enough. Dad has done what he can. Even with my weekend job, I can't make ends meet. Now, I need all the textbooks for the clinical rotations and they're out of reach."

Carl Hammerstone nodded his head thoughtfully as Tom talked. When the student finished, the doctor looked across his office over Tom's shoulder.

"Look there," his teacher said. He pointed toward the wall behind Tom.

Tom turned and looked. His eyes widened. Carl Hammerstone's library with its hundreds of volumes stretched across an entire wall.

"I have copies of every book you need. There's too much reading to do it all in a library. You need your own books at home. You can use mine. Use them as long as you want."

The student smiled with gratitude.

"And you'll need a job that pays something. One that's worthwhile. I can probably get you a job in a lab. The deans will help. Maybe there's some special interest you want to pursue."

"Infectious disease," Tom said. "I want to work with AIDS patients."

"That's not easy work. It'll drain you to the core."

"That's what I want to do."

"Then that's what it will be. On weekends, you'll have a job in one of the infectious disease labs. You can make rounds with the infectious disease team. I'll arrange it."

"Thank you sir," Tom had said when he shook the professor's hand at the door.

Soon, Tom's enthusiasm for medicine returned and he never lost it again.

The graduation program began. A woman two rows behind Tom and Katie, dressed in a bright yellow dress sang the Star Spangled Banner with a shrill church choir voice. Soon the music stopped, and the shuffling of chairs and the muffled sound of the sum of whispers began.

There was an invocation with thanks to God for all the good that had come to pass. Then Tom heard the polished voice of Raymond Cunningham ask the crowd to stand for a few moments of silence to honor the fourteen Devan medical students who died in the epidemic. Tom stood automatically though it seemed to him to be far too short a time to honor anyone. After the silence, the crowd took their seats.

Cunningham introduced Carl Hammerstone. Katie reached and took Tom's hand and squeezed it softly.

The students applauded and Carl walked toward the podium. When he reached it, he paused, adjusted the microphone, and took out his notes. For a few moments, he silently looked out over the now still audience. Then he began. He thanked the administration, the students, and then recognized the parents. "I am not ready for retirement. There is too much to be done, especially now," he said.

Soon he reached the core of his talk.

"Even with all the changes that have occurred around us, your goal, your primary goal as physicians is still to care for your patients as persons like yourselves. It is only in the context of the relationship — where one human being cares for another like himself — that true

78

healing can occur. It is only in the context of the relationship that the individual can be sustained as alive and whole, as complete." And then he added, "No technology, however advanced, will ever replace the healing force of a caring, relating person...responding to the needs of another."

There was strength, clarity, and now, still calm in the statement of his views. Once, Tom thought his voice cracked with some sadness, but he could not be sure.

Tom recognized part of his talk. The message was paraphrased from Carl's well-known book, *Doctor and Patient: The Healing Relationship.* The thin volume, with its ninety-six-pages, was the best known guide to the subtleties of the physician-patient relationship in the medical literature. "Art is just as important as science in the practice of medicine." His book stated this theme over and over.

The second speaker for the one hundred and twelve new physicians, the man who had introduced the first, was Vice Chancellor Raymond Cunningham. His tone differed from Hammerstone's. An honors Devan graduate himself and a recent *cum laude* graduate of a prestigious MBA program, he had been brought in a year before the epidemic to put the financially faltering Devan back into the black. His words drew the lines that defined a new direction for medicine.

"These are indeed challenging times. You men and women are on the frontier of massive changes in health care. The epidemic has killed well over a million of our citizens, many were our colleagues, some your classmates. Now we must move forward. There is no time to waste.

"Our technology must be carefully tuned; we must mobilize it to its fullest. We must use it in the most cost effective and resourceful manner. I am confident that the innovative PointCure system will move us successfully on our way. You new physicians are to be the managers of the new systems of health care. You are to be the custodians of the destiny of humankind. Compassionate care is our mandate, tested technology, our path. God bless you."

The crack of applause that ended the ceremony brought the proud new doctors to their feet. Parents, families, and well wishers surged forward to congratulate the young physicians. Katie and Tom found

Carl, complimented him on his talk and the three of them headed for the reception for the new doctors.

Later, at the reception, when Katie and Tom were shaking hands with Dr. Cunningham, another couple joined them. It was Ken and Laura Clark.

Ken Clark threw out his hand to Tom. "We are extremely pleased about your directing the installation of our new automated units at Starr. I'd say we have a good man on the CelestaCare team."

"Sure," Tom said.

"I think you've met my wife, Laura," he said.

"We've met," Tom said quietly. "This is my wife, Katie Sullivan."

Katie smiled politely at Ken and Laura.

Raymond Cunningham, now with his back to Katie stepped closer to Laura and smiled broadly.

"Congratulations Laura. Lilacicin was a smash success. And here's to even greater accomplishments with automated care," he said and raised his glass of champagne toward her. She smiled and quietly nodded.

Ken stared at Katie. "I think we've already met," he said. "Devan, critical care. Of course. You're the pediatrician in charge of the pediatric critical care units at Devan Hospital."

"Yes, I do work on the critical care units." Katie said.

Clark turned to Cunningham. "Ray, our CelestaCare management specialists have just completed the management study on those critical care units." Then he spoke directly to Katie. "I'm sure you found our work very helpful. The efficient administrative plans we developed will significantly contribute to point utilization and quality of care."

Laura Clark quietly observed the conversation and sipped punch from the crystal cup she cradled in her hands. Tom's eyes passed Ken face and glanced across his shoulder. Laura stood in the line of his gaze, slightly to the left behind Ken. From time to time, she looked away and shifted her body from right to left, seeming nervously to try and find her place. Why was she so anxious? Where was the confidence he had seen the day before?

Katie squared off with Ken. "Mr. Clark, it seems to me that most of your staff's recommendations have to do with time consuming meetings and staff reductions that make it impossible to spend time with our patients. If we did it your way, our patients would be totally on their own while we attended cost containment conferences."

Clark smiled. "Technology, time accountability, and cost containment are here to stay, Dr. Sullivan," he said. "We have to think of the consumer and the future well-being of humankind. And as you know, CelestaCare now owns a substantial part of Devan Hospital. Our role is to steer you in the right direction."

Tom could see that Katie was unnerved by Clark's style.

"Here to stay all right," Katie continued, "but not because you're thinking of patients. You're thinking of profits."

Clark's head snapped back.

"Well no, we're thinking of the future of humankind, Dr. Sullivan. Physicians can't begin to comprehend where health care must go. You need guidance."

Tom stepped forward to intervene. Katie's look stopped him. The fire in her eyes told him she intended to handle the matter herself.

"We can guide ourselves, Mr. Clark. Your cost containment administrators don't have a clue about how to take care of patients and that's what we're all about."

Now Laura Clark seemed to regain her confidence. She stepped forward, took her husband by the arm and turned him in the direction of the food table. For a moment he resisted. Then, having momentarily taken stock of social propriety, he moved forward with Laura's coaxing. The sparring had stopped, the round was over, and Ken Clark and Katie had disengaged. But Tom had an uneasy feeling that there would be other matches with Ken Clark to come.

Chapter 15

Mitchell R. Newman was among the consumers at one of the newly completed PointCure Check-In Centers that Tom and Katie drove past on their way to the graduation exercises. A slight man with shaggy graying hair, Newman had come for a points check and slowly made his way to the front of the modular building in the chilly morning air. As he walked through the crowd, he held his left side tightly and each time his foot hit the ground, he grimaced in pain.

He stopped to read the large sign with lilac-colored letters on the front wall of the building. The bold lettered sign informed consumers of the basic rules:

1. NO HEALTH CARE SERVICE WITHOUT A POINTS CHECK – NO EXCEPTIONS!
2. UNLESS YOUR ILLNESS OR INJURY CONSTITUTES AN IMMINENT EMERGENCY AND IS IMMEDIATELY LIFE-THREATENING, YOU MUST BE CHECKED IN BY THE HEALTH MANAGEMENT TEAM FOR YOUR DISTRICT. IF YOU HAVE A DIRE EMERGENCY, GO IMMEDIATELY TO THE NEAREST EMERGENCY CARE CENTER; CONSUMERS WITH NON-EMERGENCIES WHO PRESENT THEMSELVES TO THE EMERGENCY CARE CENTER WILL BE FINED WITH POINT DEDUCTIONS.
3. YOUR POINTS ARE YOUR MOST VALUABLE POSSESSION. TAKE GOOD CARE OF YOURSELF, BUT PLEASE REMEMBER THAT YOU HAVE A LIMITED

NUMBER OF THESE VALUALBLE HEALTH BENEFITS. USE THEM WISELY!

He felt a tap on his shoulder and turned around. "Yes, what is it?" he asked.

"You seem to be in pain. Can I help?" a stranger asked.

The man who spoke to him was dressed in a cheap, shiny blue suit. A laminated plastic badge hung from his lapel. Newman read it. "WILLIAM P. COBERN, OFFICIAL NHA HEALTH CARE ADVISOR, REGISTRATION NUMBER: NHA273016," it said. He noted that the man's shirt collar was turning yellow where it touched his neck. His tie, a frenzied, paisley print, had too much torque on the small knot. Cobern's voice was deep and he smiled broadly with his teeth showing when he spoke.

"Been here before?" Cobern asked.

"No."

"Then I can help you. My name is Cobern, Bill Cobern," he said. "I'm one of the District Health Care Advisors. What's the trouble?"

"Kidneys I believe. I had stones years ago. Feels the same. Hurts like hell." Newman groaned with pain.

Cobern looked concerned. "That's an emergency isn't it? You should go to the Emergency Center."

"That's a ton of points."

"Yes, but if you need it…"

"I need to save my points. I'll just wait in line with the rest."

"Well, have it your way, but that kidney stuff is tough business. Here's some up-to-date information for you about sale prices on health care and here's my card," he said. He handed him his business card, a booklet, and pointed toward one of the five doors. "That's where you enter the building," he said. "After your points check quote, find me. I'll be around to help you find a place to be treated. It's my job to help you find the best care for the least number of points. And I've got some really good deals today, so look me up."

"Thanks, thanks a lot," Newman said, cringing, as a sharp pain like a sledge hammer hitting him, struck the thick muscle mass next to his spine on the left side of his mid back.

Mitchell Newman felt strangely comforted by the presence of the man. The brief conversation and the stranger's interest somehow served to soothe the bewilderment he was feeling in the chaos of the new system. And even though Cobern reminded Newman of a very slick salesman, he put the card away carefully and planned to talk to him again after he had his points check.

Of course Newman already knew about the advisors. He knew that in his "Care District" he could choose among several major government approved facilities, all of which were in fierce competition for his points. For their guidance, advisors usually took a fee from the ill person in proportion to the number of points estimated for diagnosis and treatment quoted by the point check personnel.

Wooed by the highly competitive health care corporations, the advisors played a significant part in directing patients toward providers. With advertisement budgets cut, the importance of their advice had increased. And even though there were published booklets, continually updated as to where care was available and the points price, the more personalized recommendations of the health care advisors carried considerable weight. They represented some sort of remnant of a personal touch.

Newman saw still another group of people wearing badges milling around the Check-In building. He knew these to be the points merchants — the newly arrived entrepreneurs who made their living by buying points and reselling them for a profit. At first the government had been opposed to these people fearing they would undercut the NHA's control. Soon, however, it became apparent that the market they created had a stabilizing effect on the health care economy. They also curbed dissatisfaction with the system, for the rich could always pay to buy extra points.

The group had founded an organization known as the Health Care Unit Association. They requested that the government allow them access to the devices which changed the points readings, but the government felt it had best retain this function. The group developed a standardized form referred to as the "HCUA Points Certificate" whereby points could be transferred from one person to another in a legal way. The official looking certificates, which were not unlike stock certificates, were already coming to be a favorite gift for birthdays, graduations, bar/bat mitzvahs, weddings and other special occasions.

Mitchell Newman had given his place in line to a woman carrying her sick three-year-old. The feverish child was thrashing about, vomiting, and delirious. A few minutes later, an old man told Newman that he was only there for a prescription refill. He took note of Newman's extreme distress and let him enter the building in his place.

Newman crossed the threshold and looked around. Plastic vines bearing small plastic, lilac-colored flowers climbed up and trailed around the doorway. The leaves of the vines were still covered with a thin coat of sawdust left over from the recent construction.

As he entered, the sign on the dispenser instructed him to "TAKE A NUMBER IN ORDER TO BE SERVED." He reached up, pulled the white tab down, tore it off, and looked at it.

"68, step up, 68," the official at the head of his line called out loudly just as Newman looked down to check his number. Mitchell's number was "76". He leaned against the wall and waited.

"Temperature check," a short, dumpy, gray-haired older woman in a lilac smock said as she approached him, pointing to her opened mouth. Feeling dazed by his pain, at first Newman could not understand her purpose. Then, automatically, he opened his mouth and she stuck in the white plastic probe which was attached by a wire to the electronic device she was carrying.

A few seconds later, the device beeped. "Hmmm, 102.6 degrees. Remember that buddy. They'll be asking you what it was," she said, wiping the probe with the alcohol soaked gauze sponge she held in her hand.

"102.6, 102.6, 102.6, 102.6, 102.6, 102.6," Newman repeated over and over to himself, straining to hold on to the number, but being distracted by his pain.

Newman thought about his last visit to his own doctor. He recalled reading the out-of-date magazine — an ancient *Field And Stream*. He remembered the crowded waiting room and the two-hour wait. But the setting was not icy cold, like the Check-In Center, and the caregivers did not seem to be a thousand miles away.

"76, okay, where are you, 76?" the man queried, as he looked around the room. Newman waved his number to identify himself. "Come on buddy, hurry up to the table. There are lots of people to take care of here," the official said impatiently.

Mitchell Newman slowly approached the man sitting at the long counter. The man motioned again for him to come forward. A bracelet disc scanner sat on the desk. The man signaled for Newman to place his bracelet under it. He grimaced in pain as he held the left side of his back and leaned slightly forward to support himself on the table.

"No leaning on the table," the official said sharply.

The printer whirred, jerked, and whined, and produced a document of almost two pages in length. The operator of the computer terminal waited until the printer finished then tore off the sheets. He then began to talk to the sick man in a detached, distant manner.

"Let's see, you are Newman, Mitchell R., is that right?" he asked, without looking up from the papers he held before him.

"Yes."

"And your social security number is 223, dash, 37, dash 3096, correct?"

"Yes."

"And your address is 357 East Penway Road, Apartment 37, right?"

"Yes."

The man leaned back in his chair. "And what can your National Health Agency do for you today, Mr. Newman?"

"It's my back — the left side of my back, sometimes up high, sometimes in the middle, sometimes aching pain, sometimes sharp pain. I can even feel the pain in my groin sometime."

"Please wait a minute, Mr. Newman. Slow down. That's too much detail, too fast. I have some specific questions I will ask and then you can tell me about the symptoms. Now you say that you are having pain in your back?"

"Yes."

"Hmmm, back pain, let's see." He keyed some letters into the terminal and studied the information that was appearing before him on his screen. Mitchell Newman noticed that the man had a peculiar mannerism. Each time something new appeared on the screen, he would raise his bushy black, eyebrows.

"Now, just answer these questions, Newman. Pain — how long?"

"Two days."

"Did you hurt your back lifting something?"

"No."

The clerk typed all Newman's answers into the computer.

"Urinary symptoms? Pain on urination? Urinating more frequently? Pyuria?" he questioned as he read the list from the screen.

"Pyuria? I'm sorry, sir, you'll have to explain that one."

"Your piss — does it burn when it comes out of your pecker?" he explained pointedly.

"Sometimes." Newman said. He glanced self-consciously at the woman standing before the other points check clerk next to him.

"Hmmmm, pyuria. Let's see," the man said, moving the cursor to pick up the symptom on the screen.

"Family history of kidney disease?"

"Yes, an aunt."

"Mother or father's side?"

"Mother's," he answered as a shock wave of pain shot through his back. He grabbed at the place it hit. The man continued to ask his questions.

"Throat infections as a child?"

"Yes."

As he questioned the patient, the man typed the information on the keyboard.

"Now, character of pain. Is it sharp? dull? throbbing? aching? constant? intermittent?"

"That's hard to say."

"Well, which fits best?" the man asked, looking up at him.

"Wait! There it goes now," Newman said, noting his experience and trying to characterize the pain. He thought a moment.

"Dull ache — that's it — dull ache."

"That doesn't fit, Mr. Newman, that doesn't fit," the man said impatiently.

"Doesn't fit?" Newman asked, perplexed about the man's response.

"Yes, the computer algorithm won't take it. That description doesn't fit the computer's decision tree. 'Dull ache' won't work."

The combination of the pain, the man's questions and the people packing in around him was beginning to take its toll. Mitchell

Newman looked straight at the man and said angrily, "Whose damned pain is it, mine or the computer's?" Then, he quickly began wondering if he might affect the man's interest in him. Recognizing his dependency, Mitchell Newman had second thoughts. He tried to make his anger subside.

"Come now, Newman, have a little patience. It's very important to get this information correct so that the National Health Agency can do its job."

"I'm sorry. I understand. You have a job to do."

"Well, Mr. Newman, we'll just let the computer decide what needs to be done and how many points it will be. Doesn't sound like much to me, but then, I'm not a health care provider. Just a computer operator."

There was a pause while the computer processed the information. Then the man spoke.

"According to our determination, Mr. Newman, you are in need of an evaluation. You have points galore, so that's no problem. Evaluations for this problem are running from 100 to 150 points, and then, of course, if there is treatment, it will be more. If you turn out to have a stone, you might want to shop around. Someone might have a special on the new DissolvaBeam. Breaking up those stones with the vibrating, penetrating laser is quite the rage these days. They tell me they can do it in a flash." He chuckled as he said the last sentence. "That'll be twenty points please. Just put your bracelet back under the scanner and we'll collect."

"Twenty points, for what? All you did was tell me I needed an evaluation. I already knew that."

"Look Mr. Newman, the NHA did you a real service. We authorized your getting the evaluation and treatment you need. Now, you have your referral. That's no small gift. The points charge is for getting you in the system. It's an equipment and administrative fee. Administration counts for a lot you know."

Mitchell Newman knew he had no choice. He thanked the man.

"No problem. By the way, Mitch, we have a really special deal today. While you're getting your kidneys checked you can get a cholesterol check for only five points. It's usually ten, but the NHA wants to encourage cholesterol checks. Here's the special coupon.

Can't do too much about cholesterol, you know: clogs up your arteries."

He handed the coupon and the computerized authorization form to Mitchell.

"Have that treatment order certified with the NHA stamp by the aide over there." He pointed to an area where another long line of people were waiting. "Then you can decide what you want to do. But before you go, please listen to this recorded message through the earphones. Thank you. Next." The clerk looked at the next customer number on the display. "Eighty-two," he called out.

Mitchell Newman stepped aside, put the earphone to his ear and listened. The message was a familiar one:

"Your points are your most valuable possession. You should, of course, take good care of yourself, but before you use your points please remember that you have a limited number of these valuable health benefits. Use them wisely," the recording said.

The nurse stamped his form with the official NHA "points check" stamp and gave him an information booklet listing kidney treatment centers.

The pain was excruciating and Newman was starting to sweat profusely. As he walked from the building, a shabbily dressed old man pushing a grocery cart filled with aluminum cans came up to him and handed him a card. The card said, "More care for less points at CelestaCare." There was a telephone number on the card and on the back was a small map giving directions to the nearest CelestaCare Health Providers' Center. It was only a few blocks away.

"Thanks," he said to the old man, and handed him a quarter. "Thanks."

He looked through the crowd for Bill Cobern, the Health Care Advisor, and finally found him. He was sitting on a bench talking to a well dressed woman. Newman stood there a few minutes. Finally, Mr. Cobern took note of him.

"Sorry old friend, but I'm very busy. I'll be with you as soon as I can," he said. He was sitting on a bench offering his advice to a woman with dried blood on her chin.

"This is a very high point item," he said barely moving his lips so that only Newman could hear. "You understand, don't you — business is business," he said winking at him.

Mitchell Newman looked at his watch and noted that it was near noon. The pain was becoming unbearable. He decided to bypass the advisor, Bill Cobern, and simply go to the nearest CelestaCare Center. He looked at the small map on the back of the card the street person had handed him, and began his painful march.

Chapter 16

An eight-foot tall, wire, mesh fence, topped by concertina barbed wire, surrounded Starr Memorial Hospital; a folding iron gate stretched across its front door. Installed during the epidemic to stop unauthorized entries, the still in-place barriers gave the rambling building the look of a fortress. The sign over the front door said:

> STARR MEMORIAL HOSPITAL
> A CELESTACARE HEALTH ENTERPRISES —
> NATIONAL HEALTH AGENCY
> JOINT VENTURE FACILITY

As Tom walked across the parking lot, a sky ambulance painted bright lilac moved toward the heliport on the roof of the hospital. He felt the windy downdraft from the aircraft as it crept slowly to its rooftop perch. The "*flot, flot, flot, flot, flot, flot...*" sounds of the helicopter blades whirring through the air, drummed in his ears. He glanced upward as the aircraft smoothly slithered out of sight behind the protective railing that edged the flat roof.

The words, "KEEP OUT, STARR MEMORIAL HEALTH CARE PERSONNEL ONLY" were stenciled on the steel entrance door. Tom passed his magnetic card into the slot on the door, then pressed his six digit entry code number into the numerical lock. After a buzz and a click, the door opened. Inside, he walked down the hallway to the main computer station. He typed a string of numbers on a computer terminal keyboard, then typed his name. A printer rolled out a short strip of paper containing a twelve digit number — Tom's access code for the day. Without the access code each physician received daily, laboratory work and other information related to the care of patients were out of reach.

Tom smiled and spoke cordially to the hospital workers who passed him in the corridors. He turned a corner, then opened the door to the administrative suite.

This particular morning, when Tom walked into his office suite, he found a woman in his reception area leaning against the edge of the secretary's desk. She was flipping through the pages of a fashion magazine. When he entered, she acted startled.

"Lord, you scared the you-know-what out of me," she said.

"May I help you?" Tom asked.

She patted the side of her yellow blond permed hair.

"Oh yes, you must be Dr. Sullivan. I'm Jeanne Donnely," the woman said. "Personnel sent me over. I'm the applicant for the nurse practitioner job, your personal assistant, I believe."

She wore a crisp white uniform and a stethoscope with lilac-colored plastic tubing was draped around her neck. Her face was thin, Modigliani-like, her nose prominent and her eyes sky blue. Her smile was toothy and wide.

"Well when do we start rounds?" she asked.

"I beg your pardon."

"When do we start rounds?"

Tom looked at his watch. "I start rounds in about thirty minutes, but if you're going along, I need to know a bit more than your name."

The tall woman, who looked about forty, stood at attention and saluted. "Jeanne Donnely reporting, sir," she said, assuming a military manner. "CelestaCare's finest nurse practitioner comes to you directly from corporate headquarters, exiled for speaking her mind."

Tom found her appearance different, but appealing. He smiled to himself. Her demeanor was novel to say the least. "Exiled?" he inquired.

"Well, not really. It was my choice. I spoke my mind once too often. I could either hang around and likely get kicked out of CelestaCare completely or I could go back to clinical nursing. I chose the latter."

"I see," Tom said.

"I, sir, have the potential to be the interpreter of the chaotic world of CelestaCare's Starr Memorial Hospital. I believe you'll find your new assignment quite different from your old position at Devan."

Tom smiled and nodded his agreement. "Well I can certainly use some help. I've been here two weeks and I'm totally lost."

"An initial period of disorientation in the world of CelestaCare is quite normal, sir."

"That's good to know."

"I have my resume for your review. My credentials are all in order, sir. Also, please add to the information that I am single, loyal, knowledgeable, brave, clean, and reverent. CelestaCare personnel sent me over because I am the absolute best they have to offer. The choice, of course, is yours."

Tom rolled his eyes. "I was expecting an applicant for the nurse practitioner position, but I have to say you aren't exactly the person I expected." Even as he spoke, it flitted through his mind how amazingly similar her sense of humor was to his nurse practitioner, Scottie.

She smiled and said. "Dr. Sulivan, I believe you're taken with me."

"Did you know my nurse practitioner, Nancy Scott?" he asked.

"Yes, I ran into her a time or two at nursing meetings. Poor girl, she didn't have a chance, I heard."

"Yes, that's right. Strangely, there's something about you that reminds me of her."

"Flattery will get you everywhere, Dr. Sullivan. She was a doll."

He asked her into his office, offered her a cup of coffee, and began his interview. She handed him her resume, then summarized it herself. Nursing training: Blockside Presbyterian Hospital, Masters, same. Two years working in a ghetto hospital in New York City. Suffered what she called, "total despair." Entered the military and served in Desert Storm in an Army Hospital in the Iraqi Desert. Trained to deal with bacteriological warfare victims.

"Thank God, we never had to use our training over there," she told Tom. "But I did help screen for Anthrax in the events after September 11th."

He looked over her resume, nodding his head as he read. She continued talking.

"The job opening at Starr Memorial was timely," she told Tom. She had grown more troubled with the politics of the corporate structure. Her outspoken, argumentative style had brought her into constant conflict with her supervisors in the Health Care Design Division. Three call-ins and censures by CEO Sam Fisher himself.

"What happens when you disagree with me?" he asked.

"I am reformed, sir. You are the boss."

He shook his head. "That's too easy," he said.

"You are absolutely correct. I am capable of disagreeing and when I do, you will know it."

"I wouldn't want it any other way. I haven't reached the state of 'perfected excellence' yet."

"Sir, is that not a slur of Devan and perhaps its noble Vice Chancellor, one Raymond Cunningham."

He looked up, surprised. "You know about the Devan logo, the Devan slogan, and the Vice Chancellor."

"Common knowledge, Dr. Sullivan. Everybody knows about the Devan slogan and many think it's rather pompous. 'Perfected Excellence'...Give me a break. Do we disagree?" she asked, and flashed him a full, wide smile.

He slapped the palm of his open hand on his forehead. "Do you ever wind down?"

"Only after I'm hired."

She was charming. Tom liked her. Her humor would be a relief against the hard edges of the corporate health care world. She was perfect for the job.

"You're hired," he told her.

She let her head fall to her shoulder, her arms droop, and slumped down in the chair as if she were a deflating balloon.

"Wheeeeew. Thank God. You have saved me from Sam Fisher's wrath and likely ultimate dismissal. But I'm not too sure how favorably Clark will take to your hiring me. He may be guiding this hospital now, but at heart he's corporate."

"Whom I hire as my nurse practitioner is up to me," Tom told her. "By the way, Mr. Clark assumes his position here as Hospital Administrator today," he added.

"I know. It's he that you'll have to watch most Dr. Sullivan. The man's driven, plus."

"Your first assignment — fill me in," Tom said.

"Ken Clark is a difficult man. Period. End of report. I've known him since the military. The man's father was military all the way and Clark was a Medical Service Corp officer in the same casualty management area where I served. He was the Administrator of a receiving hospital near Dahran. He does things one way — his — or maybe now it's becoming more appropriate to say that he does them God's way."

A bewildered look appeared on Tom's face. "God's way?"

"At one point, Clark was studying religion you know. Lost his way for a while, but now he has gotten religion again. He believes that God is guiding the new directions in health care. You'll learn about that soon enough."

"His wife's pleasant enough," Tom interjected. "She's working day and night to get her automated units installed. We've spent a good bit of time together. She's anxious for the students to learn how to use the equipment."

"Yes," Jeanne said. "Laura is CelestaCare's brightest star, but her husband is one controlling man. It's a mystery how she can be married to him. But I suspect the glue comes from both of them having the intense interest in bettering health care."

"Maybe he stays out of the way and lets her do her thing."

"Maybe, but it's hard to believe that he could allow anyone to do anything but his thing, or God's thing, I should say."

Tom grew pensive. He recalled his drive to CelestaCare with Laura and their interchanges. Jeanne studied his face.

She continued, "But be careful. Relating with Laura Clark is like a walk on quicksand. You can't help but feel her husband's dominating style. That makes it feel like she needs your help. It's easy to get pulled in."

"I suspect I can take care of myself, Ms. Donnely."

"We'll see," she said. She looked at her watch, reached in her pocket, took out his patient list and pointed to it.

"You take care of everything," he said.

"Not everything, but I do my best," she said, becoming more serious as she looked over the computer generated patient list. "Now, Dr. Sullivan, since you've hired me, let's make those rounds."

Chapter 17

Now that the automated units were up and running, Tom could pull back and relax. He sat in front of his computer terminal in his Starr Memorial Office. He typed in the symbols, http://www.allnews net.com. Quickly he reached the web site, the home page for the All News Network, and clicked on the news update. Then he clicked on the "CelestaCare Automated Heath Care Units Installation Completed" news video. In front of Starr Memorial, an anchor man interviewed CelestaCare's C.E.O., Sam Fisher and C.O.O., Ken Clark.

"We have completed the installation of forty-two totally automated computer-controlled hospital rooms at CelestaCare Health Enterprises' Starr Memorial Hospital," Clark said into the camera. "I'm pleased to announce that we began operation a week before originally planned. The occupancy rate of the units reached one hundred percent only forty-eight hours after opening."

The interviewer spoke. "Astounding progress. And the story of your success has already reached Wall Street. This morning, in frenzied trading, CelestaCare's stock soared seventy-five dollars a share."

"Indisputably," Fisher said, "CelestaCare Health Enterprises has pulled ahead as the leading force in corporate health care. And we are deeply grateful to the man on my right, Ken Clark, for the outstanding pace he set to get these units installed."

Ken Clark tipped his hand off his brow in appreciation.

The news broadcast switched to the White House and the commentator continued. "The inventor of the automated unit system, Laura Clark, who also gave the country Lilacicin, is deservingly receiving national recognition — front page coverage in the newspapers, top of the television news.

"Last night at a White House dinner in her honor, the President lauded her accomplishments. 'First she gave us Lilacicin, now she has given us automated medicine. She is indeed a woman for all seasons,' he said."

Tom found himself smiling when the President recognized Laura's accomplishments. He knew her better now. The installation of the automated units brought them together daily. Together they conducted the staff training sessions; together they hammered out the administrative logjams to clear the way for automated care.

And it was clear that Laura was interested in more than science and computers — she was clearly interested in more and better medical care for patients.

The day the units opened, Laura and Tom toured the units together. Her recognition of his part in the project had been generous. "I couldn't have done this without your help," Laura told him. She had also mentioned Tom's help a number of times on television talk shows.

"You deserve all the credit you've gotten," Tom told her. "Now, medical educators need to teach how to use your systems in a sensible way."

On their tour, Tom and Laura paused to watch as an older woman began her stay in one of the automated care cubicles. When the "Hookup" technician completed his work, he handed the woman her copy of the *CelestaCare Consumer's Guide to Automated Care*. She briefly looked inside the booklet and then turned to ask the technician a question. "Young man, what if I need a...?" she began, but before she could get the question out, the "Hookup" technician had left the room.

Laura had quickly rushed to catch up with the technician. She had insisted that the man return to the room to answer the patient's questions.

Tom turned off the news feeling hopeful. If patients could be treated with dignity, if his teaching efforts could train young physicians to utilize the automated units in a humanitarian manner, perhaps the automated units offered hope for some answers to the health care dilemma.

His positive feelings about the new health care system were short lived. When Tom arrived at his office the next morning, he found a certified letter in a lilac-colored envelope on his desk. He read the title before his name, noting that the usual "Dr." was replaced with "Mgr." A quick reading of the information inside explained why:

Dear Manager Thomas Sullivan — Manager Number 232-37-6209,

The National Health Agency, acting under the Emergency Health Care Act, wishes to advise you that effective immediately, Medical Doctors will no longer be referred to as 'physicians' or 'doctors.' In keeping with the new directions in which health care is to be provided, you are hereby advised that all physician providers will henceforth be referred to as 'Health Care Managers,' rather than 'Doctors of Medicine.' The letters 'HCM,' establishing you as a Health Care Manager rather than the degree abbreviation, 'M.D.' will follow your name as the designation of your status. The title, 'Manager' will be abbreviated, 'MGR.'

The letter went on to say that existing medical diplomas were to be immediately turned into the government and in their place, new "Certificates of Health Care Managerial Skills" would be issued. It was obviously a play on words. Instead of doctors or physicians, managers would provide only approved "managed" care.

Tom bristled. He remembered a point in Alexander Wade's monograph on health care. The directive in his hand was in keeping with what was said to be the NHA Director's philosophy: to change a system, one must first change the names of its component parts. He dialed Ray Cunningham's office.

"This is Manager Cunningham speaking," he heard when he got through to the Vice Chancellor.

"We're physicians, doctors, Dr. Cunningham. Our history goes back for centuries. You have clout in Washington. This change in title needs to be challenged immediately. Our professionalism is on the block."

"Tom, perhaps the title 'manager' has some drawbacks. But manager, doctor, physician, what does it matter? It's what we do that counts. Shakespeare said it best in *Romeo and Juliet*: 'What's in a name! That which we call a rose, by any other name would smell as sweet...'"

"I'm sorry, but I'm not a Health Care Manager. I'm a physician and I intend to go on being called Doctor Sullivan."

"Have it your way, Tom. Call yourself what you like, but your correct title is 'Manager.' It describes more clearly what you do now. And do mail in your diploma to the NHA. Without your Manager's Certificate, you'll be deaccessed."

"Deaccessed? What the hell does that mean."

"That would mean that you would not have access to the national medical computer system. No access, no patient data. For all practical purposes, you would no longer be a practitioner of anything. There are a number of ways a manager can be subject to being deaccessed."

Cunningham told him that he understood his reaction to the abrupt change, but he'd best comply. So many things were changing, he said. He would speak to the NHA office that was responsible for the change in title about his concerns, but doubted that it would accomplish anything. The wording had originally been proposed by Wade himself.

Tom swiveled his chair toward the display of diplomas on his wall and reflected on the change. The parchment rectangle that was his M.D. degree caught his eye: "Devan University School of Medicine, Thomas M. Sullivan, M. D., Doctor of Medicine." All the hours studying, all the work, all the expenses, the loans for tuition. All the fears of death and disease, all the long nights on-call, the worries about patients. Births, deaths, joy, suffering. He felt a wave of sadness.

But why not "Manager?" What was so important about the title "Doctor?" Was it that the title carried with it a thousand-year heritage? Did it give him some special status in society? Did it give him power? Money? Was it a symbol of his knowledge? Was it that it gave him access to places in people's lives that few other people were allowed? Certainly, the title demanded that he treat his fellow human being in a carefully guarded, responsible, way, an obligation that many of his peers seemed to have forgotten. Now it was being wrested away by a letter on lilac-colored stationery.

Suddenly he felt stripped of his power and more vulnerable. Jeanne Donnely's comment to him on hearing the news later that afternoon rang true. "It's never been easy for you doctors to accept any outside controls. You people want the power," she said.

"Don't rub my nose in it," Tom replied.

"Look, I don't blame you for being pissed, Manager Sullivan."

"It's going to stay Dr. Sullivan, Jeanne. I'm going to remain a physician."

"Whatever you say, Dr. Sullivan."

At home that evening, Tom and Katie watched still another alarming development on television.

First there was commentary on the general response to the new title, Manager, from physicians around the country.

"It's no big deal," one plastic surgeon said. "Doctor, Manager, whatever. We'll still do the same thing."

"Manager is as good a title as any," another physician said. "If Director Wade feels it is best, I'm certain he has a good reason."

Like these, the vast majority of physicians voiced surprisingly little concern. However, some physicians were voicing their opposition to the change.

The scene switched. Late that afternoon, at the entrance to Devan Hospital, a dozen representatives of the media gathered around a young faculty member named Robert Kaplan as he left the hospital. Someone had informed the media that Kaplan intended to rebel.

"We understand you're unhappy about your title change. What are your plans, Manager?" one reporter asked.

Kaplan's face and voice were stern. "I plan to network with other physicians around the country. If necessary, we'll take on the NHA legally."

"Isn't it correct that the medical establishment is already federalized under the Mulholland act?" another newscaster asked.

"Yes."

"Then what recourse do you have?"

"My concerns go far beyond this title change," he told them. "Computer algorithms and automated care ignore individual needs. This kind of generic medicine is a fast food chain approach to taking care of patients. For all practical purposes, the NHA, CelestaCare, and now Devan have pronounced the doctor-patient relationship dead!"

Kaplan was in the middle of explaining his plan to take on the NHA, when suddenly four badge-carrying Agents from the National Health Agency's Investigative Division burst onto the scene. In front of the camera, one agent pressed a folded warrant in Kaplan's hand. As if planned ahead, the agent read the warrant on camera for the whole country to hear.

Standing straight with his chin forward, Kaplan listened to the agent.

"Manager Robert Kaplan. We have a warrant for your arrest. You are hereby cited for 'Interference with Compliance.' Under the provisions of the Mulholland Emergency Health Care law you will cease and desist from your protest. You are hereby deaccessed from the health care system. You will immediately turn in your National Health Agency magnetic identification cards, your medical diploma, and your license.

"Your passwords will be deleted from the information systems and you will no longer be able to obtain your daily access numbers. You will not be allowed access to the data retrieval systems in hospitals and clinics, or for that matter, any computer equipment in use in the health care system.

"You are for all practical purposes relieved of your right to participate in health care management in the usual way."

Over the signature of the Director of the NHA, at least a thousand other resisting managers around the country were similarly cited for "Interference with Compliance." They were all summarily "deaccessed" from the NHA's system of care.

"Damn," Tom said out loud, "Kaplan is one of the best residents we have ever had at Devan. What is this 'deaccessed' bullshit all about?"

Chapter 18

Bob Kaplan pondered his choices. His attorney informed him about the rehabilitation program already in place that allowed deaccessed managers to become reaccessed, but had no details. He had instead steered him to an Internet website, usagov.nat.health.agen. org/deaccess/reaccess/rehab.

Bob entered the website and studied the complicated process of rehabilitation for reaccess. First there was the enrollment cost: twenty-five thousand dollars. A clever way of extracting a hefty fine, Bob thought. Then, if accepted by the course directors, there was a one week in-patient phase, a three month out-patient phase, and a one year period of time spent in a preceptorship under the guidance of a NHA Compliance Guardian.

Non-compliance with the NHA had rapidly achieved the status of a psychiatric disorder, was entered into the psychiatric diagnostic nomenclature, and was designated "Non-Compliance Disorder, Acute, Chronic, or Intermittent-Recurrent." Already, studies of persons with the disorder had begun and the possibility of a chemical imbalance related to a genetic predisposition proposed. A few experts speculated about the problem's relationship to delayed rebellion against overly authoritative, rigid parents, but most favored the explanation based on a biochemical change.

Bob decided to turn to his mentor, Tom Sullivan, for advice.

"It's a sad day for medicine when having professional values is a psychiatric disorder," Tom told Bob Kaplan as they ate lunch together in a small restaurant down the street from Starr Memorial.

"You know that and I know that, but now the NHA has the last word," Bob said.

"I suppose you've been swamped with calls from physicians wanting to join in your resistance activities."

"Not really. Most doctors are scared they'll be deaccessed or worse — fined and slapped in jail if they persist. Being a 'manager' and taking orders is better than nothing."

Tom countered with his stance. "I won't be a 'manager,' Bob. I'm sitting tight, holding on to my old license and diploma and insisting that I still be called a 'physician' or 'doctor.' Screw them."

"You're a special case, Dr. Sullivan. They'll let you get by with it because they need you on their team. They can't slam Devan's epidemic crushing poster physician. But for God's sake, be careful how far you push it. Anyway, I've decided what's best for me. Decided to apply for rehabilitation."

"Rehabilitation for what?"

"Doesn't matter. It's all a farce. But I have to jump through their hoops. I remember what Peter Hansen said when the epidemic started." Bob took an index card out of his pocket. "I've saved this for posterity. Listen," he said, and read Hansen's words:

"Yes, unquestionably these are vicious little mobs of microbes. And they may be clever and deadly, but if we keep after them, we'll track down the little bastards and kill them off. They can't elude us forever."

"I remember Peter's determination," Tom said. "It was the first night and we were overwhelmed with that damned disease."

"Like we feel now," Bob continued. "I took down his words because I suspected that someday I would need them for motivation. If Hansen could feel that optimistic about wiping out the microbes that were causing the epidemic, then surely I can feel as sure of the ultimate fall of these disruptive, idiotic pathogens that are wrecking medicine."

"Those were inspiring words, for sure."

"Yep. I get 'rehabed,' reaccessed, I find myself a nice observation post and I watch. I just watch carefully and see what I can see. Like he said, 'The little bastards can't elude us forever.'"

"There are other ways you can go," Tom said.

"Like what?"

"Joining the 'Healers.' Carl Hammerstone is getting together a group of physicians to try to provide alternative care. I hear that he has acquired the use of an old building over on warehouse row and is making plans to build a hospital there. Carl feels that the new system can't possibly work. Patients running out of points, the falling away of the doctor-patient relationship. The NHA has their spies to watch over what's going on, but that kind of thing never bothers Carl."

"Not me, Dr. Sullivan. I need to be out in the open, in the middle of the action. I'm headed toward rehab. I'll work from the inside."

"Then you've made up your mind. Each of us has to choose our own way. In this situation, working apart may be just as good as working together. But If you need me, let me know," Tom said.

"You can count on it. You've got your own special inside position in the middle of the action, you know."

"What do you mean?"

"I have a hunch that Ken and Laura Clark know as much about the ins and outs of the points machinery as anyone. And they might tip their hand. I'm pretty sure how he votes, but I'm not sure which side she's on."

"I'll get the check," Tom said.

"Thanks, I'm short on cash. That's another side effect of being deaccessed."

Leaving the restaurant, they walked by a bookstore across from Devan.

"Take a look," Tom said as he stopped in front of the book store window and pointed to several tall stacks of books occupying the display window. A fanned-out spread of copies surrounded the piled columns.

"These people are convinced that they know the way," Tom said, pointing to the display. "Out a week and this book has already sold more than two million copies."

"Who is this Oliver Sellers?" Bob asked.

"He's the leader of the Theotechnicist movement."

"What the hell is the Theotechnicist movement."

"They believe that technology will show us God's way of selecting people for eternal life," Tom said. "It's dangerous stuff. I've heard that my boss, Ken Clark is a Theotechnicist. Not surprising. When he was pushing me into the Lilacicin project, Cunningham told me that Clark dabbled with theology before he went into health care administration. That was supposed to prove that he's a humanitarian."

"Wait here a second," Bob said and went inside the bookstore. Soon he returned, a copy of the book in a plastic bag.

"If I'm going to accomplish anything in my efforts, I need to understand the thought processes," Bob told Tom.

"I've already told you the gist. Just keep in mind that these people feel that out of points will come redemption." Tom said.

"We'll be in touch," Bob said shaking Tom's hand.

"I'm sure." Tom said.

Later that evening, at home, Bob Kaplan followed instructions on the website, and dialed the NHA rehabilitation direct line, 1-800-UACCESS, to secure the application forms for the reaccess program.

"Hello this is Mgr. Clyde McIntosh," a friendly voice answered. "Welcome to the manager rehabilitation program information office hot line."

"Mgr. McIntosh, My name is Robert Kaplan. I've been deaccessed and I'm interested in learning more about the reaccess program."

"How about the twenty-five grand. Can you pay, Kaplan?"

"I can handle it."

"Wonderful. Might I have your social, Mgr. Kaplan?"

"Sure," Bob said cooperatively, and told him.

"Yes, here you are Mgr. Kaplan. Yes, you're right here in the computer. Let's see. You got your Manager's degree at Devan Medical Center in Middleside, Pennsylvania. Now it seems you've developed a Non-Compliance Disorder, Acute with Chronic features. Looking this over, I suspect that you're suffering from Control Addiction, Mgr. Kaplan?"

"Excuse me?"

"Control Addiction is a basic cause of Noncompliance Disorder. Too much control can be intoxicating. Now, how long have you been addicted?"

"Manager, I don't believe I have an addiction."

"You're in denial, Manager. I have your profile right in front of me. Says you're organizing a movement resisting the NHA's new regulations. Establishing counter-authority through coalescing a group is an age-old method of holding on to control. Oh no, Manager. No doubt about it, you're addicted to control. Your response to authority is characteristic. Don't be ashamed, control addiction is a brain problem; it's an illnesss."

"Is this a joke?" Bob asked, with an incredulous tone in his voice.

"No, on the contrary. Your addiction was serious enough to cause legal intervention. Turning over authority to others means relinquishing control and respecting higher powers. Control addicts can't do this. You'll have to admit you've lost control and want it back. Admit it, that's the first step. Turn it over to a greater authority and forget about trying to always be in control. Wanting control at that level will only get you into more trouble."

"Damn, I think you're serious. And if I don't admit it, what then?"

"No rehab, Manager. You stay deaccessed and we say, 'lots of luck.' Basically, you're stuck in this terribly dysfunctional state of having lost control of your life and being miserable. And you can forget about being a manager."

McIntosh paused a moment to give Bob time to think. "Now can I sign you in?"

"Seems to me that wanting some control is good," Bob said.

"Right, a man can lose too much control, Mgr. Kaplan. But we don't really expect the candidates to understand all the subtleties of control addiction at this stage of recovery.

"Join the program and you'll learn, Mgr. Kaplan; you'll learn. There are didactic lectures, teaching videos, instructional computer programs, one-on-one and group counseling efforts, and a host of other methods designed to help you learn to give up control. After you complete the course work, you'll be assigned to a Reaccess Counselor. You'll have to report in regularly. So, please be advised, this is no simple path; recovery is a long, arduous process."

"I'm sure Mgr. McIntosh, but you can count me in."

Chapter 19

Long before Wade was appointed Director of the National Health Agency, Tom had done his best to try to better understand the theorist's philosophy of health care. He had read the copy of Alexander Wade's monograph on health care that he had secured from an out-of-print book agency in New York. Even using the Internet, it had taken months for him to find his own copy; few were in print.

Tom learned that at the time of the writing three years before, Alexander Wade had been unable to secure a publisher. He had published the book himself through a vanity press in Detroit. When the monograph was first printed, only five or six hundred copies were sold. After Wade's appointment as Director of the NHA, copies of his book flooded the bookstores, but Tom had already done his homework.

In his book, *One Health Care, Under God*, Wade urged that the public claim its "God given right" to medical care. In the text, he was quick to point out that, "…concessions will have to be made. The cost of medical care is skyrocketing and everyone can not possibly continue to receive the same level of care." He made references to the selection committees who chose "deserving" candidates during the early days of kidney dialysis when dialysis machines were in short supply. Then, dialysis might be made available to those who were felt to contribute most to society — examples being scientists, ministers, boy scout leaders, and the like. At one point in his discussion, Wade suggested that a society should deliver care to those "most deserving," but his methods of choosing the recipients of treatment were unclear.

Now it was clear that Ken Clark's administrative policy at Starr followed another principle stated plainly in Wade's Health Care monograph: "To be available to all, the technique or method of health care provided for any given disorder must be reduced to the lowest common denominator of its essential parts." Bob Kaplan was right, Tom concluded. Wade and CelestaCare were aiming toward generic care. They had little interest in anyone's individual or unique needs and responses.

But what about his teaching program? Why was there no movement toward establishing the instruction? Tom finally discussed the situation with Carl Hammerstone over coffee.

"I think the teaching program is a ruse," Tom said. "I've been at Starr for six months and nothing has happened."

"What did you expect from those entrepreneurs? They have a different agenda than yours," Carl said.

"Why would they move me to Starr Memorial to begin a teaching program then drag their feet like this? I've put in a dozen calls to Cunningham, but he won't return them. I've faxed him, e-mailed him, and still no answer."

"Talk with Clark. Not that you'll get an answer but it can't hurt," Carl suggested.

Tom called Clark's office for an appointment. Ken agreed to meet with him three days later.

When the time for the appointment arrived, Tom waited in Ken's reception area. He glanced at his watch. Ken was already thirty minutes late. His eyes drifted toward a side table to the most recent issue of *Health Care for All,* the monthly magazine published by the NHA. Ken's picture was on its cover. While he waited, Tom perused the feature article that Carole Weeks had put together to honor the administrator of the hospital that premiered the automated treatment units.

The article reported that Ken's family traced their military history back to the Revolutionary War. His father, a high ranking Army surgeon, had encouraged his son to follow the family heritage and pursue a military career. According to the article, Clark always worked under his "father's watchful eyes." Indeed, a photograph in the article showed Ken at his Starr Memorial desk with a large oil painting of his father looking down from behind.

The young Clark had received his education at Westpoint. First trained for Airborne Infantry, then as a Chemical Corp officer, he was assigned for a number of years to a post in the Pentagon. The article attributed his abrupt decision to leave the army in favor of pursuing an understanding of theology as a means of better grasping his role in doing "...God's work on Earth." Later, he moved to a career in health care administration as a path designed to realize his "visionary insights about making the world a better place."

CelestaCare was a fledgling health care corporation when he later came to Middleside, took a job, and began his ascent up the corporate ladder. At CelestaCare, he met and married his wife, Laura. Retaining his commission in the reserves, for a brief period in the early 90s, he was called back to active duty to serve in the war against Iraq.

The article included a picture of Ken's engaging in his favorite after hour activity, sky diving. It made note of an unusual art collection in his home: seventeen death masks of famous people.

Finally, Ken appeared at his office door after concluding an interview with a young manager.

Tom stopped the manager, Trim Willingham as he left and shook his hand, recalling that Trim had been a medical student and then a trainee in internal medicine on his ward at Devan.

Ken ushered Tom into his office.

Tom scanned Ken's desk as he sat down in the chair in front of it. On the desktop, stacks of papers were neatly arranged in perfect order. The edge of each pile, as if carefully measured, rested exactly the same distance from one another. A book with a purple cover lay centered on his desk blotter.

Tom read its title. The book was the physician, Oliver Sellers', *Prayers for Technology and Tomorrow*, the best selling recently published testimony of the value of health care technology in determining the future of a "moral" humankind.

"Willingham will be joining our staff to work on our automated unit," Ken told Tom.

"I know Trim well. He will be a fine addition to the staff. He was a top student at Devan."

"Now, what can I do for you?" Ken asked.

"I want to talk with you about my teaching program."

"Yes, Willingham is interested in your teaching plans also. I suspect that your being here has a lot to do with his wanting to work at Starr. He's also interested in health care education. You'll need to get him involved in the teaching program."

"That's precisely why I want to talk with you. There is no teaching program," Tom said. "The automated units have been operational for months. I want to know why no Devan medical students and residents have been assigned here."

Clark shrugged his shoulders. "Look, don't blame me if Cunningham doesn't send any students and residents to Starr."

Tom stiffened. "No! You look! I was told when I was sent over here that I would be used to teach the trainees and staff how to integrate the physician-patient relationship and automated care."

"Okay, Sullivan, the fact is we think it's questionable if this kind of technology requires such a traditional kind of teaching program. At least at this point."

"Then why the hell am I here if there's not going to be a teaching program?"

Clark looked Tom straight in the eyes. "Cunningham and the NHA want you here. You were chosen to have a role in the future of humankind."

Tom scratched his head.

Ken reached for one of the files from a neatly piled stack and placed it in front of him. Tom saw the imposing NHA "Red Security" stamp on the file's front.

"We're poised and ready for the next step in the system installation. Do you know what it is?"

"No, I don't," Tom said angrily. He rubbed the tense muscles at the back of his neck.

"It's Phase II. I want you to go over these plans in detail."

"What the hell is Phase II?"

"Central lines. Mandatory Central lines," He said, pointing to his neck. "If you think the automated units are efficient and cost effective, just wait until you see this."

Suddenly Tom remembered the patients on the gurneys in Laura's lab with the central lines leading to the jugular veins of their necks. He felt himself quietly shudder.

"The installation demonstration will be this weekend, here at Starr. There will be high level dignitaries and top drawer media coverage. It should be spectacular."

"Damn. You people are moving at blitzkrieg speed."

"Cunningham and I will rethink your teaching program. But for now, the top priority is getting Phase II in place. Starr Memorial is CelestaCare's flagship hospital, the key hospital in the development of the new system of care, the model for the rest of the country. You should be pleased. Your reputation will help us a great deal. Participating in the preparation for the future of humankind is nothing to be sneezed at," Ken said.

Chapter 20

"Ladies and Gentlemen: the President of the United States."

The words, "United States" were hardly out of emcee, Stu Sizemore's mouth when his booming voice was drowned out by loud applause. Sizemore, a big, beady eyed man with a high forehead and a full head of gray, wavy hair that cascaded in the back down to the top of his coat collar, smiled broadly.

Sizemore took his cues and directions from Carole Weeks via an earphone. The two media masters were standards in NHA productions. Sizemore's convincing canned sincerity ("Your greatest wealth is your good health!") and Carole Weeks' five star productions were winning NHA supporters from coast to coast. Today, as was her usual practice, Carol was stylishly dressed in a chic lilac-colored outfit. She stood with her crew, out of camera reach, glancing at the notes on her clipboard.

The President of the United States, a tall man with dyed jet black hair, entered at a crisp pace. Behind him, three other men, flanked by secret service agents, marched through the open door. Walking just behind the President was Alex Wade with his shiny, bald head reflecting the overhead television lights. The NHA Director's eyes darted quickly from side to side as he scanned the large crowd of dignitaries assembled in the hospital auditorium. Behind Wade was Senator Ross Mandell. He swabbed his face with a handkerchief, wiping away the sweat that beaded out on his cheeks and forehead.

"Sir, please come with me," Ken Clark said to the President. He ushered him to a set-up model hospital room in the center of the room. There, resting on a small table near the head of the stretcher, was a vase of plastic lilac plumes. At the gurney's side was a surgical instrument table with an unopened, rectangular, surgical procedure pack resting on it.

Clark pointed toward the stretcher. "If you would be so kind as to lie down here, Mr. President, this will be where our managers will put in the central line," he said.

The President graciously complied.

The crowd grew still and quiet. Sizemore, with a portable mike in hand, continued. "This morning, ladies and gentlemen, the President of the United States is going to be the first to demonstrate a real breakthrough in health care delivery — the Universal Central Line.

"But first, we want to welcome your friend and mine, Manager Alexander Wade, Director and Chief of the National Health Agency. Let's all put our hands together to welcome him."

The crowd responded with a loud round of clapping.

"Director Wade is going to explain the benefits of the central line to all of us. Director, just what is a central line?"

The camera spun around to catch Alex Wade's face as he spoke. The full face screen alternated with a wider angle shot of the President lying on the stretcher.

Wade began his explanation. "The central line is an established method of maintaining direct access to the blood stream. It's a very minor procedure, which simply involves threading a small, plastic tube into the internal jugular vein in the neck. This catheter runs down into the superior vena cava, the large vein that brings blood back to the right side of the heart."

An artist's representation of the tube inserted into the neck vein, threading its way down close to the heart, appeared briefly on screen.

"This, my dear friends, is a central line." Wade said.

A health care manager had already attached the small plastic analyzer cube onto the President's forearm. The device straddled the raised blue ridges that were the veins running through the surface of the President's right wrist. Instantly, the monitor screen over the President's head began to roll out a string of blood chemistry values.

"But why put in this central line, Director?" Sizemore asked as he arched over to get a better view of the area on the side of the

President's neck where the HCMs would be working. "What's to be accomplished?"

Wade responded. "With the central line in place, we have a direct hook-up to the consumer. Health care will be provided in the hospital without the consumer swallowing pills and without using the old-fashioned IV needles and the tubes of the past. No more pills, no more nauseating liquid medications. All health care formulas, all medicinal treatment will be dispensed through conduits coming directly from the central formula supply units and will be given as necessary to each patient in the hospital exactly as the computer orders. The levels of control this method allows us to have over diagnostic and treatment procedures will be phenomenal. And the savings on drugs and fluids bought in bulk by the hospitals will unquestionably lower costs."

Sizemore beamed. "That's wonderful, Director, but surely this procedure isn't going to be free. How many points is this innovative approach itself going to cost?"

"Stu, here's the unbelievable part. This service will involve absolutely no additional expenditure of points. In fact, it will not only reduce the chance for error and mixups and save dollars, but it will also reduce point requirements and allow the consumer to get more care for the points he has."

Out of the corner of his eye, Wade saw Carole Weeks point to the stretcher bearing the President. "I believe we're just about ready to move ahead," he remarked.

The country's top health care man walked closer to the stretcher where the President waited. He looked directly into the camera and spoke to the television audience with what sounded like his most earnest tone of voice. "The President of the United States has been good enough to offer to demonstrate this procedure." He rested his hand on the President's shoulder. "Thank you, sir, for coming today. I'm sure that your being here will place the mind of every citizen at ease," Wade said to the President. "How are you feeling, sir?"

"Alex, I'm fine, and to my fellow countrymen, I say it's really my pleasure and honor to be first in this history-making time in health care. We won't waste time with speeches," he said with a nervous laugh. "Let's just get on with it!"

The President eyed the masked, gowned Health Care Managers standing nearby. A look of terror flashed across the Chief Executive's face, but he cleared his throat and quickly regained his composure. He glanced toward the monitor next to his head and eyed the cluttered readout of physiological functions crammed onto the screen.

There were a few hand claps, a few chuckles, and some anxiety-laden shifting around in the crowd. Alexander Wade moved away from the President's side and backed up from his position at the microphone.

As instructed, the President turned the right side of his neck toward the camera. Two aides tilted the stretcher down at the head, elevating his feet. A nurse tore open the sterile, disposable, central line kit sitting on the surgical table, making it ready to use. The camera zoomed in for the close-up, recording the bulging distention in the President's neck veins where the inclined posture caused them to fill with blood. Soon, one of the Health Care Managers plunged his hands into a pair of sterile gloves, took a packet of antiseptic soaked swabs from the sterile procedure kit, and opened it. Meticulously, he rubbed the swabs containing the amber-red iodine solution on the President's neck to create a bacterial free skin area. Then he began to skate his fingers across the President's lower neck muscles to pin-point the precise anatomical location for insertion of the central line. Finding the place where the two sides of one of the neck muscles merged together, he signaled to a gloved nurse who removed the surgical drape from the kit and placed its precut opening over the work site. Once the drape was in place, the HCM identified the pulse of the carotid artery that lay next to the internal jugular vein.

The gloved Health Care Managers moved closer to the President and pulled the skin of the President's neck taunt while the chief operator injected a small puff of anesthetic into the skin over the insertion site. Then he worked the needle deeper into the flesh to further deaden the area. Next he took a long, plastic cannula sheathed needle and positioned it over the insertion point. A moment of quiet stillness followed when the HCM's rubber-gloved finger tips stretched the skin of the President's neck even tighter and the needle point touched the skin. Suddenly, the HCM plunged the cannular cloaked needle through the President's skin. Having hit the mark, he attached a small syringe and pulled back on the plunger. Dark red blood flashed into the barrel of the syringe. A loud gasp sounded, as if everyone in the audience took in a simultaneous deep breath.

The President winced in pain. "Damn it!" he said, almost inaudibly.

"Are you alright, sir?" one of the managers asked.

"No problem, Manager. No problem."

More deft hand movements followed, as the HCM removed the needle and then treaded a thin wire through the remaining plastic cannula into the internal jugular vein. He then removed the cannular and moments later, after pushing an expander through the flesh of the President's neck, he threaded the larger plastic central line over the guide wire into the vein, skillfully sending its end down into the jugular vein and then advancing the tip to rest near the heart. He flushed the in-place central line with an anticoagulant to prevent clotting and used a strip of tape to secure the line in place. He capped off two of the central line entry ports, then connected the third to an intravenous line the nurse handed him. He regulated the flow of fluid dripping from the fluid sac into the intravenous line. Momentarily the manager stepped back and nodded to indicate that he had completed the installation. There was loud applause.

"It's in! Wow! It's already in!" Sizemore shouted. "History in the making. It's in! Look at that! It's in!"

On tiptoes, the crowd strained forward to see the accomplished deed. Smiles appeared on the observers' faces. Then there were sighs of relief and hand shakes. Excited interchanges rippled through the audience.

"Manager," Sizemore said to one of the gray coated managers who performed the procedure and was now taking off the latex gloves. "That was wonderful — marvelous. May I have a few words with you? Could you tell the television audience a little more about what you've done?"

"You bet," the young manager said proudly with a wide grin on his face. "The small, plastic tube is much smaller than a soda straw, and I slipped it right in there, into the vein. Like Director Wade said, now we can get those medications and intravenous fluids right on in there to do their job. And Stu...," He stopped a moment, while a young blond female nurse wiped the sweat from his forehead with a gauze pad. "Because the tubing has several channels, we can also extract blood samples if we need them and use more than one channel if medications interact adversely. Every consumer will have one. It's nothing to be afraid of. The universal central line is a sensational breakthrough in reducing the costs of health care and ensuring efficiency"

"I'll say!" Stu Sizemore commented. "The NHA really has the best interests of the consumer in mind. The NHA cares! And with CelestaCare, you're in the best of hands!"

"You bet your life!" the manager continued. "And the line can be hooked up to monitors to allow us to track all important body functions, even some we can't pick up with the external analyzer cube. With the monitor system and our other diagnostic technology, we can obtain virtually any information we need about a person's body." He smiled, then winked. "You might say we have an inside line."

Sizemore guffawed and slapped the young man on the back. "Hey, that's a good one. Thanks Manager," the interviewer said appreciatively. "And I might add," Stu Sizemore said, "With the central line, we'll have better and more cost efficient health care for us all. That's what this is all about. As we all know, our greatest wealth is our good health."

Sizemore looked around the room and scanned the crowd.

"Now, let me point out some of the people who have had a part in making this day a reality. There, over there is Tom Sullivan, the Medical Director of CelestaCare's Starr Memorial. The camera pointed toward him. "Manager Sullivan is one of the most outstanding Health Care Managers in Middleside or anywhere else in the country for that matter. His reputation as a researcher and manager is well known. He himself used the central line in the epidemic to cut down on the chance of the spread of the disease to others. He tested Lilacicin and now he's overseeing the birth of the new era of health care taking place in his hospital. What a proud man he must be!"

"Laura Clark! Laura Clark!" Carole Weeks said to the newscaster through his earphone.

Sizemore looked around. "And over there, there's lovely Laura Clark, the lady who designed the miracle drug, Lilacicin, and invented the automated care system. What a proud day for that genius of a woman. She deserves a hand."

Laura Clark looked down when she heard her name and the applause. The camera hardly caught a glimpse of her face before her green eyes looked toward the floor.

Carole Weeks held up three fingers of one hand, then made a zero sign with her other. "Thirty secs to kill," she advised Sizemore.

The announcer searched the audience for someone to interview. He decided on the young curly haired man standing beside him. "I'll have a few words with this young Manager. Your name, sir?"

"I'm Manager Robert T. Kaplan," the young man said, appearing surprised to have been chosen to be interviewed.

"Robert T. Kaplan. You're kidding. Ladies and Gentlemen, this is one of the first doctors to be deaccessed when the title 'Doctor' was changed to 'Health Care Manager.' Isn't that correct Manager?"

"It is correct, Stu. And you might also mention that I was also the first manager in this area to be rehabilitated and reaccessed. Yes, I am recovering. I've served my time in the rehabilitation program, made my official apology, took the oath of allegiance, and now I'm back in the game."

"Oh I know that's so gratifying, Manager. And I see by your ID, that you're on the staff at the Devan Medical Center. I suppose that you academic folks are closely watching the advances made by CelestaCare aren't you?"

"We sure are. We're installing the new CelestaCare systems soon ourselves. But I came over for this ceremony to see history in the making. And I want to commend you. The television coverage of this moving event was fantastic."

"Thank you, sir. And Manager Kaplan, perhaps you can share a personal comment about this wonderful moment, an observation from your heart."

"Yes, I can say that I think the universal central line program is a giant step for humankind. In fact, I think it could easily be said that it's one small step for human beings, one giant leap for humankind."

"Sir, the language you're using, are you comparing this to the first moonwalk? Are you saying that this is that monumental a happening?"

"No less," Kaplan answered. "I'm somewhat of a space buff and I think the language fits it perfectly."

"God Bless the National Health Agency," the newscaster said. Kaplan smiled. The interviewer turned and looked straight into the camera. "That's it, for now. For Good Health 93, this is Stu Sizemore signing off and saying — for the love of God, let's all care a little more for each other."

The prattle that began among the camera crews and production staff told the audience that the broadcast was over. While the secret service surrounded him, two health care managers removed the central line tubing from the President's neck. When a trickle of blood seeped from the puncture site, one of the managers held a four by four gauze bandage tightly against the bleeding insertion site. After a few moments, the secret service agents helped the President sit up and swing his feet over the side of the stretcher. His eyes appeared glazed; his mouth hung open.

"Are you alright, sir?" one of the HCMs asked.

"Of course!" the President answered with a note of bravado.

The energized audience of dignitaries surveyed the hall and located the tables loaded with lavish hor d'oeuvres. They surged *en mass* toward the food. Servers in short, lilac coats passed through the audience, offering plastic glasses filled with champagne and handing them out with lilac-colored, paper napkins.

So this is history in the making, Tom mused. What's next?

Chapter 21

Jeanne stood in front of Tom's desk and gave him the news.

"Carl Hammerstone? In the hospital? Here? At Starr?" Tom instantly reached for the phone. Jeanne lurched forward and slapped her hand across his.

"Hold it, Dr. Sullivan. Before you call the floor, let me tell you what's going on," she said. "I was up on the ward when they brought him in. It's a grand-scale nightmare."

"Okay, what is it?" Tom asked.

"He's had a MI."

"Carl! A heart attack? No!"

"Severe substernal chest pain, radiation down the left arm, diaphoretic, began about an hour ago," Jeanne said. "He was brought in by NHA ambulance, and admitted to one of the automated units. So far he's doing fine. The problem is he's refusing to let them use monitors or put in a central line. He says that's not his kind of medical care."

"Thank God he's okay," Tom said. "We'll need to get him out of the automated treatment track right away."

"You know the NHA treatment protocol," Jeanne remarked. "Acute Myocardial Infarction falls in the automated unit treatment category."

"Well the hospital is going to have to make an exception."

"I'm not sure another treatment channel would help," Jeanne said. "Manager Hammerstone is refusing all treatment. He has his full allocation of points left on his bracelet. He could have any treatment he needs, but he says 'absolutely no.' He's insisting on giving away his points to lash out against PointCure and the automated units."

Tom rolled his eyes. "Let's go. I'll talk to the health care team when we get on the unit. I can reason with him; he'll be more cooperative."

When Tom reached the unit, Carl Hammerstone was resting in a hospital bed in his darkened room. Tom paused in the doorway. Soon Carl felt his presence, opened his eyes, and spoke.

"Who's that? Now what? When are you people going to hear me? I'm not having a damn thing to do with you. This isn't medicine; it's dehumanizing torture. Take your damned technology and go to hell!" he shouted.

A group of unsettled staff milled around muttering outside his room. The monitor team, the central line team, and the consumer data gathering team stood lined up in the hallway ready to do their job. Tom glanced at the irritated, impatient looks on their faces.

"The manager must go along with the automated protocol," an angry nurse said to Tom. "It's for his own good."

"Let me talk with him," Tom said.

Carl heard Tom's voice. "Tom, that's you isn't it?"

"Yes."

"I knew you'd be here soon. I asked them not to get you involved. The damned ambulance brought me here. I asked them to take me to Devan to spare you this. Guess you're going to try and force me to go along with the fancy new equipment too."

"Carl, You know better."

"Not anymore. Don't come in that door. The only real doctors left are those deaccessed souls who sit in front of the PointCure Check-In Centers and take care of a few people with scrapes and colds. They may not get paid in your fancy point system, but they haven't forgotten what it means to treat patients like human beings. They don't use computers and machines or try to play God."

Tom paused to frame a response. Carl was talking about the group of physicians who called themselves the "Healers," the group he was organizing. They were volunteers from the ranks of the aging, already retired doctors, the deaccessed managers who did not apply for reaccess or failed to complete the rehabilitation program for "Non

Compliant Managers." They made a pittance income treating minor illnesses and injuries for people who didn't wish to use their points unnecessarily.

The Healer's persistence was the outcome of the "Thomas Jefferson" of health care, Allan Mulholland's one weak point in his masterful, legal instrument. The Supreme Court had recently ruled that under the Constitution, without proof of criminal action, and with credentials otherwise in order, managers could not be deprived of their right to practice health care outside of the points system. They could not collect points, but because of an oversight in the lawyer's legislation document, the physicians retained their health care managerial licenses. The NHA had no choice except to look the other way.

"Universal central lines, hmmmphf!" Carl growled. "I watched the demonstration on television. You, standing there like you were proud of it. What a bunch of crap. No central lines. No computers. Understand?"

"Carl, at least let them put the monitors on so you can be treated. You know that the first hours are the most risky…"

"Absolutely not! You don't understand. These people want total control over medicine and now they have it. They even have control of you. This plan is much bigger than it looks. Someone smart as hell has figured it out down to the last letter."

The nurse standing beside Tom whispered to him. "He's paranoid. He's delirious. Maybe we need to call in a psychiatrist."

Tom shook his head.

"Ask yourself, Tom. Why would the NHA do it? Why would they dynamite the whole medical system under the guise of giving more medical care to people?" He was breathing more rapidly. "They're power hungry and have a weapon stronger than any sword that's ever been held over the heads of any people. They know that this is the ultimate method of control."

"That's a little extreme isn't it?" Tom said, mulling Carl's words over in his mind.

"He is delusional. That's a paranoid delusion if I ever heard one," a young manager standing beside Tom whispered.

"Carl, this isn't the time to prove a point or hypothesize about conspiracies," Tom said. "You've had a serious heart attack. At minimum you need to be monitored for arrhythmias or other complications. The EKG showed a definite ST elevation. You have a hell of an infarct!"

"I'm doing this my way," Carl said.

Tom looked at the old professor. Here was his mentor, his medical professor in his training at Devan. Here was the man who taught him to care for patients. Now his idol had a massive heart infarction and was refusing treatment. Tom began to feel desperate. A gnawing heaviness ran across his chest.

"You need acute care — we've got to do something about that clot. At the very least you need a cardiac cath. Maybe a balloon angioplasty will do it, possibly a stent. But you could need bypass surgery. You have all the points you need."

Carl was sweating profusely. He held the left side of his chest, clenched his teeth and struggled against the crushing pain. "I know my rights — at least what rights I still have within this system. There's no way you can overrule my decision without going to court. If you want to do that, I'll welcome it. I'll have my say in public." He held up his points bracelet and shook it in Tom's face. "I want you to find someone, a child, a young person, someone who can use these points. It doesn't matter who. My only stipulation is that the points can't be used for the automated system. I want the person to be treated as a human being by human beings."

"At least let me order some morphine. We can arrange to do something with the points."

"No morphine. The pain's not that bad. Didn't you hear me? I've given away my points, every damned one of them. My points count is zero. I can't have morphine. I can't have anything. That's it."

"Listen, Carl," Tom said. "if you give away your points, that takes you out of the managers' care and puts you in the hands of the administrative staff. Clark will have the legal authority to do whatever the protocol says. Without points, he'll transfer you over to the New Directions program. That's the way it is now. Please let us treat you."

"I've made my decision. Go ahead and notify that Clark character."

Jeanne Donnely tapped Tom on the shoulder and leaned close to his ear. "He's here. Ken Clark is already here. He wants to talk with you," she said. "He's in the Central Control Center."

Tom left the room and entered the control station. Ken was reading the computer printout of the events surrounding Carl's care. He looked up at Tom over his reading glasses and spoke. "If he wants to give away his points, that's his business. NHA protocol is clear on this. We have to send him to New Directions," Ken said. "The old man is trying to make a fool of us, trying to make us look bad."

"He's frightened. He knows what that kind of chest pain means."

"I'm no fool, Sullivan. He's trying to make the program look bad."

"Can't we make some kind of special arrangement? Carl Hammerstone is a close friend and one of the great physicians in Devan's history."

"I don't give a damn if the man is Hippocrates. If he gives up his points, it's New Directions. I have the authority to make this decision and I intend to do it." Clark's voice was growing louder and louder.

"Besides, he supports the Healers. I have no use for managers who operate outside the NHA system. It's New Directions. And now!"

"Then at least let him sign out. Send him home and let him treat himself." Tom implored.

"Send him out? You must be crazy. All we need is some grand old man like this dying on us because he was unhappy. There's no way I can let him go home after we've gotten that messy EKG tracing on him," he said. "He has a clear cut diagnosis of a massive infarct and that's unquestionably a hospital treatment category. It's protocol. Like it or not, he has to stay and we have to keep him."

"You can override all the protocols; you know that."

"True, but not in this case. The man's is giving up his points. It's a slap in our face. It's blasphemous. Downright sacrilegious."

"Sacrilegious? Now that's a peculiar way to look at it. What the hell has this got to do with religion?"

"It's New Directions now," Ken said. "The old man brought it on himself. He gives away his points and it's my call." He nodded to the nurse to begin the transfer process. A thin smile crossed his face.

Tom slammed the door to the control station. He walked over to where Ken was sitting. "I've had it. I've had it with this whole fucking mess," he said.

Ken ignored him. He was busy signing the transfer document the nurse had put in front of him.

Tom glanced out toward the hallway. The stretcher carrying the sedated Carl Hammerstone passed by the Central Control Station on its way to the New Directions treatment program area.

"I'm resigning, damn it," Tom said.

"I think not, Manager Sullivan," Ken shot back. "Or should I say Doctor Sullivan, as you insist. You're in the service of the United States Government and your actions are governed by the Mulholland Act."

Then Tom remembered. His position at Starr had been designated by the NHA as "necessary for the welfare of the country." Mulholland's Health Care Laws prohibited resignations from assignments of his level without endless hearings and probable punitive action by the authorities.

"You're going to stay in this hospital if I have to force you to do it with armed guards. You may get by with insisting that you be called Doctor Sullivan, but make trouble with a noisy resignation and I promise you, you'll end up in prison."

"Okay, Clark. But you had better understand. I'm going to do everything I can do to expose this outrageous system. You'll be able to use my name, but you're going to have a hell of a time using me."

"Think through your actions well, Sullivan. Both you and your activist wife could force our hand. Join the team and do your job. Don't put yourselves in harm's way."

Tom clenched his fist, then stood back. Though the threat was vague, it was a threat. He would think through the best course of action. He recalled Bob Kaplan's observation that waiting and working from the inside may be the most effective way. But at this point, there was little he could do. Ken Clark would have his way. Carl's transfer had already taken place.

Chapter 22

Sitting at his desk, Tom perused the New Directions unit brochure. It was titled: "NEW DIRECTIONS — REACHING TOWARD THE FUTURE." It pointed out that the New Directions unit at Starr Memorial Hospital offered the very latest and finest in cutting edge health care. "That's bullshit," Tom concluded. "'New Directions' is no more than an euphemism for human experimentation."

The New Directions unit was close akin to a medical side show. People without points and patients who refused to participate in the new system of health care could be sent there. The unit used technology largely for spectacular effects, and the results were used as part of the advertising programs for CelestaCare. Recently, massive media coverage told of a New Direction patient's headless body that was kept alive for two weeks. "We're funded by the NHA," a CelestaCare spokesperson had answered when asked on television why the health care corporation would conduct such research. "The NHA wants to demonstrate the amazing techniques we can use to sustain life."

On Ken's orders, Tom had accompanied representatives of the media to view the living, decapitated body. The man's trunk and extremities had just lain on the hospital bed and twitched. Machines had done it all.

Catchy slogans like "The Health Care of Tomorrow, Today" captured public attention for the "New Directions" project. By and large, the procedures had no positive effects and even worked to patients' detriment, but the New Directions program had become a central place for health care research. It also served as an ideal stage for the showman manager who wanted the spotlight. There was even talk of "New Directions" becoming a health care specialty — complete with training programs and certification. The specialists would be called "New Directionists." A New Directions text entitled, *New Directions: The Sure Way to Life Eternal,* had already been written and published by a prominent surgeon manager at Devan.

A short while later, when he went to visit Carl on the ND Unit, Tom spoke to a young New Directions manager. He leaned over and whispered so that only Tom could hear him. "Manger Hammerstone's condition has stabilized. I'm taking my time deciding which direction to go," the young manager told Tom. "I know it's risky to drag my feet; Clark won't like it. But, some of us still have feelings left. Manager Hammerstone taught me at Devan. He's not going to be in any experimental protocol if I can help it."

"Has Clark been around?"

"No, for some reason he seems to be looking the other way."

Tom blotted his brow, thanked the young man, and walked toward Carl's room.

"It's not your fault," Carl told Tom. "I was angry about everything that's happened — this damned heart attack, this screwed up medical system, my own helplessness. You got caught in the crossfire."

Tom pulled up the single chair in the room. "The control the administrators and the NHA have is enormous."

"You're right," Carl said. "And they'll have even more control before it's over. The government is using this joint venture business to set up an operation that will give them unshakable power and control."

"I don't like anything about it. I should never have trusted Cunningham or Clark," Tom commented.

"Don't blame yourself. These people are playing hard ball," Carl continued, "but I have to believe that something this destructive will destroy itself." He winked at Tom and smiled. "Maybe we can help the process along."

"What do you mean?"

"There will be an opening, a window; there's always one. We just need to wait."

"What kind of opening?" Tom asked.

Carl placed a finger on his lips and motioned toward the microphone over the bed. He leaned close to Tom and whispered, "They're listening to everything we say."

Tom told Carl goodbye and left. On his way out of the New Directions unit, he passed a room where New Directions scientists were testing mechanically provided care. On the other side of the glass he saw two patients in care situations totally devoid of people. Robots whirred around the room attending to the patients. "HUMAN BEINGS MUST STAY OUT!" the sign on the door said. The two isolated patients inside the chamber looked gaunt and their faces wore blank stares. "This can't be," Tom asserted. "I can't let this be."

Jeanne met him when he returned to his office. She was breathless. "I'm so happy for you. Something very unusual has happened," she said. "The unit nurse just called about Manager Hammerstone. Clark has reversed his decision. Carl Hammerstone is going to be allowed to go to Devan and direct his own treatment. They're probably afraid that your manager friend might die on the New Directions unit. I suspect Ken knows that would be terribly bad press."

Tom slumped into a chair. "Thank God," he said with a sigh of relief. "I'll go back up and tell Carl."

"That will have to wait," Jeanne said. A young manager named Willingham has been calling here for the last hour. He's called from the ward five or six times. He said he needs to see you as soon as possible. Now he says it's urgent."

"I'll see what he needs."

Minutes later, Tom punched in his access code and passed through a door into the control station on an automated unit where Trim Willingham, the newest addition to the managerial staff at Starr worked. Two health care assistants busily rushed from console to console adjusting the dials and levers controlling the automated units. Above the consoles, twenty monitors ringed the half-circle of solid gray wall. On the other side of the wall, circling the central control station, were twenty patient cubicles. A camera aimed at each patient beamed a picture to its corresponding monitor screen. Across the control room stood Trim Willingham, his eyes fixed on a monitor with a large black number "18" painted above it. When Tom entered, Willingham cast a quick glance at him, then looked back at the monitor.

"Thanks for coming up," Trim said, as Tom walked up behind him. "Take a look at the man on number 18. His name is Mitchell Newman. Maybe there's nothing you can do," he told Tom, "but I'm not big on sitting comfortably in this control station while my patient is suffering on the other side of this damned wall. Look at that poor man. Came in with kidney stones a month ago. They DissolvaBeamed them. Did fine and was discharged. Now he's back with a dissecting, aortic aneurysm and he's uremic. Look at his chemistries. He's in big trouble."

Tom studied the closed circuit television monitor. Mitchell Newman had a pained look on his face. His eyes were glazed and widened, his pupils large. Tom's eyes dashed to the console monitor screen. He noted the patient's elevated blood urea nitrogen and creatinine readout. The patient's BUN and creatinine were dangerously high — a sure sign of kidney failure.

"Trim, get some lytes."

Willingham quickly keyed in a request for electrolytes. In seconds, the electrolyte report appeared. Sodium, potassium, chloride, carbonate: all dangerously out of balance.

Tom found the room camera controls. He switched to a panoramic view of the cubicle. The man's hands clutched at the sheets. Tom narrowed the field, zooming back to Mitchell Newman's face. He was moaning with pain. Tom leaned over close to the microphone.

"I'm Doctor Sullivan, Mr. Newman. Can you hear me?" Tom asked over the microphone connected to the speaker in the cubicle.

The patient looked around for the source of the voice. He squinted as he tried to make out Tom's face on the television monitor in front of his bed. His hardly audible reply came over the speaker in the control center. "Ye...ye...yes," he said.

"Can we do anything for you?" Tom asked.

"I want my family. Call my wife, my son. I've been here for hours by myself. I have no idea what's going on. My chest, my stomach, and my back are killing me. Help me. Tell me what's going on."

"We'll get you something for the pain."

Tom switched the microphone to the cubicle off.

"What the hell *is* going on, Trim?" Tom asked.

"When the aneurysm of his abdominal aorta dissected, it split the wall of the vessel and sheared off both his renal arteries. He slipped into renal failure. Here, take a look. There's no blood flow to his kidneys."

Trim flashed a picture of Newman's aortagram on the console screen. Tom looked at the outlines of the large artery that traversed the patient's abdomen then branched into the two large arteries that fed the legs. From the large artery's truck came smaller ones to the intestines, the kidneys, and other organs. Trim was right. The blood flow to the kidneys was almost gone.

"This man needs surgery. He needs it fast."

"Negative authorization from the NHA." The surgeons can't touch him. Not enough points," Trim told Tom.

"But he's blitzed his kidneys."

"I know. But with his point level, about the most we can do is put him through dialysis a couple of times. I've put the surgical treatment request in several times. They're holding the line."

Tom heard Trim's words, but couldn't believe them. He shook his head. "Damn the NHA. That's rationing care and they are doing the deciding," he said.

Tom switched on the room communication system again.

"Mr. Newman, we're working on your problems now," Tom said. "We'll get you something for your pain. We'll be in to talk with you in just a minute."

"Where is my family? I'm lonely and scared," Newman said faintly.

"We understand," Tom said through the microphone, when he saw the distressed look on the man's face. "We'll see about calling your family."

"No one's been in for hours," the man said. His voice was tremulous. "What's happening to me?"

"We'll have someone in there soon," Tom said.

As he spoke, Tom saw Trim Willingham shaking his head. He turned off the communication system again.

"Where is his family?" Tom asked. "There's no one in the cubicle with him. Why is this man all alone?"

"New visiting regulations. The close circuit visiting system became operational today. No visitors except by the close circuit televisions when someone's this ill."

"No visitors? When someone's this ill, that's when they need their family. I was told the closed circuit visiting system would only be used for patients with highly contagious diseases."

"No sir, these directives are straight from the NHA. They say it's less costly to manage patients this way. Forget visitation in the rooms. The NHA says family members get in the way when someone is this sick. Too many costly complaints. It's a universal application, like the central line. No managers in there either."

"This man's on the edge of a delirium," Tom said. "You need to get in there and talk to him. He needs some orienting stimuli from the environment. He needs to know what's happening to him."

"We can't go in there. Look at this memo," he said, handing Tom what looked to be ten pages of information. "It was just distributed this morning."

Tom read the title: "TO ALL STARR MEMORIAL HEALTH CARE PROVIDERS: DIRECTIVES FOR CONSUMER VISITATION."

Willingham pointed to one of the sections on page 7 and Tom read it. "Routine maintenance of the system connections and central line will be accomplished by the hospital's System Maintenance Team. The hospital Waste Products Team will attend to patients' excretory function needs on a scheduled time basis to which the consumer will be expected to conform. Costs must be reduced."

Now Tom realized why the units had more of a urine and fecal odor. The patients weren't conforming to the "scheduled time basis." It was impossible. Each patient was different. Some were incontinent; some couldn't urinate and defecate while lying in the bed. There was no way to superimpose these rigid demands. He read on.

"Health Care Managment Staff are not to enter the patient cubicle areas. Communication is to take place only over the electronic system. Exceptions to this rule will be made only when it is determined that entering the cubicle is designated as an 'Unquestionable Health Care Necessity.' If this is felt to be the case, the manager is to call the Quality Assurance department, discuss the need with one of the QA personnel, and enter the room only if authorized to do so. In case of cardiac arrest, the Cardiopulmonary Resuscitation Team (CPRT) should be called immediately. Managers should remain in the treatment control centers."

Trim spoke. "When I told QA I needed to go in and talk with this patient, they said, 'no'. I explained that this man needs me to be with him. He needs support; he's dying. I said it's an 'unquestionable medical necessity,' but the Quality Assurance clerk disagreed. 'Do what you need to do over the speaker. Use the closed circuit television,' she said. I couldn't convince her or her supervisor otherwise.

"She said that we have to conserve managers' time. What she really means is that they want to hire fewer managers to run these damned machines. Mr. Newman needs someone desperately. That's why I called you."

"Clark didn't tell me about any new NHA directive. I've never seen this. I've never heard of anything as ridiculous as the NHA mandating universal closed circuit family visitation," Tom said angrily. "And these damned rules about urination and bowel movements by the clock. Absurd! Having to get clearance to comfort someone this sick. It's madness." Tom said, "This man is near death. We're going in there."

"I'm ready." Willingham said. "You call the directions and I'll follow them. To hell with the NHA."

"Mr. Newman is already scheduled for dialysis isn't he?" Tom asked as they headed toward the door leading to the patient cubicle area.

"No. We're waiting for clearance from the NHA. Their software is raising a question as to whether or not his condition warrants dialysis. And to make matters worse, there's some kind of screw-up in the computers about his points."

"Waiting for clearance from the NHA? That won't do. This man needs immediate attention. His BUN is soaring. And look at that creatinine and those lytes. He's already uremic. He'll be delirious in no time. We have to buy some time."

"I know, but there's nothing more I can do. I tried to ask them to rush the decision, but I couldn't get through on the 1-800 number. For a long time, there was nothing but a busy signal. When I did get through, I got a menu. Then, I got a voice-mail instead of a person. It was a dead end."

Tom saw the pained look of frustration on Trim Willingham's face. He knew that the bright young man had come to Starr to learn more about caring for patients in his teaching program. He had been deceived. Now, Willingham was little more than a powerless technician, manipulating the controls at a computer terminal. His patient, on the other side of the wall in a small cubicle, was dying.

Tom looked across the control station at monitor number 18 and saw the patient's face. "Let's get in that room. At least we can try and comfort the man," he said, beckoning the young manager to follow him.

Seconds later the two managers entered the cubicle.

"Mr. Newman, we want to talk to you," Tom said, pulling a chair close to the bedside. You shouldn't be left all alone like this." He placed his hand on the patient's arm. The man opened his watery eyes. His breathing was shallow and labored.

"We're not your family," Tom said, "but we'll stay in here with you and help explain what's happening and how we plan to try and help you."

"Yes, Mr. Newman, we're going to try and help in any way we can," Willingham assured him.

Mitchell Newman raised his head slightly from the pillow, looked at them both, smiled faintly, and then lowered his head back down. Tom noted the shiny plastic tubing of the central line running from beneath the gauze pad on the patient's neck to the outlet on the wall beside his bed.

"Thank God you're here," the patient said, gasping between words. "I don't want to die alone." His breathing was becoming more labored. He closed his eyes.

Trim quickly turned up the oxygen flow. He began to tell the patient the treatment plan. He told him that he was still hopeful about his condition. Then it struck him. Mr. Newman was almost motionless. He was not hearing him.

The room grew quiet. Tom looked at his young colleague. Tears were welling up in Trim's eyes. "I think I'm learning what is most important in medical care," Trim said.

"It's a human being's ability to be-there and respond to the needs of another human being like himself," Tom said.

A minute later, Mitchell Newman gasped a deep breath. His arms and legs quivered. His eyes opened and stared straight ahead. A peculiar smile appeared on his face. Suddenly, his head fell to the side. His breathing stopped; his pupils dilated; his body was still.

Number 18 was dead.

Chapter 23

When Katie Sullivan looked down at the chart on a new patient admission to her unit at 8:30 a.m., she noticed that the words on the admission sheet briefly blurred. She shook her head to try and clear her vision and felt a pain shoot across the back of her neck.

"I need a couple of acetaminophens," she said to the nurse standing next to her. "I think I'm getting a cold."

The nurse shook two pills from the bottle and gave them to her. She filled a cup with water and swallowed them. Her assistant, Mgr. Sam Berman saw her take the pills and walked over.

"You're okay?" he asked.

"Just a cold."

"Kate, you have to stay well. We're going to need more meetings like the one yesterday," he said.

"Yes, we have to band together," Katie said. "I'm not going to put up with these new regulations, especially with children. I'll do whatever I have to do to change them. Organizing Devan's managers is a beginning. I don't know who's advising those NHA turkeys, but most of their regulations won't float."

"Cunningham won't be happy. You're brave to lead the group."

"Someone has to."

"People listen to you. You have a following, you know. Nurses, physician assistants, residents, medical students…"

She smiled appreciatively. "I think you left this cold virus I'm getting off the list," she said. "We need to take a look at this child that was just transferred to the unit."

"Sure," Sam said, walking next to her down the hallway.

What a change, she thought as they walked along quietly toward the room housing the sick child. The wards were nothing like they were six months ago. Automated computer care had changed everything. She looked at the corridor. The colorful, old, fairy tale figures painted on the walls were gone. Now the walls were painted a drab gray.

She glanced through the observation windows into the patient cubicles. Each child lay alone in a small, sparsely furnished space, the parents nowhere in sight. There were no toys or television. Even the very small children lay motionless and quiet with shiny plastic central lines running from their small necks to the outlets above their beds. The stillness is bizarre, she thought. Then she remembered the new regulations — "All children are to be heavily sedated. Wide-awake children are costly consumers."

Pediatrics, the noisy specialty. How many times in medical school had she placed her stethoscope on the chest of a crying, screaming child and not been able to hear the breath sounds or the sounds and murmurs of the hearts? How many times had she wished the child would be still and quiet so that she might do her work? How many times had she felt self-conscious while protective parents hovered nearby?

Now, there were no parents with the children. Now the children were still and quiet. Morbidly quiet. Too quiet. She listened carefully, but heard nothing. The place was like a tomb. She craved noise.

They reached the child's cubicle. Katie stopped suddenly and peered in through the glass observation window.

"What's wrong with that child, Sam?"

Sam studied the boy through the glass. "I'd like to think it's sedation — possibly too much sedation. At least that's what we're hoping. We can reverse that."

"No, this is something else," Katie said. "His eyes are slightly open. But look at that facial expression — that's a mixture of sadness and fear. And his little arms are so thin." She held her fingertips to her lips. "He looks like a starving child from a third world country. Sam, what's wrong with him? This isn't sedation!"

Berman looked through the observation window and shook his head. "The truth is no one really knows, Katie. This little fellow has everyone stumped. The child stopped eating five days ago. Then he began wasting away at an unbelievably phenomenal speed. Now he's stopped communicating. This morning he developed a 105 degree temp. He was getting shocky, so we transferred him to the ICU. I've got blood cultures and a dozen other tests working." He paused. "I'm afraid it's hit Devan," he added.

"What?" Katie asked.

"A description of an illness like this was on the pediatric update website last night. Some strange new kind of wasting syndrome. They call it AMS — the acute marasmus syndrome. Cases are beginning to pop up all over the country." Sam said.

"Acute marasmus? What do you mean?" Katie asked. "Marasmus is a slow wasting process."

"I know, but this happens fast," Sam remarked. "It doesn't make sense, but six cases were reported in this week's *Northeastern Journal of Health Care* yesterday. Two are children. Usually the patient has been in the hospital for several days when the illness begins. Once the illness starts, the patient becomes withdrawn and sad, stops talking and eating, and rapidly begins to waste away. They all present this way. After a few days, they go on to develop high fever. No one has been able to explain the illness. Some people feel it may be related to the epidemic..."

"And the treatment?" Katie asked.

"So far there isn't any," Sam said. "Every patient who has developed the syndrome has died."

"That's horrible," Katie said. She stared through the observation window.

Sam nodded quietly in agreement.

Suddenly Katie felt faint. Her vision blurred. She felt unsteady. Still another, more severe pain shot across the back of her head and neck. She staggered briefly, then regained her equilibrium. She placed her palm on her forehead.

"Sam, this is crazy, but I feel like I'm coming down with something and it's not a cold. I'm going down to the emergency department to let someone check me over."

"Want me to go with you?" Sam asked.

"No, that isn't necessary. I'll catch up with you in a little while," she said, then turned down the hallway toward the emergency department. "Keep a close eye on that child," she called back. "See if anything new turns up on the pediatric update website this morning."

Chapter 24

The afternoon news shocked the country. Fifty-eight patient-consumers at the CelestaCare Ritter Park Hospital in Houston were dead — killed instantly. Another forty were in cardiovascular shock — dangerously ill. Hazy information about the catastrophe slowly seeped out of the hospital's public affairs office. At first, the cause was said to be an oxygen fire. Then it was rumored that escaped chemical fumes swept through the halls asphyxiating consumers. Finally, the truth emerged.

Jeanne Donnely printed out the news sheet from the high security CelestaCare hospital Internet link, quickly scanned the freshly printed message, and rushed into Tom Sullivan's office. There, she found Tom watching the news report on his monitor screen. The two watched as the television camera focused on the frenzied crowd standing in front of Ritter Park Hospital.

The newscaster in the foreground was anxious and breathless. "I wish we could tell you more," he said. "At the moment all we know is that many consumers have died in an accident. I've been informed that the cause of their deaths is being investigated as rapidly as possible.

These people are bewildered. Family members, friends, and concerned citizens are all gathered here, waiting for news.

Wait. Hospital personnel are beginning to come out of the hospital. They're calling out names and handing out envelopes to family members. I'll try to talk to one of them."

POINTS

Momentarily, the reporter stood next to an elderly man who had removed his glasses and was blotting his eyes with a tissue.

"Sir, the country is waiting. Please, can you tell us what the message in the envelope said?"

The television lights glared in the stunned man's eyes. His lip quivered. "It says that my wife is dead — there was an accident."

"That's all? No other explanation?"

"It says representatives of the hospital will contact me as soon as they have further information."

"Oh God, is someone with you?"

"My daughter's with me."

The man broke into tears and was comforted by his daughter.

Others cried out in anger when they received the news. Some wailed loudly.

"My God, what a catastrophe!" Tom said, finally acknowledging Jeanne's presence.

"Bad as it gets," Jeanne said.

"What the hell happened?"

She showed him the printout. "This just came through on the high security Internet link. It was a glitch in the computer program. They suspect a treatment program dumped a drug overdose into the central line system."

Tom's forehead wrinkled. "You mean they don't know for sure?"

"Not yet. They're still piecing the clues together. The consumers all showed a slowed heart beat on their monitors. The ones that died immediately went into irreversible shock, developed arrhythmias, and then experienced cardiac arrest.

"As best they can tell, it looks like a consumer with migraine headaches was to be started on a beta blocker. Instead of the system treating one patient with a standard dose, the computer dumped the whole pharmacy supply into the system. The main trunk fed the drug into the central lines of every consumer on that floor. The toxicologists don't have all the studies complete, but they're pretty sure."

"Those poor souls. All overdosed on a beta blocker. Fifty-eight people dead because of some damned computer error — that's real medical progress. How many more are likely to die?"

"Shhhh," she said, putting a finger to her lips and pointing toward the television. "This looks official."

The screen filled with the now familiar NHA logo with its lilac background. "Ladies and Gentlemen, the Chief Manager of the United States, and Director of The National Health Agency, Manager Alexander Wade."

On screen, the unruffled Director sat relaxing near the fireside in his comfortable high back, leather chair. He spoke calmly.

"My friends, it is with great sadness that I make this announcement. As you have heard, there has been a tragic accident at CelestaCare Ritter Park Hospital in Houston. Thus far, sixty people have died under circumstances which remain unclear. It appears that there was a problem with an automated treatment medication dispenser, an unexpected happening in the course of these patients' health care, a rare side effect.

"This is undoubtedly an isolated event. Its cause will be subjected to the most thorough investigation. As we progress, your National Health Agency will make every effort to bring you the most up-to-date information on this tragic event. But let me assure you, your loved ones now being cared for in our nation's hospitals are eminently safe."

Not once did Alexander Wade stammer or pause. He concluded with, "I will be talking with you again, as soon as we know more. You may be sure of that. Thank you, and may God bless you all with good health."

The lilac plumes of the NHA reappeared on the screen. Then the picture flashed back to the CelestaCare Ritter Park Hospital in Texas. Standing in front of Ritter Park Hospital, with the American flag rippling behind her, another newscaster announced that a statement from George Turpino, the Hospital Administrator, was immediately forthcoming.

Turpino, dressed in a fashionable double breasted suit, thanked her, smoothed his hair in place, and took out a written statement. He began to read.

"I regret to say that our automated treatment program has today made an error and contaminated the central line inflow fluids of ninety-eight people. Some have unfortunately died; others are quite ill. The majority of the people who were killed in the incident were over seventy, on the geriatric units, and had most likely lived good lives."

He cleared his throat.

"Every treatment method has risks, potential side effects, and unknowns. Today's happening was simply an unfortunate side effect, something no one could control or have predicted. Let me assure you that CelestaCare and the NHA have only your best interests at heart.

"Having no better answer, we can only conclude that God's will has been done. Thank you."

When he finished, Turpino folded his papers, then turned and walked quietly through the crowd.

"That son of a bitch!" Tom shouted. "How the hell can he dismiss sixty deaths as a side effect? And what does he know about God's will? That pompous bastard doesn't give a damn that these people died. Not a word of comfort for those families."

"I think you're being a bit hard on him," Jeanne said, looking at Tom directly. "These kinds of things happen. The administrators have to make statements. I think he reported the facts as best he could."

Tom said nothing. Jeanne's statement had an unusual quality. She usually was not so understanding of the presumptuous statements of the NHA and CelestaCare.

"Side effect," Tom muttered. "They shouldn't be so quick to dismiss a tragedy of this magnitude as a 'side effect.'"

"It doesn't matter," Jeanne said. "They're dead. There'll be an investigation and the problem will be corrected."

"I'm afraid it does matter," Tom said.

"I guess that every now and then, computers make mistakes," she said. "They screw up, like people do, but probably a great deal less. You could call it a side effect."

Tom listened, still surprised at Jeanne's position.

"And when did you get to be so damned accepting?" he asked.

She placed her hands on her hips. "Why get upset?" she asked. "Look, all we can do is the best we can do. Sometimes, we just have to accept things as they are. A side effect is a side effect.

"I've got to get to work. Life at Starr goes on, Houston or no Houston. Do you want your door open or closed?"

"Just close it when you leave," he said, still puzzled and irritated by Jeanne's reaction.

The latest issue of the *Northeastern Medical Journal* topped the stack of mail in front of him. Still agitated, Tom perused the Journal's table of contents. An article containing case reports about a newly described syndrome caught his eye. "Acute Marasmus: A Wasting Syndrome Leading to Death: Report of Six Cases." He skimmed the article, reviewing the symptom complex found in the six patients. They had been admitted to the hospital for a variety of illnesses. All six had become progressively more agitated, restless, and withdrawn. They were all noted to manifest a peculiar look on their faces, a mix of terror and sadness. They had refused food, lost weight rapidly, and deteriorated physically. Rampant blood borne infections of various kinds had lead to death in all cases. The syndrome was unresponsive to any treatment.

The last statement that appeared in the report was particularly bothersome. All six patients were being treated on CelestaCare's new automated treatment units when they developed the syndrome, but the paper's author capped his article with, "We are certain that these deaths have no relationship to the use of the automated unit treatment modality."

Tom's scientific training incited suspicions. How could they be so absolutely sure so soon?

Tom sat for a moment, gazing off beyond his desk. Suddenly he noted a newly framed Certificate of Health Care Management Skills hanging on his wall. He rushed to the wall, removed it, held it in front of him, and scrutinized it carefully.

"Who put this HCM certificate up in my office?" he momentarily asked his secretary.

"Maintenance came by yesterday afternoon after you left on rounds. Said you requested that it be put up immediately," his secretary responded.

"That's crap! I've never turned in my medical degree, never asked for one of these certificates."

"Dr. Sullivan, you know all health care managers have to have one of those certificates."

"Do me a favor, Betty, call maintenance, and tell them to get over here, pick this up, and give it back to whomever requested that it be put on my wall. And you can tell them that here is where I think it belongs. He tossed the certificate into the trash can next to her desk."

"I suppose I should come clean," his secretary said. "Mr. Clark sent it over. Said that he feels responsible as administrator for bringing you in line with regulations. I told him you wouldn't be happy."

"You're right, Betty. And now you can call Mr. Clark's office and tell them that they can come over and pick it up. Have them tell Mr. Clark that the Medical Director said he doesn't need this hokey certificate to know how to take care of his patients or to know that he is a physician."

He was still fuming when he sat down at his desk. Sixty fatalities in Houston dismissed as a "side effect", "Acute Progressive Marasmus" leading to wasting and death. This is progress?

Moments later, he was shuffling through the correspondence on his desk when the call system on his desk sounded.

"Doctor Sullivan," his secretary said.

"Yes."

"It's Consumer Information Services at Devan Hospital on the phone. They want to speak with you right away — it's an emergency."

"Sure," he said and picked up the telephone.

"Yes, what is it?" Tom asked.

"Thomas Sullivan. Your wife is quite ill," a voice on the other end said officially.

"What? Who are you?"

"I'm Don, in the Consumer Information Office. Manager Katherine Sullivan is being admitted to the hospital at this very moment."

"What's wrong with her?"

"Try not to get alarmed. I will read you the consumer information report."

"Katherine P. Sullivan entered the emergency department at 1005 hours. She was found to have a temperature of 104 degrees. She complained of a severe headache. It was the decision of the admission computer system that she be admitted to the hospital. The exact nature of her difficulty is unknown at this time. Diagnostic procedures are in progress. The most probable diagnosis derived from the Diagnosi-Stat program is acute encephalo-meningitis."

"For God's sake, what else?" Tom demanded.

"This is the extent of the report," the clerk answered.

"Surely there's more information," Tom said.

"This is the extent of the report," the clerk repeated.

The clerk's monotone voice sounded like a computer synthesized voice. "Look, I want more information. I'm a physician."

"A what?"

"Oh please excuse me," Tom said sarcastically. "I'm what you would call a manager. My wife's a manager also."

"I'm very sorry, Manager. This is the extent of the report at this time."

"Where is she now?" Tom asked.

"She's in an automated unit room on the fourth floor. I'm sure they will be putting in a central line and we'll have more information soon."

"A central line? Damn," Tom said, his mind immediately flashing to the Houston incident.

"I want to visit her. I want to see her," Tom said.

"I'm afraid they won't allow that yet. The regulations state that you can't visit, except by closed circuit video visiting, at least until a diagnosis is made."

"Who's listed as manager?"

"Robert T. Kaplan."

Tom sighed a deep breath. He felt a sense of relief. At least he knew that Bob Kaplan would do his best. For a split second, the impersonality fell away. But he still felt terrified and numb. Whatever Katie had, the illness had progressed with unusual speed. The indefinite news about the deaths of patients in the computer treatment units in Houston added even more concern. He put on his gray coat and went out into the secretarial area. Jeanne Donnely stood there, just back from rounds. He quickly gave her a complete accounting of the Information Service call.

"She'll be alright. I know she will. Probably some viral illness," Jeanne said.

146

"It'll be another hour before I can see her, even on that damned video visitation setup, but I need to be there. Hopefully I can get more information about her condition."

"Is there anything I can do to help."

"Not with Katie. Not right now. But I want you to read about 'acute marasmus' in the Northeastern Journal. It's some sort of acute wasting syndrome. The journal's on my desk. Check out the hospital adverse development report section and compare them with the case reports in the *Northeastern Medical Journal*. Be sure we don't have any cases at Starr that we might have missed."

"If you're talking about the people who stop eating and rapidly waste away, we have had four in the hospital. They have been like this for the past week. One died yesterday afternoon, and this morning there was another death."

Tom stopped short of going out the door and turned to look her square in the face.

"Jeanne! No one has mentioned anything about that to me. I should have been informed about this."

"Mr. Clark didn't feel it was necessary."

"Look, Clark is not the Director of Medical Care in this hospital."

"They call these people "DUEs" don't they? Isn't that a strange name?" Jeanne commented. "I think it means 'deaths of unknown etiology.'"

"I have to go. Get me reports on those patients. And have them on my desk when I return."

"Yeah, 'DUEs.' You could say that some of the people on those units are paying their dues," Jeanne said, faintly smiling.

"It's pretty hard for me to find any humor in that, Jeanne."

"God, I'm sorry. I forgot about Katie," she said and sheepishly covered her mouth with her hand.

Chapter 25

At Devan Hospital, Tom took his place in line in the family area and waited for his turn to use one of the closed circuit, television, visiting booths. It was a cold day and the heat inside the waiting area was inadequate. He pulled his overcoat up around his neck and surveyed the room.

The place resembled the waiting room of a large bus station. The people waiting to take their place in line sat on long benches that were bolted to the bare, gray, concrete floor. Rows of patient's names filled overhead monitors, like those showing arrival and departure times in airports. After each name came a series of code letters denoting the patient's location, visiting privileges, and condition. Tom checked and Katie's name was not yet posted.

The lines of people waiting to get to the video camera, visiting booths were similar to those at the PointCure Check-In Centers. Tom wondered if he had the same fatigued, pained look on his face as the other visitors waiting in line for a glimpse of a loved one or friend.

While he waited, he read through the small instruction booklet that had been handed to him by the uniformed guard at the entrance gate. It summarized the instructions and regulations for the visits:

Each visitor will be allowed ten minutes at the closed circuit television system in the visitor's station. The instructions for operating the video camera are in each booth. By typing in the patient's name, you will receive an update of the patient's progress in the form of a computer printout. The update is revised every eight hours for adults, every six hours for children under 16. Specific questions can be addressed to the Management Care Team via the patient progress information data system. Instructions for its operation are posted in the visitor's station. Usually, encoded answers to your questions will not be available for at least twelve hours. Answers to your questions may be obtained by returning to the visitors' area, securing a booth, and typing in the patient's name and the inquiry identification number. At this time a printout of the answer will be retrieved.

If authorized by the patient, a family member may request a face-to-face conference with a manager, if it is desired. These are scheduled in the order that the requests are received. There are no exceptions. Usually, at least twenty-four hours is required to secure these appointments. Each of these services, like the treatment itself, requires a certain number of points. The numbers of points required for various services are listed in the appendix of this booklet and will be removed from your family member's point bracelet.

At last, Tom's turn came. Neatly affixed to the window of each booth was a large lilac-colored sticker, "REMEMBER THE EPIDEMIC!" He stepped into the booth and typed Katie's full name into the visitor request program. Then, as the instructions directed, he typed Katie's hospital control number into the program. A woman with a respirator apparatus protruding from her mouth appeared on the monitor screen in front of him.

Stunned, he stared at the respirator. Surely the clerk would have said if Katie were on a respirator. He heard the rhythmic pumping of the air stream. Was it possible that Katie had to be intubated in order to breathe? He shuddered with fear.

Then it registered. The patient was not Katie, but an older woman with a puffy face and gray hair. Her skin was the color of putty.

Something was wrong. He looked back at the number he had typed in and realized that he had misread his hastily handwritten "5" as a "6." He pressed "exit" on the program board and was back to the beginning. Repeating the process with the correct number, the screen now showed Katie lying in the hospital bed. A control knob like a video game joy stick allowed him to move the viewing field in closer, broaden the field or move the view in different directions. He reflexively called out Katie's name, and despaired when he realized that she could not hear him, nor could she respond. As he watched, she shifted restlessly around in the bed, tugging at the sheets. He wanted to reach out and touch her or hold her hand, but the painful distance would not allow it. "Poor Katie, dear Katie, you're all alone," he said.

Tom requested a patient progress report and the most recent one began to print. It was 5:45 p.m. and the most recent report had been prepared at 4:00 p.m. He read the report.

38-YEAR-OLD CAUCASIAN FEMALE ADMITTED AT 2:45 P.M. WITH SYMPTOMS OF INCOHERENCE, TEMPERATURE ELEVATION, STIFF NECK, AND LOSS OF MUSCLE TONE. PRELIMINARY DIAGNOSIS: MENINGITIS. DIAGNOSTIC PROCEDURES — BRAIN, SPINAL SCAN, FULL MONITORS, LEVEL OF CONSCIOUSNESS OBSERVATION, BLOOD CHEMISTRY SURVEY, URINALYSIS. AT THIS TIME IT IS BELIEVED THAT K.P. SULLIVAN HAS VIRAL MENINGITIS OR ENCEPHALITIS. HER CONDITION IS CLASSIFIED AS SERIOUS. SHE IS EXPECTED TO IMPROVE, BUT THERE ARE POSSIBILITIES THAT COMPLICATIONS WILL DEVELOP OR THAT THIS PERSON WILL HAVE RESIDUAL BRAIN DAMAGE AS A RESULT OF THE DISEASE PROCESS. FAMILY REQUIREMENTS FOR PATIENT — NONE. WORK STATUS: UNABLE TO WORK. CURRENTLY HAS ADEQUATE POINTS AVAILABLE FOR APPROPRIATE CARE. YOUR NATIONAL HEALTH AGENCY TAKES PLEASURE IN PROVIDING THE BEST OF CARE FOR YOUR FAMILY MEMBER. PLEASE DO NOT REQUEST ON-SITE VISIT AT THIS TIME — DIAGNOSTIC PROCESS STILL IN OPERATION. WE REQUEST THAT YOU READ THROUGH THE NATIONAL HEALTH AGENCY FAMILY CARE MANUAL IN ORDER TO BECOME

MORE FAMILIAR WITH THE HEALTH CARE OPERATIONS SYSTEM. END REPORT.

> A special notice to the Devan Hospital consumer:
> For just a few points, you can now call in for a progress report — 24 HOURS A DAY. Simply dial 1-800 DEVPROG and use the patient identification number shown below.
> The report is updated every six or eight hours just as is the written printout. For problem resolution and complaints, the Consumer Service Number is 1-201-643-2191. This is another timesaving service provided for you by CelestaCare-Devan Hospital in collaboration with your National Health Agency.
> Patient Identification Control Number: DF6097342

Tom glanced over his shoulder through the glass door. A man about his age was glaring at him, impatiently shuffling back and forth with a disgusted look on his face. The man's eyelids sagged with fatigue.

The man leaned closer to the glass. "Hey Buddy," he said. "I've got a sick wife in there. How about hurrying up."

He tried to ignore the man, but found himself empathetic rather than irritated. He stood quietly, staring at the blank monitor, realizing that Katie's care was totally out of his hands.

The man who wanted to use the booth began to rap loudly on the glass and point at the digital clock above the monitor. Nine minutes, fifty-five seconds. A loud buzzing alarm went off. Tom pushed the "clear" key on the program, opened the door and stepped aside to let the man come in.

"Bastard. No respect for anyone else's feelings," the man said when he passed Tom to enter the booth.

The hour was late. Tom felt nauseated and drove directly home. The house was still and when he walked into the bedroom, he felt more than alone. He fell onto the bed exhausted from the day's activities and, still in his street clothes, fell asleep.

An hour later, he awoke to the sound of a ringing telephone and reached across the bed to answer it. It took him a moment to orient himself. He quickly realized that Katie was not in the bed next to him. Then, remembering what was happening, he felt a painful pang of loneliness.

"Hello," he heard a woman's voice say. "Tom, this is Laura Clark," the voice on the line said.

"Oh, hello," he said. He shuffled around and tried to become more awake.

A pause.

"Hello," Tom said again.

"Sounds like I woke you. I didn't know; I thought you'd still be up."

"That's okay. Guess I fell asleep before I realized it. Exhausting day."

"I don't want to bother you, but I heard about Katie. I wanted to let you know that I was thinking about you. I hope she's okay."

"Thanks Laura."

"How is she?"

"It's hard for me to tell. All the news I can get is the progress report print-out. I did see her on the video visiting set. She looks pretty sick, but I'm hopeful that things will go well. At this point, it's hard to know."

"She's on an automated unit, isn't she?"

"Yes."

"I know the distance and separation is hard. The way they have it set up, it's pretty impersonal. I know that. That's not how I intended it to be."

"Yeah, I feel pretty closed out."

"Tom, I'm really concerned about Katie and what you are both going through. I know you must be frightened."

"Thanks Laura, you're kind to call." He recognized that she sounded quieter and more tentative than usual. "Are you all right?"

There was a moment of quiet. "I'm feeling a little overwhelmed myself — about the Houston hospital situation. I feel responsible and pretty disturbed about what's happening."

"I understand. It's very unsettling."

"I know I had a big part in the creation of these units. I don't know exactly what's going on, but I don't like being a part of it. I feel very guilty."

Tom thought he heard her softly sobbing. He recognized her need for support but had little energy to give it. "I know all this is hard for you, but they'll find out what the trouble was in Houston," he said.

"It doesn't make any sense. There are too many safety checks in those systems for anything like that to happen," Laura said. "Since Katie's in an automated unit, I wanted you to know so that you won't worry about her."

Another pause in the conversation.

"Katie is safe. I'm sure. Is there any more news from Houston?" Tom asked.

"Wade spoke about an hour ago."

"Yeah? And what did he say?"

"Wade had Sam Fisher from CelestaCare with him. Fisher said that with this level of technology and all its benefits, we can expect some happenings like the one in Houston. He said that we have to realize that there may be side effects or problems with any new kind of procedure. Wade supported his position."

"I'm sure that's comforting to those families."

"Fisher needs to do something. Junk the whole project if necessary. I feel terrible about all that's happened."

"I doubt that they'll junk the project. There's too much invested in it."

Tom's head felt heavy. He was nauseated again and Laura's words were running together. He had to bring the call to an end. "Laura, you're kind to call, but to be honest with you it's been a terribly draining day and I need to rest. I just hope that Katie will be all right."

"I'm sorry. I guess it wasn't really very appropriate for me to call. You do know that I want Katie to get well quickly."

"I know you do."

"Goodnight, Tom," she said. "If you need me, let me know. I just had to talk to you. I wanted to let you know that I was thinking about you both."

"Thanks for calling. Goodnight," he said, so tired that he was not even sure that he heard the last few sentences she spoke.

He got up, went into the kitchen, and poured himself a glass of milk. His eyes ached; his neck was rubbery. Finally, he undressed and got back in bed. A thousand thoughts rushed through his mind.

He thought about Katie. He thought about Laura's call. He wondered if she might have been crying. More unanswered questions, he thought, and soon, beyond exhaustion, he fell asleep again.

Later that night, he had a dream about Laura. She was in a hospital bed, asleep, with a central line in her neck. Suddenly she opened her eyes and screamed. Her eyes were lilac-colored and when she shrieked, bright red blood spewed out of her mouth.

The dream jolted him awake. He sat up in bed, filled with terror. Looking at the clock, he saw that it was only midnight. After a full hour of tossing and turning, he finally fell back asleep.

Chapter 26

The next morning, Tom was the first person in line at Devan Hospital for the 6:00 a.m. family visitation. When Katie appeared on the screen, she was alert and gave him a big smile.

"I think I'm going to make it," she said.

"I miss you terribly," he told her.

"Me too. It's so lonely in here."

"I spoke with your parents twice last night. I'll call them again this morning and let them know that you're better."

"And how are the Owatuga, Oklahoma Perrys?"

"Your dad's as feisty as ever. Gave his usual speech on how you should have been a journalist instead of a doctor. Said you probably caught this illness from some patient. He's mad as hell. Wants to write an editorial on the devotion of the medical profession and how pediatricians are underpaid."

"Small town newspaper editors have their own ways of saying how much they care about their daughters, don't they?"

"Your mom wants to fly in. I told them I would call first thing this morning and if you weren't better, she could come on."

"Well, I am better. And Oklahoma is a long way away. My mother should stay home. I have enough problems."

"Katie, you sound like yourself. Thank God."

"I've never been anyone else."

"Let me see what the official word is on your condition. I'll get a progress printout."

"Be my guest. I'm not going anywhere. The plastic tube in my neck and the hundred wires running from these monitor electrodes don't exactly allow me to run marathons."

Tom hurried to key in the proper numbers and information, and in seconds, the printout appeared. He scanned it quickly. It said that Katie was still intermittently confused, but her mentation was clearing rapidly. She was being treated with a new antiviral agent and her fever had almost subsided.

He felt relieved. The automated system was treating Katie successfully. Surely, everything would be all right. He remembered Robert Kaplan's comment about the moon walk at the central line ceremony and smiled. Perhaps the new system was a "giant leap."

"Well, how am I?"

Tom chuckled. "Getting well. The printout says that by tonight, I'll be able to see you in person."

"I like that printout."

"I miss you. Home is miserable without you," Tom said. He looked behind him, half expecting someone to shout at him or rap on the glass.

"This place is desolate," Katie said. "My friends have tried to come by my cubicle, but they've refused to let them visit. I feel like I'm all alone on a desert island. Sometimes I drift off into the loneliness and feel disconnected from everything – a little strange. But I'm going to make it. Don't worry."

"I love you."

"I love you too, Tom Sullivan. Always."

Tom left for work feeling more confident about Katie's recovery. Twenty-five minutes later, he pulled into the Starr Memorial parking lot.

"Thank the Lord she's better," Jeanne said when Tom told her about his visit to Devan. "She really had us all worried."

"The new antivirals are amazing," Tom said. "With this kind of progress, she should be out of there in a day or two."

"Clark wants to see you. He asked me to tell you to come to his office as soon as you came in. He wants to give you the word on the Houston disaster."

"Thanks," Tom said, setting down his brief case and putting on his gray coat. He checked to make sure his stethoscope was in his pocket, and found it in its usual place.

Jeanne watched the stethoscope ritual.

"Old habit," Tom said self-consciously.

"Real old. It dates you," Jeanne said. "No one uses those anymore."

Tom threw her an irritated look. "I do," he said forcefully.

Ken Clark's office was only a short walk down the hall. When Tom entered, he encountered the imposing oil painting of Ken's military surgeon father hanging in an inescapable view behind the desk. In the picture, Ken's father stood tall, posing regally as if he had just emerged from an operating suite. He was fully garbed in a green, scrub suit, complete with cap and mask. In his hand, he held a scalpel. His small, beady eyes stared out over the mask at everyone who visited his son.

"Your wife, how's she doing?" Ken asked.

"She's certainly improved, but I'll be happy when she is out of the hospital and home."

"God and technology working hand in hand," Clark said.

"Sure," Tom said.

Tom scanned Ken's desk again and sat down in the same chair as before. The stacks of papers were still neatly arranged. Oliver Sellers' book, *Prayers for Technology and Tomorrow*, lay in front of him on his desk.

Ken picked up the book and held it so that Tom could see the title.

"You've read this, I hope."

"I know as much about Oliver Sellers as I want to know."

Clark sighed. "You should read it carefully. It's the Theotechnicist's bible and it could be the future of health care."

Tom nodded, looking down.

"If you want Katie moved to Starr, I'll arrange for the transfer," he said.

"No, leave it like it is for now," Tom said.

"At Starr, you would be certain to have God working on your team."

Ken's comments about religion struck Tom as increasingly odd. Then he saw Ken tuck in his chin and look at the insignia pinned on the left lapel of his CelestaCare blazer.

"You know what this emblem is, don't you, Sullivan?" Ken asked.

Tom inspected the emblem. The lapel pin looked like the letter "T." It was a full inch in height and gold, with an enameled purple face. Its cross bar and vertical arm flared out slightly at the ends. Tom thought it was a St. Anthony's cross, the so-called, "tau cross" with the crossbar running across the top of the vertical arm rather than placed lower as on the more well-known Latin cross.

"I've seen it on the cover of Sellers' book. It's St. Anthony's cross."

"Wrong. It's simply a 'T' for 'Theotechnicism.' Any similarity to a T-shaped, St. Anthony's cross is purely coincidental and irrelevant. Theotechnicism stands on its own and has a unique higher meaning. We are not connected to Christianity or any other religion. Of course if the emblem is confused with a cross, or a powerful religion, that can't hurt, can it? We want as much of the religious market share as we can get. The fact is that this icon has become the symbol of Theotechnicism."

"Oh, I see," Tom said.

Ken picked up the purple covered book on his desk and held it up again. "You must read this closely, Sullivan. It's inspiring. Oliver Sellers spells out a spiritual direction that we all need to pay close attention to."

"Maybe I'll do that at some point, Clark. But right now, I have other matters on my mind."

"Tom, I certainly understand. And anyway, that's not what I want to talk with you about. I want to give you specific directives as to how the Houston matter is to be handled. You probably know by now that the beta blocker overdose at Starr is going to be dealt with as a rare, automated unit side effect."

"Yes, I've heard and I think that's a pile of crap," Tom said.

"You managers are all the same. You have doubts about everything."

"Medical science depends on the ability to avoid premature closure, to remain skeptical, to raise questions, Ken."

"The directive from the NHA is irrefutable. Other than the routine checks of the system, no further investigation will be necessary. The problem in Houston at Ritter Park was a rare side effect, a happening inherent in our new technology. Henceforth, side effects of this sort will be categorized as due to a risk factor in the new system which we will call the 'T-effect.' The 'T' stands for Technology. The 'T-effect' is simply a risk, which one encounters in any nearly perfect technology. It's unavoidable."

"Unavoidable? How can you say that?"

"Because CelestaCare says so, and the NHA concurs! It's the administrative position, so it's *the* position. The exits of those patients were due to the 'T-effect.' No one is to blame and there will be no further investigation."

Tom shook his head. "That won't hold up. People won't accept an explanation like that."

"People will accept what we want them to accept. Public Relations is already at work. It's no problem — a few news releases, some advertising campaigns, a couple of talks by experts on TV. The public will accept anything as long as they believe they are going to get the best in health care and that *is* what they believe."

"You'll be challenged by every manager in the country," Tom said.

Clark laughed. "In the past, maybe, but with the change to administrative decision priority, that's unlikely. Administrators, not managers, now have the last word. Cost effectiveness, efficiency, and productivity are the most important considerations in health care now, and those are administrative matters, not medical ones. The 'T-effect' is non-negotiable."

Tom looked at him in dismay.

"And of course, there's always the deaccess process for persistent disbelievers," Clark added.

Tom stood up. "I was transferred to Starr to run a teaching program, not to run a hospital based on a phony system of health care. I didn't come here to implement some hokey 'T-effect' bullshit that undoes all accountability.

"I was told that Devan and CelestaCare wanted young managers to learn to treat patients in the automated system with dignity. So far, not a single health care student or resident has rotated through Starr.

Dignity is out the window and the NHA program to save health care and lower costs gets more and more bizarre," Tom said.

"Now, I have to get to work." Tom turned and began to walk toward the door.

"Hold it, Sullivan!" Clark called out. "There's one more matter we need to discuss. It has to do with saving consumers' lives. Does that still interest you?"

Tom stopped and looked back toward Ken.

"I need your help with the unexplainable deaths, the DUEs – the acute marasmus syndrome, AMS. We want to know what's causing it."

"Let the administrators figure it out; maybe it's a 'T-Effect.'"

"No, Manager, this is an official order from the NHA. The numbers are increasing. Unfortunately, all the cases are occurring in the computer controlled diagnostic and treatment units.

"Point requirements have been reduced enormously in those units, so they're of great advantage to both the consumer and to CelestaCare. The units have significantly increased accessibility and reduced the cost of health care for everyone. The NHA wants every manager looking into this problem as soon as possible."

Tom listened carefully. Ken was acting tough, but he was defensive and Tom knew it. The marasmus syndrome spelled bad press for the automated units. Ken was more upset about the problem than he was saying.

"Let me know immediately if you come up with anything."

"Is that it?" Tom asked.

"That's it."

"Then, if you don't mind, I have work to do. Yesterday was a nightmare — Katie's illness, the Houston accident."

"I'm sure you're pleased that your wife is so much better. It's splendid witness for the new system isn't it?"

Tom did not answer. Instead, he walked out of Ken's office and slammed the door behind him.

Chapter 27

At 7:00 p.m. that evening, the iron gate to Devan's visitors' entrance opened.

A guard scanned the magnetic strip on Tom's consumer's family card to verify his visiting privileges. He had Tom sign the register, then motioned for him to pass through the turnstile.

Ten minutes later, Tom entered Katie's cubicle, Unit 406. Struggling with the tubes and wires, and careful not to disturb the central line, he embraced his wife. Then he pulled the one straight backed chair over to the bedside, sat next to her, and took her hand in his and held it tightly.

"I can't believe how much better I'm feeling," Katie said. "Of course I know that's because I knew you were coming. How do you think I picked up this virus?"

"It happens. I'm just glad that you're better. You're moving your neck fine now."

"Yeah, except for this central line."

"Have you talked with Bob Kaplan? He's the manager assigned to take care of you."

"He stuck his head in for ten seconds to say that he wasn't allowed to visit."

"That's strange; Bob's so outgoing and caring. And we have our history. But I suppose he's saddled with rules because of the reaccess process."

"Contact with people is minimal. There was one monitor technician in here this afternoon for about a minute. She checked the monitor leads and that was it. Never said a word. There's no communication with anyone. In fact, I've been completely isolated." She took his hand in hers. "Oh, I'm so very glad to see you."

Tom smiled. "You know, I'm still surprised that Kaplan hasn't contacted me."

She tugged on his hand and motioned for him to sit on the side of the bed. "Watch these damned wires and tubes!"

He stroked her hair.

"I've got to get out of here," she said. "The Devan manager's meeting in two days is a very important one. If we don't get organized soon, we're in trouble. They're slipping those new regulations in right and left."

Tom looked at the camera pointing toward them. He put his finger to his lips. "Later, Katie, later."

"It's already later. The administrators are becoming more and more powerful. Lying here, I've had a lot of time to think about all this. I think there's more than one reason why they pushed you to Starr Memorial. Sure CelestaCare needed your name and image to develop the automated units and Cunningham wanted CelestaCare's money. But you also have too much clout at Devan, too big a following. If you were still on staff, you would be up in arms, protesting, slowing them down. You'd be kicking and screaming about their administrative mandates. You wouldn't put up with medical students and residents being taught this hands-off approach to medical care. You wouldn't put up with this impersonal approach. They know that. You would have the faculty organized into an army. At Starr, you're on the sidelines."

"You're right," he said. "Clark is making sure that he has the last word, but I'll find a way."

"Fine, but for now, it's left up to me to do something about it at Devan."

"Be careful Katie."

"I'll be just as careful as you would."

"I want you out of here for other reasons. The house is empty without you. I can't sleep without your being next to me. I miss seeing you in the mornings when I get up. There's no one to sing my beautiful Irish ballads to…"

"That was so romantic," she said. She smiled, looked at him longingly and when he kissed her cheek, she whispered softly in his ear. "I'm almost well enough. Know what I mean?"

"You're recuperating. That's for sure."

There was a sound of chimes and then a saccharin recorded female voice came over the speaker:

Visitors, we must request that you now leave the floor. Your time for visitation is over. It is most important that your family member or friend get adequate rest. We are sure that you are pleased to find your family member or friend doing so well. Your National Health Agency, in cooperation with this fine hospital, is proud to be able to provide the finest in quality health care to you and your family. Good night.

Tom told Katie goodnight.

"Will I see you in the morning on your way to work?" she asked. He was holding her hand and she seemed reluctant to let him go.

"You betcha." He kissed her on the forehead. "I love you," he said.

She smiled another satisfied smile.

Outside the unit, he walked slowly down the hall toward the exit. Devan Hospital had changed dramatically since he had left. The CelestaCare financed hospital reconstruction was complete. He hardly recognized the hallways where he had trained and learned to take care of patients.

He was unable to tell who was who among the few health care personnel who passed him in the halls. Everyone wore gray coats of the same length and style. Old titles on name badges had all been replaced with a generic one that said, "HEALTH CARE PROVIDER." The gray color seemed appropriate. It captured the feel of the drastic changes and the drab terrain.

At home thirty minutes later, he thought of Katie's improvement and felt a little brighter. At least, he could expect that she would be home in a few days. He looked at the unmade bed and the dirty glasses and coffee cups on the bedside table. Then he thumbed through the mail. His fatigue became mixed with a kind of vague sadness.

So many disturbing happenings in only two days, but some good events also, he thought as he turned off the light to go to sleep.

For Tom, a telephone ringing in the middle of the night was not a new experience. But he was more tired than usual, and the phone rang several times before he picked it up. He fumbled with it for a moment, then placed it against his ear.

"Is this Thomas Sullivan?" the unrecognizable woman's voice inquired.

"Yes, this is he," Tom answered with a drowsy voice.

There was a pause. The caller then identified herself as Vera Pledget, a spokesperson for the Devan Health Care Center Consumer Information Service.

"I have some very bad news. It's about your wife. She suddenly took a turn for the worst. It happened so fast that the managers aren't sure exactly what caused the reversal. She was asleep when the monitor alarms went off. They began to pick up abnormal electrocardiogram data on the tracings. She developed an unusual arrhythmia, then suffered a cardiac arrest."

Tom could not believe what he was hearing. "This isn't real, this is a dream," he said.

The spokesperson continued, "The manager went on the automatic cardiovascular assistance program as soon as she developed the irregular heart beat. The cardiac arrest team was there almost immediately, but nothing positive happened. She was officially pronounced to have made her exit about five minutes ago. We're terribly sorry. Everyone in the hospital will miss her. She was such a fine person."

For half a minute there was silence. Only the sounds of breathing could be heard on the line. Then Tom spoke. "Yes she was," he said, hearing his use of the past-tense and feeling stunned. "God, I just saw her a few hours ago and she was doing fine. This is impossible! All the reports were positive. Did they check electrolytes? What could have happened?"

All of a sudden, he realized that he was not talking to another physician or even a nurse, but rather to a hospital spokesperson, Vera "something." She wouldn't know any of the details or be able to answer questions.

"Manager Robert Kaplan said to be sure to tell you how much he regrets this happening. He said he will communicate with you concerning his findings in regards to her exi…"

"Put him on," Tom interrupted.

"I'm afraid that's not possible. He was exhausted. He left to go home and get some rest."

"Left to go home? Exhausted? That's absurd!"

"I hate to ask you to do this," the woman said. "I know that you are a health care provider yourself and this probably seems very unnecessary, but the NHA asks us to give this information to family members when someone exits."

Bewildered and overwhelmed, Tom spoke automatically. "Go ahead."

"Well, first, I need to tell you that Mrs. Sullivan had some points remaining. As you know, you can redeem them for cash, take them for yourself, or you can donate them to indigent care. You don't have to decide that now. You can let us know later."

Her words were followed by silence.

"Hello. Hello, are you there? Hello, hello," she repeated.

Tom said nothing. He held the telephone out at arm's length and stared at it for a few moments. Then he quietly placed the telephone on the receiver. He laid back on the bed and looked up at the ceiling, feeling immobilized.

Waves of disorganized feelings washed over him shattering his sense of connection with the world around him. Thoughts of Katie rushed through his head, feelings about Katie, images of Katie. Katie as a medical student, their wedding, her smile when he said, "I do." His senses filled with her, their closeness, her smells, intimate physical times in bed with their naked bodies next to each other. He thought about their long philosophical conversations, her assertive style, her tenacity. Was she really gone? He was sure that was what the woman had said, but still, he could not really feel that it was true.

Then came an image of cubicle 406 and Katie with the central line in her neck. Too suddenly, the whip-like emotional pain of reality slammed across his senses. His emotions jammed, then released, and a few moments later, he felt a peculiar still calm. Lying in the dark, alone in the quiet of the early morning hours, he began to weep softly. His whole self tried to say that it was not true, but he knew it was.

Katie was dead and medically her sudden death made absolutely no sense.

Chapter 28

Nearly two hundred of Katie's and Tom's friends and co-workers attended the memorial services for Katie in the small on-campus church at Devan. Ray Cunningham had asked to speak briefly and did.

"Katie Sullivan was one of our finest managers. Her untiring devotion to her duties is well known to us all. We will miss her," Devan's Vice Chancellor said. Tom noted that Ray Cunningham appeared curiously moved by Katie's untimely death. A number of times during his talk, his voice faltered.

Tom sat with Katie's parents. A recovering Carl Hammerstone sat next to him. Ken and Laura sat a few rows away. Ken held a small purple "T" in one hand and Oliver Sellers' book of prayers in the other. From time to time, he opened the Theotechnicist prayer book and appeared to be reading it. Laura blotted her tears throughout the service.

After the closing prayer, Tom shook hands with everyone who attended. Laura hugged him and momentarily, he felt comforted.

"What a dreadful happening. What a loss," Laura said.

"Having these people around helps," Tom said. "As much as anything can."

"Give yourself time. Don't rush back to work."

"I'm not sure how long I'll take off. Right now, I'm not sure of any directions. I feel lost without Katie."

The group dispersed shortly before noon and an hour later, Ken Clark was in Ray Cunningham's Devan office for a meeting.

"Only one month to go," the Vice Chancellor proudly told CelestaCare's Chief of Operations. "You were lucky enough to have the President for the central line insertion; in one month Alex Wade has agreed to come to Devan for the announcement of Phase III."

"Yes, the new system is taking shape," Clark said. "All that remains is the final software." He smiled and fondled the purple "T" emblem hanging around his neck.

Cunningham sighed. "But as near as we are, there's still cause for caution. If the automated treatment units are implicated in this acute progressive marasmus mess, the whole program could go right down the drain. Billions of dollars worth of technology and all of our..."

Clark interrupted and leaned forward with a serious look on his face. "That's precisely why CelestaCare wants an explanation for this wasting syndrome. Get one of your Devan research people on it. Come up with something, something treatable. And come up with it fast."

"I've given this a lot of thought. This strange disease is illusive enough to be a psychiatric illness. Maybe a neurotransmitter problem, perhaps a biochemical aberration," Cunningham suggested. "I'll speak with Devan's number one psychiatrist, Manager Taylor Blaine, as soon as possible. He's a psychiatrist with an imagination. He'll come up with something."

"How about Leo Strasberg?" Clark asked. "Isn't he the grand old man of Devan psychiatry?"

"Strasberg's time has passed; he's a dinosaur. The man's senile," Cunningham said. "He has already come to talk to me about some foolish theory about consumer's isolation in the automated system. That's all we need — a theory like that. No, Blaine is our man. He's contemporary."

"Sounds like the way to go."

"And in the meantime we harvest more points."

"God rewards his workers in wondrous ways," Clark said with a thin smile.

"Ross Mandell will be coming to Devan Hospital with Director Wade. Mandell is making his bid for the presidential nomination. He's the President's first choice. I suspect he'll get the nomination."

"Not a chance. I believe that Alex Wade will be the candidate," Clark said.

"Oh?" A surprised Cunningham remarked. "How do you know that?"

"Intuition."

The meeting over, Clark returned to Starr Memorial.

"The manager you had the 'shoot-out' with this morning won't comply," Jeanne Donnely told Ken as he walked to his office and set his briefcase and book of prayers on his desk. "Manager Boyd said she doesn't give a damn what you say, she's not treating this man against his wishes."

"Get the NHA on the phone. I want Compliance Enforcement. I want Susan Boyd deaccessed immediately," Clark shouted. "Get the papers together! Fax them to Washington. Change her password and access code. I want that headstrong woman out of my hospital!"

Jeanne smiled and ran her index finger across the purple velour spine of Oliver Sellers' Theotechnicist prayer book. "No problem," she said.

Clark's eruption related to a young oncology manager who refused to continue treating a point-rich, dying man with the specified NHA treatment protocol: highly toxic chemotherapy, radiation therapy, and extensive neurosurgery for widespread carcinoma of the lungs.

Cancer riddled the patient's lungs and liver. The MRI showed a number of golfball-sized lesions in his brain. The program insisted that the managers, "PROCEED WITH TREATMENT."

"Ridiculous," Manager Susan Boyd had protested in an angry confrontation with Ken Clark earlier that day. "I'm not going to treat this poor man aggressively just because he has an abundance of points. He and his family want him to die peacefully. What you're doing is not a damned thing but 'point harvesting.' You're pouring government money into CelestaCare's pockets."

Clark sat at his desk brooding about the matter. "That woman just doesn't get it," he said under his breath, as he recalled the interchange with Manager Boyd. "Doesn't she have any respect for the work of the powerful One who directs our lives?"

Chapter 29

The founding father of the Theotechnicist movement, Oliver Sellers, an aging family physician, came to Philadelphia from Beaumont, Texas, to lead the giant gathering assembled to further the movement's cause. His story, he was fond of telling his audiences around the country, was a "simple one." A devoutly religious man, he had practiced medicine for forty of his sixty-five years. Severe headaches and a saddened mood had come to interfere with his practice routine and his life. During this rather deep depressive episode, he had undergone magnetic resonance imaging of his head as part of a neurological workup for headaches. When he emerged from the noisy enclosed space of the MRI machine, Sellers reported having had a revelation delivered to him by the voice of God. The revelation led to his elaboration of what he called, "a theology for the times." His mood lightened almost immediately, and he set out to "spread the word," devoting his life to conducting his rallies.

At the giant, public rally in Philadelphia almost forty thousand devotees packed the huge, modern, sweeping, steel beam and glass arena. A huge pipe organ pounded the air inside the domed coliseum, booming out a number of hymns while the throng of people scurried about to find seats.

Promptly at 8:00 p.m., the house lights dimmed and a spot light beamed on the announcer as he surveyed the packed house. When he moved his arm, reflected rays of light angled off his diamond-studded, gold watch. Behind him a giant banner bore the words,

"GOD, HEALTH CARE TECHNOLOGY, AND LOVE – THE PATHWAYS TO ETERNITY."

"A hearty welcome to you, Ladies and Gentlemen. We welcome each and every one of you to our 'Quest for Eternity' rally. Soon we're going to hear from our inspired leader, Oliver Sellers, but first, let's get our souls in tune with the message by welcoming one of our country's most beloved performers, direct from Nashville, the one and only, Mr. Whit Whittier."

Seconds later, country and western singer, Whit Whittier, wearing a large, black Stetson and a shirt emblazoned with dozens of lilac-colored "T" shaped symbols, bolted up the stairs to the stage. Ecstatic cheering followed as the spotlights crisscrossed the stage and the audience.

"I know what you want to hear," he told the jubilant audience, "and I am gonna sing it for you," he said. "Here's your favorite song and mine, 'Eternity Is Waiting.'"

Cheers rose from the audience; the back-up singers took their places, Whit strummed a few introductory notes on his guitar, and soon he launched into a fast-paced chorus of the song:

Eternity is waiting for the ones who will survive,
For those who use their loving points and keep themselves alive.
For those who, growing old or ill, can find the way to cure,
For those whom God has chosen, for those who will endure...

Cheers, shouts, and applause broke out in the audience as they rose to their feet, clapping in time with the music. Whittier sang on:

Now, I'm not saying that I'm better than any other man,
And I'm not saying that there is on earth anyone who can.
But we all know who cares for the sick from way on high,
And we know why he lets some live, while other people die.

Still standing, the audience swayed with the music, pointing up to the heavens. Whit repeated the chorus, *Eternity is waiting for the ones who will survive, for those who use their loving points...,*" then moved to the next verse:

171

Those who live can use this earth to make a sacred way,
A path that leads to heaven where the blessed may always stay.
So please dear God, if I fall sick, let health care help me live.
And guide my heart to goodness and to me blessings give.

Eternity is waiting for the ones who who will survive...

The performer finished out the song with licks of chords and twangy notes that reverberated though the arena, and when he took his bow, thunderous applause and cheering echoed through the vast space.

"Thank you, thank you, thank you friends and neighbors," he said, bowing and holding out his hat toward the audience in appreciation.

Moments later, the announcer was back on the stage. "Bless you Whit. Bless you, bless you!

"And now, folks, here's the man we've all been waiting for, your prophet and mine, Oliver Sellers. Folks, stand and be blessed." The audience was instantly up on their feet applauding and cheering. "Let's all welcome the man who has showed us the way."

The spotlight caught Oliver Sellers as he made his assent to the podium. Amidst deafening cheering and applause from the still standing audience, he took the steps to the stage holding his hands above his head, intermittently turning on the stairway and throwing kisses to the audience. A man who looked strikingly like Mark Twain, he was dressed in a solid, white suit and wore a white hat. Around his neck hung an oversized purple "T", the now well-known Theotechnicist symbol. Once at the podium, he stood holding his hand over his heart and acknowledged the thunderous applause with strings of, "Thank you, thank you, thank you." As the applause and cheering came to an end, he paused until a solemn stillness and quiet came over the crowd, then began.

"Thank you and God bless you, Ladies and Gentlemen, thank you. And special thanks to Whit Whittier for singing my favorite song." He paused a moment, looking out at the crowd, then began.

"My story is a simple one. It began with headaches, headaches, and more headaches. Doctor after doctor told me it was my nerves, my sinuses, told me it was stress. Not so, I said. Not so. 'Then it's depression,' they said. 'You have a chemical imbalance, a clinical depression.' But I knew all along that it didn't make any difference what the cause was, it would be God's direction of the health care technology that would save me — God working hand in hand with the technology of health care that would show me the way to a better place both on earth and in heaven."

He took off his white hat and held it over his heart.

"My health care managers did test after test, x-rays of this, blood tests for that. And then one day, my doctor ordered a magnetic resonance imaging study, a MRI. And there, in that machine, over the noise of the banging and clanging, the Lord chose to speak to me. Yes, just as the Lord spoke to Moses at the burning bush, this time the Lord chose the noisy tunnel of that MRI. The banging noise of that machine was so loud you couldn't hear yourself think, but I could hear His voice telling me what would be my mission. 'Write this down,' the Lord said. 'Write this down, and go forth unto my children and tell them the truth.' Well, I told the Lord there was no way I could write anything down in that cramped steel tube, but the Lord told me that didn't matter. When I emerged, I would remember it all, every last word as clear as could be. And He was right on target. With the help of my dear wife, Elizabeth, that is exactly what I have done."

"Glory be," a young man in the third row stood and yelled.

"Eternity is waiting," another called out, waving his hand above his head.

"Speak out for all time," another shouted.

Sellers continued. "I am a humble man, but I believe that I, like others who have come before me, have been told by God that a new way has come about. Modern day health care technology was brought about by divine inspiration in order to allow certain ones of us a longer time on earth.

"But this is for a reason. We, who are chosen to live on as I was, must take on the task of improving the earthly universe while we prepare ourselves to take our places in the highest part of the Kingdom of Heaven. We are the selected ones. So I bring you God's message.

"Yes, those who are granted long life are given this blessing directly by the man upstairs. And we all know that Heaven itself will be an even more desirable place with this select group of people as its population. We know now that this 'superior' afterlife is the 'Heaven above Heaven.'"

He took out a large, white handkerchief and wiped the sweat from his forehead, then went on.

"Now I'm here to tell you, regardless of your previous lifestyle or morality, if you keep on living and live a long life, that longevity brought to you by our glorious technology is a direct indication of God's blessings. Your life is blessed. And if, with the help of our magnificent technology, you do survive, you can see your survival as a mandate from God that you are being allowed to live longer in order to achieve the ultimate development of more righteous forms of human beings.

"Folks, if we hope for survival of the human species itself, we can no longer depend on evolution, even if there were such a thing. Survival must rest on the deliberate use of technology to foster the spiritual survival of the deservingly technologically salvageable. The lot of perpetuating the ultimate good of humankind will fall to these people, the chosen ones. We now have millions and millions of followers and I assure you there will be more."

 A salvo of applause rose from the audience. After almost a full minute of shouts and clapping, Sellers raised his hands for quiet.

"And friends, we have been sent a kind of savior. The man now in charge of health care in Washington, Manager Alexander Wade, is somewhere between a man and a saint and we fully support his endeavors. Unquestionably, God has placed the technology in the hands of selected persons to do His will and we Theotechnicists believe that our National Health Agency director is inspired by God. Yes, my friends, these God-inspired individuals in the new order will determine who is deserving of health care and we will abide by their decisions.

"If you have any doubts, go get you a copy of my three-hundred and two page prayer book, *Prayers for Technology and Tomorrow*. Read it everyday. Read it cover to cover, teach it to your children. It has already sold millions of copies and has been translated into thirty languages."

Throughout the audience, waving hands clutching copies of *Prayers for Technology and Tomorrow* stretched upward.

"But we must be cautious. There will be disbelievers who will try to disrupt our plan. But the Lord has said that interfering with the careful use of our health care technology is no less than tampering with the future of humankind. And you should know that there will be those who speak out against the overuse of technology. These people, friends, are interfering with the work of God. These sinners must examine their motives and repent — or else."

The audience stood and applauded, hoisting placards emblazoned with purple "T"s.

Sellers caught the end of the applause with perfect timing. "Folks if you believe in what the Theotechnicists are doing, I say join with me to make a better world for us all."

With these words out of his mouth, a group of about seventy-five members from the Church of the Holy Theotechnicist began their chant:

"You bet we will, you bet we will, you bet we will, you bet we will, you bet we will…"

Moments later, the vast crowd had picked up the words, and the volume of their voices reached roaring heights.

While Oliver Sellers captivated the group in Philadelphia, thirty miles away in Middleside, Carl Hammerstone unlocked a rusty padlock guarding the door to an abandoned building on Warehouse Row and stepped inside with three other members of the organization now known as "The Healers." The four physicians watched as a flock of pigeons, stirred by their entry, took flight through one of the broken warehouse windows. The musty smell of old wood and debris filled their nostrils. One of the men took a handkerchief from his pocket and covered his nose and mouth.

"This space was donated anonymously for our group to use as a clinic and hospital. Take a look; it will be fine," Carl said to the three men as they gazed around the large, open warehouse room.

"What about equipment and supplies? There's nothing here," Richard Caldwell, an aging surgeon commented.

"Nothing here? Just wait. There'll be plenty here," Carl replied. "We have interested people, caring physicians, and attentive nurses ready to take care of those people who are being tossed out of the hospitals because they've run out of points. That's the best equipment of all."

"I understand, Carl," Caldwell continued, "but we have to be realistic. I'm as idealistic as you, but we'll need drugs, instruments, equipment, all the things that the NHA controls."

"There're others who feel like we do about the NHA. I suspect we can count on them to siphon off some of the supplies to us," Carl said.

"You know the punishment for doing that. It's health care fraud, and the NHA would be happy to expose anyone doing it. They would get prosecuted criminally. And besides, how many of the doctors who stayed with the NHA will do that?"

"A lot more than you think," Carl answered. "Of course they stayed. What choice did they have if they wanted to continue to practice medicine. So far, there's been no option. Give them some way to fight the iron grip of the NHA and they may have enough strength to move in another direction. I suspect we'll get as much help as we need."

"What about this marasmus mess?" the other healer asked. "We could be on the edge of another epidemic."

"I have some theories about that," Carl said. "We may already have the cure and not know it."

"What do you mean?" Walter Baker asked.

"They could be suffering from the lack of a commodity that's not even available as a treatment in the NHA systems."

"A kind of antibiotic, a laboratory test, a procedure, a protocol?"

"I can't be sure yet, but let's see what old fashion human contact will do," Carl said.

Baker was thoughtful. "Count me in," he said after a brief pause.

"Okay men, let's get going," Carl said, taking out a notebook and pen. "How do we want to organize this place?" He pointed to one section of the warehouse. "Shall we wall off that portion of the room and make a clinic space?" Carl asked. "And what about that area over there for surgical suites?" he said, transferring his ideas to a sketch on a notebook page.

After his rally was over, Oliver Sellers met his driver behind the coliseum.

He slipped into the back of the white, stretch limousine, pulled down the portable bar, poured himself a drink, then leaned back against the plush leather seat. He sighed, turned to his wife Elizabeth sitting next to him, smiled, and said, "What a crowd! We are indeed spreading the word."

"Glory!" Elizabeth replied lyrically. "Glory!"

Chapter 30

The event ushering in Phase III would be aired just before the seven o'clock news. In a prime-time, live, television broadcast from Devan Hospital's pediatric floor, Director Alexander Wade would visit with seven-year-old Melanie Wilson on camera. "Mellie" was in the precarious predicament of being out of points.

Down the hall from Mellie's room, Alexander Wade chatted with Ray Cunningham and Ken Clark. Nearby, an aide was whispering a message to Carole Weeks. She stood, clipboard in hand, nodding her head and listening intently. Ms. Weeks was wearing a tailored, lilac, suede suit with a NHA logo sewn in multicolored sequins on the jacket back.

Wade looked at his watch. "Where the hell is Mandell?" he asked.

"My aide just told me," Carole Weeks said. "The Senator should be here any time. But there's trouble. On his way from the airport to the hospital, some idiot hurled a bomb at his car. Exploded just short of its target. The Secret Service is being extra careful bringing him in."

"Was he hurt?" Wade asked.

"He was thrown around by the shock waves from the explosion, but he's not hurt badly. They say he's shaken up a bit, and nervous as hell," she told them.

"Can't blame him," said the broad shouldered NHA agent Victor Brandt, Wade's special assistant.

Seconds later, disheveled, unnerved, and out of breath, Mandell came rushing down the hall. Over his left eyebrow, where he bumped his head when he was thrown around in the car was a gaping cut. "…and they weren't able to catch the person who did it," he was saying. "Dis…dis…dis…disappeared in the crowd."

"Are you all right, Ross?" Wade asked with a concerned look on his face.

Carole Weeks interrupted. "Excuse me, but it's show time," she said and began to herd the group down the hall. "We're on the air!"

On a mobile cart, a cameraman behind a television camera preceded them, capturing the procession scene. They soon entered the child's automated cubicle and, on cue, Alex Wade walked toward Mellie's bedside. Off to the side, a group of smiling adults watched.

"Hi, Mellie," the Director said, standing at the bedside of the little girl. "I'm your good friend Manager Alexander Wade, Director of the National Health Agency. I'm visiting the hospital to see how our agency is taking care of important people like you."

The little girl smiled a broad smile and waved the small American flag she held. "Hi," she said, and blew him a kiss.

Mandell stood in the background nervously looking around the room. A manager had loosely placed a bandage over the cut above his left eyebrow. Blood had already seeped through the gauze.

Carole Weeks watched the monitor, checking to be sure the scene was on camera precisely as she wanted it.

Alex Wade turned to Ray Cunningham. "Please tell me about this lovely child, Manager Cunningham," he said.

"Why certainly, Director," Cunningham replied. "As you can see, little Mellie is a real dear."

The child began to cough deeply and could not seem to stop. Cunningham paused to let her finish the noisy paroxysm, then started up again. "Mellie has a chronic lung disease called cystic fibrosis and she has run out of points. Her hometown folks have been good to her. They've donated a lot of points for her care. They want her to have the best, but there are limits to what they can do. They need their points too."

"Of course they do," Wade said. "But the National Health Agency can take care of little Mellie." He patted Mellie's head. "The selection process has determined that she is to receive any and all care that she needs."

Cunningham backed away and Wade moved in closer to the child and continued, "There was a great American president who had the same last name as yours, Mellie. He wanted peace and happiness for the entire world. He started a great world organization to bring that about."

"I want that too — peace and happiness for everyone," the child said precociously. In one hand she held an American flag, in the other the flag of the NHA.

"I'm sure you do, Mellie. And, so do I. So do we all. You have exemplary values and this is America, the greatest land there is," Wade said.

There was applause. The cameras cut away to the smiling friends and family standing about the room. Some waved small American flags. The camera focused on one of the women as she wiped tears from her eye.

The blond haired, blue eyed child's front teeth were missing; her broad snaggled-tooth smile highlighted her captivating little girl charm.

"Who got your teeth?" Wade asked playfully.

She giggled. "The tooth fairy," she said.

"Ah hah, and what did she leave you."

"Five points for each one."

"What a lovely gift."

"I'm getting new teeth too, just like I'm getting new lungs."

"Of course, and we're going to see that you, and all the other deserving children like you, get whatever you need to live a long, long, peaceful, and happy life, Mellie."

"Thank you, sir, for coming to see me," the child said with coached poise.

"I wouldn't have missed seeing you for anything, Mellie, because it's people like you, the children, the youth of this nation, that have caused us to look very closely at our health care system. We want you all to have the very best of what we have to offer, Whatever you need — lungs, livers, kidneys, hearts, whatever..."

Mellie offered a wide smile.

"I know that you've run out of points, but I want you, your family, your friends who are here from back home, and all our citizens across this fair land to know that in cases like yours a shortage of points will not be a problem. If you are a deserving child or adult, the NHA is going to give you as much care and treatment as you need. You can quit worrying about points and put all your energy into getting well." Again, he patted her on the head.

The child looked up at Wade and gave him a big smile. He paused a moment, then reached down and held her hand.

"You, Mellie, are what this country and this new health care system is all about — giving free health care to those who merit it; giving free health care to those who will make America remain a great land."

Guiding the woman by the arm, Carole Weeks coaxed Mellie's mother, a woman of about thirty who looked at least ten years older in front of the cameras. "Oh thank you, Director; God bless you." She looked upward. "Oh thank you dear Lord," she said. When she held her hands together in a thankful, prayer-like fashion, the camera zoomed in on the emblem she wore on her dress – an oversized purple "T."

"Now, Senator, now," Carole Weeks whispered and nudged Mandell toward the child's bed. Taking his cue, the shaken Senator Mandell limped over to the bedside.

"Director Wade, I'd like to say a few words to Mellie." Mandell's voice was weak.

"Why certainly Senator," Alex Wade said. He graciously extended his arm pointing Mandell toward the child.

"Mellie Wilson, this is Senator Ross Mandell," the NHA Director said. "He is the man who is largely responsible for bringing American Health Care to where it is today."

"Hello Melanie."

"They call me Mellie," the child said. She frowned for a moment then quickly smiled again.

"Well hello, Mellie," Mandell stammered uncomfortably as he vigilantly surveyed the crowd for a suspicious face.

His glasses broken, he squinted as he read the lines from the teleprompter. "Mellie, in order to provide its citizens with the best that life has to offer, this country needs the finest leadership available.

I want you and the people watching to know that in the coming election, I will be seeking the presidential nominat…"

"How did you hurt your face?" the little girl asked, interrupting and pointing toward the bandage above his eye.

"It was an accident."

"Fall down?"

"No."

"Were you in a fight?"

"No."

"Well your bandage is coming off," the child observed, seeing the gauze coming loose and leaving the cut exposed.

Mandell fumbled awkwardly with the loose bandage, trying to put it back in place. In the background, Carole Weeks waved frantically to the camera crew to pull the cameras off of him. It was too late. He stayed on screen.

"Ooooooo, that's gross," the little girl said pointing to Mandell's face as blood oozed out of the cut and rolled across his eyebrow. A large drop dripped onto the child's bed sheet. The child's smile faded. She looked at the drop of blood in horror.

"It's nothing," Mandell said mortified. He struggled to get the bandage back in place and frantically tried to fold back the bed sheet to hide the splotch of blood.

Alex Wade quickly rushed forward and took over. Maneuvering Mandell out of the way, he moved in closer to Mellie and gave her a big hug. The camera caught her smiling face next to the Director's, then zoomed out to get a shot of her waving the miniature National Health Agency flag. There was applause, a fade out on the monitor, and the show was over. The crowd began to talk.

"Damn, those lights are hot," Mandell said, relieved to be off camera. He blotted the blood on his face with a handkerchief and wiped the sweat from his forehead. "Thank God there were no more attacks on my life," he said, and turned and faced Alex Wade. "How do you think the show went?"

"It could not have gone better," the Director said. He tilted his head back and inspected the cut above Mandell's left eye. "Nasty cut you have there. You'll have to get that taken care of right away."

"Yes, I must," Mandell said, his hand pressing the bandage against his forehead.

Brandt nodded to two health care managers standing close by and they followed his cue. They took Mandell by the arms and escorted him down the hall to render the proper treatment.

Chapter 31

Director Wade charmed his audience at the reception given by the Cunninghams after the television event. He told of the gracious welcome he had received at Devan and complimented his alma mater. "All of you have done a masterful job for the NHA and your country," he said to the doting group gathered around him.

Laura Clark was one of those listening until she turned and saw Tom standing alone across the room. She left her place in the circle and walked over to greet him.

"Hello Tom," she said. "How are you?"

"I'm fine," he said, but he could tell she knew better. He questioned if she had heard about his behavior after Katie's death. He concluded that she probably had.

"I miss seeing you," she said. "I don't get to Starr as much since we began setting up the units in all the other hospitals around the country," she said apologetically. "They have me on the road most of the time."

"I know. It's been a while," he said.

She took in a deep breath, and sighed. "Did you meet Wade?" she asked.

"I shook his hand. That's as close as I want to get. And he didn't seem to be any happier to meet me. I suspect that he has learned that I'm not on his team. You may know. The day after Katie's death, I lost it and crashed into the records room at Devan and tried to get into the records to see what happened. I didn't believe that she died a natural death and I still don't. Devan security tossed me out of

records and told me not to come back. There were moves to arrest me
and even some talk about deaccess. Cunningham himself came to my
rescue. Even said my behavior was understandable in view of my
wife's death. The man has a soft spot. 'Not guilty by reason of
grief,' he said. They backed off on any NHA action and sent me back
to Starr, but I suspect the story made it to higher levels like Wade."

"I heard the story," Laura said. "Gutsy."

"I won't be satisfied until I know what happened," Tom said.

"I wish I could help to shed more light on Katie's death."

"Stick around, you may get your wish,"

"Did you ever get to talk to Bob Kaplan?," Laura asked.

"I didn't get to talk to anyone. There's a cover-up," Tom said,
seeming preoccupied. He was staring at the group chatting with the
director. "We can't talk about this here, Laura."

Laura followed the direction of his gaze.

"So what do you think of Wade's new direction in medical care?"
Tom asked.

"He's a sharp cookie," she answered. "Ken's convinced that
Wade will be the next president."

"I thought Mandell was on deck."

"Right now, Mandell is being admitted to Devan Hospital," Laura
said. "They're suturing that cut and checking him out to be sure he
wasn't injured in the explosion." She took a sip of rose colored wine
from the crystal glass she was holding. "He's dead politically. He
looks like an idiot next to Alex Wade and the Director is doing
everything he can to keep it that way."

"God, what craziness. Mandell's an old fashioned politician, but
he's honest. I suppose you're already doing the programs."

"What programs?" she asked.

"The selection programs. They have to have selection software to
pull off rationing on a national scale. I would think you would be
very much in demand to put them together after doing such a good job
before," he said.

"I haven't done any programs," she said with mild irritation.
"They haven't let me near a new program in months. Government
informatics people in Washington do programs now. All I do is
supervise the installations and trouble shoot." Her eyes moistened.

"I'm sorry, Laura, that was cruel," he said. "But this is all madness. Patients treated like cattle. Patients wasting and dying with the acute marasmus syndrome. Points for deserving patients. Wade, a hero. It's a nightmare."

"You're right," Laura said.

"You're not one of them, are you, Laura? You never really have been."

"I feel relieved that you know that," she said, and took another sip of wine.

He watched her tilt the glass up.

"I know you miss Katie," Laura said quietly.

"I do, terribly. I don't expect that to change anytime soon."

"I feel horrible about what happened, a kind of complicity."

"No, Laura, you're a scientist. It isn't your work; it's the misuse of your work that's the problem. But I've had enough. I have no idea how I'll do it, but the time has come to see what I can do to change what's happening. I have to do something."

She shifted nervously. "Looks like people are getting ready to go to dinner. But we must talk again soon," she quickly added, "over coffee or somewhere." She set her wine glass down on a nearby table and stood up straight. "Yes, maybe you and I will take this on together. Who knows? Maybe we can even go further than that — even solve all the problems of the world."

"I'd like that," he said through a thin smile.

"Friends?" she asked. She put out her hand to shake his like when they first met. With their hands together, he felt the warmth and sincerity of her grip. She wrapped her hand around his for a long moment.

"For sure," Tom said.

She felt comforted by his answer. Perhaps her anguish would have a chance to quiet itself, her guilt a chance to diminish.

Out of the corner of her eye she saw Ken coming toward them. He stood straight, swaggering when he walked.

"I'm so glad you could come, Tom," he said and slapped him on the back. "You need to get out more and be with people. Let's see, how long since the wife's death? It's been months now, right? What a tragedy. Death of a spouse. That's at the top of the scale in the popular stress rating scale."

Laura looked at Ken contemptuously. Tom glared at him angrily.

"Can't imagine what went wrong," Ken said. "She had the finest medical care in the world. It's really hard to believe, but you know what they say. If something's going to go wrong, it'll happen to a manager's wife every time. Can you imagine? I understand she was doing so well. Then a T-effect exit. Well, you know how sorry I am. I wish we could have gotten you a better outcome. I guess sometimes things just don't work out. Sometimes even God deals from a dirty deck."

"I don't think God had anything to do with it," Tom said. "But you can believe that I intend to find out who did."

Later, at the banquet, seventy-six carefully selected notables drank and ate from the fine crystal and china dinner wear in the CelestaCare Health Enterprises dining room. An animated Carole Weeks conversed in a lively fashion with the enraptured high level city officials seated around her.

Calvin Cimmaron, of *The Minneapolis Sun*, represented the Midwest Newspaper Syndication Bureau. Wade spoke to the influential group and told them that health care would be rationed across the nation. "A system will be designed to provide distribution of services and resources to those most deserving of such care," he said. Cimmaron listened closely with a sense of *deja vu*. He remembered being at a small press conference years before when Alexander Wade had published his little known book on the utilization of health care resources.

Then, Wade's discussion of the rationing and the selection of the benefactors of expensive health care technology was little more than an intellectual, ethical controversy – something to discuss. Now, it was far from a philosophical discourse. The message was clear. What Wade believed, what had long been Wade's way, was to become reality with Phase III.

Cimmaron interviewed Ken Clark after the banquet. He asked Ken how Wade had managed to realize his philosophy of rationing health care. "It's God's will," Ken said, pointing to the T-shaped emblem on his lapel.

Chapter 32

That night, after the reception and banquet, Laura lay still in bed in the dark, her mind churning. She visualized the lilac-colored PointCure Check-In Centers with the people waiting. She thought of her work with the automated units and the universal central line. She dwelled for a while on the Houston tragedy. She thought of Katie's death. Flooded with feelings of guilt, she placed herself on trial over and over and could not arrive at a favorable verdict. Finally she fell asleep.

Into her light sleep, a dream floated. She was a patient at Starr Memorial on an automated unit. Rope-like monitor wires were wound tightly around the length of her body, imprisoning her so that she could not move. She cried out, but made no noise. Ken stood above her with a raised machete in his hand about to bring it down across her neck. She was certain that death was near.

Terrified, she awakened and glanced at the clock. It was 2:00 a.m. She struggled to slow her rapid breathing. The panic lessened, but sadness crept over her, settling on her shoulders and neck like a cold steel mesh shawl.

"What have I done?" she asked herself, still trying to get back to sleep.

Her thoughts flashed back to her conversation with Tom at the reception. Somewhere in their exchange she had found a faint promise of relief. "Solve all the problems of the world…" she had said. Something had made her optimistic, but even the recollection of that interchange was elusive. Soon, she could not find a glimmer of comfort anywhere. Her guilt returned.

Laura's restless mind took charge; sleep would not come. The night seemed endless. Ninety restless, sleepless minutes crept by. She got out of bed, put on her robe, and walked down the stairs.

In the kitchen she felt the still silence of the dark house around her. For half an hour she sat at the kitchen table and tried to read. Then suddenly, she felt another person's presence. When she looked up, she saw Ken standing in the kitchen doorway. He was wide awake, holding his briefcase in his hand.

"Thought I heard you get up," he said.

She did not look up from her book.

"Alex Wade has asked me to supervise the new plan for choosing the deserving," he said with pride in his voice. "He met with me today before the Phase III television event for almost an hour. He wants me to direct the operations division of the selection program."

She marked her place in her reading and looked up.

"We'll need you to do the software," Ken said.

"You never stop do you? Well, I've had enough bogus health care for today," Laura replied. She stood and turned her back to him.

He came closer. "I'm excited about this new project. We have to try and work together on the new programs. There's a great deal more to do."

He reached into his briefcase and took out a thick stack of papers. "I want you to look at these program proposals."

His presence had changed to intrusiveness. She felt the anger surging within her, burning away her despondent mood. "No more programs, I said. I've told you that I've done all I will do."

"We're at a new juncture. I need your help. The system needs your help."

She spun around and faced him. "Screw the system. I've had it with the damned system," she said and glared at him angrily.

"Look Laura, look at these," he said.

"Ken, this is bizarre. It's four a.m."

"See for yourself. Take a look!" Now, he was shouting. He grabbed her roughly by her shoulders and forcefully turned her toward the papers he had spread out on the table. "See how exciting this is going to be," he said shaking some of the papers in front of her face. "Here it is, the basic plan of the selection programs. This is the beginning of the ultimate truth."

She looked at him, terrified.

"Listen to this array of attributes — vocation, religion, race, personality traits, physical descriptions, medical history, life styles, political inclinations, sexual choices — there are dozens of other possibilities."

She folded her arms and shook her head.

"Can you imagine the challenge of integrating these characteristics into the treatment programs? Can you imagine the challenge of distributing health care based on peoples' places in society, their contributions to humankind, their value systems? Not only will we be able to define the most deserving individuals to be given points, but with our advanced data retrieval systems we can determine just how deserving a person is as compared with every other person in the country. Why we're changing history."

"You're playing God, Ken. The whole damned group of you is playing God."

He reached out and gripped her shoulders tightly. "We're not playing God, Laura, we're playing for God. Every one of us is involved in a project that will shape eternity. In that sense you are correct, Laura. This *is* a God inspired, holy effort."

She stared at him with an astonished look. Her eyes caught the flash of the purple T-shaped totem he was wearing around his neck. His words had the feel of intention approaching madness. A shudder of fear ran over her.

"You must understand, Laura. All of us are involved in a sacred mission: Wade, me, you, even people like Sullivan. That's why it's so important that you help. You must do the programs."

"Ken, leave me alone," she said. "You're hurting me."

"No, listen. Economics can't be the only determinant of the health care system forever. We need to turn to a higher order of motivations, a higher cause, a higher power."

"Please, Ken," she pleaded. "Some other time."

"Look at these directives. Don't you see. We're going to have to determine who gets points and who doesn't. Decisions will be made on the basis of which individual is deemed most deserving of a particular intervention. We have some precedents for this, you know.

The plan is similar to the decision-making to decide who would have dialysis when it was in short supply back in the 1960s."

"Most deserving?" Laura asked incredulously. "Who decides who's most deserving?"

"With the help of the Holy Father, your software will. You'll begin work immediately with a team of computer experts. You'll create software programs that will consider these personal descriptive categories, ranking them for each individual. Holt has all the information we need in the national data bank. We'll assign a numerical value to every person on the basis of the ranking. We'll call it a 'Procedural Priority Rating'. You will construct the programs so that our leaders can rearrange the variables and alter the values as they deem necessary. It's the only way to do it: scientifically, economically, and..." His eyes widened; his face glowed with excitement.

"And what?"

"Spiritually, Laura. Scientifically, economically, and spiritually. Alexander Wade has the good of all people at heart, for now and for the future. What he is doing is spiritually directed."

"Spiritually directed? Please."

"We're going to have to set some limits and this is the best way to do it. Alex Wade is a spiritual being. I am sure of that, as sure as I am that there is a God."

"I don't want any part of this."

"It's rather late for you to divorce yourself from the development of the system, isn't it? The original programs were your idea. You created them. We couldn't have gotten where we are without you. It was your research, your knowledge of technology that enabled this kind of health care to develop. You needn't act so self-righteous."

"You're right, I had a role in the early phases and I feel guilty as hell. But this plan has become an open invitation for some kind of strong-arm use of health care. You need to hear me. I've had enough."

"Laura, for God's sake, we have to have some trust in Manager Wade and the NHA."

He gripped her shoulders again. She was trembling.

"You're hurting me Ken. Stop it!"

His hands dropped away.

"An amalgamation of government, science, and religion is the only answer, Laura. Millions of people are putting their faith in science. A new religion has sprung from the technological Garden of Eden. Our piety will assure the survival of the best of humankind. Our work is divinely inspired." He was glassy eyed, staring at his papers, absorbed in his own world.

"I'm going back to bed — in the guest room We'll talk about it in the morning," Laura said and left the kitchen.

For months, Laura had watched Ken's involvement with the new religious order deepen — meetings at night, copies of the purple covered prayer book lying around the house, his insistence on wearing the T-shaped lapel button, and now the large purple "T" around his neck. It was apparent. He had become obsessed with his so-called "mission."

She made her way to the guest room, got in bed, and pulled the covers up. She had just closed her eyes when suddenly the door opened and Ken switched on the light.

"Laura, we cannot judge the value of our efforts. That will have to be done by others, religious leaders who are theologically devoted to this direction. The Theotechnicist leaders will evaluate our intentions; they will bless our work; they will guide us. My contribution to the process is my knowledge of economics and business operations. Yours, Laura, the automated units, your computer programs, your research. Each of us has our place in the plan. And now as we step into the future, as we progress, I believe that we will bring great benefits to humankind."

"You've gone mad." Laura said calmly. "This is another power move."

He acted as if he did not hear her. "There is no choice," he continued. "We must and will proceed with our task. The power of the technology is a gift which has been handed to us to do the will of God. As Chairperson of the NHA Task Force for Choosing the Deserving, I will do my part. All Theotechnicists must unite!"

Then, with the index and second fingers of his right hand, he made a religious sign on his chest with his two outstretched fingers. It was a crossing of a sort, a crossing sign in the configuration of a "T." He outlined the crossbar from his left to his right shoulder, then dropped the vertical from its center down the center of his chest in the design of a *tau* cross. He looked straight into Laura's frightened eyes. "I trust that you will join us in our mission."

Chapter 33

Every day, Tom found more and more deaths listed in the obituaries as due to the automated system side effect the NHA called the "T-effect." When the media raised questions about the increase in deaths caused by the "T-effect," Alexander Wade appointed a special commission to study the problem. The commission's consensus report stated, "The incidence of T-effect exits is less than 1 in 15,000 to 20,000, approximately the same risk as dying in an automobile accident each year." The NHA then concluded, "The T-effect exit is not a matter of major consequence. The automated systems are no more dangerous than riding in ones own car."

The Theotechnicists proposed their own explanation for the phenomenon. The T-effect tract mailed out to every home in the country stated, "People who exit from a T-effect simply are not destined to participate in the future of humankind." In a television interview, Oliver Sellers, the father of Theotechnicism, told of a personal disappointment. With tears in his eyes, he sadly noted, "My own dear, departed brother suffered a T-effect exit. I regret that we will not be together in the life to come."

When a rash of managers around the country openly questioned the validity of the "diagnosis" in talk-show interviews, they were deaccessed immediately without the opportunity to apply for readmission to practice. The NHA administrative offices in Washington continued to insist that the explanation for the T-effect exits was crystal clear. They reiterated: "The matter has been carefully studied. The explanation is that there is no earthly explanation; ultimately, we are all in the hands of God."

The NHA Commission on T-effect exits appointed special teams of pathologists to perform the toxicology studies and autopsies on persons who exited because of the side effect. These managers reported directly to the Commission and in the interest of national health care security, the reports were handled as top secret.

The Commission did establish an information center to assist the public. But all health care records involving equipment failure, information system error exits, or exits of questionable cause were immediately secured by the NHA and sent to Washington to be reviewed by special teams in the unusual exit investigation division. The teams reportedly studied all the records in great depth to attempt to determine the basis of the occurrence.

After the review, the families and managers of the patients might ask for a report of the postmortem study and one would be sent. But, the NHA continued to hold the actual charts in secret, inaccessible files.

Tom found the phrase "T-effect exit" ludicrous. It made no medical sense. And sadly, the T-effect was only one more of many administrative terms that had come to be accepted as causative explanations for disease. The labels: "terminal event leading to exit," "sudden exit," "favorable exit," "exit of unrelated determinants," "unusual exit," and "T-effect exit" had all become terms that supposedly told all about a disorder but said nothing. He was convinced that the categories were no more than misleading informational gaps perpetrated by the new order. But what could he do to expose the hoax?

As the weeks and months went by, the number of consumers who exited on the automated treatment units from one cause or another grew, but the exit that initially attracted the most attention was that of Senator Ross Mandell, the presidential hopeful.

Mandell had exited in Devan Hospital three days after his admission for "tests" to determine his well-being, after his close brush with death when the car bomb was hurled. All of the data that was accumulated before his death had showed no evidence of serious injury from the explosion that had shaken the car in which he was riding. He had exited suddenly, ostensibly due to a massive pulmonary embolus: a deadly blood clot that raced through his veins and instantly blocked the blood vessels to his lungs causing instant suffocation.

The media graphically reported the terminal event: "Senator Ross Mandell sat up in the bed, suddenly gasped, grabbed his throat, turned purple with cyanosis, and fell back dead." Fortuitously, the fatal episode of his exit was recorded on digital video equipment when a health care professional of unknown training background had accidentally switched on the camera recording device while in the control center making rounds that night. The recording clearly showed what had happened.

"Ross Mandell's exit was a most unfortunate happening," Alex Wade said on the news reports. "He was a man who gave his all to the health care system. His untimely exit leaves us all deeply saddened and bereft."

With Mandell's death, the speculation as to whom the President would endorse as the next presidential candidate increased.

"The fact is, the T-effect is absolute nonsense," Tom said. He handed his report from the NHA regarding Katie's mysterious death across the table to Carl as they lunched together in a small diner. "Here, take a look."

Carl adjusted his glasses and began to read:

Dear Thomas Sullivan:
In response to your inquiry regarding the exit of Sullivan, Katherine P. (SS# 192-34-6643), we have subjected the computer printout documentation of your spouse's departure from this earth to the closest possible scrutiny. Our review has led us to conclude that Sullivan, Katherine P. developed an arrhythmia which led to a cardiac arrest.

We are unable to explain the cause of this cardiac disorder. We are unable to find any indication of incorrect administration of medications; toxicology reports reveal no irregularities. We located no deficiencies in the monitoring apparatus or managerial control malfunctions. The search revealed no program failure in the automatic treatment system and no problems occurred in the manual management phase.

It is our final view that the terminal event of Sullivan, Katherine P. warrants designation as an EXIT OF THE T-EFFECT VARIETY. We sincerely regret this unfortunate happening and want you to know that your National Health Agency is always ready to serve you.

Carl handed the letter back to Tom. He took a swallow of his coffee then set his cup down. "I'm damned tired of this NHA health care exit-babble. They come up with a euphemism for everything. The word 'death' isn't mentioned anywhere in that letter."

"I remember the day Clark first used the word, exit," Tom told Carl. "In the middle of a staff meeting when everyone was shattered by the horror of the Houston tragedy, Clark stood and quoted from Shakespeare's *As You Like It.* 'All the world's a stage, And all the men and women merely players: They have their exits and their entrances…' he said. Since then, I haven't been able to separate the word from Clark's theatrics."

"Clark's bright, but he's an officious bag of wind," Carl said.

"Naming a phenomenon doesn't explain what causes it," Tom said. "This so called 'side effect' of a perfect technology has become a separate reality, a bogus term that's used as a definitive explanation."

"You're right," Carl said. "It's administrative subterfuge."

"Complete with meaningless statistics. The informed consent treatment permit for the automated units might as well say, 'anything is possible,'" Tom said.

"Listen, those statistics compiled by the National Health Agency are bogus too," Carl said. "Statistics are based on the chance of a random happening. You don't really believe these so called 'T-effect exits' are all random happenings, do you?"

"Not a chance. But how to prove it; that's the question," Tom said.

Carl looked across at Tom's plate. "You've hardly touched your lunch."

"Not hungry. Katie's death is weighing on me. I miss her."

"I understand, but you have to eat."

Tom pushed the plate to the side and picked up the check. "Your work on Warehouse Row is getting the NHA's attention. I want to take a look."

"Be careful. Mixing it up with me may not be in your best interests. The greatest risk is that I might put you to work."

"I'll take my chances."

Tom found himself obsessed with the cause of Katie's death. That night at home, he reread the letter from the NHA Unusual Exit Investigation team. He retraced the final hours of Katie's life. The most obvious possibility would have been a pulmonary embolus, a blood clot thrown to the lungs from a deep vein thrombosis in the legs. The immobility associated with being on the central line would explain the tendency for this to happen. Yes, like Mandell she must have had a pulmonary embolus. But surely Kaplan would have made the diagnosis if that had been the case. Perhaps it was an overwhelming infection spread through the blood, a septicemia. But if so, why didn't she have a fever and other symptoms of an infection? She did have a viral infection.

Could the cardiac arrest have been secondary to her having developed a cardiac myopathy? A viral infection weakening the cardiac muscle might cause a cardiac arrest, but she had no signs of heart disease.

She was recovering from her illness and should not have died. Perhaps Clark's vague threat was more than a threat. But surely, even these people, as devious as they might be, wouldn't deal in murder. But then why, when Katie was almost well, would she have had a cardiac arrest? Perhaps it wasn't a cardiac arrest. The thought that it was a bogus system problem crept back in.

Painfully pondering his wife's untimely death, he could come to only one absolute conclusion. Clark, Cunningham, and the NHA should damn well know his intentions. He would do his best to find out exactly who or what had actually killed his wife. And once he found the answer, if there was foul play, he would see that the guilty parties were brought to justice.

Chapter 34

Abandoned for decades, the old buildings on Middleside's Warehouse Row had again become familiar landmarks. When the Healers occupied them, the NHA public relations department photographed the warehouses for scare-tactic publicity. They touted the warehouse hospital as "The disastrous alternative to National Health Agency provided care."

Flashed on in prime time television spots, glaring out from posters stapled to utility posts, mounted on subway walls, and posted around clinics and hospitals, pictures of the tumbling-down buildings appeared everywhere. "CONSERVE YOUR POINTS, OR BE CARED FOR HERE!" the NHA message accompanying the scenes warned.

"We have three hundred deaccessed physicians and nurses, all working to take care of patients in these old warehouses," Carl told Tom on the telephone. "Come take a look. These patients are being treated like human beings."

Tom placed the phone back on the receiver. Carl's call was timely. All day he had been mired down in his ruminations, feeling powerless about Katie's death.

A few hours later, Tom walked from his car toward the red brick warehouse. A few flakes of snow gently floated down from the late winter sky. Carl Hammerstone, in a heavy coat and fur hat, waited at the bottom of the front steps to greet him. He shook Tom's hand, smiled a warm welcome, and then lead him up the steps.

When Tom stepped through the door, the heated air washed over his chilled face. He recognized the characteristic antiseptic smells of a hospital. Long rows of fifty gallon steel drums converted to wood stoves radiated warmth to the dozens of patients housed in the large room. Sheets hung from lengths of cord tied between the beams, dividing the space and providing the patients with privacy. Healers in crisp white coats, scurried in and out of the patient alcoves. Bright colored paint coated the studded walls, and in one area, set aside for children, cartoon characters danced across the partitions.

Carl led Tom through the passageways. "Families of patients and volunteers have been working for months to turn this place into a refuge. They've painted and patched the walls. They've brought in old furniture. They've built the wood burning stoves to provide warmth. We're taking care of over a hundred patients here now," Carl told him.

"A working hospital inside a ramshackled old building. It's like something out of a fairy tale," Tom said.

"We have our problems — shortages of supplies and equipment, small quantities of drugs, but we do all right."

Tom's eyes shined when he surveyed the room. "Impressive," he said.

"For some reason, the NHA allows us to go on with our work. I suspect there's something in it for them; they have a reason for everything they do. My guess is that they probably don't want to risk making us into martyrs. And we make good material for their public relations campaigns — they think."

The two men walked along the creaking boards. Tom peered into the patient alcoves. Carl stopped for a moment to warm his hands in front of one of the heaters. Tom did the same and felt the welcomed heat against his palms.

Carl turned to Tom. "What we're doing for these patients is treating them like human beings. When there's nothing else that can be done for someone, that's the most important thing a person can do."

Tom looked admiringly at his mentor. The new system could not dampen Carl's values. His way of doctoring and caring for people remained the same.

"Come over here," Carl said. He held back a flap of sheet. "See if you think what we're doing is worthwhile."

Behind the sheet, a child of about eight or nine lay on a cot. The boy's arms were stick-like. His respirations were shallow; his skin pale and dry. He lay still and quiet.

"Good afternoon, folks," Carl said to the boy's parents. The man and woman glanced up and gave tired "hellos."

Carl introduced Tom. "Doctor Sullivan here is taking a look at our hospital. Believe it or not, I taught him when he was in medical school. And I can still teach him a thing or two." He winked at the parents.

Carl picked up the boy's wrist, felt the child's pulse, and then placed his limp arm back down by the boy's side. He gently stroked the boy's forehead, then softly smiled at the woman and nodded his head.

Tom noted the healing puncture mark on the boy's neck where the central line had been. The skin around it was bruised blue.

The boy's mother followed Carl outside the cubicle. "Is there any hope for Samuel?" she asked.

"There's always hope," Carl said. "Please try to get some rest. I'll be back soon."

"Thank you, Manager Hammerstone."

When Carl and Tom were some distance away, Carl spoke. "That boy is very sick, isn't he?"

"Sure. Looks like acute marasmus."

"That's right, but as soon as his points were gone, he was ruled undeserving. Then he was discharged from Devan Hospital immediately."

"Surely they would keep on treating a child."

"Not a chance. The Blochs are openly anti-Theotechnicist. Oliver Sellers and his followers are becoming more and more influential."

Tom shook his head. "A make-believe religion to go along with the make-believe medicine."

A few minutes later, Tom sat down beside another patient, a young policeman. He talked with the man for a long while. His history: a rookie, a walking beat, finally a promotion to a patrol car.

Suddenly one night, a high fever and a stiff neck — meningococcal meningitis.

Carl motioned to Tom to look at the patient's hands. When Tom inspected them, he found that the man's fingers were wrinkled, black, and dry.

"Sepsis. D.I.C., "Carl said.

Tom recognized the putrid smell. The man's fingers were gangrenous; disseminated intravascular coagulation had taken its toll. When the infection spread to his bloodstream, the man's blood coagulation mechanisms collapsed. Blood clots blocked his peripheral arteries and blocked the blood supply to his fingers. Without oxygen, the flesh of his fingers could not survive.

After their visit with the policeman, Tom and Carl walked down the pathway between the hanging sheets. "Fine young man," Tom said. "Why was his treatment denied?"

"He got through the treatment for his meningitis, but complications of the illness stripped him of points. When he developed D.I.C., it became obvious that he would need months of treatment, rehabilitation, and thousands of points. He also was ruled undeserving and sent out to die."

"Deserving, undeserving — sounds like a pretty arbitrary call."

"Exactly. His family thinks that he was found undeserving because he can no longer work as a policeman. But who really knows the reason? Maybe it's his race. Maybe it's the way he smiles. Maybe it's his religion. Maybe his politics are wrong. Whatever, the computer spit him out."

"He could appeal," Tom said.

Carl rolled his eyes. "With the red tape the NHA has built into the appeal process, he would have been dead long ago.

We had enough antibiotics and other medications to keep him alive. Now he's better. There's a deaccessed hand surgeon who's willing to do reconstructive surgery as soon as we get our operating suite set up."

"He'll do fine. He seems to have a lot of courage," Tom said. "And he has a tenacious man for a physician."

They toured the hospital for over an hour. Clearly, though the NHA had ruled every patient in the Warehouse undeserving, Carl Hammerstone was determined to provide them all with care.

"I only wish that Katie could see this," Tom said. "You have human beings taking care of people. Your philosophy of care has survived through it all."

Carl placed his hands on Tom's shoulders and looked him squarely in the eyes. "Tom, ever since we first met, I've always felt that you're a healer to the core," Carl said. "You've always talked and acted like one and you've always cared for patients like one. You know that don't you?"

"I'd like to think I have those characteristics," Tom said quietly, "but I should be helping you here. Starr Memorial is a dead end street."

"We all have our roles in dealing with these destructive changes," Carl said. "It's the ability to put tension in the equation that counts. When one person or a group swings too far to one side, they may see this as having found the absolute truth. Then it's a healer's job to restore the play, to add tension, to put the ball back in motion and generate a sense of movement. It's out of this activity that we can turn the play that is part of life itself back toward a constructive direction, a direction with meaning."

Tom glanced toward the wall next to Carl's card table desk. Carl's medical school diploma hung there, clearly displayed. He had refused to turn it in to the NHA.

Carl continued, "I understand your feelings about being at Starr, but we're doing our job here and you can help from where you are. I would say you may have gotten yourself in a good place at Starr Memorial. You're a healer, still inside the loop, close to Clark. You need to stay right there. I have a feeling that there may be answers to some of our questions in the shadows of Ken Clark. Keep your eyes and ears open and keep stirring the pot. Keep the tension in the system."

Tom's mood brightened. His mind flashed back to that day when Carl called him to his office, when he was a despondent and discouraged medical student running out of financial support. Carl's wisdom and guidance had allowed Tom to emotionally move forward. Now, in a makeshift hospital on Warehouse Row, it was happening again. He took in a deep breath.

"I'll do it," Tom said, standing tall. "You can be sure of that."

Chapter 35

A few weeks later, when Tom returned to his office from his morning rounds, he found Jeanne Donnely curled up on his couch reading a newspaper.

"Well, your friend called. She's coming over," Jeanne said without looking up from her reading.

"What?" he asked, still pondering Carl's words about Ken Clark and Starr Memorial.

"Your good friend Laura Clark is on her way over here now."

He noted Jeanne's sarcastic tone. "What?" he asked again.

"You're not listening to me. L — A— U — R — A   C — L — A — R — K," she said, spelling out Laura's name. "Supposedly, she's coming to run another check on the information system's control unit, but between you and me, I believe that Laura Clark has a special interest in Y — O — U. She's spending a lot of time around here lately."

"She's trying to be helpful," he said.

"Sure she is. Remember, she's the babe who did the informatics for the automated care system, Manager, the very system in which your wife, Katie Sullivan died."

"Thanks for reminding me. And Jeanne, you know how I feel about being addressed as "Manager."

"Orders are orders, Manager Sullivan. It's a different time."

"Maybe, but I expect you to be on my team."

Jeanne looked up from her newspaper. "I don't understand how you can be so pleasant to her. You're so against all the changes in health care she's been so intimately involved with from the beginning. And Katie's death..."

"I believe she knows she had a part in creating this monster. She regrets it," Tom said. "She had no idea that automated care would turn out to be so damned impersonal. And she didn't invent the T-effect bullshit."

"Okay, okay, she's terrific," Jeanne said. She folded the newspaper, stood up, then tossed it on the sofa.

"I don't know how terrific she is, but I plan to be pleasant to her and you had best do the same."

Jeanne glared at him. Her eyes flashed anger. Then she quickly smiled. "You are outrageously forgiving, Manager Sullivan. I love you for it."

"Don't get in my way, Jeanne. I'm not as forgiving as you might think."

Jeanne shrugged her shoulders. "Some of us have work to do," she said, as she shuffled a stack of papers under her arm. When she leaned over to pick up her brief case, Tom caught a glimpse of a thin wire winding its way down the inside of her jacket. Was it a microphone? A recording device? Was their conversation being broadcast to another place?

She noted his eyeing the wire. "Don't get paranoid on me. It's a monitor to check for an arrhythmia." She showed him the device attached to her belt. "I had this weird dizzy spell a few days ago — almost went out like a light. They want to be sure it's not cardiac, so they're doing the old twenty-four hour electrocardiogram tracing. I hate to wear this silly thing."

"Hope it turns out okay," Tom said, feeling reassured by Jeanne's explanation and uneasy about his heightened vigilance.

Jeanne left to make rounds and ten minutes later, Laura arrived. She looked at him for a moment, then smiled. Her eyes brightened when she saw him. "Hello Tom," she said.

"Another check on the control unit?"

"Yes. Ken insisted. The last thing CelestaCare wants is for anyone to think that the acute marasmus syndrome is linked to the automated systems. Every time the equipment checks out okay, it strengthens CelestaCare's hand."

"They've had you trouble-shooting the system for weeks now."

"Yeah, they're a little compulsive. But you can bet that CelestaCare will do anything not to have to junk all the machinery."

"I'm sure of that."

"Millions and millions of dollars would go down the drain. But still, there's a limit to what people will tolerate. Consumers are becoming more and more frightened about being on the automated units."

"I know, and I can't say that I blame them. At this point, the syndrome has us all stumped."

Laura opened her briefcase and began thumbing through her papers. "You mean you don't agree with Ken that it's part of God's plan to weed out unsavory characters to ensure the future well-being of the universe? Why surely you know that the syndrome is punishment for spiritual inferiority."

"I keep thinking that AMS may be related to some unusual psychological disturbance," Tom said. "The patients show all sorts of emotional reactions: anger, fear, sadness, withdrawal."

She stopped going through her briefcase and looked up at him. "An emotional disorder, like depression?"

"Possibly. They act depressed. They withdraw from the environment, stop relating; they refuse food and waste away with malnutrition. But there are physical events too. Their fluids and electrolytes become impossible to control. They get overwhelming infections in their blood streams. Usually, it's the uncontrollable blood-borne infection and vascular collapse that kills them."

"That's horrible."

"We're missing something, but I don't know what," Tom said.

"Take me to see one of the patients," Laura suggested. "Maybe seeing what's happening will point me to a particular place in the programs."

"It's not in the programs. And if it is, you didn't put it there."

They walked toward the treatment unit through the stillness and quiet of the halls. Tom glanced over at Laura. She looked and acted very different from the time when they had first gone to see her laboratory. Now she was thinner and more mature. She had been chatty before; now she was quieter. Her enthusiasm about her work had slipped away.

He remembered her call the night Katie was admitted to the hospital, her guilt about the accident in Houston, and her concern about Katie. His memories caused him to ache; he longed for the past. He had Katie. And Laura was happier then too.

They walked past an entrance to a critical care unit. Tom glanced through a half-open door and saw a surreal scene. Inside the unit, jammed-together gurneys packed every inch of space. Patients lay side by side with little room between them. Cables and tubing ran back and forth across their bodies. He saw no attendants or nurses.

Katie would find these crowded, impersonal places totally unacceptable and the distance from caregivers abominable. He recalled her plans to lead the physicians at Devan in rebellion.

Laura spoke quietly. "You're thinking about Katie."

"How did you know? Was it that obvious?"

"This place, critical care. You were so quiet, and when you're quiet like that, I know that you're upset. I understand. I was thinking about her too."

They stopped a moment and peered into the unit.

Laura shuddered. "These are not good times for people who care about people," she said.

"Yes," he replied, "and people who care about others can't let it stay like this."

He squeezed her arm gently and she instinctively moved closer to him, clearly feeling a need for more human connection.

Moments later, they reached a control center for patients dying from the marasmus syndrome. Inside, they stood watching a large monitor with the number "23" above it. Tom spoke quietly, almost in a whisper, and Laura listened carefully to every word:

"This is a thirty-seven-year-old man who was admitted for elective surgery. He was doing fine until he had a post-operative incision infection. He seemed to be recovering, then began to show all of the symptoms of acute marasmus. Now look at him."

Tom leaned forward and moved the controls on the console to scan and view the man's face and body. The man looked as if he were dying of starvation. He lay perfectly still except for his almost imperceptible shallow respiration. His gaunt face and sunken, closed eyes gave him a look closer to death than life. The veins bulged on his temples; his carotid arteries pulsated visibly in his neck. His skin was dry and clung, without benefit of any fat-tissue, to the bony structures of his arms and legs. The man was little more than a skeleton.

Laura placed her curled fingertips over her mouth. "Oh, Tom, this is horrible, just horrible. He looks like someone in the final stage of cancer. These people are so sick. What in God's name have we created. I never intended for my work to lead to this. Isn't there anything that can be done?"

He took her arm and held it firmly. She leaned against him, her head lowered. "I'm sick about this."

"Don't blame yourself. We don't know that the syndrome is related to the automated systems."

"I will blame myself until we find the cause," she said, looking up at him. "I don't mind knowing that I've screwed up. Then at least I could correct my mistakes and do something for these people."

"You're doing your part to discover the cause."

"I'll help any way I can. Please let me know immediately if you find out anything. Please."

Tom stared at the pained expression on her face. "This can't go on forever. I'm sure something will turn up. When it does, I promise you'll know," he said.

"For God's sake, call me anytime you need me," she told him. She forced a quiver of a smile, then turned and stared at the image of the emaciated man on the monitor.

Chapter 36

The message on Tom's e-mail said, "MANAGER SULLIVAN —
AS SOON AS YOU ARRIVE, COME TO MR. CLARK'S OFFICE
IMMEDIATELY."

As he was leaving his office, Jeanne came from the hallway into
his reception area. She put her hands on her hips. "The top man is
looking for you," she said firmly.

"I'm on my way," Tom said and stuffed his stethoscope into his
gray coat pocket.

"Look this over first," she said and passed him the morning
edition of *The Middleside Times*. "The media is going after the NHA
full blast. The Chief is having a fit."

Tom took the paper from her hand. The bold black headlines set
the tone for the series of articles that followed. "ACUTE
MARASMUS BRINGS DEATH TO THOUSANDS ACROSS
NATION — PUBLIC ASKS WHY?" Then, underneath the headlines
in smaller headlines: "NHA EXTENDS RESEARCH —
CELESTACARE INSISTS DISEASE UNRELATED TO
COMPUTERIZED AUTOMATED TREATMENT SYSTEMS."

The theme continued down the page in several front page articles.
Tom scanned the titles: "People Waste Away Like Corpses;"
"Marasmus: System Side Effect or Disease?" "Emaciation Kills
Thousands;" "Deminhart Takes Stand — Questions Wade's Motives."

"Who the hell is Deminhart?" Tom asked, when he saw the name
mentioned a number of times.

"Malcolm Deminhart happens to be a very powerful politician."

"Afraid I don't know the man. Never big on politics."

"Deminhart was Mandell's understudy in the old health care drama with the HMOs. Now he's filling in for Mandell as the Colorado Senator. And he's full of questions about the new health care."

"I have to get to Clark's office."

"Take my advice and look this over. You need to know what's going on before you talk with Clark."

Tom hesitantly looked at the paper. On the front page, column after column addressed the horrors of the syndrome. Tom's eye found the column entitled "Deminhart Takes Stand — Questions Wade's Motives." He read it. "In an interview earlier this week at his ranch in Colorado, Malcolm Deminhart boldly challenged the operations of the National Health Agency. 'Where are all the excess profits being made in health care going?'" he asked. Deminhart said he was particularly interested in knowing why more was not known about the devastating acute marasmus syndrome. "Why is this serious problem being swept under the carpet?" He called for the NHA to "…get the research going and get to the bottom of this dilemma. If there's a problem with CelestaCare's Automated Systems, we need to know and we need to know fast."

But as Tom scanned the paper, he quickly saw that everyone had an answer to Deminhart's questions. In fact, the responses covered almost a full page. The other sides had countered in their own interviews. Sam Fisher said there was "…absolutely no evidence that the illness was related to the automated systems." He supported a popular current theory about the disease, attributing it to a latent autoimmune response left over from the epidemic. He also mentioned an interesting new finding by the CelestaCare-Devan researcher, Dr. Taylor Blaine that related the devastating syndrome to brain chemistry.

In response to the allegations about taking excessive profits, CelestaCare's CEO Sam Fisher announced that, "Money was most certainly not CelestaCare's first interest." In fact, the corporate giant was offering "double points" incentive coupons over the next two weeks. CelestaCare had also put a rebate program in place. "If money were the prime interest, why would CelestaCare be giving double points and discounts?" Fisher asked. Fisher said that the company currently offered "point rebates" for high ticket items such as heart and lung transplants and brain surgery.

The Theotechnicists also issued a statement: "The technology is sending a clear message. These people are damned. They are simply not in God's plans for the future of civilization. No wonder they are not responsive to the healing powers of the technology." Their religious leader, Oliver Sellers, was quoted: "Don't blame the computers and technology, citizens. Nothing's going to save those people. They just aren't being chosen as a part of society's renewal team." Sellers went on to say that "...this work isn't for the spiritually weak. We're shaping the future of humankind and not everyone is qualified for the job."

Alexander Wade, Tom saw, had declined to respond to his attackers. Tom guessed that once again, Wade concluded that if he held comment, the factions would soon be fighting among themselves. After all, he had repeatedly insisted in his television interviews and in other media that the new health care, PointCure was a vast improvement over the health care of the past: "...a step into the future."

Tom slammed the newspaper down on a nearby desk. "It's about time the press picked up on AMS," he said. "Somebody needs to do something. We can't just stand by and let thousands of people die."

"Come on, Sullivan, you know how the media exaggerates," Jeanne said. "CelestaCare and the NHA have done a lot of good. And the Theotechnicists make a lot of sense."

Tom glared at her expressionless face and headed down the hall.

When he arrived at the administrator's suite, Ken's office door was closed. The secretary told Tom that Ken was expecting him and signaled for him to go in. Outside the door, his hand raised to knock, Tom heard what sounded like gasps and heavy breathing coming from inside the room. A coarse, cawing sound, like a crow's call blasted out. The piercing cry persisted for a few seconds. Then there was silence. He waited for an uncomfortable half-a-minute and then knocked loudly.

Seconds later, the door opened and Ken Clark looked at him, squinting at the bright light. Inside, his office was in total darkness except for the glowing, bright screen of the giant, flat-screen television set in the corner of the room.

"Come in," Ken demanded. "Come in quickly and close the door." Tom did as he was told, and then took a seat on the couch by the door. Ken had a wild look in his eyes. "Watch this," Ken said, "I have an actual DVD of Mandell's death. It's spectacular! It's as close as you can get to death without dying. I've watched it at least ten times."

Tom felt his body muscles tighten, ready for action. "Fasten your seat belt," he told himself under his breath.

Ken pushed a switch and waited while the DVD loaded and the menu appeared. "There," he said. He pushed another switch then stood back in the darkened room, his eyes fixed on the huge high-clarity, wide screen television screen.

For a few seconds, a title appeared on the display: "MANDELL, SENATOR, R.M.; EXIT; PULMONARY THROMBOEMBOLISM; EXIT, UNTIMELY." Then, the picture shifted abruptly to the subject, Ross Mandell. It showed him lying in his Devan hospital bed beneath a lilac sheet with a central line coming from his neck.

For a few moments, Tom watched while the video disk showed the Senator resting quietly. The volume was turned up and the sounds of Ross Mandell's heavy breathing filled the office. Ken looked over at Tom and smiled ghoulishly.

"Now watch this. Don't miss a second of it. It happens fast," Ken said in a loud voice.

Tom watched as Mandell suddenly kicked out wildly at his lilac-colored sheets and slammed his hands down on the sides of the bed. Two of his heart monitor wires came loose with a twang. Mandell's stentorus breathing blasted out with a roar. A hoarse, staccato crowing sound blasted through the surrounding sound speakers. Mandell's hands reached for his throat. He sat up with a look of grim horror on his face. The color of his skin changed quickly from oxygenated pink to air-starved, purplish-blue. He let out a piercing cry, like a trapped animal. Reddish foam poured from his contorted mouth.

Tom watched the macabre show with dismay. Within a second or two, the stunned Mandell fell back toward the pillow. The Senator's head rolled over toward the side of the bed and his tongue protruded from his mouth. A section of plastic tubing from the central line dangled down, swinging in a small arc at the bedside.

"Now, that's a death! It's sheer poetry," Ken said, going over to the set, turning it off, and then turning on the office lights.

Has this man gone mad? Absolutely mad? Tom thought.

"They loved this in Washington," Ken said. "It wowed them! You can imagine. The top administrators from all around the country sat in the NHA conference room and watched this DVD with the best in surrounding speaker sound. The only problem is that Cunningham is getting all the credit for this gem."

"Is that what you wanted me for? To watch this?" Tom asked. "This is sick, really sick."

The smug look on Ken's face melted to one of dark seriousness.

"Look, it's not every day you get to see a scene like this. But no, that's not the only reason why I wanted to see you. Sullivan, I need your help. I was in Washington for an emergency meeting. We were doing what should be managers' work. We were brainstorming about the acute marasmus syndrome situation to try and stop it from ruining the nation's health care system."

"Well, now I feel better knowing that the health of the nation is in good hands," Tom said.

Clark ignored his remark. "Yes, the main reason I wanted to see you has to do with this blasted syndrome. The newspapers are giving us a rough time." He picked up the morning newspaper and held it out for Tom to read.

"I've seen it," Tom said.

"Then you know how important it is that we find the cause of this plague," Clark continued.

"That's simple isn't it?" Tom stated. "It's the T-effect. Isn't that what it is? Now, why don't you people just do your usual magic routine? Pull your T-effect out of the hat."

This time Clark heard Tom's sarcasm. "Listen," he said. "In the people's minds, the acute marasmus syndrome is already associated with the automated system. No, we can't blame the T-effect this time around. Even if it were the T-effect, a system side effect of this magnitude would deliver a deadly blow to our mission and our cash flow. The NHA must identify a disease as the cause — a *real* disease, a definite disease. And it has to be one we can do something about."

Tom shook his head, but kept quiet. "Keep your eyes and ears open," Carl had told him. Good time to follow his advice, Tom thought, holding back his comments.

"With a real disease, the problem can't be linked to the system," Clark continued. "The automated treatment units are our top point maker, you know; we've got our money bet on them. They've got to be seen as safe and sound. If people reject the automated units, that won't be good.

"Long and short of it, Manager, is that we have to find the cause of this disease soon and treat it. Otherwise the future of humankind will be threatened. I suppose you have some ideas about the cause, right?"

"Nothing that's certain," Tom replied. "The Administration won't let us get close enough to the cases to research it. You know damned well that the maramus syndrome death records are being managed the same way as the T-effect records. We have no access to them."

"To be honest, they haven't come up with anything in Washington. We'll have to do our own research. This is a high profile matter. It has the potential to cost us a pile of money."

"People are dying, Clark, and you're worried about CelestaCare's bottom line."

"Well, that's just fine. You don't have to be working on the money angle. There are higher causes to work for if you need that. There're spiritual issues involved. Now, I know you're not a believer, but even so, you can still be one of God's workers." He smiled and crossed his arms. "You, Sullivan, can be a worker in the vineyards, and if CelestaCare makes a few bucks while you're picking grapes, well..."

"Screw your damned grapes! I'm interested in finding out why these people are dying and doing something about it," Tom shot back.

"Sullivan, I know that I'm not one of your favorite people and to tell you the truth, you're not one of mine. But right now, that's not the issue."

Suddenly, Ken banged his fist on his desk. Then he stood and shouted directly in Tom's face. "Listen to me! We want to know what's causing the syndrome and we want to know soon!"

Tom's expression did not change. Ken stood there looking at him for a moment with his arms at his side, his fists tightened. Then, as fast as Ken had exploded, he calmed down. Now, Ken's voice became quieter.

"CelestaCare's research indicates that the disease is a physical disorder with emotional symptoms, a brain disorder, like a chemical imbalance. Perhaps you saw the article in the recent copy of the CelestaCare New Directions Newsletter. There's a psychiatrist over at Devan Medical Center that is on to something. His name is Taylor Blaine. He's working on a project using the new CelestaCare high chromatic, positron emission tomography scanner. And he's developed a promising theory about the cause of this syndrome."

Tom had read the article about Blaine's work with the high chromatic PET scanner. Blaine was totally convinced that he had discovered the cause of the acute marasmus syndrome. The psychiatrist claimed to have developed a new use for a kind of brain imaging using the chromatic PET scanner. Using his own newly developed process that he called "programmed recalculation of the secondary maximized image," and combining this with "deep focus brain wave studies," and a new image printer software program, he had reported he was able to get specific images of the brains of the acute marasmus sufferers. In these consumers, he said that he had demonstrated an unusual distribution and concentration of colors in the limbic system, that part of the brain associated with emotions.

In the literature, Blaine claimed that the colors were indicative of the specific kinds of brain functions and dysfunctions that caused the marasmus syndrome. Clearly, there was no way yet of knowing exactly what the significance of the rearrangements and varying intensities of the colors in his newly derived images were, but Blaine had come up with his own interpretations and was essentially treating his pure speculations as facts.

Utilizing his own printer software which he had dubbed "the reverse chromatic derivation program" for printing the images, in Blaine's construct, brain parts that showed up as green were brain centers that were "on-the-go." Centers that showed as yellow were neither stop nor go, but resting somewhere "cautiously in-between." Red, according to Blaine, meant that the brain part's function was "coming to a stop." Blaine equated the red images with the syndrome's clinical features of slowing, fatigue, withdrawal, and the cessation of eating. He called the phenomenon, "limbic halt." His logic was filled with bias and holes, but with economics driving research, science had come to this.

And to make matters worse, Blaine had developed several behavioral treatment techniques for the illness and one physical treatment method that many scientists thought to be extremely dangerous. With a pharmaceutical company's grant for a clinical trial, he was testing the use of unusually high dosages of psycho-stimulants to "speed up" the brains of the patients. He reasoned that this would likely switch them to green and "...get them on the go again."

Blaine's whole scheme would not only provide a treatable entity, it could also be the basis for a "scoop" to bring in consumers. There was no proof that his treatment modalities were of any benefit to the patients he was treating. Even so, CelestaCare was already milking the project for all the publicity it could get.

Tom surmised that Ken would have his own reasons for being interested in Blaine's work. Not only would this explain the acute marasmus syndrome as a so-called, "real" disease, a definite disorder of the brain itself that would get millions of dollars of technology off the hook, but the theory also offered a variety of business opportunities in the form of patents. And Tom knew, that in these times, health care patents seemed to have become more important than patients.

Ken soon confirmed Tom's intuitive assessment when he commented further that, "Blaine's studies are sensational. They're clear cut, marketable, and potentially big sell items. And what a name he has come up with. It's perfect! He calls it the 'stoplight syndrome.' Get it? Red, yellow, and green. The 'stoplight syndrome.'

"Can you imagine the marketing potential? We can easily change the name of the marasmus syndrome to the 'stoplight syndrome.' Why, we'll have toy stoplights and traffic cops for kids to play with. And there'll be little stoplight models with the CelestaCare logo on them, flashing their colors on everyone's desk. Billboards and signs will be flashing red, yellow, and green colors that will jump out at you. Every stoplight on the street will be a reminder. Stick-on notes, ball point pens, paper weights. What a scoop this will make! We might even be able to get the government to fund routine screening brain checks for every citizen. High chromatic PET scans by the millions. And think of the points, millions of points for the procedures."

Tom shook his head in disbelief.

"I want you to talk with Blaine. Check his theory out. I want to know if you will stand with us and support Blaine's theory. It would be worth your while, I assure you."

Again Tom heard Carl's words, "Keep your eyes and ears open and keep stirring the pot." And Tom was curious. Blaine's work was so ludicrous that it might be amusing to see.

"I will check it out, Clark. But I can tell you now, his work sounds like the most ridiculous excuse for research I've ever heard. The man is dangerous."

"Reserve comments until you see the research. Here is your mission, Manager Sullivan. Find me a disease that is causing the syndrome. Just be sure that whatever you turn up is a disease and not a problem with my computers and my automated care units. I want a real live disease, do you hear me?"

Ken then sat behind his desk and opened a small rectangular box. In it was a diamond-chip, sharpening stone. He then took a stag horn knife from his desk drawer, opened its blade, and then carefully angled it on the stone in front of him.

Tom watched incredulously as he placed the knife on the stone.

"Oh, one more thing," Ken said to Tom without looking up.

"Yes?" Tom answered impatiently.

Shereeeet, Shereeeeet, the knife sounded as Clark pulled its edge down the length of the stone.

"I understand you are spending a lot of time with Laura. I suppose that you are sleeping with her," Ken said without looking up.

Tom glared at Ken.

Shereeeet, Shereeeeet, the steel blade of the knife screeched as Ken stroked it along the stone again.

"Don't worry," Ken continued. "It's okay. I've had it with that unholy woman. She doesn't understand the importance of our mission. And besides, it's really no problem anyway. I'm using all my energies to better this world we live in and to prepare myself for all eternity."

Tom felt himself struggling through his rage to reply.

Ken drew his finger lightly across the knife blade to check its sharpness, closed it, and put the knife back in his desk drawer. Then he picked up a box of felt-tip colored pens from his desktop and opened them.

"Good God, Clark, you've gone mad," Tom said, then turned and walked toward the door, shaking his head.

Ken appeared oblivious and did not reply to Tom's parting words. When Tom reached the door, he glanced back and saw that the administrator had begun to sketch a traffic light on a CelestaCare note pad with one of the colored pens.

Chapter 37

CelestaCare's corporate headquarters pulled strings. Taylor Blaine agreed to see Tom at Devan Hospital that same afternoon, and Tom agreed to go. He wanted to get the assignment behind him, so he pushed aside his lingering feelings of anger about the madness he had encountered in Clark's office earlier in the day.

He took the elevator to the third floor at Devan. On the third floor, when the elevator doors closed behind him, he eyed the locked entrance to the psychiatry unit straight ahead. There, affixed to the unit door, was a large, yellow traffic light with its red light lit up brightly. He walked closer, inspected the light, and touched one of the metal sun shields fastened above each saucer-sized red, amber, and green lens. It was authentic, a genuine traffic light, exactly like those on the streets of Middleside.

He pushed the button on the communication box to the right of the door.

"Yes, who is it?" a voice asked over a small speaker. At the same time, the traffic light changed to a bright yellow.

"It's Doctor Tom Sullivan. I have a two o'clock appointment with Manager Blaine."

"Oh yes, Manager, he's expecting you," the welcoming voice said. "Do come in."

The traffic light changed to green and a loud buzzing noise on the lock sounded. Tom pushed the heavy door forward and entered, gazing around for a moment to orient himself.

A woman dressed in a brightly colored outfit walked toward him. She wore a red blouse with scarf to match, a wide yellow belt, and a bright, green skirt. Her hair was dark with strands of gray and was neatly pulled back in a bun. She wore small, oval, black rimmed glasses, which were obviously of designer grade. A plastic name badge attached to the lanyard around her neck identified her as "Manager Monica Muntero-Blaine," and beneath her name, a designation unfamiliar to Tom identified her health care specialty. She was, the name tag said, a "BOARD CERTIFIED LIMBICOLOGIST."

She introduced herself and told Tom that she was Manager Blaine's assistant and, in "real life", as she called it, his wife. Taylor had asked that she show Tom around the unit before their meeting in his office. Barring the garish blouse and skirt, Tom found her demeanor to be far more professional and engaging than he would have expected from the bizarre theory Taylor Blaine was advancing.

Tom looked down the corridor toward the unit control station. At least twelve traffic lights lined the long hallway and simulated roadways had been painted on the floor. Most of the traffic signals were of the usual red, yellow, and green variety; a few were the "WALK," "DON'T WALK" pedestrian type. Some bore the "stop" hand, and the "go," walking figure. Walking down the hallway, he noticed that the patients and the staff stopped and moved forward, in keeping with the traffic lights' directions.

"Excuse me Manager Muntero-Blaine," Tom said politely. "I'm not familiar with that specialty designation on your name tag. Just what is a 'limbicologist'?"

"Oh," she said, "surely you know that the limbic system is that part of the brain where the emotional centers are located. Remember, it's the old brain, the part of the brain that functions without the benefit of the higher centers of knowledge. Originally parts of it had to do with smell," she said. "Old brain: smell, limbic system, powerful, primitive emotions. You know."

"Of course I am familiar with the limbic system," he said, "but not the term, 'limbicologist.'"

She went on in a very serious tone. "Taylor has founded a new health care specialty based on his theories. It's called 'limbicology'. It will soon be a subspecialty of psychiatry; we've already been approved for board certification. The International Board of Limbicology will be issuing the certificates; Taylor is President of the Board."

"Board certification? Why, that's incredible. I've never even heard of this medical specialty and there's already board certification," Tom said.

"Taylor's been working at this project for several months. High level training and board certification is a must. After all, we can't have just any run of the mill psychiatrists working with something as important as the limbic system. Stoplight therapy is a very precise treatment modality. We need credentials to protect consumers."

"You're telling me that you have to be board certified to have people going and stopping like this in front of stoplights? We have no proof that these theories are valid. Isn't the formation of a certifying board a bit premature?"

"Perhaps, but you can't be too careful. We need to have board certification in place as soon as possible," Manager Muntero-Blaine confided, "to keep out the untrained and unduly biased. There are, you know, many psychiatrists who want to cling to the 'dark age' theories that focus on the importance of relationships, archaic psychoanalytic, interpersonal, and psychosocial frameworks. Taylor says that these people have never entered the new millennium. They can only contaminate the new direction he's discovered."

"Well, it does seem that relationships are important for good mental health," Tom commented.

"Yes, there are still many who seem to believe those out-of-date ideas," Manager Montero-Blaine replied, obviously undeterred in her conviction.

"If it's just becoming a subspecialty, how did you get certified so quickly? Is there an exam?"

"There will be, but some practitioners we are training now will be judged to be exempt from the exam. 'Grandfathered in', as they say. As Taylor's assistant, I was 'Grandmothered,'" she said and smiled proudly.

Tom squinted his eyes in disbelief.

The light in front of them turned a bright green. Monica motioned for Tom to move down the hallway. As she showed him the ward, she explained more about stoplight therapy.

221

"The treatment method is called 'neuronal intersection reprogramming therapy,' or 'NIRT.' The consumers are required to spend at least four hours a day 'on the streets' in the ward doing reprogramming exercises. Taylor's research demonstrates that the aberrations in color on the high chromatic PET scans represent chemical shifts that are at the root of the acute marasmus syndrome.

"More recently, he has expanded the use of "NIRT" to treat the entire spectrum of emotional disorders. We now believe that all psychiatric illnesses are related to these chemical shifts. Interesting findings. Yes?"

"Er, indeed. Very interesting."

Monica and Tom went on to tour the special acute marasmus ward. A few weakened, frail people in the early stages of the disorder marched on foot, but for the most part, the patients were all being moved around in wheelchairs and on gurneys. Ward personnel moved them up and down the hallways in the painted lanes, stopping and going in response to the traffic lights. As he and Manager Montero-Blaine stood observing the treatment setting, two men rolled a gurney by them, removing a recent casualty of the illness: a body covered with a lilac sheet.

Tom stared at the scene, bewildered.

"Death is a part of life," Manager Muntero-Blaine stated solemnly and resolutely. "Let's move on."

Monica Muntero-Blaine escorted him to her husband's office. Another large traffic light was mounted on his door. When she inserted the key in the door lock, the light turned green.

"We'll wait here, Taylor will be along any minute."

Tom looked over Blaine's diplomas. The largest one, his certificate for his Board Certification in Limbicology, signed by himself, hung in the center. Next to it was a large plaque that had been given to him by the National Health Agency for his outstanding work in applying the scientific method to human behavior.

On a side table was a large book entitled *Traffic Signals of the World*. Tom picked it up and thumbed through it, finding pictures of traffic lights and roadside signals from a dozen different countries.

"Interesting. Most interesting," he said to Monica.

"Yes," she commented, "stopping and going are indeed aspects of human behavior that deserve far more research and attention."

A few moments later, Taylor Blaine entered. He was a large, imposing man with a full head of thick, solid black hair and a ruddy taut-skinned face with rounded eyes. At first, Blaine appeared to be in his early forties, but a closer look told Tom that the thick, black head of youthfully styled hair was a toupee, and when he looked more closely, he saw Blaine's ageless features to be the effects of all that cosmetic surgery had to offer.

"Welcome, welcome, welcome, Manager Sullivan," Blaine said with a grating voice and broad smile. "So glad you came; yes, this acute marasmus syndrome is certainly a problem these days isn't it."

Tom nodded a yes.

"Well, it's most definitely a biochemically caused, purely organic, psychiatric disorder," Blaine told him. "And I'm delighted that you've come over to take a look at our work. Neuronal intersection reprogramming training is the answer. We're sure."

Tom knew. For Blaine as well as Clark, it would be a plum for a manager of Tom's status to endorse the "Stoplight Theory." But the tour only made him more skeptical, more convinced that Blaine's work was a hoax. Now, he was certain. Blaine's gracious welcome was as phony and self-serving as the cockamamie unit.

"Are you sure that what you've found is actually the cause of the syndrome, Manager Blaine?"

"Of course."

"Isn't this explanation a little too simple? It's such a complex illness."

"It's not that complex. It's a chemical rearrangement."

"Chemical rearrangement?"

"Yes, it's very similar to what we used to call a chemical imbalance, but instead of an imbalance, it's a rearrangement, a neurotransmitter rearrangement."

"Oh," Tom said, his eyebrows raised.

"Now, you understand," Blaine said, proud of the apparent acceptance of his explanation.

"What causes the rearrangement?"

"At this point, we can't be absolutely sure," Blaine said. He was mildly irritated by Tom's probing questioning. "But whatever it is, it's closely related to some problem in the limbic system — probably reactivation of a dormant virus, maybe an autoimmune phenomenon, or perhaps, an enzyme abnormality. It could even be a genetically determined disorder.

"But we're positive about one thing. It has to do with color shifts, simple biomolecular color shifts. There's simply too much shift away from the green and toward the red, and that causes things to come to a stop. Good feelings about relationships, happy moods, eating, all of these functions come to a dead stop. And when we reprogram the consumer's neurons, the colors shift back in place and it's back to go."

Tom was thoughtful. Blaine's logic was obviously full of holes, yet the man was frighteningly sure of what he was saying.

Blaine pointed to a framed blow-up of one of his chromatic PET scans on his wall. "They're shifts, simple biomolecular shifts," he said. "It has to be related to neurochemical rearrangements. We only need to discover which chemicals are rearranged and then we can successfully treat the disorder with an effective drug. But for now, we have to effect the correction of the rearrangement by using the behavioral treatment with traffic lights."

"But people are dying by the droves and your methods aren't really bringing about any changes."

Blaine sighed deeply. "Science is not perfect. We need time. We've tried all of our traditional treatment methods. Admittedly, some of these new methods appear rather desperate, but we have little to lose."

"Exactly what is your cure rate, Manger Blaine?" Tom asked.

Blaine's irritation had increased. "Humphhhhh! What a question," Blaine said. "Please. Have a little trust. I have every reason to believe that most of the consumers we're treating are moving along the road to health. Let me show you the proof."

He took out a series of high chromatic positron emission tomography images of brains of marasmus patients. He explained that they were cross sections prepared with his newly developed programmed recalculation of the secondary maximized image process combined with his deep focus brain wave database program. "Look at these colors, aren't they terrific?" Blaine said.

Tom looked carefully at the images Blaine handed him while Monica looked on with pride. The parts of the brain near the limbic system appeared in varying shades of the stoplight colors. The color distribution and intensity had obviously been altered by Blaine's methods of imaging and printing. The colors indicating low and high levels of brain activity were exactly opposite of what they should be.

"The reds, the yellows, the greens. Aren't they vibrant? Aren't they beautiful?"

Tom did not answer, and Blaine asked the question again.

"Why yes, they are," the pressured manager finally conceded.

Blaine leaned over closer to him. "I'll let you in on a personal secret. I really wanted to be an artist when I grew up, but a very special kind of artist. Even as a child, I used to say that when I grew up, I wanted to paint the lines on the streets. I've always had a fascination with traffic and traffic lights. The progression red, yellow, green is sheer genius."

"Fascinating," Tom said.

"Yes, my dad was an artist, Sullivan, but the poor man was run over by an automobile. When I was six, he was run over and killed while he was crossing a street. Someone ran a red stoplight."

Tom noticed that for a brief moment Blaine had a sad expression on his face. But the psychiatrist quickly regained his smile.

"The brain can be just like one big congested traffic jam, like rush hour, with tracts of all kinds running all over the place and little electric impulses, like tiny cars, running everywhere, carrying messages here and there. It's a magnificent piece of equipment."

"I certainly agree, Manager Blaine," Tom said. He realized that he was dealing with the psychiatrist carefully.

"Look at these," Blaine said, picking up still another stack of image prints. "I designed the image printer color distributor program myself. It's designed to register only the clearest shades of red, yellow and green and distribute these in a way that definitely supports my theory."

"That's unbelievable! You're telling me that you are arranging the colors yourself?" Tom remarked.

"Tell me Manager. How could we demonstrate the stoplight theory and use NIRT, the stoplight therapy if the images showed other color distributions? Our studies would be contaminated."

"Manager Blaine, Manager Blaine," Tom said with frustration, "you're a trained manager, a scientist. I can't believe that you don't see that your theory doesn't hang together."

"Possibly, but it doesn't really matter, does it? There's no business like show business; that we all know. The public wants a show and what the public wants, we'll give them. Right?"

"Well, Manager Blaine, I'm trying to clarify my ideas about acute marasmus. That's why I'm here, and I'm not impressed with your 'play.' So, I'll have to be honest. I can't say that your work is very convincing. Demonstrating a phenomenon with a biased test and developing treatment techniques doesn't mean you've found the cause of an illness."

A bewildered look appeared on Blaine's face. "What? Why, there is no question that chemical rearrangement is the cause. You saw our Marasmus Unit. Isn't that enough proof for you?"

"Those people don't look like they're getting any better," Tom observed. "They are draped over wheel chairs and laid out on stretchers like corpses. The ward personnel are the ones who are stopping and going. How does the cure come about? By osmosis? And why didn't we see the acute progressive marasmus syndrome before we had the automated units?"

Blaine stood up straight and glared at Tom seriously. "The technology is brand new, Sullivan. We've only recently demonstrated the red, yellow, and green distribution phenomenon. How could there have been a stoplight disorder without the test to demonstrate its presence. And treatment results? Give us some time, please. You're in such a hurry. Slow down. Think of your own stoplight system. You don't want to end up in a jam yourself."

Tom turned to look at Mgr. Montero-Blaine's face, expecting to see some response to his questioning of Blaine's theory. What he saw was an unchanged expression of dead seriousness. Tom's critical comments were going nowhere.

"Then, I take it that you don't think the syndrome has any relationship to the new system of health care, to the automated units or to the computers," Tom said.

"Of course not! It's a real disease, a bonafide disease, and a colorful one at that," Blaine said. Then he slapped his thigh and smiled broadly, savoring his own sense of humor.

Monica Montero-Blaine looked at her husband admiringly.

Tom felt edgy. "I have to go now," he said uncomfortably, "but thank you for the informative tour."

"We're grateful to you for coming over. The NHA, CelestaCare, and Cunningham are behind us all the way you know, and we have the support of the highway department and city traffic engineers," Blaine said. "We want your endorsement also." They shook hands and Tom prepared to leave. Blaine reached into his pocket and took out what looked like some kind of brochure.

"Why don't you look this over," he said, handing Tom a shiny pamphlet with a picture of a large traffic light on the cover. You might have a little cash lying around that you'd like to invest in a little venture I'm getting together. I can get you in this for thirty-thousand. Check out our website: www.celestacare/stoplight.com."

Tom looked at the booklet. It was a prospectus for a new company, a subsidiary of CelestaCare: "Stoplight Industries Incorporated."

"If we're lucky the government will decide to foot the total bill for people with the syndrome and we can cash in. There'll be a lot of money to be made in traffic lights; the treatment units will need thousands of them.

"There'll be hundreds of units just like this one all around the country, all run by limbicologists. It's simple. We franchise them and supply the traffic lights, and the government health program picks up the tab, while we make giant profits. Sullivan, I can get you certified, even if you are in internal medicine."

"Still another increase in the cost of health care; more points down the drain," Tom said.

"Manager Sullivan, you know better than to worry about that. As long as you've got your health, you've got everything."

"It's Doctor Sullivan, not Manager Sullivan," Tom said.

Chapter 38

Driving back to Starr Memorial, Tom eyed the PointCure buildings along the way. Constructed quickly, with substandard materials, the centers were already rundown and in disrepair. The lilac-colored paint was starting to blister and fade. Foul graffiti and misshapen art covered the outside walls. Duct tape held together broken window panes. Weeds overran the grounds. Strangely, however, the neatly planted lilac trees that encircled the centers were still well tended and healthy. Their buds were full and poised to bloom.

Back in his office, Tom pushed his chair away from his desk, swiveled around, and looked at the wall graph plotting the numbers of marasmus syndrome deaths. The curve was ascending rapidly.

He reflected back to Monica Muntero-Blaine and her husband. He shook his head, and again concluded that Blaine's therapeutic milieu was total madness. The ward, with its traffic lights and painted highway lanes was dream-like. It was like a plunge though a mirror into another world.

His thoughts were interrupted by his secretary's voice on the intercom.

"Manager Hammerstone wants you. He says it's urgent," she said.

Tom quickly picked up the telephone.

"Get down here right away," Carl said. Come down here immediately. No questions. Do as I say. Can't talk. Most likely, this phone is tapped. NHA agents are here, all around the neighborhood."

Twenty minutes later, Tom entered the healer's warehouse hospital. Soon, he was standing with Carl at the bedside of Samuel Bloch. The child was alert, sitting up and eating cereal from a bowl.

"Look at Samuel. Can you believe it? He's getting well," the child's mother said.

Tom turned to Carl. "What happened? How did you do this?"

"I didn't do it. They did it. All the people who took care of him: his parents, his brothers and sisters, and the volunteers who sat by his bed through the long nights did it. People did it, not high priced medicines — people, not fancy technology — people pulled him through."

Tom felt overwhelmed. "This is phenomenal," he said.

"At least ten acute marasmus syndrome patients are recovering. As best I can tell, we entered into the patients' detached, disconnected worlds. We overcame some force that was hurling these people toward death. I can't say for sure, but the reversals seem to have something to do with their being cared for by people instead of machines."

"Manager Hammerstone has kept someone with Samuel around the clock," Mr. Bloch said.

"Our goal was to reestablish contact, to overcome the withdrawal, and to create a sense of security, a safe place," Carl said. "Family, relatives, friends, and volunteers stayed with the patients day and night. We tried to feed the patients even when they refused to eat. We talked with them even when they wouldn't answer. We made certain that they were kept clean and warm. At first, they didn't want anyone around and if a strange person came near, they withdrew even more."

"Go on," Tom pressed, hanging on Carl's every word.

"But we were persistent. We kept trying to relate with the patients and gradually, they came around. It was amazing. When they first began to talk, they just babbled unintelligible words. Coming out of the withdrawn state, they displayed all sorts of wild emotions. Later they became calmer. I think we've discovered something. These are damned important findings."

"Your perseverance has paid off."

"But we've got to do something fast. It looks like the acute marasmus syndrome may be linked to the isolation that patients experience in the automated treatment systems."

"The NHA and CelestaCare won't be happy," Tom said.

"Your job is to use this information. You have to get it out in front of the public. This has to be studied."

"The last thing CelestaCare will want to do is to dismantle all their automated units," Tom said. "They'll do anything they can to discredit everything I say."

"Do what you can," Carl said. "That's all any of us can do."

"I'll do my best."

"Do it soon, Tom. People are dying."

A few minutes later, driving through the cobblestone streets that marked the old area of Middleside, Tom reviewed Carl's findings. Then for some reason, a name popped into his mind. The name was Leo Strasberg. Strasberg was one of Tom's psychiatry professors in medical school. Strasberg? Why Leo Strasberg?

He scanned his recollection of his contact with the man, but his memory gave him no clue. Finally he remembered — "Isolation," he said out loud. "Isolation and loneliness." Pathological emotional states related to isolation and loneliness, he recalled. Strasberg used to talk about isolation and loneliness as causing emotional disturbances. But how could isolation cause this disease?

Within half an hour he was searching for the answer to his question. He was back at Devan about to enter the vast medical library. There he planned to comb the scientific literature for writings that might show a connection between isolation and marusmus.

On his way down the hallway, in a ritual of admiration, he paused to view part of the permanent collection of the memorabilia of the medical school's founder, Dr. Paul Devan. Displayed in a glass case, he saw Devan's personal copy of *Therapeutica Medica*, a book of the treatment methods of his times. Next to the book stood a small brass microscope, its primitive mechanics assuring one that it was an authentic relic of a bygone era. Beside the microscope was the primitive wooden stethoscope sent to Devan by its inventor, Rene Laennec. Devan's handwritten journal, filled with faded cursive writing, lay open near the center of the case. Inches away, a mottled, leather-bound, antique book also lay open on display.

A description accompanied each item. The tattered journal contained Paul Devan's brilliant accounts of his patients' illnesses. The printed book, an original copy of Devan's *De Morte Subita*, was a compilation of minutely detailed descriptions of the sudden deaths of a number of his patients.

A printed card above the book explained:

When *De Morte* was first published, critics derisively called Devan's fascination with death 'morbid and maudlin.' 'Perhaps he has become a physician more interested in death, than in life,' one of his old professors said of him. Now, this book has come to be considered one of Paul Devan's greatest contributions to medicine and the brilliant descriptions of sudden deaths contained in his book have survived as a mark of his genius.

In the introduction to his book, *De Morte Subita,* Devan wrote that, '…death is a part of life and should be so studied,' but his close scrutiny of sudden deaths was felt by the then reigning medical authorities to be a useless exercise.

Devan suffered a bout of severe melancholia, closely related temporally to the publication of his book. Then, about a year after the period of his dark mood, as if to balance his preoccupation with death, Devan focused all his energy on establishing this medical school and committing himself and his faculty to enhancing the lives of the living.

Tom felt his interest in the display growing. He quickly read the first few lines on the open page of his handwritten journal. The journal was open to the point where Devan described sudden death resulting from pulmonary emboli:

The patient suffering from traveling blood clots, which have caused the sudden closure of the large arteries traversing the chest from the heart to the lungs, and stopping blood flow though them, is prone to the most terrible and catastrophic state of acute distress. The ill man suffers from a deficiency of breath and of air entering his lungs, and is likely to grasp and tear frantically at his own neck, with his own fingers, even leaving nail marks and true lacerations in his own skin. He gasps desperately for air, and taking it in, still gets no oxygen. As his blood darkens from the lack of vital gases adhering to the blood chemicals, his skin, first around the mouth, turns as purple-blue as the lilac blossom. The color spreads across the cheeks, and then can soon be seen in the fingers of the hands. The face is drawn up in a frenzied, contorted expression of suffocation and terror, the chin twisted to the side.

The eyelids blink as rapidly as a leaf doth flutter and the colors of the eyes drive upward, leaving only the white to show. The sounds made are distinct and close akin to those made by terrified, trapped animals. The raspy call of the crow is all too often reproduced in the midst of the torment...

That detail is uncanny, Tom thought. And Devan's description of this acute, clinical event is remarkably similar to Ken's real-life digital video of Senator Mandell's grotesque death.

A short time later, in the library's reference section, Tom sat, pouring over the computer-derived medical literature search on the effects of interpersonal isolation. There were articles on disturbances related to sensory deprivations, and others referred to the effects of interpersonal deprivation on infants. Still others dealt with attachment and loss, separation and grief.

He thought of Katie. In the hospital, before her death, he remembered her mentioning a deep sense of loneliness and sadness connected with the scarcity of people taking care of her. Was she experiencing the preliminary symptoms of the marasmus syndrome? He felt his motivation surge even more.

Skimming through book chapters and articles, he found a plethora of theories and observations by a variety of theorists, researchers, and clinicians. But hours passed and still he found nothing that he could put together that made sense. Finally, he left the library to take a short break.

He walked through the still hospital halls near the room where Katie had died, hoping for some breakthrough in his thoughts. A hospital aide passed by, pushing a surgical patient on a stretcher down the hallway to the operating suite. The patient's monitor cords hung down over the sides of the stretcher and a fluid bag dripped small drops of dextrose in normal saline into the patient's central line. A long loop of the central line dangled dangerously unprotected over the side of the gurney and skipped along the floor.

Disconnected imagery floated in and out of Tom's mind. Suddenly, the image of a developing fetus floating in its mother's uterus fixed in his imagination. He imagined its dangling, unprotected umbilical cord to be kinked. Starving for nutrients, the fetus had become separated from its tenuous attachment to its mother and its link to life was endangered. He followed the image in his mind, imagining the fetus in severe distress, struggling helplessly in the fluid of his mother's womb. The fetus' desperate movement continued, then slowed, and after a few minutes ceased. Its exhausted, lifeless form floated weightlessly in the yellowish, amniotic fluid.

Preoccupied, Tom wandered onto the pediatric unit. In the distance, he heard a small child crying and cocked his head to locate the sound. He entered the control station and scanned the bank of monitors. His eyes fixed on Monitor 16. On the screen, in a sterile, automated cubicle sitting on the bed, was a newly admitted four-year-old child dressed in a lilac hospital gown.

Not yet sedated into the standard zombie-like pediatric patient, the wide-eyed boy was filled with terror and clung helplessly to his mother. The child's shrill cry penetrated the dim stillness of the otherwise quiet ward. His mother stood close to him, holding his hand.

Gasping for breath, the child sobbed loudly. "Don't leave me mama, no mama, don't leave," the child cried out. "They're gonna hurt me and you don't care. Please, mama, don't leave, I'm scared, they'll hurt me. I love you. Don't leave me. Don't."

"You move on out of here lady," the health care assistant said. "This baby will be fine. A little crying has never hurt a child," the woman said as she slipped the hard foam pillow she held under her chin into the lilac-colored, disposable, paper pillow case.

The child held on to his mother's arm. "My son's burning up with fever," the worried woman said.

"Look, I said the kid will be okay, lady. You've got to leave," the health care aide said as she mechanically continued the admission tasks.

The anguished mother reluctantly began to leave the room. Twice she moved back toward the child and was admonished by the aide.

Finally she left.

"Lie down, boy," the aide barked at the child.

The trembling, terrified child, his fingers stuffed into his mouth, compliantly obeyed. The aide attached the monitor leads and left the room. Moments later, the central line team came in and, moving swiftly, the blank faced workers installed the plastic conduit in the child's neck.

Then, one of them took a disposable, loaded syringe from a packet. He thrust the needle into the receiver on the central line and injected a drug. Almost immediately, there was evidence of the drug reaching the child's brain. His mouth drooped open and he slowly closed his eyes, becoming sedated and quiet. The team then gathered up their gear and left the child alone in the cubicle.

For a few moments, Tom shifted his weight from one foot to the other. Then, drawn toward the empty, sterile silence of the cubicle, he broke all the rules, as he and Trim Willingham had done with Mitchell Newman. He dashed through the control station door and entered the child's room.

Once inside, Tom noted a barrenness that extended beyond quiet. The room was brightly illuminated. The shining stainless steel machinery stood out starkly against the backdrop of the pale-cream color of the walls and ceiling. The camera was aimed at the child. He looked for a window in the room, but there were none.

His eyes focused on the form of the boy beneath the lilac-colored sheets. A dozen wires crisscrossed the bed. Tom listened in the quiet and heard the distant, muffled rush of fluids passing through the treatment tubing valves to reach the central line. The television camera whirred from side to side. The only human sound that Tom heard was the child's shallow breathing.

Painful feelings of loss swept over him as he stared at the helpless boy. He felt a peculiar array of feelings: sadness, anxiety, anger, mild confusion, and vulnerability. With these, he experienced unsteadiness and even blurring of his vision. There were no human beings anywhere nearby. As if floating out in space, Tom felt removed from any kind of connection with other human beings. Alone in the peopleless quiet, he felt himself empathetically identify with the abandoned boy, lying motionless in the bed.

Suddenly the puzzle began to fall into place. It was as if the experience had released a flow of images and associations that could be integrated and come to have a meaning. Katie's death rushed through his mind and he felt his own grief and turmoil. He recalled his own anxiety, his loneliness, his withdrawal, his isolation and his hopeless despair after she died. He remembered feeling abandoned and recalled his anger, his guilt and his belief that, without Katie, he also would perish. He remembered that for days he could not force himself to eat. He remembered how disoriented and insecure he felt without her.

It's as if this child is being left to die also, he thought. Abandoned, endangered, and uncared for in this strange environment, the isolation raises the specter of death. As he stood watching the still form of the child lying on the lilac sheets, he realized that total separateness from people was in itself a form of death.

Now he knew why he thought of Leo Strasberg. Now he knew why he kept coming to his mind. He remembered a conference Strasberg had conducted in the old Devan amphitheater when Tom was a medical student. It was a time when psychiatry was more concerned with relationships and peoples' needs than with neurotransmitters.

There was a conference about a two-year-old child who had been unexplainably abandoned in the hospital by his youthful mother. The authorities had not been able to locate the child's mother and the toddler had suffered a period of severe physical deterioration of unknown cause. Strasberg, basing his discussion and formulation on the works of those who observed similar physical reactions connected with such abandonment, had argued for an emotional basis for the child's disorder.

Later the child's gentle, devoted grandparent had come forward and offered to stay with the child. She stayed with the child constantly and the sickness reversed. Tom remembered the names, "Spitz" and "Engel" in connection with the conference. He knew then that Strasberg could tell him more.

Chapter 39

Back in the library, Tom thumbed through the Devan telephone directory. Unable to locate the number for Strasberg, he turned to the librarian.

"Manager Leo Strasberg's extension number, perhaps you have it somewhere. Do you know where I can reach him?" Tom asked.

"The man who used to be the Chairman of the Department of Psychiatry?"

"Yes, he was Chairman," Tom said.

"They moved that crackpot to the basement over a year ago and that's a good place for him. He may not even have a telephone."

For some reason, she seemed irritated by his asking about Strasberg. "Leo Strasberg hasn't looked at a single journal since the new health care system was installed," she told Tom. "I asked him about that once. He says there's nothing of any value in them. Now, isn't that presumptuous? Shunning the current literature like that."

Tom's eyes cut across to the periodical rack. *Money and Medicine*, and *Harvesting Health Care Dollars*, were the first two journals he saw. "Perhaps," Tom said.

Tom looked through the Devan telephone directory again and finally found Strasberg's number. It was listed, in error, in the student section.

"If there's something you'd like to know about psychiatry, I would suggest you call Manager Taylor Blaine," the woman volunteered.

"No it's Strasberg I want, not Blaine," Tom insisted.

She begrudgingly moved a lilac-colored extension phone to the counter. As Tom reached for the phone, he noticed a large stoplight shaped pin-on button on her sweater. Its printed message said, "Stop the marasmus syndrome, Get in the Blaine Lane."

Another librarian who had been standing nearby grew interested in the interaction, and moved closer as if listening in. She bore more than a slight resemblance to Katie. She stood a few feet away and watched him, appearing strangely captivated by Tom's look of distress.

Tom punched in the number and it rang. A man's voice answered and identified himself as Manager Leo Strasberg.

"Manager Strasberg, I didn't expect you to answer the phone yourself."

"Yes, I'm between patients and there are no secretaries in this division of the department. What can I do for you?" he asked, his words leading directly into a paroxysm of coughing that went on for at least twenty seconds. "Sorry," he said breathlessly, "I used to be a heavy smoker."

Tom told him who he was, what he was doing at Devan, and why he was calling. He mentioned his attendance at one of Strasberg's conferences years before, described the case discussed, and told the psychiatrist of his search for the cause of the acute marasmus syndrome.

"Oh yes, I remember the conference," Strasberg said.

"I'm interested in the literature on separation and loss. Spitz, I believe, was the investigator you quoted most in your conference."

"A CelestaCare hospital director interested in psychiatric literature on separation and loss? And Spitz, you remember Spitz. That's amazing," the old man said.

Tom mustered his courage. He decided to go ahead and tell Strasberg about his conclusions. Tom advanced the idea that the acute marasmus syndrome was connected to the interpersonal barrenness in the workings of the new medical system. Strasberg listened, coughing every few sentences, and politely excusing himself. "I'm sure there must be a relationship between the syndrome and separation and loss — a direct relationship," Tom said.

"Of course, there's a direct relationship," Strasberg said immediately. "There's no doubt about it."

Tom's jaw dropped. "You've already thought of this?"

"Certainly."

"Then I'm sure you've already brought this to the attention of the health care center administration," Tom said with relief.

"Exactly. I've talked with Vice Chancellor Cunningham. And to put it bluntly, my effort went absolutely nowhere."

"Excuse me, sir, but if that's true, it's unbelievable. This syndrome is devastating. Thousands of people are dying from it."

"It is, isn't it, and the fact that the administration isn't paying any attention to it can only mean one thing."

"Yes." Tom said, anxiously waiting for him to continue.

"Young man, we're dealing with the powerful force of Destrudo. In fact, it's pure, unbridled Destrudo. We're headed in a cataclysmic direction. It's a deadly force. I am in the process of writing a paper on the subject now. It's titled 'The Destrudo Direction.'"

"Destrudo? I don't understand, sir."

"Oh, yes you do. You just don't know it yet," Strasberg said with a soft, raspy cough followed by another polite, "Excuse me".

Strasberg told Tom that he would be glad to see him, but that he could not meet with him until the next day. He had patients scheduled for the rest of the afternoon, but had some free time around ten the next morning.

"I'll be there," Tom assured him.

"We'll talk about it then. For now, take down these names and find these peoples' articles and books. Look them over; read every word you can. If you've already read them, read them again. These authors worked at life's crossroads. I think you'll find their observations illuminating. Do you have something to write on?"

Tom looked around for a piece of scratch paper. Still working nearby, the librarian who resembled Katie quickly handed him a piece of paper and a pencil and smiled.

Tom wedged the telephone between his cheek and shoulder and wrote down the names and references as Strasberg gave them to him. "Okay, I've got it, Engel, and Bowlby, and the paper by Cannon. What's the source again?" Tom asked with excitement. "And Spitz, of course Spitz, he's the one I remembered from your conference. What's that reference?"

Strasberg commended him on remembering any of these authors during times like these. He told Tom that he recently met another manager who had knowledge of these authors' writings. They had met in Cunningham's waiting room the day he went to talk with the Vice Chancellor about his theory of the cause of the marasmus syndrome.

The other manager, a young man, also had an appointment with Cunningham. It seemed that there was a disciplinary matter of some sort that needed to be settled. He had told Strasberg of his concern about the horrors of acute marasmus as the two waited together. The manager was most interested in what Strasberg had to say, and was the only other person that the old psychiatrist had encountered thus far that seemed to even have the faintest investment in an interpersonal explanation for the syndrome.

"What was his name?" Tom asked him. "We may need to look him up. We need all the help we can get."

"I believe his name was Kaplan. Yes, that's right. It was Robert Kaplan."

After the conversation with Leo Strasberg, Tom turned to the young librarian who looked like Katie and introduced himself. "I'm Tom Sullivan. I used to be Chief of Infectious Diseases here at Devan. I work at Starr Memorial now, but I still miss being at Devan."

"Yes, I am familiar with your work. You're the manager who tested Lilacicin, right?"

"Yes," Tom replied.

"You did us all a tremendous favor. I was at the conference when you and Manager Hansen presented the results of the Lilacicin trials to the media. Bonnie Glass is my name." She glanced down at the paper resting on the counter where Tom had scribbled the references given to him by Strasberg.

"I can help you find those books and articles quickly," she said, and they went off together toward the stacks.

As they walked along, Tom caught himself staring at the young woman.

"Is there something wrong?" she asked.

"Excuse me. You look very much like someone in my life who was very important to me."

"Oh, really? I suspected that you might notice."

"It's striking," Tom said.

"I knew your wife. Every time she came to the library, someone would point out our resemblance. We used to joke with people about being twins. She was such a dear person and I was very sad to hear about her death.

"My father died over a year ago. He collapsed on the street on his way to work. We were told that he died in transit after being picked up by an NHA ambulance. They were extremely vague about the cause of his death and we asked for an investigation. His death was finally ruled a T-effect exit."

"That isn't much comfort, is it?"

"No, we still don't know what really happened. But someday, somehow, I believe this whole crazy system will fall apart."

"You may be right. I see that you're wearing a stoplight badge," Tom said.

"As of this afternoon, every employee at Devan Medical Center has to wear one — orders from Personnel. Yesterday, we had a two hour lecture on Manager Blaine's work. Public Relations insists that we get his name in front of everyone anytime we can. As for myself, I'll wear the badge because I have to if I want to work here. But if you ask me, Manager Blaine's work is pure, unadulterated crap."

Tom smiled at her terminology. Her likeness to Katie was more than skin deep.

Four hours later, Tom handed the stack of books and journals back to the young woman at the desk. He thanked her for her help and left the library.

He picked up dinner at the drive-through of a fast food restaurant and was off toward home with the bag of food on the seat next to him. Each time he stopped at a traffic light, he thought of Taylor Blaine's weird ward and his bizarre treatment methods. Arriving home, he thumbed through the mail, sat down in the kitchen, and finished off his fries and hamburger. He thought about the feisty, young librarian he had met at Devan. She did look like Katie.

The day began catching up with him. He was exhausted, but had reached a new level of understanding about the marasmus syndrome. Once in bed, he had no trouble falling soundly asleep.

Chapter 40

The next morning, Tom checked the hospital office directory to locate Manager Strasberg and confirmed that his office was no longer in the psychiatry department. Replaced by Taylor Blaine as departmental chairman, Strasberg's office had indeed been relocated to the hospital basement.

At nine forty-five, Tom left the Devan hospital lobby through a door marked "Exit To Basement" and walked down a flight of stairs leading to the underworld of the giant health care center. There, where the air was still and a haze of fine dust seemed permanently suspended around him, he wandered down the cream-colored, tiled corridor.

He passed the entrance to the morgue, and further along, the trash disposal area. Workers in gray scrub suits, their hair covered by lilac-colored bonnets, passed by him pushing the large, gray rolling carts piled high with red, plastic bags of odorous, biomedical waste. Wandering further into the building's bowels, beneath the exposed water and sewage pipes near the ceilings, Tom made his way toward Leo Strasberg's office.

The directions given to him by a security guard led him to the end of a long, blind corridor where he came to a varnished oak door with a frosted, glass panel in its upper half. A piece of yellow legal paper was taped to the glass. On it, written in black marker, was the notation, "Department of Psychiatry Annex: Office of Leo Strasberg, HCM, Emeritus Professor of Psychiatry." A barely legible note at the bottom of the paper was obviously scribbled at some time of haste and said, "Please knock before entering."

Tom waited a moment and then rapped tentatively on the glass.

A few moments later, a man who was almost a full head shorter than Tom opened the door. The slight little man was bald and had a beard. His eyes were kind and soft and his facial expression gently asked for the telling of a life story. He wore a crumpled, brown-gray, tweed sport coat with leather patches on the sleeves — a piece of clothing from another era.

"Come in, young man," the old gentleman said. "You are Tom Sullivan, right? I'm Leo Strasberg." He coughed a deep cough, cleared his throat, then invited Tom to sit down in an old, leather covered recliner with worn arm rests. Tom assumed it was the chair he used for his patients.

Strasberg plugged in a hot pot and then sat down across from Tom. "Would you like a cup of tea?" he asked.

"No, thank you," Tom said.

A few moments of silence followed, while Strasberg studied him with a penetrating look.

"And where are you from?" Strasberg asked.

"New York City," Tom replied.

"And the outspoken, young woman, Katie Sullivan, was your wife?"

"Yes."

"Aha, I thought so. You are struggling with death. Your quest has a driven feel to it, like the forces in an opera."

The psychiatrist then poured himself a cup of hot water and placed a tea bag in it. He leaned back, sat quietly for a few moments, and then invited Tom to talk.

Tom told him that he had reviewed the literature in the library as he had advised. He found it to be extremely informative. Extrapolating to the acute marasmus syndrome was easy once the connection was made. He told Strasberg that he suspected that acute marasmus was similar to an "anaclitic depression," as described by Spitz. He had learned that the word "anaclitic" designates a depression that comes about when an infant is deprived of someone to "lean on."

"When we are severely ill, we all become like dependent infants," Tom stated. "We want to be nurtured and cared for."

"Exactly right, and not bad thinking for an internist," Strasberg said with a twinkle in his eye. "René Spitz wrote about that in the nineteen forties," the aging psychiatrist told Tom. "The infants who developed 'anaclitic depression' were bonded to a nurturing mother, then separated and cared for by strangers. Their depression was a kind of grief related to separation and isolation from a mothering person. They became sad, irritable, and withdrawn. They refused food and became emaciated. Past a certain point of deprivation, without a nurturing person to care for the child, the devastating reaction to separation could be irreversible. Many of the youngsters became very ill or died from infections."

"Like patients with the marasmus syndrome," Tom commented.

"Exactly. The acute marasmus syndrome is a similar state, but a more acute and a very rapidly progressing illness. One might view this illness as being like a fulminating 'anaclitic depression' exaggerated by the post-traumatic stress disorder that all of us now suffer in this time of overwhelming exposure to the threat of death. Because of terrorists' activities and our recent immersion in the horrors of the epidemic, we are all more insecure and fragile. We are all more likely to experience these deadly responses to isolation and interpersonal loss."

Strasberg continued, "The psychological injury caused by the automated units is compounded by the technology. The lack of caring relationships denies personage; patients are treated like nonhuman objects, as persons who are nonexistent or dead. And when caregivers react to a living person as if he or she is dead or nonexistent rather than behaving toward them as living, we have the painful situation of social death. You likely read about this in the writings of Kastenbaum or Sudnow.

"A dramatic form of social death is found in Canon's writings in which he refers to tribes where natives are treated as if they are nonexistent. Shunned by their fellow tribesmen, they feel dead and may actually die a 'Voodoo death,' victims of these reflected appraisals.

"Undoubtedly, the patient's experience of social death is devastating. For when there is disruption of the caring relationship —

that activity that affirms a person's aliveness and promotes the experience of human meaning — then life, itself, can quickly be compromised."

"Amazing." Tom was awed by Strasberg's formulations.

"There's more. There's also Engel's 'giving-up — given-up' complex."

Tom looked at Strasberg with a questioning look.

"Engel described this complex as occurring in response to overwhelming feelings of powerlessness or exposure to extreme real or fantasized personal danger. The response is associated with feelings of utter helplessness and hopelessness. The person feels unaided by the environment and inadequate to alter the threatening circumstances. In this 'giving up, given up' state, a person's capacity to fight off pathogenic processes is lessened and susceptibility to illness is likely to be substantially increased.

"And, of course, there's Bowlbys' work on separation, loss, and grief. Reactions of protest and despair, detachment, and disorganization. It's all relevant."

Strasberg took out his handkerchief, held it over his mouth, and coughed. He took a sip of his tea. When his coughing subsided, he began again.

"It is true, Doctor Sullivan, that the new technology reduces the need for human caregivers and it saves money and increases profit. But in the process, our patients are removed from familiar surroundings, distanced from their families, and bereft of care by healing, nurturing people. They are abandoned and are literally starving for care, for human presence. They are no longer treated as being alive and so they perceive themselves as dying or even dead. The person is, in essence, 'given-up' and then 'gives up.'"

"And now they are dying by the thousands," Tom added.

"Yes, once the wasting sets in, there are undoubtedly extensive biochemical and physiological changes. As the syndrome progresses there's massive interference with the immune response. This deceased immunity increases predisposition to infection. The patients develop a sepsis. The infection in the blood leads to multiple organ system failure, and then, death.

"Most regrettably, this horrible epidemic of acute marasmus is, in fact, being manufactured by the creators of the new health care system. They are the system's primary benefactors as well as the purveyors of the syndrome."

Strasberg's explanations made it crystal clear to Tom.

"And you say you talked with Cunningham? You told him all this, the same as you've told me?" Tom asked.

"Of course, I told him."

"Well, I would expect even Cunningham would find your explanation convincing."

"No, as I told you, Cunningham said he thought it all very speculative. He plans to do absolutely nothing."

"That's absurd," Tom said.

"Yes, but it's what I would expect at this point."

Tom then told Strasberg of Carl's recent findings. He told him how the Healers' persistent efforts to relate, nurture, and care for the marasmus syndrome patients had reversed the syndrome. He told him about Samuel Bloch's recovery. Surely, these new findings would convince Cunningham.

"Fascinating, Doctor Sullivan, and certainly consistent with investigators' findings that timely restoration of a nurturing environment by persistent caregivers may overwhelm the effects of isolation and lack of nurturing. But I fear that even proof of this sort will be of no avail. It's too late."

Tom looked at the old psychiatrist skeptically. The wise old professor's pessimism seemed excessive.

"You see, the motivation and intent go beyond mere human maliciousness. It's far more dangerous. It's the power of Destrudo, pure unbridled Destrudo," Strasberg told him."

"The same words you used yesterday," Tom reminded him.

"And the ones I'll use tomorrow and the next day if anyone will listen. We're in precarious times, young man." Strasberg's hands began to tremble. He set his tea cup down. "Let me explain, as I promised I would. I suppose that you're familiar with the Libido theory."

"Yes," Tom told him. "Freud's Libido theory."

"Most people know about Libido, but not as many know about Destrudo, or if they do, they don't really understand it. It has to do with the forces within us that lead us toward destruction. Libido is the life force, and Destrudo is the energy of aggression and destruction. It is the force of death and destruction itself."

"The death instinct?"

"Yes, Destrudo is related. But it's far more than an intellectual concept. It's very real and it's going full throttle right now. The very people that were the caretakers of life have rapidly become the providers of death. The entire system of health care has tipped toward the Destrudo direction."

Strasberg leaned closer. "How long have you been a physician?" he asked.

"About fifteen years."

"Then you know. In medicine, the dictum, *'Primum non nocere,'* 'First do no harm,' recognizes the dangerous junctures where our judgments may cause our actions to either help with healing or do injury and harm. Our work gives us the potential to align our energies with the forces of life or closely by, those of death. In our profession, we walk a fine line.

"Those people who put the 'new medicine' in place have their energies caught up in the forces of death. They cannot listen to anything that would move them to a different course. They have lost sight of human needs outside their own narcissistic ones. They can no longer respond to 'the other.' Do you understand?"

Tom slowly nodded his head yes.

Strasberg continued, "As I told you on the telephone, I'm currently writing a scientific paper entitled, 'The Destrudo Direction.' It deals with this very matter. The conflict is nothing new. Paul Devan himself was caught up in this same struggle. His book, *De Morte Subita,* is good evidence that he too was fascinated with Destrudo. He toyed with it and even studied it in depth. But instead of embracing it and mobilizing his energies toward destruction and death, he mobilized his efforts in a creative direction, toward life. He wrote his classic book on sudden death and then established a medical school to try and help people live. In him, the struggle for creativity and life won out. He devoted his passions to helping others. But for a very long time, he too was absorbed with death."

Tom was speechless. What a strange coincidence that he had looked at the display containing Devan's book the previous evening.

Strasberg continued, "The struggle with Libido and Destrudo is a balancing act every one of us does, you know. It's like a walk on a tight rope. Our profession's heritage is one of dedication to protecting life and promoting healing. In times past, we made good livings; our patients respected us. Then the corporate entrepreneurs and their applied economics took us directly to the market place. And certainly among them there were physicians who took part in this transformation or later rushed to reap rewards. Medicine became big business and economics became primary. And now, there are forces in health care that seem to have embraced power and destruction. We have tipped the other way."

"In your paper, I'm sure you've considered what we might be able to do to reverse the Destrudo direction," Tom asserted.

The old man was thoughtful, but then a saddened look crossed his face.

"No, I'm afraid it has gone too far," he said with remorse. He looked up at the wall at a framed letter in the midst of his hanging diplomas and certificates.

"I had thought there may be an answer. So did the writer of that letter; so have many others, but I fear we have all been proven wrong."

"May I read it?" Tom asked eyeing the letter.

"Of course, please do."

Tom stood before the framed document, an old letter, which had been written to Sigmund Freud. It was dated February, 1921.

My Dear Doctor Freud,

I have just read your essay, "Thoughts for the Times on War and Death," in which you discuss the death instinct. We all live in the shadow of the horrors of the Great War that ended in 1917. I trust that the insight and understanding your brilliant essay conveys will allow us to have some power over the destructiveness that you deem to be an inherent part of the makeup of mankind. It is my humble intention to do my best to teach others about your work in order that we might all learn to control our innate destructive nature.

Your sincere and devoted student,
Doctor Abraham Strasberg

"My father wrote that letter to Freud," Strasberg said. "He studied with the great man in Vienna. Historians found the letter among some old papers in Germany after the second war. One of them forwarded it on to me."

"Your father was a psychiatrist?"

"Yes, and his father too. My grandfather was a Frenchman who worked with the great French school of psychiatry in the nineteenth century. My grandfather immigrated to Austria toward the end of the nineteenth century. We are wanderers," he said with a thin smile. "Not always by choice."

Strasberg paused and looked dreamily toward the letter. He stroked his beard.

"My father was a very wise man," he continued, "but he wasted a great part of his later years. When the Nazis were coming to power, he was able to get our family out of the country and immigrate to America. I was just a small boy, but I remember. He never practiced psychiatry again. He spent his last years going from door to door in Washington, trying to tell the politicians what the Germans were doing to the Jews, but no one would listen. No one would do anything."

"Why didn't they listen?" Tom asked.

"It was a manifestation of the power of Destrudo, similar to now. Initially, people seem to be unable to see, hear, or otherwise detect the forces of Destrudo. Perhaps it is a form of denial. Then it's too late."

"It doesn't sound like what your father did was really a waste, Doctor Strasberg. He did his best to let people know what was happening. That may be the most any of us can do. Perhaps in the end, what he did had some impact."

"Maybe. Perhaps you are right. It would be good to believe that, young man," the old psychiatrist said with misty eyes. He looked up at the letter, and back at Tom. He held his hands together against his lips in a supplicatory manner and gently nodded his head.

"It is a blessing to be hopeful," Strasberg said. "May you find a way to turn these destructive forces around."

Chapter 41

After his visit with Leo Strasberg, Tom returned to his office at Starr. When he entered, the e-mail alert icon was blinking on his desktop monitor. He punched in his password and then clicked on the mailbox. A new letter appeared on the list and when he opened it, the message read: "CALL MANAGER ROBERT KAPLAN AT 391-8904 AROUND 5:30 p.m."

Bob Kaplan? It's about time I heard from him. But, why would he be calling me now? Tom jotted down the name and number on a slip of paper, placed it on his desk, and left his office to make his rounds.

After his rounds, he called Laura at her CelestaCare office. She recognized his voice.

"Free for lunch?" he asked.

"Sure," she answered.

"I told you I would call if I had any news about the marasmus syndrome. Well, I have news."

"Thank God. I can't wait to hear."

"I'll be there for you around noon," Tom told her.

Laura waited for Tom beneath the CelestaCare corporate building portico. At noon he pulled up in his Jeep Cherokee. Soon they were on their way.

"I met with the Devan psychiatrist Leo Strasberg this morning," Tom told her.

"I thought you were going to meet with Blaine."

"I did, yesterday. He's a screwball. But Strasberg is solid; he was one of my psychiatry professors at Devan. Before all the changes in medicine, he was a much respected man. He confirmed my suspicions about the marasmus syndrome."

"That it has an emotional basis?"

"Exactly, and it's potentially reversible."

"Thank God."

"But Doctor Strasberg doubts that there's much we can do about it at this point."

He led her through Doctor Strasberg's formulations. She was amazed. He told her about Strasberg's discussion with Cunningham and explained the psychiatrist's conclusion that little could be done to turn the destructive process around. She paled when he described the power of the Destrudo direction.

"I feel so guilty," she said.

"It's not the technology; it's how people use it. You didn't build Destrudo into the programs, Laura. You were invested in improving life; you wanted more people to have medical care. Destruction wasn't your goal."

"How do you know that? Maybe it was unconscious. Perhaps I am involved in the Destrudo direction."

"I know you. Clearly you were used. CelestaCare and Ken kept you in the dark."

They lunched together, then took a quiet walk through the Devan campus. When they neared the Green, she pointed out the new, giant, digital, computer-driven, television display she was installing at Devan for CelestaCare's consumer education programs.

"It's huge," Tom said.

"The display screen is one hundred feet high and two hundred feet wide. The image is projected by a complex new computer system cable hookup. It's totally digital. With the high quality, in-depth sound equipment and the fine-tuned resolution, the reality-factor rating in the picture approaches 100%."

"Impressive," Tom said.

Tom drove her back to CelestaCare. "We'll think of some way to be heard," were her final words before she shut the car door. It was the very encouragement Sullivan needed.

Back in his office, he paced the floor. He glanced at the acute marasmus syndrome chart and saw the still ascending curve of new patients. He looked at the picture of Katie on the shelf next to his desk. An image of the child in pediatrics rushed to his mind. Then, Samuel Bloch. Enough is enough, he told himself. He grabbed his gray coat and his stethoscope and headed for the wards.

Tom rounded on every unit. He told the managers they were to feel free to interact with the patients. No more of the Clark's hands-off approach. "Ignore the NHA regulations," he said. "If anyone asks what you're doing, tell them I personally gave you orders to relate to the patients."

An hour later, Clark called to question his behavior.

"What are you doing? Have you gone mad?"

"No, I've gone sane," Tom told him. "And you had best leave my new instructions to the managers as I gave them."

"This is treason. You know about the Mulholland Health Care Act. This is treason. I'll have you behind bars."

Tom slammed down the receiver. The telephone rang again and this time Clark threatened to have him deaccessed.

In response to his threat, Tom calmly replied, "You wouldn't dare Clark. I know too much and I have too much clout."

"What do you know?" Clark asked.

"I know that you were doing studies on human interaction deprivation in automated care in the New Direction section. I suspect you know a lot about patient isolation. And I know that you already know what I found out today about the acute marasmus syndrome. While you're trying to come up with some cheap way of managing it, or not planning to deal with it at all, thousands of people are dying."

There was silence at the other end of the line.

That afternoon, Tom sent an e-mail memorandum to Ken Clark. He typed the message in rapidly:

TO: KENNETH CLARK, CHIEF, HEALTH CARE ADMINISTRATION, STAR MEMORIAL HOSPITAL:
TOMORROW, I WILL BEGIN CONDUCTING CONFERENCES AT STARR TO TEACH THE STAFF ABOUT THE IMPORTANCE OF HUMAN INTERACTION WITH PATIENTS. IF YOU INTERFERE, I WILL SPEAK WITH THE MEDIA. YOU ARE TO CONTACT

RAY CUNNINGHAM AND HAVE HIM INSTITUTE THE
SAME KIND OF INSTRUCTION AT DEVAN — STAT!
THOMAS SULLIVAN, M.D.

An hour later, Tom's e-mail display appeared. Clark had sent a response. "WILL YOU BACK US ON TAYLOR BLAINE'S FINDINGS? REQUEST IMMEDIATE REPLY."

Tom sent back a terse response. "TAYLOR BLAINE IS FULL OF SHIT!"

Ken replied, "THERE'S NO WAY YOU CAN PROVE ANYTHING. YOU'RE ONLY GETTING YOURSELF INTO DEEPER TROUBLE. OUR METHODS WILL BLOW YOU AND ALL OF YOUR THEORIES OUT OF THE WATER."

It was almost five-thirty. Tom remembered the message in his desk about returning Kaplan's call. He reached for the phone to dial.

What does Kaplan want? He never said a word to me after Katie's death and wasn't even at the memorial service. He won't return calls; it's strange behavior.

Three rings and no answer. Then a fourth ring. An answering device switched on.

"Hi, this is the Kaplan residence," the recording said. "Can't get to the phone now, but leave a message if you want. And remember… life's filled with small steps for human beings and giant leaps for humankind."

Tom couldn't help but be amused. More of the "giant leap" stuff. Kaplan and his interest in space travel never stops.

The beep went off. Tom debated for a brief moment about leaving a message, then decided to speak.

"Bob, this is Tom Sullivan. I'm returning your call. It's about five-thir…"

"Hold it," a man's voice said. "Let me cut this damned thing off."

"Sure."

"There." There was another beep. "Now, Doctor Sullivan?"

"Is this Bob Kaplan?"

"For sure," the man said. "Doctor Sullivan, I need to talk with you."

"It took you long enough to call, Bob."

"I don't blame you for feeling angry, but I had my reasons."

"Go ahead."

"Not on the phone."

"Let me get my appointment book. I'll find a time for you to come over to Starr."

"No, not there either. I'll meet you at Flint's — the magazine shop."

"I would never have thought of meeting you there," Tom said with surprise.

"Neither would anyone else. Please. The magazine shop – Flint's." There was a note of distress in Kaplan's voice.

"When?" Tom responded.

"In about an hour and a half, around seven. It's important, very important."

"I'll be there," Tom said.

"Take a look at a copy of *The Opera Review*," Kaplan told him. "It's on the rack, halfway down the store on the right."

"I'll just be browsing."

"No, I remember once that you told me about your love of opera. I believe you said that *Turandot* was your favorite."

"You remembered that?"

"I remember a lot of what you had to say, Dr. Sullivan. When you get to Flint's look at a copy of *The Opera Review*. It's good that you know a lot about opera, because we're in one."

"What do you mean?"

"You'll see."

"I'll be there, Bob," Tom said. "Flint's, around seven. For sure."

Tom was hanging up the telephone, thoughtfully puzzled by the conversation, when Jeanne Donnely came through the door.

"Oh excuse me," she said. "I didn't know you were on the phone."

"I'm through."

"I just wanted to drop off this stack of print-outs for you to look over."

She set them on the edge of his desk and looked down and read the name and telephone number on the slip of paper Tom held out in front of him.

"Damn, you're intrusive!" Tom said. "If I didn't know better, I'd say someone has you watching me."

"No, just watching out for you," she said. "Now what in the world does that guy want with you? He's the guy who took care of Katie at Devan, isn't he?"

"You know the answer to that, Jeanne. But he's calling me, not you."

He folded the slip of paper, placed it in his desk drawer, and began to get ready to leave for the day.

"Nervy guy," she said shaking her head. "Nervy guy. Protested the title change. I'd stay away from him if I were you."

"I believe that's my decision, don't you?" he asserted.

"You've already made Clark furious — real furious. That's serious business. He says you're interfering with the work of God."

"Whose God?"

Her eyes flashed anger. "Have it your way, Manager," she said, and walked out the door.

Chapter 42

Flint's Books and Magazines occupied the first floor of an old, two story, red brick building in a block long strip of small shops and restaurants across the street from the Devan University campus. Tom hesitated briefly outside the newsstand entrance and watched the throngs of students walk up and down the sidewalk outside the shops and eateries. The scene was almost the same as when he had first arrived on campus years before.

As he passed through the arched doorway to enter Flint's, he saw the old, cork bulletin board on the wall in the entrance arcade. He quickly scanned the announcements for self-help groups, activist lectures, and the scattered, thumbtacked index card listings of used bicycles, furniture for sale, and apartments for rent.

Inside, he passed the cash register where three people stood in line to buy evening newspapers. He made his way past a table piled with discount books and walked down an aisle toward the racks of magazines in the back of the store. He excused himself as he squeezed passed four or five men and women absorbed in perusing the periodicals they held. Slowly, he moved toward the area where he saw Bob Kaplan leaning against a rack, studying a copy of the magazine, *Out Into Space*.

He moved closer to Kaplan, found a place where there were no other people standing, and looked over the tiers of magazines in front of him. On the shelf near him was the latest copy of *The Opera Review*. Tom picked it up and thumbed through its pages. Near its center was a preview of an upcoming television presentation of *Pagliacci.*

His eyes darted to a picture depicting the vicious stabbing scene at the end of Leoncavallo's opera. The photograph captured the point when the staged comedy within the opera becomes all too real and Canio, the cuckolded clown, stabs his stage wife, Nedda in a jealous rage. Tom read the description beneath the picture: "In the play within the opera, the audience watches in shock while the farce becomes reality and the dying Nedda calls out her true lover, Silvio's, name. As he rushes forward, he too is stabbed by the half-crazed Canio."

The final dramatic words of Pagliacci ran through his mind: "La commedia et finite...," "The comedy is over..." Some comedy, he thought, momentarily remembering the scene of Ken Clark sharpening his knife while alluding to Tom's relationship with Laura. He put the magazine back on the shelf and picked up another one.

Dressed in a hunter green hiking jacket with the hood thrown back behind his head, his black, curly hair wet with perspiration, Bob Kaplan edged closer to where Tom was standing.

Tom watched him move among the browsing customers. He remembered Kaplan as a third year medical student. Together they had drained fluid from an air-starved dying patient's chest cavity to help him breathe. Working together, the two had inserted a long needle into the man's chest and removed fluid from the space around the man's cancerous lung. Kaplan had calmed the patient with reassuring words throughout the procedure. "Lie still now, it's going to be all right. Easy now, easy," he had said repeatedly. It was then that Tom had first been impressed with Kaplan's gentle way of relating with patients.

Kaplan could also be antagonistic and rebellious with authority. His personality traits gave him the character that made him stand out as being of a different cut than the other student doctors in his class. When he protested the new title, "Manager", Tom was not surprised. Tom had concluded that Bob's failure to contact him after Katie's death was out of character.

Finally, the two men came close enough to speak.

"How goes it, Doctor Sullivan," Kaplan said in a whisper. He kept his eyes focused on the magazine.

"Careful with the 'Doctor' title in public," Tom said, and continued browsing.

Bob Kaplan put the magazine he was holding back on the shelf, glanced at the rows of magazines for a moment, and then took down another and began to turn its pages. "I'm sorry. I'm not going to call you Manager. I'm not about to give up my heroes and have you all ride off into the sunset. You'll always be Doctor Sullivan to me."

"Then call me 'Tom.' You know it's fine with me, but addressing me as 'Doctor Sullivan' is particularly dangerous for you."

A young woman walked by, excusing herself as she passed. Kaplan was quiet while she moved by, but after a few moments, he spoke again.

"I'm deeply sorry about what happened to your wife."

"I guess you did everything you could. Right?"

"I did," Kaplan said.

"I wish you would have contacted me. I can't say I wasn't angry. It was out of character for you, Bob. I kept waiting to hear from you."

"Couldn't. At least not then. I can understand your anger, but I was very upset myself and also, I didn't want to lose my perch. You're doing okay?"

"I'm okay, Bob. But what's this all about?" Tom asked.

"I'm sorry to have to meet like this, but I thought it best under the circumstance. I think I'm on to something, but I'm not exactly sure what."

Tom listened intently. He was having trouble keeping from looking directly at Kaplan. He forced himself to continue perusing the magazine.

Kaplan leaned closer and whispered. "Over the past year or so, at least five of my patients have died in *exactly* the same way."

"I don't understand," Tom whispered.

"The five deaths were all T-effect exits," Kaplan said, putting his foot up on the lower shelf of the magazine rack.

"That's not unusual. There are a lot of those occuring. Too many. At Starr, we…"

"No," Kaplan interrupted. "I'm not making myself clear. I mean the ways that these patients died were identical — absolutely identical — the pulses, the blood pressures, the respiratory rates and patterns, the blood work, even the electrocardiograms, everything. They were all *absolutely* identical."

"What are you saying, Bob?"

"These five patients died identically. All their monitor tracings, all their laboratory work, everything about the clinical picture around their deaths was exactly the same. I mean exactly the same, like a textbook picture. Do you understand?"

Tom's thoughts raced back to his third year in medical school. He remembered reaching the clinical clerkships, studying the various syndromes, and being shocked that patients did not conform to the textbook descriptions. Every patient with pneumococcal pneumonia did not present as having the night before, developed chest wall pain when breathing in deeply. Every pneumonia patient had not spiked a high fever. Every patient did not cough up rusty colored phlegm. There were a multitude of variations. Every patient suffered a disease a little differently.

And the deaths were different also. Every one of them was individual and uniquely different in some way. Carl Hammerstone had taught him that the real skill in medicine lay in appreciating the subtle differences in individuals. That was what Carl felt medicine was really all about.

Now Kaplan was telling him about another curious side effect of the new system that fits with its reductionistic way of dealing with people. For any given illness, the automated units treated every consumer the same. There was no consideration of individual differences. Now he was hearing about a new twist in the system: even the clinical picture surrounding these patients' terminal events and deaths were identical. They were generic deaths — exactly the same.

Kaplan's face became somber. "I need to apologize. I couldn't talk with you when your wife was admitted. The regulations prohibited it and my reaccess status was still fragile. I couldn't speak with you after she died. I was too overwhelmed myself. Her clinical picture — it was so absolutely clear cut. Something was wrong, but I didn't know what. I've never seen anything like it. I couldn't get the scene out of my mind."

"Her cardiac arrest?"

"She was one of the five, Tom — the first. Her terminal event was just like these other patients I'm telling you about. All of them had identical cardiac arrests. It's like I was listening to the same song being played over and over."

"You're sure of this?" Tom queried.

"I'm certain. The clinical pictures and all the findings down to the last heartbeat were exactly the same."

"I've never really understood why Katie died. She was doing so well. She was completely alert, and…"

"You don't want to hear me, Doctor Sullivan. There's something very screwy about five people's deaths being *exactly* the same."

Suddenly, what Kaplan was trying to tell him became blatantly clear. "Oh my God," Tom said under his breath. He tried to exercise restraint in the public setting.

"Sorry, I didn't mean to push, but there's more," Kaplan said. "I've talked secretly to other managers. All of the T-effect deaths — they're cardiac arrests or massive bleeds, pulmonary emboli, anaphylactic shock. Acute, sudden deaths, and they're all like classical textbook clinical pictures; it's like they've been lifted right off the pages of a medical text.

"Every one of these patients seemed to be been getting well. Then bang! It was over! Not an easy fact to live with."

"You reported this to your supervisors, didn't you?" Tom asked.

"Sure, I completed an 'Unusual Circumstances Report' on each of the patients.

And each time, I got the same reply."

"Which was?"

"Administrative bullshit that amounted to 'forget it' and a reminder that I'm a rehabilitated, reaccessed manager. I haven't been able to get anywhere with the information."

Tom rolled his eyes.

Bob continued, "Then there's the Mandell situation."

"Go on."

"I was one of the managers taking care of Mandell. He was doing fine too. They say he injured his knee having his MRI. After that, he needed bedrest to keep off of his leg. Otherwise he was fine, just like Manager Sullivan and the others. They say he had a pulmonary embolus. They had it on the monitors and some crazy bastard

259

recorded it. Caught the actual death scene on video. I saw it later. It was super grim."

"How's that related?"

"Mandell's death. The clinical picture. It was too damned classical. It was too much like a textbook pulmonary embolus — like the cardiac arrests. Like someone has put together a too-perfect case report. Too textbook!"

"Why haven't more people noticed this?"

"They have. It's not a matter of noticing it. It's a matter of being able to do something about it. They've got us by the balls. All of the T-effect deaths that I know of have been on units that are run by rehabilitated, reaccessed personnel. I'm sure I'm not the first person to bring this up in an Unusual Circumstance Report. Other managers must have reported it too. But the records are whisked away to Washington, handled by the administrators, and that's the end of it."

"So, now what?" Tom asked.

"I'm going to have to hand you the baton," Kaplan said. "I have some ideas what this is all about, but I can't be sure."

"This is mind boggling."

"I agree," Kaplan said.

"What do you suggest?"

"You might want to run this by Laura Clark," Kaplan suggested. "She's an insider, one of them. A friend in hospital informatics told me that she was working on Devan's automated system computers the very day your wife died. You're tight with her and if you ask me, she knows all about this. In fact, I would suspect that if she wanted to, she could give you an earful."

Tom swallowed. He felt a sinking feeling in his chest. He thought a moment, then spoke, "What about you. How can I help you, Bob?"

"You showed up and listened. That's enough. It's not all on me now." He sighed deeply, then surveyed the crowded store. "That's it; that's all I can tell you now." He closed his magazine and returned it to the rack.

Tom glanced toward the front of the newsstand. A young student had pushed open the door. Behind him was Jeanne Donnely. She took a newspaper from the rack, looked around, then saw Tom. She caught his eye; he saw her smile. She started toward him, then looked beyond him toward Bob Kaplan. She stopped abruptly. The smile faded. She turned and moved quickly toward the cash register.

"You know that woman?" Kaplan asked with concern.

"Yes, she works for me."

"You mean she works for CelestaCare. She and that woman who's been standing across the way watching us. They're spies for CelestaCare and the NHA."

Tom glanced across at the woman Kaplan had mentioned. She was putting something in her purse.

"I've got to go now," Kaplan said. "There are more planets to explore." He looked at Tom and smiled.

"Thanks Bob."

Bob Kaplan walked around the magazine racks toward the newspapers. He picked up a copy of the late edition of *The Middleside Times*, and took his place in the checkout line to pay for it. A few minutes later, he gave the cashier a dollar bill, got his change and walked out of the store. Tom watched through the window as Bob walked his bike across the busy street dodging in and out between the moving cars without waiting for the light to change to stop the traffic.

Chapter 43

Tom punched in the CelestaCare Health Enterprises number on his cell phone. He listened to the lengthy recorded message touting the many marvels of CelestaCare, and after hearing a complex menu, finally reached a switchboard.

"This is Manager Thomas Sullivan. We're having a problem with one of the automated units at Starr Memorial. I'm trying to locate Laura Clark," he said to the operator. "I thought she might still be in the building."

"I can try the Informatics lab if you like. Sometimes she's there quite late."

"Please do," Tom said.

The operator rang the extension, and almost immediately he heard Laura's voice.

"Laura, it's Tom," he said.

"Hi," she said. "I'm just finishing up some work in the lab."

"Listen, I've had this crazy thing happen. Bob Kaplan just gave me some very disturbing information."

"About what?"

There was silence.

"Tom, are you there?"

"Yes, but once I tell you, you're going to be involved in this nightmare with me. It might be best that you not be."

"I want to be involved, and besides, I'm already involved," she said. "Now what is this about?"

"It's information about the T-effect exits. It might explain Katie's death and maybe the deaths of many others. I need your help, but it could spell big-time trouble."

"I'll do anything I can."

"What time will you be finishing there?"

"Whenever you need me to finish."

"We need to talk privately."

"Why don't you come here? I'll put on some coffee."

"To CelestaCare — this late? You've got to be kidding. Someone will see us and then you'll really be implicated in all of this."

Laura paused for a moment, then spoke. "I'm sick of being so cautious, Tom. We have to do what we have to do."

"What about Ken?"

"Ken's gone to Washington. He left, very upset. I think Wade called some kind of special meeting. He won't be back until tomorrow morning."

"I'll be there in fifteen minutes."

"I'll meet you at the front door. Bring your Starr Memorial pass. It'll get you in."

"You're sure that's what you want to do."

"I'm sure. I'll be waiting for you," she said.

Later, in Laura's CelestaCare office, Tom told Laura about his meeting with Kaplan. She listened, absorbed in his story. The fear that he saw appear in her eyes let him know that she felt as unsettled about Kaplan's information as he did. He was sure that she was not connected with the T-effect deaths as Kaplan had suggested.

He drew in a deep breath. "Laura, Katie didn't die of natural causes," he said. "She was murdered. Now, I'm certain."

"For God's sake, Tom. What are you saying?"

"Everything Kaplan told me points in that direction."

"Sure they were upset with Katie, and I suspect with others too, but murders? That would be absolute madness."

"Katie was over the worst of her illness. A cardiac arrest at her age would be rare. Whatever she died from had more to do with her being in the hospital in that vulnerable situation than with her illness. I believe her death was some kind of sick expedient solution. It may have been because she was becoming too outspoken. She had too much clout at Devan.

I don't know exactly how it was done," he continued, "but I suspect that it was an entry into the program that delivered a lethal drug. Maybe that caused the cardiac arrest. There must be a way for them to enter commands into the system to make it do whatever they want."

Laura looked away, uneasy.

"They called Katie's death a T-effect exit, but I believe that the T-effect is a hoax," Tom said. "I believe it's a form of blatant deception to allow them to manipulate outcomes. They can use the automated system to do whatever they choose. So far, the cover-up has worked well."

Laura looked dismayed.

"So do you believe that what I'm saying is madness?" he asked.

"No, unfortunately, you could be right on target. I've never been allowed to view the actual programs of T-effect exit patients. They don't trust me enough to let me have that kind of access. They know that I could spot a false entry into the programs.

But I can tell you this. The central mainframe computer in the National Computer Center is, for all practical purposes, a direct connection with any consumer, on any automated unit, anywhere, any place in the country. I can also tell you that it wouldn't be difficult to enter the system and alter a program or alter a patient's treatment. All a person would need is the passwords to get through the program locks."

"Then we're on the right track."

"The commands could come from anywhere, even at a distance," Laura continued. "It's no different than the points bracelet monitoring system. Each day when the point reading is taken on a patient, it goes by internet to Washington. There, the programs automatically change the treatment methods on the basis of the number of points remaining. That's a Washington mainframe function. The treatment program changes to make it economically fit with the person's points. Other changes could be made just as easily."

"Damn. Now that the selection programs are in place, they can easily manipulate those too," Tom said.

"Yes, their choices are as close to the consumer as the main frame computer keyboards."

Tom thought for a moment. "Do you have the passwords? Can you get into the mainframe system?"

"Not legally. An unauthorized entry into the mainframe is a very serious criminal offense. They can track a break-in to the exact terminal."

"We need to see those records."

"Then I'll have to get to work," Laura said picking up her notebook computer and a box of CD-Recordable disks.

Walking through the CelestaCare lobby, Tom and Laura passed by the security desk. One of the guards was sitting on the edge of his seat watching television.

"Goodnight Dr. Clark," he said, never looking up from the television. "Looks like they've finally gone after those Healers."

Tom and Laura stopped abruptly. "What?" Tom asked. Their eyes fixed on the screen.

A newscaster was speaking: "…repeating this bulletin: in the face of what amounted to futile resistance, at 6:00 a.m. this morning, troops evicted a group known as the 'Healers' from the makeshift hospitals they operated on Warehouse row in Middleside. The facility is located only a short distance away from the pinnacle of American Health Care, CelestaCare-Devan University Health Care Center. Unfortunately, force became necessary when the Healers barricaded themselves inside the building, encouraging the families and patients with whom they worked to join with them in the resistance.

"Minutes ago, in a news conference, a spokesman for the National Health Agency told why this action was necessary."

Standing in front of a seal of the United States, the government official spoke:

It has unfortunately been necessary for the government to put a stop to the activities of the irresponsible group of individuals known as the 'Healers.' The National Health Agency, under the informed and able leadership of Director Alexander Wade, has determined that it is no longer in the best interest of the public to have this band of improperly equipped, medically incompetent individuals operating with the misguided conviction that their efforts are beneficial to the people.

The President has ordered the closing of these dangerous facilities and will prohibit any further delivery of health care by the Healers. Once again, you may be assured that the National Health Agency is acting in your best interest to insure that you will continue to receive the best in competent health care. God Bless the National Health Agency...

"This looks like more Destrudo," Tom said. "The NHA will do whatever is needed to keep the truth from coming out."

On the screen, there were scenes of the rout of the Healers by the National Guard. The live newscast showed vivid details of the destruction: the entrances to the warehouse were sealed with boards; large piles of equipment were stacked in front of the building; bonfires of sheets and bedrolls burned in the streets.

Ignoring the screams of protest from patients' families, emergency health care teams rushed the sick to NHA ambulances waiting nearby. Members of the Investigative Division took Healers into custody, dragging some away by the collars of their white coats.

"Hammerstone. Have they said anything about a manager named Carl Hammerstone?" Tom asked the security guard.

The guard turned to Tom. "He's the leader isn't he? Oh yeah. They showed him earlier, near the beginning of the coverage. He tried to keep the forces from entering the warehouse. He was injured. There was blood all over his face. But a few minutes ago they said he escaped."

Tom's shoulders dropped. Laura squeezed his arm.

"It's about time they blew those Healers out of the water," the security guard remarked. "Bastards couldn't fall in line with all the other managers."

Then Tom noted the purple Theotechnicist "T" around the guard's neck.

Tom and Laura left through the main CelestaCare entrance. The wide, glass entrance doors to the lobby parted automatically and they walked though. They stood for a moment on the broad steps in front of the building.

The famous Spanish sculptor, Juan Pallado's thirty-six feet tall, stainless steel statue of Caesar's Assassination towered imposingly over them on the entrance plaza. CelestaCare recently purchased the piece of art for close to a million dollars. Tom looked up at the huge, purple-lettered CelestaCare International sign attached to the building facade, then glanced at the massive Roman figures engaged in the violent act of murder. On Caesar's face, Pallado had fashioned an expression of uncanny agony. On Brutus' face there was a cool, sadistic half-smile.

Tom studied the statue. Before he left Starr to meet Bob, he had glanced at an afternoon newspaper. The paper carried a story about the President's emergency hospital admission for what sounded to be no more than a gastrointestinal virus — hardly a basis for inpatient treatment. And the admission was to a Washington CelestaCare hospital rather than the usual military hospital at Andrews Air Force Base. The President was on an automated unit with a central line. Now it occurred to Tom that the admission might be a ruse. Might Alexander Wade be the up and coming Brutus?

The row of lilac-colored National Health Agency flags that jutted out from the CelestaCare building facade cracked noisily in the April wind. Tom thrust his hand upward toward the waving flags and made a hand sign that spoke his true feelings.

Then, he turned and looked at Laura walking next to him.

"Thank God you came into my life," he said to her. "I couldn't deal with this alone."

"Thank God, you came into mine," Laura replied.

Chapter 44

The next morning, when Tom walked into his office, Jeanne Donnely handed him a lilac-colored envelope.

"What's this?" he asked.

"Open it. Now!" she said insistently. "There's going to be a party."

He opened the envelope and found a formal invitation engraved in formal type. It said:

> The National Health Agency, in collaboration with CelestaCare Health Care Enterprises, cordially invites you to attend scientific proceedings to examine current clinical and research considerations regarding the acute marasmus syndrome. The conference will convene in the historic Franklin Amphitheater at the Devan University Health Care Center...

An R.S.V.P. was requested and admission required the presentation of the invitation at the door.

"You *will* be there, won't you?" Jeanne Donnely asked. "Unquestionably you'll be one of the star contributors."

He turned to answer her, and then noticed. She was wearing the lilac-colored uniform of a NHA nurse.

"You're damned right I'll be there," he said, eyeing her outfit. "Look for me."

"You'll be swimming upstream against a strong current," she said, "like your friend Carl Hammerstone."

"Get out of my office, Jeanne."

She gave him a condescending smile, then strutted through the door.

The next morning, on his way to the amphitheater, Tom sidestepped the thick network television cables running to the famous room where countless medical deliberations had taken place. In the round, walnut paneled amphitheater with its worn walnut benches, Paul Devan, himself, had once presented his brilliant, detailed clinical descriptions of sudden deaths. More recently, at the meeting organized by Tom and the epidemiologist, Peter Hansen, a group of eminent microbiologists met there to confer about the causes of the epidemic. Now the room was filling with over one hundred acute progressive marasmus syndrome conference invitees.

Outside one of the entrances, two security guards had taken aside a grey coated manager. Short in stature, with curly black hair, the manager had his back turned to Tom, but Tom immediately recognized him as Bob Kaplan. Bob grasped a camera tripod in one hand and a molded black, plastic camera case in the other. As Tom came closer, the taller security guard, who towered over the shorter manager spoke gruffly to Kaplan.

"Okay, what's in that case?" the guard asked.

"It's no big deal, just a video camera," Kaplan responded matter of factly.

"*Just* a video camera? Are you part of the official conference camera crew?"

"No, I'm a manager on the staff here at Devan," Bob Kaplan answered with a straight face.

"A Devan manager, hmmm? Well, we have orders. No recordings, no video cameras, and no photographs of these proceedings unless you're a member of Ms. Weeks' special media crew. They all have special badges, like that one," the guard said, pointing toward a woman holding a camcorder. She wore a lilac-colored, plastic badge clipped to her pocket and stood a few feet away talking with Carole Weeks. "I don't see any ID badge like that on you, buster," he said.

"But I'm not filming the proceedings, I'm filming Ms. Weeks," Kaplan said, raising his voice, "...every move she makes. I want to preserve her spectacular style of producing and directing for future generations of media students."

"You're what?" the guard asked incredulously.

"Recording Ms. Weeks' production technique. Her brilliance, her aplomb, her style," Bob said even more loudly.

Carole Weeks, only a short distance away, could not help but overhear him. She stopped her own conversation abruptly.

"Her work is superb! It's brilliant," Kaplan continued. "What she's done for the country has helped us take a giant leap, sir, a giant leap indeed."

Kaplan had captured Carole Weeks' attention. Her head was turned and she listened with curiosity to the conversation. In a few moments, she moved closer and joined the three men.

Carole Weeks was dressed in her most daring outfit to date. She wore a lilac-colored, skin tight dress with large, open, diamond shaped areas cut out both in front and in back.

Tom stopped and stood off to the side, watching the action unfold.

"What's going on here?" Carole Weeks asked. She looked Bob Kaplan over and inspected the tripod and the camera case he held.

"Ms. Weeks, we've told this man — no unauthorized videos of the proceedings. He insists that he isn't videoing the proceedings; he says he's videoing you," the guard said.

"Videoing me? Why that's so dear. And who is this lovely gentleman who wants to film me? He looks familiar," she said.

"He says he's a Devan manager," the guard said. "He has a video camera, Ms. Weeks, and he says he..."

Bob interrupted. "Yes, the man's absolutely right, Ms. Weeks. Like many people, I have an interest in your media productions. I want to capture your work for posterity, and produce a living record of how you create these spectacular NHA events."

"How thoughtful," Carole Weeks said, glancing downward. "And just who are you?"

Kaplan gave her a salute off his forehead with the fingertips of his right hand. Then he bowed. "I'm Manager Robert Kaplan, ma'am, at your service. What you're doing here today will definitely be a giant leap and the way you bring it about should be recorded so that it will last forever. It's people like you that make the future happen."

Clearly Kaplan was engaging Carole Weeks' narcissism.

"Why, that is so gracious of you. I am indeed flattered," she said, as she studied the large camera case that he held. "Hmmm, isn't that a Shinakawa 125 SX digital camcorder," she said noting the markings on the case. "Why that's the newest in digital cameras, the very one that's on its way to Mars. You're an amateur and you own a camera like that?"

"Nothing but the best to film giant leaps, Ms. Weeks," Kaplan said. "You probably know that this camera is an update of the ones used on the NASA trips to the moon."

She chuckled as she nodded yes. "Don't you move. Wait here a moment."

Carole Weeks walked over to Devan's Director of Public Relations. She cupped her hand around the man's ear. When she finished whispering, she listened as he said something back to her. Soon, she returned to where Kaplan was standing.

"You don't come with the best of recommendations," she told Kaplan. The Devan Public Relations Director says that you're a troublemaker. He says to watch you closely. He says you're a case of 'caveat emptor.'"

"Some people feel that way. You be the judge."

"You seem to have your head on pretty straight to me. And you look sincere enough. I'm a pretty good judge of character. I'm going to let you do your thing," she said.

Kaplan winked at her and gave her a "thumbs up" sign.

She dismissed the guards, took a media pass from her waist belt carryall, and handed it to Kaplan. He sat the tripod and camera down next to him and looked over her gift. Laminated in plastic, the card said, "MEDIA PASS — ISSUED BY CAROLE WEEKS, CHIEF, PUBLIC RELATIONS DIVISION, NATIONAL HEALTH AGENCY." Wasting no time, Kaplan penned his name in the signature space on the back of the card.

"When you have your documentary edited and finished, do give me a ring," Carole Weeks told him. "I want to see that recording."

"You bet you will," Kaplan said, beaming. He took the badge and affixed the clip to his pocket.

Tom Sullivan entered the amphitheater, found a seat, and surveyed the scene.

Draped festoons of red, white, and blue, star-studded flag cloth ringed the entire circumference of the old amphitheater. Above the stage, ten foot high replicas of the logos of the National Health Agency and CelestaCare Health hung side by side from thin wires.

Kaplan soon entered the amphitheater, armed with his camcorder. Tom was seated near the aisle on the second tier of benches. Kaplan moved toward him, nodded a friendly hello, and stood by the seat next to him.

"Mind if I sit here?" Bob asked.

"Of course not," Tom said.

"No need for Flint's Book and Magazine Shop meetings now," Kaplan said as he set up the tripod between his legs and began mounting the camera. "They know quite well that we're on to them. But the NHA is so powerful and cocky and sure of their PR, they really don't give a damn."

Tom looked around suspiciously.

"This is going to be quite an affair," Kaplan said to Tom. He adjusted the tripod and screwed the camera in place on its mount. "Wade, Cunningham, Clark, Deminhart: the main players, the whole group; they'll all be here in the same room. We would have had the President too, but I understand that the poor bastard is sick."

Tom continued to look around the room eyeing the crowd.

"Look at that Weeks character," Kaplan said. He pointed his video camera toward her and watched her though the viewfinder. "She's really something, isn't she? I love to watch her work," he said, shaking his head in disbelief. "She's a phenomenon — the lead soprano in today's opera. What she has done is undoubtedly one giant leap for mankind."

"A giant leap for mankind?" Tom commented. "You're stuck on that phrase. You keep saying it."

Suddenly Kaplan looked up from the viewfinder toward Tom.

"Because it's true, Doctor Sullivan. I say it because it's absolutely true!" His voice and the look on his face had become totally serious.

"I heard you say it on camera in an interview when they installed the first central line, and now here," Tom said. "I'm not sure that I would agree that the central line, what Carole Weeks does, or for that matter, any parts of this crazy screwed-up system are really giant leaps forward for mankind."

"Come on Doctor Sullivan, who the hell said anything about giant leaps forward? These aren't giant leaps forward; they're giant leaps backward — way backward. This is primitive stuff, regressive primitive stuff," Bob said, leaning back as if he were going to fall backward to emphasize his point.

Tom broke into a wide smile.

"Whoaaa, steady now," Kaplan said, flapping his arms and regaining his upright position. The two men looked at each other grinning.

"With the information you gave me, I think I'm beginning to understand," Tom said quietly.

"I would suspect so," Kaplan said. He continued putting the camera together and adjusting it.

"But Laura is on our team, not CelestaCare's," Tom said. "I'm confident of that."

"Then we have a chance," Kaplan confided. "I have a plan that involves using her new, giant, digital screen on the Devan campus. But pulling it off will be difficult, dangerous, and maybe even impossible."

"You know more than you've said, don't you?"

"Yeah," Bob said. "As the saying goes, I know too much, far too much for my own good."

There was a flurry of activity near the door. Secret service men entered the room and formed a guarded pathway. Alexander Wade followed and took his place on the first row of benches in the center. Brandt and Cunningham were with him. A personal aide escorted Senator Deminhart into the hall. He paused a moment near Wade, waiting to be invited to join him, but Wade only nodded a cool hello. Deminhart looked around and moved toward a seat some distance away. Soon Ken Clark came in, accompanied by Jeanne Donnely in her lilac-colored nursing uniform.

Kaplan was back at the viewfinder recording Carole Weeks' activity.

"Yeah, they probably know that I know too much," Kaplan whispered to Tom as he swung the camera around to catch a shot of Carole Weeks walking over and greeting Cunningham and Wade.

"I'm afraid you're right, Bob. The NHA investigative division has a crack intelligence unit. They see all and know all."

"Hey, the big boys are on camera, right where I want them," Kaplan said, positioning the lens while he looked through the viewfinder. He pulled the trigger on the camcorder, turned a dial, and aimed his eavesdropping microphone toward Wade just as the Director leaned forward and whispered to Carole Weeks. "Lovely shot. Perfect," Kaplan remarked.

"Tom, my guess is that they're expecting big things from you in this conference. You're the closest person to Carl Hammerstone and they need some force to counteract all the news that's leaking out about the wasting syndrome."

"Yeah, I think I see their scheme. They'll present the marasmus syndrome in Taylor Blaine terms and then want me to give it a stamp of credibility. Then the press reports that the automated care machines are as safe as mother's milk and everyone lives happily ever after."

"No way. They're too smart for that. They know you won't go against your conscience. As a matter of fact, my guess is that they want the strength of your story. They need it so that when you're shot down there'll be a very loud, ear-drum-bursting bang."

"Strasberg will be here. He'll support what I say."

"I'm not sure that they'll give Strasberg a chance to say anything. There'll be too many people here who would still respect his opinion. He's well known to the press."

"Then I'll have to present my case as best I can."

Tom sat quietly. His brow wrinkled. After a few moments, he spoke, "Bob, did you see Katie in person the night she died?"

"Only after her death. When the crash team came in to attempt the resuscitation, they told me to stay in the control center. I watched their so-called 'resuscitation' on the monitor. Later they called me in to pronounce her dead. That was very painful. When I entered the room, the crash team had finished."

"You would recognize her, right? You knew Katie, didn't you?"

"Of course. I had seen her around."

"Was that Katie on the monitor?"

"It was until the arrest and the resuscitation began. Then the crash team was between her head and the camera. At that point there was no way I could positively identify her. And here's the real rub. What I saw next on the monitor was the attempt at resuscitation. I don't believe that was really Dr. Sullivan. I think it was a fake, a video, one made just for the record, similar to the other textbook exits."

"The sons of bitches! I suspected that might be the way it was done," Tom said.

"Same with the other cardiac arrests. They did the same thing. Before each death, the arrest team insisted that I stay in the control room. They said someone should be at the controls in case they needed to run a special antiarrhythmic or airway program.

"When I finally went into your wife's room, it was to pronounce her dead. That wasn't easy, Tom. I was in tears. As soon as I confirmed that she was dead, they rushed her body out. Said if there was to be a post-exit exam, it would be done in a special pathology unit."

"And Mandell, did you go into his room? Did you see him in person?"

"That was different. There was no cardiac arrest. I just happened to go to check on Mandell right before he died, but I never got into his room. They were busy at work."

"Who was busy at work?"

"I can't say. One person knowing too much is enough. First, let me figure out what to do about that situation. We have to be real careful."

Kaplan reached into his pocket and took out a slip of paper. He handed it to Tom.

"But take this. It's the names and access numbers of the textbook cardiac arrest patients. If Laura Clark is on our team, I have a feeling that she'll find these helpful."

"Thanks," Tom said. He folded the slip of paper and put it in his pocket.

The noise level in the amphitheater was becoming louder as more of the participants arrived. Leo Strasberg entered, looked around, stroked his beard, and then glanced over at Tom. He waved a gentle acknowledgment, and then took a seat over near the side of the hall, coughing noisily as he sat down. Peter Hansen entered. He waved to Tom and then made a "V" for victory sign with his fingers.

Several trainees of varying levels, students and residents entered and took their places on the bench near the open area in the amphitheater center. Then Taylor Blaine and Monica Montero-Blaine entered the hall.

The time had come for the conference to begin.

Chapter 45

"Thirty seconds," Carole Weeks shouted, fanning her outstretched arms to bring quiet to the room. "Five, four, three, two, one, go! We're on the air!"

The program title appeared on the screen:

A NATIONAL HEALTH AGENCY PRESENTATION
IN COOPERATION WITH DEVAN MEDICAL CENTER:
ACUTE PROGRESSIVE MARASMUS — THE ANSWER

The sound man threw a switch and a voice synthesized version of "God Bless America" began playing. Head-on shots of the regal crests of Devan and the National Health Agency, hanging above the podium, appeared on the oversized monitors attached to the side walls of the auditorium. Then the picture faded to panoramic views of the flag colored festoons, and finally, to top off the program's introduction, there were shots of the packed-in audience.

Carole Weeks stood at the side of the stage area. Like a conductor blessed with perfect timing, her hand cut the air with a swift wave and the music abruptly ended. She pointed to Cunningham, held up five fingers, then folded them one by one counting off the seconds. Cunningham picked up his cue and moved forward.

At that very moment, Leo Strasberg hacked loudly, cleared his throat, and coughed into his handkerchief. Carole Weeks paused for a second, looked up toward Strasberg with disgust, and then motioned to Cunningham to begin.

Cunningham gripped the podium edges firmly with both hands, then spoke. "We at Devan are honored to host this important conference in this historic hall. For one hundred and fifty years, the Devan Health Care Center has been guided by four Cs: caring, commitment, conscience, and credibility. Our Center represents the essence of perfected excellence. That's what Devan is all about. It is a fitting place in which to discover the absolute truth."

The audience welcomed his comments with applause.

Cunningham continued, "Over the years, the most esteemed men and women in health care have gathered in this amphitheater to solve the mysteries of the diseases that have plagued humankind. Today, health care's greatest minds are assembled in this hall. We welcome you all to Devan and praise you for your quest. We will begin with the case presentation."

He nodded to a wavy haired, young man in the front row who responded by coming forward, adjusting the microphone, and then presenting a consumer's health care history.

"The consumer, Mary Adkins, was a lovely, twenty-six-year-old woman who struggled for her life against what finally proved to be insurmountable odds. She was admitted to a Devan Health Care Center automated care unit with severe, lower abdominal pain. Diagnosi-Stat software, version 5.9, quickly determined that she had an abnormal conception dangerously nested outside of her uterus, and made the diagnosis of ectopic pregnancy. Autostereotaxic laser surgery, using the intra-abdominal video scope, enabled the managers to swiftly remove the misplaced, non-viable products of conception."

The manager then called for the first slide.

A color image of the pathology specimen of tissue removed at the time of surgery appeared on the screen. A ruler lying next to it showed it to be about ten centimeters in diameter, irregularly globular, greenish yellow-brown, and bloody.

"This is the specimen that Devan health care providers so skillfully removed."

After a few moments, he nodded to the projectionist and the image faded from the screen.

"Mrs. Adkins was in shock when she first arrived at Devan. Surgery proved to be life-saving and she did remarkably well during the postoperative phase.

"It was during a monitor-booth visit, on the fourth post-surgical day, that her husband, a construction worker, noticed her unusual irritability and saddened mood. He was alarmed and tried to comfort her, but unfortunately a faulty chip in the closed-circuit video system brought the visit to a premature end.

"When Mr. Adkins returned to visit the next day, his wife was withdrawn and mute. I must tell you, however, that before she lost the ability to communicate, her last words to our attentive nursing staff were, 'Thank God for the National Health Agency.'

"The progression of her symptoms was typical of the so-called acute marasmus syndrome, and she died six days later. It is probable that in the last days of her illness she developed Pneumocystis canni, a type of pneumonia that tends to develop in people with an extremely weakened immune system."

Grinning sardonically, the manager then called for the second slide. "Now ladies and gentlemen, for your viewing pleasure, this slide will show you how Mary Adkins looked shortly before she exited this world."

The projected image was a picture of the attractive, curvaceous, young woman in a scanty bathing suit in a beach scene.

The audience snickered. The manager smiled broadly and cleared his throat.

"I will conclude my presentation with one last comment," he said, and glanced over his shoulder at the image on the screen behind him. "That one last comment is Wow!" The audience broke into laughter and then applause.

Tom shook his head, astounded by the manager's demeaning display. Where were the more clinically relevant pictures of the emaciated Mrs. Atkins, dying from the deadly acute wasting syndrome? Tom followed the audience's response as the bikini pin-up drew cheers, loud applause, and a few cat whistles. The image had carried the audience to another realm.

The next person to come forward was the Chief Administrator of Devan Hospital.

"It could not have gone more smoothly," she told the audience, carefully reading a prepared statement. "The finely tuned Devan informatics infrastructure contributed substantially to the excellent management of Ms. Adkins. The point reading was taken speedily and the questionnaire-derived symptom list keyed into the computer data base with haste. The registration of the new patient was accomplished in two minutes flat, a full minute less than the national average."

Applause shook the amphitheater and, when it subsided, the administrator continued.

"We regret that this lovely, young consumer died, but we have no doubt that our administration managed her stay in the system with the greatest skill. Outstanding judgment was used with her point utilization," she said, twisting her own points bracelet as she talked. "And because she was such a lovely, deserving person, on two occasions, the National Health Agency graciously awarded her additional points so that her care plan might be extended.

"Mrs. Adkins received quality managed care. Even though her treatment employed big ticket items, it was delivered with complete efficiency and unquestionable cost effectiveness."

There was more applause during which the administrator returned to her seat.

"Thank you for your informative report," Cunningham said. He glanced up at the slide of Mary Adkins and then continued.

"This case presents us with an incomprehensible happening, a completely unexpected outcome. How, when someone receives the ultimate in health care, can this have possibly happened?

"The truth is, such things do happen," he said. "Unexplained mysteries are something we are all usually forced to live with. However, one of our most brilliant scientists has found answers to some of our most perplexing questions about the wasting syndrome."

Tom heard a commotion near the entrance to the amphitheater. He saw three voluptuous young women in simulated traffic light costumes making their way to a place just inside the doorway of the conference hall.

Cunningham spoke on. "Once again, diligent scientific research is conquering the plagues of humankind. Devan's own Taylor Blaine has illuminated the highway to the cause and treatment of this dreadful disease. His high chromatic imaging techniques unquestionably demonstrate that the acute marasmus syndrome is caused by the slowing of brain function due to a neurochemical rearrangement. It's indisputable. His description of the 'stoplight syndrome' will take its place in history as one of health care's most brilliant discoveries.

"And there is more. Now, this talented man has developed an equally innovative treatment for this disorder called Neuronal Intersection Reprogramming Therapy. Thank God that with NIRT, at last afflicted persons now have an avenue for recovery. Ladies and Gentlemen, Manager Taylor Blaine's work is Nobel Prize material."

Having said this, Cunningham pointed toward Blaine. The lights went down and four lilac-colored spotlights beamed on him. The limbicologist stood and bowed. The audience rose to their feet, cheering and applauding. Blaine extended his hands to accept the recognition.

Next came a drum roll and then, from their place near the exit, the three dancers costumed as traffic signals, with their lights blinking red, yellow, and green, glided into the room and shuffled onto the stage of the amphitheater. The audience remained standing, clapping rhythmically while the "Stoplight Girls," backed by a Gershwin ragtime tune, danced for nearly three minutes in a chorus line. When the music ended, all the traffic lights turned green and the trio bowed to the audience.

Cheers and applause thundered through the amphitheater. Scattered "bravos" rose from the crowd. Carole Weeks made a twirling motion with her finger and pointed to the draped festoons. Then she pointed to the camera on her left. The red, white, and blue, flag-like folds of the festoons appeared on the monitor screen. From his seat, Bob Kaplan watched Carole Weeks' motions and carefully captured her techniques for posterity on his video camera.

"This is a total mockery of medicine," Tom said to Bob. "It's absurd. They know damned well what Carl's findings were."

"No, it's worse than mockery; it's show business," Kaplan said. "It's denial in its worst form and Carole Weeks knows exactly how to package it. The public will eat it up."

Tom was growing more furious. He looked around the packed amphitheater. The hundred-plus faces with glaring eyes focused attentively toward Cunningham momentarily blurred.

Tom's eyes darted to the logo of the National Health Agency, then quickly over to the smug faces of Wade and Cunningham. Suddenly, the sound of Cunningham's voice became distant and the giant picture of Mary Adkins in her bikini, still on display, faded in Tom's mind to images of infants, deprived of nurturing caregivers, emaciated and wasting with gaunt, hollow, faces like starving children in some distant land.

Then Tom looked over toward the entrance. A group of personnel from the Health Care Center crowded in the doorway to catch a glimpse of the historical proceedings. There, he saw the young woman from the library who had helped him with his research, the young woman who looked strikingly like Katie. His emotions turned to sadness, then anger. Cunningham's pompous voice droned on.

Tom remained in his reverie for a full minute before the Vice Chancellor's voice drifted into focus again.

"Yes, it is becoming clear that we are dealing with a neurochemical rearrangement of the most vicious variety. Thank God, the wasting syndrome is completely unrelated to our lifesaving automated system of care," he said with heightened drama. "Manager Taylor Blaine has shown us that it is a clear-cut case of neurochemical malfunction."

Suddenly, Tom sprang to his feet. "This is absurd!" he shouted. "A circus! People are dying by the thousands and you people are gawking at a woman in a bikini and cheering for burlesque dancers."

Whispers floated across the audience. Cunningham held up his hands for quiet and spoke. "Manager Sullivan," Cunningham said, "I take it that you wish to address the group?"

Amidst the mutterings of the audience, Tom quickly moved down to the speaker's podium. The television cameras moved in to get a close-up. His eyes flashed with rage.

"This is a hospital, not a zoo. This conference is a sham," Tom said. "For God's sake, we are responsible for people's lives."

"Make no mistake," Cunningham said. "All of us are interested in what you have to say."

"Then look at Doctor Carl Hammerstone's findings. We know exactly why these people are dying," Tom said. "Acute marasmus is due to the isolation connected with the use of the automated treatment technology."

Leo Strasberg began to cough loudly.

"I want to tell you what I know about this deadly syndrome. You must listen!" Tom said.

"Why certainly," Cunningham said. "Please tell us your ideas."

Strasberg's relentless paroxysm of loud coughing continued. Carole Weeks looked over toward him. She whispered into her microphone.

Within seconds, three security guards were loping up the aisle to where Strasberg sat. One leaned over and whispered in the old psychiatrist's ear and seconds later the guard was escorting him down the steps.

"Then you're willing to look at the real issues?" Sullivan asked.

Cunningham answered. "We are scientists. We would never dismiss ideas that may help save lives. But we must ask that you keep to the business at hand. Please avoid conjecture and personal attack."

Tom gained control. "This disease, as you call it, is directly related to the interpersonal isolation of our patients, to their sense of abandonment and loss. It is a form of acute grief, a psychological reaction to separation, that progresses to a psychological disaster. There are indeed underlying physical consequences of the emotional state, but these are not explained by the stoplight syndrome. The illness is directly connected with the barrenness of the automated treatment settings. I'm certain that Doctor Leo Stasberg can and will present data from the scientific literature that will support these statements."

Filled with the emotion of the moment, Tom had not seen Strasberg being removed from his seat. He searched the area and could not spot him. He frantically surveyed the hall and finally saw the security guards with Strasberg at the amphitheater exit. On his way out, the old man looked back at Tom sadly. Tom swallowed.

"I'm afraid that Manager Strasberg would only give us philosophy. Science is another matter," Cunningham said. "Surely you don't really believe that such a complex disease as the marasmus syndrome could be a consequence of an unseen, immeasurable, subjective feeling-state of a patient. For a man of your stature, your ideas are quite out of date."

Tom glanced toward Wade, Cunningham, and Clark and watched the guard lead Strasberg from the amphitheater. Then he spotted Bob Kaplan, holding his camera on its tripod, quietly tiptoeing toward the door. He was following the guards and Strasberg out of the hall.

Wade signaled for Cunningham to come over to where he was sitting. "Who the hell is that man with the video camera?" Wade asked.

"A Devan Manager named Bob Kaplan," Cunningham said. "You remember his protests about the title of Manager. Kaplan used to be outspoken and rebellious, but believe me, he knows where he stands now. He's harmless."

Chapter 46

Outside the amphitheater, the guards led Leo Strasberg down the corridor to a small emergency clinic.

"Come in, Manager Strasberg. I'm Manager Rob Glade," the Provider-in-Charge said. He smiled a broad smile and thrust out his hand. Leo Strasberg shook his hand and walked into the office. "I'll take over now," Glade told the guards, and dismissed them.

The televised conference beamed onto a small television set on Glade's desk. Carole Weeks had called for a commercial break to mask the unrest in the amphitheater. On screen, a clip was pouring out words of praise about the National Health Agency and CelestaCare.

"You know me?" Strasberg asked Glade. "Hmmm, that's interesting. I don't think I know you."

"You're a famous man. I'm pleased to have the honor to assist you."

In less than a minute, Glade recorded Strasberg's updated consumer identifying data and took a brief history. He entered the information on the keyboard in front of him. Then he took the points scanner out of its sheath and aimed it at Strasberg's bracelet.

As Glade started to view the readout, the clinic entrance doorknob began to turn. The two men heard the thud of a shoe kick and the door swung open. Outside, Bob Kaplan stood looking through the viewfinder of his video camera, the lens and microphone pointed directly at them.

"Who the hell are you?" Glade asked.

"Kaplan, Bob Kaplan," the manager replied, holding up his media card. "I'm the official behind-the-scenes cameraman."

Strasberg grinned when he recognized the brazen, young manager as the person he had met in Cunningham's office.

"I saw them take you out of the amphitheater, Manager Strasberg. I'm certain that Ms. Weeks would want shots of this manager providing health care for you. You're an important man."

Glade spoke up. "That's crap. Carole Weeks doesn't want anything of the sort."

"Not so, Manager, I work for Ms. Weeks. I'm filming a documentary to archive the way she produces her famous public relations and marketing events. You can contact her staff if you'd like. Unquestionably this scene belongs in the show."

Glade lunged toward Kaplan, then suddenly halted his charge when he realized that Kaplan had turned on his camera.

"Careful, Manager Glade. We wouldn't want to capture any violence on this tape, would we? Just ignore me. Go ahead and treat this fine gentleman. Manager Strasberg needs to get back to the conference as soon as possible. He's the primary support for Manager Sullivan's position on the marasmus syndrome, you know."

"Damn you," Glade said, pulling back.

On the small television set in the emergency clinic, the commercial came to an end. Tom Sullivan had the podium and was speaking again.

"Please," Strasberg pleaded to Glade, "some cough syrup will be fine. Let me get back to the conference. It's extremely important that I be there."

Glade studied the computer monitor showing a printout of Strasberg's preliminary treatment plan, then shook his head. "Based on the reading I'm getting, we have to call in a consultant immediately. You will have to be admitted to the hospital."

"Oh no. I have to get back to that conference immediately. I must speak."

"Impossible. There's no choice," Glade said. "You'll have to wait. I'll put in the admission call right away."

Glade left the room to use the phone in another office, and Kaplan and Strasberg were left alone. On the television screen, the men could see that Tom was presenting his case. The slide of Mary

Adkins in a bikini remained on the screen behind him. Tom was carefully explaining the dangers of the automated system. As he did, a number of the participants stood and left the conference, some yawning as they passed the camera.

"They are completely disinterested," Strasberg said. "This whole conference is just more of that Destrudo business."

"Right on target," Kaplan agreed. "That's exactly what it is. It's one more giant leap backward for us all. But I promise you. We're going to get our point across somehow." Kaplan reached into his pocket. He took out a photograph and held it in front of Strasberg. "This is Mary Adkins shortly before she died. This is the way she really looked."

Strasberg raised his head to place the photograph of the sunken eyed, wasted, dying woman in the path of his bifocals. He studied the picture closely.

Kaplan spoke. "Now tell me what happened to this woman. What made her die? You know more about this syndrome than anyone else in the world and there are still people who will listen and believe what you say. Hurry! Tell me. Look at the camera and tell me."

Strasberg looked up at Kaplan. "Now? You want me to explain the theory again? Here? Now? On camera?"

"For God's sake, Doctor Strasberg. Please, hurry. This is our only chance. It's now or never," Kaplan said and frantically switched on the videocamera.

Holding the picture in his hand, Strasberg obliged.

In less than three minutes, Rob Glade rushed back into the room. "Wait here, Manager Strasberg. The admission consultant will be right along," he announced.

Kaplan gathered up his equipment. On the television screen, Tom was still talking in the auditorium. He turned to Strasberg.

"Thanks for all you've done," Kaplan said. "Thanks for telling me about the Destrudo direction that day when we were waiting in Cunningham's office. You gave me the impetus to do what I had to do. I hadn't really understood before then and now it all makes perfect sense. When Manager Sullivan and I can get others to understand, it will be a giant leap forward."

Strasberg smiled appreciatively. Glade looked puzzled.

David Barton

A few minutes later Kaplan was back in his seat in the amphitheater with his video camera set up in front of him. The conference moved on.

Cunningham had come forward to the stage and was sparring with Tom. "Manager, are you saying that 'human contact' is superior to the advanced automatic programs, the very latest in health care technology? I doubt that the many thousands of individuals who have survived because of the blessings of automated care would support your views."

Tom pleaded his case. "It is imperative that we look at Manager Hammerstone's findings. Acute marasmus can be reversed with appropriate interpersonal contact."

"Absurd. Ridiculous," Cunningham replied. "Psychiatric hogwash."

Laughter rippled through the audience. A few echos of the word "hogwash" came from the crowd. More participants stood up and moved toward the exits.

Standing behind Tom, the "Stoplight Girls" blinked their yellow lights. With fingers fanned and palms toward the audience, they made circles with their hands.

"Manager Sullivan, regretfully your dear friend and mentor, Carl Hammerstone is a relic of the Dark Ages of health care. He has treated untold numbers of consumers with substandard equipment simply to fulfill his own needs. I hardly think we can rely on the observations of someone so disinterested in quality of care. I ask you to stop filling this hallowed hall with comments about his inane work."

The "Stoplight Girls'" lights turned red. Carole Weeks was at work.

The hand that went up next belonged to a friend and classmate of Tom's. Cunningham invited him to come forward. "Thank God," Tom said under his breath as he waited to hear his colleague's supportive remarks.

"I have to disagree with my good friend Manager Tom Sullivan," the manager said. "He is sorely mistaken. I do not believe that a lack of relatedness had anything to do with Ms. Atkins' death. I was personally involved with her care and I can assure you all that there was more than adequate interpersonal contact provided for this lady.

288

As managers, we must deal with science, not mystical attitudes about human relationships. The wasting syndrome is a disease of the body and perhaps a sickness of the soul. It has absolutely nothing to do with relationships."

The audience cheered wildly. Tom was shocked. His shoulders slumped.

A flood of comments supporting the Stoplight theory followed. Blaine showed his green-yellow-red high chromatic PET scans of Mary Adkins' brain. "Please note that Mary Adkins' neurochemicals were 'in the red'," Blaine said confidently. Taylor Blaine looked at Monica Montero-Brown and smiled, gloating with pride. A few minutes later, Tom returned to his seat.

"Bob, there's no way we're going to be able to do anything here," Tom said.

"Then we'll find another way," Kaplan said. "Something must be done to turn these destructive forces around."

Carole Weeks pointed to Cunningham. The Vice Chancellor took the cue, nodded his head, and extended his arm out pointing toward Wade. "I am delighted to say that the man who has made the changes in health care possible is here with us today. This man alone saved American health care from disaster. This man dismantled the archaic medical system that was our legacy. I say, God bless the National Health Agency. And I say, God bless you, Director Alexander Wade."

The audience was on their feet giving the director a standing ovation as he stood in the spotlight. "God Bless America" began to play. Some people threw spiral strands of colorful lilac streamers. Others hurled confetti of various shades of purple. After an extended period of cheering and applause, Wade held up his hands for quiet, then spoke.

"My friends, today, I will authorize the funding of one hundred new stoplight treatment units across the land. You may be sure that the National Health Agency has every intention of bringing the acute marasmus syndrome under control. Manager Taylor Blaine's work is a gift from above. God bless you, Taylor. God bless us and grant all the deserving, eternal life."

Thunderous applause capped Wade's comment. Soon the hand clapping took on a metered cadence and was followed by metered foot stomping that shook the hall. The "Stoplight Girls" twirled through the room and danced up and down the aisles amidst the cheering audience. Their traffic light costumes flashed alternating, vibrant reds, yellows, and greens.

Outside the hospital, hundreds of people watched the proceedings on huge television monitors. A chant spread through the crowd: "We want Wade! We want Wade! We want Wade! We want Wade!"

Alexander Wade, flanked by Cunningham and Clark made his way to the door of the hospital. Wade raised his arms in a victorious salute.

"You're a shoe-in for President," Cunningham said.

Wade seemed not to hear him. Instead he stood with a broad smile frozen on his face, absorbed with the adoration of the crowd.

Chapter 47

Tom made his way through the crowd to the place where Laura waited. Soon they were driving back toward Starr Memorial.

"You saw the conference?" Tom asked.

"Every minute of it," she said. "I suspect that ninety percent of the people in the country had their televisions tuned to that conference. The acute marasmus syndrome is big news."

"It's clear at this point; the NHA and CelestaCare have the power."

"Tom, you know for sure; that conference was completely contrived. Carole Weeks produced the conference from beginning to end and she did her work well. They designed it to make you look like a fool and Alexander Wade, a god. The system came out looking like a faultless, futuristic dream and your ideas, relics from the past. But she underestimates the importance of your ideas. They have to survive. They have to and they will."

He told her that Bob Kaplan had given her a list of the patients he had observed dying in exactly the same way.

"Brilliant move. That's exactly what I need. We may soon have more information about all this madness," she said. "We'll need to go back to my office at CelestaCare."

"When?" Tom asked.

"Tonight. The CelestaCare people will be tied up entertaining the dignitaries."

That evening around eight, they arrived at Laura's CelestaCare office.

Laura unlocked her office door.

"Did Kaplan give you any other informatation besides the list?"

"He knows something about Mandell's death, but wouldn't tell me. He said one person knowing too much was enough."

"I have an idea what he's talking about. We'll see if I'm right. I'll take that list now."

"Laura, be careful," he said and handed her Kaplan's list.

She walked over to her desk, switched on her computer terminal and took a deep breath. "Here goes. You'll visit me in the penitentiary, won't you?"

She moved the mouse, clicked open a file, then another, then another, and entered a password. Then she took a disk out of a locked drawer in her desk and installed a program.

"I put this software together to use if I ever got brave enough to enter the central mainframe. With the program, I can enter any NHA system in the country."

"Laura Clark. You're a genius!"

"Hang on, we're going into Ken's terminal in his office. It's connected with the CelestaCare operations mainframe."

"If he's out of his office, won't the terminal will be switched off and locked?"

"No problem. My interactive program will unlock it and switch it on."

She booted the program and punched in the keys. Then, she held up her hand. "Don't be afraid of what you hear next," she warned.

Seconds later, the sound of a whooping siren screamed outside her door in the hallway.

"What's that?" Tom asked.

"The system's break-in alarm. It's signaling that someone is breaking into Ken's mainframe-linked system."

"Great, we're discovered. Now, how do we get out of here?"

Laura looked at him and smiled. "Oh no, Tom. Next, I'll turn Ken's system off and when Security runs the check on Ken's computer for a break-in, the window will show a 'FALSE ENTRY ERROR - UNACCEPTABLE EXIT.' My program encoded that response. Security will think that the illegal entry alarm is due to

Ken's shutting down his computer system without exiting correctly. Everyone knows that Ken is not the greatest with computers. It's happened before. They'll think the alarm is of no significance. But their break-in check program interacting with my programs should deactivate the alarm system on the terminal. Then we'll reenter Ken's system."

"How will we know that the alarm has been deactivated?"

She looked at him with apprehension. "I'm afraid we won't know for sure until we reenter."

Tom rolled his eyes. "That's comforting."

"Come on Sullivan. Stick with me. You need a little excitement in your life."

Laura followed the progress. "There, computer security is working in Ken's computer. I'm getting a signal that they're running the check.

"Good. They've gotten the 'false entry' reading. 'System error' message is showing. Well, we know that part of my program works. They'll run a few checks to be sure the correct passwords are in place. It's routine. You can see that happening on my screen now. We'll have to wait until they finish their checks and leave.

"When we reenter the program we'll know. If there's another alarm, we've got a program failure and we're in big trouble. The guards will never buy two false entries." Tom glanced at the clock then back at the monitor screen. Laura poured them each a cup of coffee.

"Sugar or sweetener?" she said calmly.

"Sweetener."

She looked at him as he nervously watched the clock. "I like your style, Tom Sullivan."

"Thanks," he said, "and I like yours."

Suddenly a string of small, military figures marching through an obstacle course appeared on her screen. Tinkling music accompanied their advances.

"What in the world is that?" Sullivan asked.

"Believe it or not, that security guard is playing a videogame on Ken's computer. It's comic relief. We'll have to wait him out."

Tom paced around Laura's office. Laura watched the monitor.

"He's not bad," she said, "but he's about to lose to the mother board. There, he's given up. He'll be out of there soon. He knows that what he's doing is strictly against regulations."

Seconds later, the screen went blank. "Now it's our turn," Laura said, back in front of her computer terminal.

"Okay Sullivan, here goes the big one," she said as she typed in the entry symbols. "Now we're going to find out just how good my work really is. If there's no alarm in thirty seconds, we're in."

Tom watched the second hand on the clock. Ten seconds, fifteen, twenty, twenty-five, thirty seconds…No alarm.

"Thank God," Laura said. "The program worked." She positioned and clicked the mouse, typed in a string of words, and then leaned back. Unintelligible symbols, completely foreign to Tom, flashed across the screen. Tom noted that Laura seemed to be reading them like a book. Intermittently, she would type in a series of numbers and letters, then lean back and watch again. A minute later, Tom saw a menu screen appear. Laura leaned back and sighed.

"I'm still closed out by the password locks. That's as far as I can get."

"So what happens now?"

"This," she answered and opened a locked file behind her desk. She took out another CD ROM disk and put it in the drive. "It's an interactive password extraction program. Something I whipped out one evening when I was bored."

"Laura Clark, I'm glad that you and I are on the same team."

She typed another string of symbols into the computer. More unintelligible symbols appeared.

The room was still and silent; the only noise was the clicking of the keyboard keys. Laura had been working at the keyboard for almost five minutes when a clump of letters followed by a long number appeared at the top of the screen.

"I think we've done it," she finally said. Look at those beautiful letters."

On the screen were the symbols: "CALGRAFLCIENRA 236/549-30-03-4307"

"It has to be unscrambled," she said, and punched in a string of commands.

"LILAC FRAGRANCE 623/495-00-33-7430" appeared on the screen.

"There it is. LILAC FRAGRANCE. We should have known they would use something that has to do with lilacs."

"To cover the smell of death," Tom said.

She smiled. "That never worked, did it?" she commented.

"Nope, Paul Devan was wrong," Tom said.

With the password, she was soon in the mainframe program. She worked for several minutes with the names from the list. At one point, Tom saw the name, "Ross Mandell" fly across the screen.

The computer groaned. The disk drive whirred. Laura leaned back in her chair and waited.

"There," she said. "The records are retrieved. But we better have something that will nail these people. If not, when they find out we've been in their mainframe, they'll nail us. Using the password establishes a traceable path leading right to my computer."

"What's on the records? Can you tell?" Tom asked.

"We'll need to take them to another place to find out what's on them. I'll need a different system."

"Take them where?" he asked.

"My lab," she said. "You'll recognize it. You've been there before — long ago."

Chapter 48

"Hold it," the guard in the lilac-colored uniform shouted as Tom and Laura stepped out of the door of her office. His hand was on his pistol.

They froze and waited while he approached. Tom felt his heart racing. He turned to look.

"Dr. Clark, is that you?" the guard asked.

"Yes," Laura said.

"You're working awfully late. Did the alarm scare you?"

"Sure did," Laura said.

"It was nothing. A system error in the Chief's office. Don't worry. It was nothing," he said.

Laura took a deep breath. "Thanks for the information," she said.

"Where you headed," the guard asked.

"My lab."

"I'll walk with you and let you in."

"Thanks. That'll be helpful," Laura said. She looked toward Tom. "Manager Sullivan is helping me with a project."

The guard looked Tom over suspiciously. "Sure," he said. "No problem."

A few moments later, at the entrance to the laboratory, the guard slid open the large door. He clicked the rows of light switches on, and section by section, the overhead lights illuminated the vast space.

Tom eyed the gymnasium sized research lab, recalling his last visit. The banks of electronic devices with their connecting wires and the colored cables crisscrossing the floor were still in place.

In contrast to the noisy chatter of the scientists and technicians when he last visited the lab, now there was utter stillness. Only the reflections of light shimmering on the polished stainless steel surfaces of the equipment gave the slightest hint of any movement in the space.

Tom's eyes darted to the gurneys across the room. An image of the "volunteer" patients with the still-to-be-perfected central lines emerging from their necks flashed in his mind. Now the stretchers were starkly empty. Tightly stretched lilac-colored sheets held in place with neatly folded hospital corners, covered the thin, foam mattress pads.

When the guard left, he slammed the thick, steel door shut. A loud clang echoed through the giant room. Laura motioned in the direction of a control center. Tom followed her as she moved toward a glassed-in control deck.

They passed a cubicle where a flesh-colored, plastic form of a woman lay in a hospital bed. The mannequin's red lips were tightly closed and her smoothly sculpted, expressionless face held two pale, blue eyes that stared blankly at the ceiling. Pulled across her chest, near her naked shoulders, was a lilac-colored neatly folded sheet. Her slender waxen arms extended down her sides beside her torso. A simulated points bracelet encircled her left wrist.

Inside the control center, Tom and Laura briefly glanced at each other. Tom looked at the control panel with its dozens of dials and switches, digital indicators, keyboards, and banks of monitor screens.

"Brings back memories," he said.

"Yes," she said, "a lot has happened since then."

Laura motioned toward a swivel-base, desk chair and Tom sat down.

She hit a series of switches and green lights flashed across the console. The video monitors blinked, and then lit up brightly. Colored bands began to roll across the rectangular screens. The measurement devices glowed and beeped, the vital sign displays flashed random numbers, and the speakers emitted muffled noise.

Tom watched the flicker of the video monitor brush colored light across Laura's face as she adjusted switches and turned more dials. Then she opened her brief case, took out a disk, and inserted it into the drive.

Instantly six names followed by social security numbers appeared on the menu on the screen. There were three men's names, Katie's name, and another woman's name. Laura had added Ross Mandell's name. She moved the mouse and highlighted the woman's name, then turned to the console and dialed the program switch to on. A click of the mouse and the retrieved record of the woman's hospital stay began to play.

Digital indicators flashed her pulse and respiration rate, blood pressures and oxygen saturation. Electrocardiographic tracings began crossing the cardiac monitor screens.

Above the vital sign readings, the monitor showed the patient lying in the hospital bed. When the image appeared, Tom reflexively looked through the glass to check the picture against reality. There, he saw only the lifeless, female mannequin lying in the bed.

The digital clock on the console clicked off the time. The electrocardiographic tracing glided along, showing the characteristic saw-tooth squiggles and low arcs of the normal QRS-T heart beat conduction pattern on the small green screen.

Laura paged through the record. Day 2 in the automated unit. Day 3. Suddenly, the words "T-effect exit" began to run as an overlay on top of the picture. They had reached day 4 of the patient's hospital stay and the record of her exit. Laura advanced the record and scanned the scenes. Suddenly, she halted the fast-forward action.

The timer clock marking minutes clicked to 2:22 a.m.

The record continued for nearly a minute, then suddenly Tom saw the electrocardiogram tracings begin to move up and down in a strange pattern. A few seconds later, lightning fast slashes of abnormal heart rhythms raced across the electrocardiogram display. Then the tracing flashed the life-threatening fluttering of ventricular fibrillation. Tom knew that the fibrillation pattern heralded the heart's inability to pump blood.

Almost instantly, the high pitched blast of the emergency monitor alarm squealed. Red lights flashed on the panels. The pulse indicator numbers tumbled precipitously. The blood pressure reading careened downward and the patient's respirations became shallow, erratic, and then ceased. The patient's oxygen saturation measurement dropped precipitiously.

"A classic cardiac arrest. It's textbook," Tom said.

On the screen, the patient lay motionless with her arms resting limply at her side. Her face was lifeless, her color, a pale white. Tom glanced at the picture, then at the vital sign display.

Within seconds, a team of cardiac resuscitation managers rushed into the room on the monitor screen. Hurrying through the door, they pushed the equipment loaded crash cart next to the bed and hastily readied the patient to begin the defibrillation to restore the patient's normal heartbeat.

Tom cast a look out through the window. He saw no busy arrest team in the simulated room, only the corpse-like form of the female mannequin lying beneath the lilac-colored sheets. Laura's replay of the medical record was driving her point home. Were the direct view into the cubicle blocked, a manager would assume the scene on the monitor to be real, medical events.

On the video, the cardiac arrest team managers grabbed frantically to pull back the sheet. They tugged at the patient's lilac-colored hospital gown, baring her chest. Her naked breasts exposed, they positioned the shock electrodes over her heart. Instinctively, Tom positioned himself to see the patient's face, but an interposed manager blocked the camera's view.

"Watch it, damn it, stand back!" one of the cadiac arrest code managers on the screen shouted just before the electrical jolt surged through the paddles on the patient's chest.

The electrocardiogram continued to show the pattern of ventricular fibrillation.

"Breathe for her. Now, surge electrodes on the chest. Shock for defibrillation again."

Again, Tom looked out through the control station window at the woman in the hospital bed. An eerie feeling came over him. The mannequin lay as still as death, staring her empty stare at the ceiling. On the control deck, the vital sign indicators and the video continued to play out the findings and the scenes of a cardiac arrest on the monitor.

An image of Katie in the automated treatment unit at Devan rushed through Tom's mind. He remembered the woman's telephone call in the middle of the night, "It's your wife, Manager Sullivan, she's dead," the woman had said. "A cardiac arrest."

On the monitor, the managers at the bedside attempted the defibrillation shock a third time. Each time the current flowed, the patient's body jerked in response to the electrical jolt and the arrest team stepped back to avoid the shock. The team administered emergency medications and rushed to insert a breathing tube into the trachea, then tried the defibrillation procedure again. Almost a full minute passed and still the display showed the heart muscle continuing to quiver ineffectively. Another shock. No sustained heart rhythm or effective beat. For thirty seconds, the tracing ran along with only an occasional spasmodic discharge of electrical activity from the heart muscle interrupting the flat line. Soon the spasms disappeared and the monitor showed only the continuous flat line of a non-beating heart.

The few minutes flurry of noisy activity in the room faded to a still, vacant silence. "She's dead," Tom said and sighed.

Laura nodded yes.

On the screen, two managers stood back with their arms folded, quietly talking. In an ancient ritual to separate the living from the dead, another manager pulled the sheet over the woman's head. The technician had already begun to order the cardiac defibrillation apparatus and was putting it back on the crash cart.

Laura leaned forward, threw a switch, and stopped the program. The scene instantly froze on the screen.

"Hold on," she said.

Tom watched as she reversed the record to just before the abnormal heart rhythm began. "What's going on?" he asked.

She let the record begin to move forward again. After a few moments, she nodded her head.

"Yes, I was right. I was right, Tom."

"About what?" Tom asked.

"I think I see something that might just hang these people." I'm moving the record back again. Now look carefully at the patient's bedside table and tell me what you see." She reversed the record to 2:22 a.m. and froze the frame.

"Usual objects," Tom said. "Box of tissues, pitcher of water, a paperback book."

"Right, now let's go forward again," Laura said.

The record flowed along. Again the clock reached 2:23 a.m. Then, the abnormal cardiac rhythm appeared, the plummeting pulse and blood pressure, the alarm.

"Now, keep your eye on the bedside table," Laura said and switched the video to slow motion.

The record ran on. The cardiac arrest team entered the room.

"Look!" Laura said.

"Damn!" Tom said. "When the arrest team arrived, a vase of lilac plumes magically appeared on the bedside table. It wasn't there before."

"Exactly!"

"Someone must have moved them there to get them out of the way of the crash cart."

"Tom, lilacs don't bloom in Middleside in January. And that's when this patient died."

They watched another record, this one an older man. Again there was a cardiac arrest and again a team identical to the one in the first record rushed in to do a resuscitation. Again, it was a classical cardiac arrest just as if it had been lifted from the pages of a textbook. Again there was a vase of lilac blossoms on the bedside table that wasn't there before the life-threatening heart rhythm began.

"This man died in early February. Lilacs bloom in Middleside in May."

"Now I understand. I see exactly what happens," Tom said. "CelestaCare makes sure a manager's only contact with the patient is through the monitors and the electronic devices. A substitute digital program is faded in. The manager believes that what he's seeing is happening to his patient, but the display in the control room may have nothing to do with what's really going on. In the hospital room, something totally unrelated could be taking place — like a murder."

"Right," Laura said. "Even if the patient is getting well, like Katie, the authorities can still make things go their way. A quick acting, lethal poison through the central line kills the patient, but the murder is not recorded on the record. The event looks like a spontaneous happening in the patient's clinical course. The digital film fade-in could come from anywhere in the system. But to the manager, it seems to be a clear-cut clinical reality."

"Run Katie's record," Tom said.

"No Tom. Let someone else examine her record. You're too close and so am I. It's not fair to either of us."

"You're right. But I know now how she died."

"Yes, what you suspected all along is true."

Laura gently squeezed his shoulder and gave him time to have his feelings.

Chapter 49

"And Mandell?" Tom asked quietly after a few minutes. "What about Mandell?"

"I'd say they murdered Mandell too," Laura said, "for their own political reasons. In Mandell's case, I'd say there was a little different twist. They needed an indisputable account of his death to cover up the murder. Somehow, they quickly produced their own video using someone who looked like Mandell for the cover-up, then pulled the stunt about the video of his death having been accidentally recorded. I'll run a segment of his exit."

Laura keyed in a sequence of commands. On the monitors, another sequence immediately appeared. This time, the patient resting quietly in the mock-up room was an obese, middle aged man. After a few moments, he suddenly grabbed his throat and croaked a loud crow-like sound. He choked, gasping frantically for air. His skin turned bluish-purple. After a few moments, he fell back on the bed motionless. Quickly, the vital signs and chemistry indicators faded to zero. The man was dead.

"It's the Mandell video that Ken showed me," Tom said. "Another textbook death."

"There's a good reason that all of the fake programs look like textbook descriptions of sudden deaths," Laura said. "They are."

"When all this began," Laura explained, "Ken wanted a surefire way to sell the idea of the automated units to the government. The link between CelestaCare and Devan Medical Center had already been established. I've learned that Cunningham was one of

CelestaCare's biggest stockholders. When Ken consulted Cunningham about the best way to sell CelestaCare's automated system idea to the government, he told Ken that programs illustrating sudden deaths would surely grab their attention. 'Scare the shit out of them with gory, death scenes. In these times they'll rush to buy anything that gives the slightest promise of being life-saving and cost-cutting,' Cunningham told him. He suggested that Ken carefully read a special book. In fact, he gave him this very copy."

She reached into her brief case and took out a mottled brown book carefully wrapped in plastic film. She removed the wrapping and handed the antique book to Tom. Handling it carefully, he opened the front cover and inspected the frontpiece. "This is an original edition of Paul Devan's *De Morte Subita*," Tom observed.

"Yes, the book that captured Ken's morbid imagination and probably gave them all the idea for this plan. The detail that Devan captures in his descriptions of sudden death is phenomenal. When you read his observations, you can almost see the patient. Devan's observations and writings are pure precision."

Tom thumbed through the pages of the book, perusing its contents. Laura continued, "It's clear that Devan himself became obsessed with death. There was a diphtheria epidemic in Philadelphia and people were dying all around him. He confronted his own mortality. He became terrified that he too might die suddenly. To combat his own phobia, he developed an insatiable fascination with watching people die. Psychiatrists call it counter-phobic behavior. It led to his journal observations about sudden death. Once he had collected the material, he wrote and published *De Morte Subita*.

For a period of time, Devan couldn't seem to decide where to direct his energies, toward his absorption with death or toward his work facilitating life. Devan even collected death masks, made from the very patients he wrote about. That's where Ken got the idea for his collection. But once he wrote the book, he was released from his total immersion in death. He insisted that the death masks of his patients be destroyed. He turned his energies toward the founding of his medical school."

"Another struggle with Destrudo," Tom said, "but with a creative outcome on the side of life forces."

"Yes, in keeping with Strasberg's theory. But Ken's fascination took a different turn. Driven by economics and his grandiosity, Destrudo won. His motives tilted toward the destructive and stayed that way.

"I remember clearly. Ken demanded that I produce a series of software based on Devan's classical descriptions of sudden death. As Cunningham had suggested, he would use them to sell the system. The idea was gruesome." She paused and swallowed.

"I resisted, but he had a driven need to push ahead. He was convinced that my work could save millions of lives — and health care. He gave some persuasive arguments. The health care world was spinning out of control and I wanted to make a positive contribution. Health care had become unaffordable. Finally, I gave in. We used actors to simulate the clinical situations, combined realistic animation techniques with digital editing, and added matching vital signs and laboratory values to make them seem even more real. The actors followed Devan's descriptions to the letter.

"Later, CelestaCare presented these computer programs to the NHA. Cunningham was right. They bought the idea of the automated systems. The horror show immediately put CelestaCare out in front in the race for government support."

Tom glanced up at the picture of the purple faced man electronically frozen on the monitor screen. "The video Ken showed me was exactly like this one. I would have sworn the person was Mandell."

Laura shook her head. "I don't believe for a minute that Mandell died from a pulmonary embolus. The scene we're seeing was made for the record. It's not what actually happened. If you read the description of death from a pulmonary embolus in *De Morte Subita*, you'll see that the Ross Mandell exit is an exact copy of Paul Devan's description of death by a blood clot to the lungs. God knows exactly how Mandell died, but there's little doubt that he was murdered. That's what Kaplan knows, and somehow he probably knows that the person on this film isn't Mandell."

"By coincidence, I read Devan's description of death by pulmonary embolus when I went to Devan to do the research on the wasting syndrome," Tom said. "His book was in the display case outside the library, opened to that page. It seemed unbelievably familiar. Now I understand why."

"The promotional programs I made to sell the system were amateur productions compared to these, but I'll bet that's where they got the idea. The cardiac arrest programs we've watched are polished, professional jobs. Near one hundred percent reality index. They were digitally worked into the treatment records as required. They even have interactive capability to be sure that if the managers responded, the programs would take over and lead them to the desired endpoint. But their zeal for reality in the sudden death videos carried them overboard. In order to be sure that the viewer would think it was Devan, they even put the plastic lilacs on the bedside table."

"To try to cover the smell of death," Tom said quietly.

Laura put the copy of *De Morte Subita* back in her brief case.

"I believe it was pure coincidence that Katie had viral meningitis and entered the hospital. A case of their having her right where they wanted her. But after you talked with Kaplan at Flint's, and later spoke with me, I kept asking myself: If Tom's hypothesis is correct, how do they get people on the central line when they want them there? And I guessed it. Here's the key," she said and held out her left arm displaying her points bracelet.

"I had a theory and checked it out. I played sick and went to CelestaCare's Employee Health Service. Before I went, I used my own scanner program to look at my points bracelet codes. I had the feeling that the bracelet was being put to more uses than we know. When I looked at the point strip and the identifying data space, I soon noticed still another available data strip on the bracelet format. At that reading, the extra data strip was blank.

"I made up vague complaints about pains in my knees. I said I was concerned that I had injured myself jogging. They did the points check with their scanner. I was frightened and I later learned that my fear was justified. If they had wanted me on the central line, my less-than-dramatic symptoms could have gotten me there. Until then, I must not have posed that much of a threat — at least not enough for a fake T-effect exit."

She took in a deep breath, and then exhaled. Her face grew pale.

"Are you okay?" Tom asked.

"I think so. The manager told me that he wasn't able to explain my symptoms. 'Just be careful. A little less mileage, try some new shoes,'" he said. "He prescribed a non-steroidal anti-inflammatory and told me if I wasn't better in a few days to get the prescription filled. He instructed me to return in a month. When I left, he told me to stop by the scanner desk to have them subtract the points for the visit.

"I did. Then I came back to my lab to use my own scanner to read my bracelet. The points scanner in the clinic had done exactly what I suspected. On the auxiliary data strip, a string of new messages had been encoded. Look," she said to Tom.

She picked up a pistol grip scanner lying on the desk and plugged it into her laptop. She aimed it at her points bracelet, pulled the trigger, and a picture of the data bar from her bracelet appeared on the screen.

"Check the readout. On the left is the point reading. '4,673 Points.' Next is my identifying data. And to the right of that, the inscription in that extra data strip. Well, that's the area that they would use to tell my fortune. When they subtracted the points, the laser put machine language symbols in that space on my bracelet."

"That looks like hieroglyphics on the strip. What does it mean?" He turned to Laura with a questioning face.

Laura continued, "In plain English, those are the machine symbols ordering a T-effect exit decision. It means that the next time I'm admitted to a hospital or go to a health care facility for any reason, unless I erase this marker, they may play Destrudo."

"That's total madness." Tom said.

"That little message was put on by a direct electronic message from the mainframe in Washington. They no longer depend on coincidence to get their victims. Now it's a smooth, well designed, deadly system. They use a high tech version of stalking their prey."

"Unbelievable!" Tom exclaimed.

"I suspect it works like this. The code is a red flag for the killers. If I go for health care for any reason, the scanner will immediately alert the mainframe that I'm a special person. A consulting manager will be called in, probably a reaccessed manager with an incentive to keep his mouth shut. If they're ready for me to die, the computer will tell him to admit me to the hospital regardless of my complaint. He'll come up with a bogus reason for my hospitalization and insist that it's urgent. And if I refuse, they'll just wait for another chance. Sooner or later they'll put me in an automated unit and then, whack!"

"Can you erase the T-effect exit alert?"

"My program can." She pressed several keys on the keyboard and pointed the scanner toward her bracelet. "Done," she said.

"I'm afraid there have been many deaths like Katie's and Mandell's. Anyone against the regime is likely to catch it.

"In fact, I checked through the list of the T-effect deaths. A significant number were people who opposed the new system of health care. Some were anti-Theotechnicists. Others were rebellious administrators, physicians or academicians. One was a noisy, critical CelestaCare stockholder. Another was writing a book about the exorbitant profits being made in health care. It obviously posed too much of a threat."

"Bastards," Tom said.

Laura clicked on a program description and booted up another program in her notebook computer. She pressed a key and a decision tree for the diagnosis and treatment of gastrointestinal bleeding appeared on the screen. "Let me show you something else. Fake programs are just one possibility. There are other kinds of destructive games." She keyed in a command and the decision tree flipped upside-down.

"In the conventional use of the decision tree, symptoms, physical findings and laboratory results lead to the diagnosis and treatment. What you're seeing now is what computer engineers call a 'reversed algorithm.' It's simply a decision tree that's reversed.

With this technique, an operator could key in whatever clinical situation or disease they want to produce. Then the program artificially creates the disease in the patient. Symptoms, lab results, you name it. Using the central pharmacy and the central lines, they use drugs to produce nausea or headaches, sedatives to produce stupor or fatigue, medications to make blood pressure and pulses go up or down, injections of bacteria to cause infections."

"Or a blood thinner like heparin to cause a bleed," Tom added.

"Exactly. It's extreme irony: a health care system that deliberately causes illness, a technology that can cause any symptom, disease or medical disaster they choose. It has to be the ultimate in managed care."

Tom shook his head. "Amazing. And incredibly sadistic."

"It's not what I had in mind for my programs," Laura said. "I wanted to help treat illnesses, not mimic or cause them."

"It's like Strasberg said. It's Destrudo. The emphasis is no longer on life, it's on death," Tom said. "It's on the side of 'first, do harm' rather than being focused on 'first, do no harm.'"

"Yes, I'm afraid so. Except for those supporters that the Theotechnicist want to live."

"And physicians have gone along with this?" Tom questioned. "That's hard to believe. Surely someone would have noticed that the T-effect exits are faked."

"Tom, the times have changed. The physicians have become more and more apathetic and demoralized. They've progressively given in to the controls. They're so distant and removed from the patients, so lulled into complacency by the automated programs and the technology, so detached from anything related to direct care of human beings that most of them couldn't care less. They do their work and get their paycheck. Being a doctor has become a nine-to-five job.

"The truth is they can't talk with their patients. They can't talk with families. They're so busy being productive with the machines that they can easily miss the deceptions. And worse of all, the majority of them don't give a damn."

Tom shook his head.

"Besides, the authorities don't let just any manager oversee the real dirty work. I scanned the profiles of the managers who were assigned to take care of the T-effect patients. Every single one had been deaccessed and granted reaccess — sworn back in with the reaccess oath. They know that if they make any trouble it's all over for them for good: at least ten years in prison or worse. But regardless, Kaplan wasn't going to buy in. That's why he met with you."

"The question now is how to bring this system down," Tom said.

"I think it's time for you, Bob Kaplan, and me to sit down and talk," Laura said. "We have to think of some way to put all this information together and get in out in front of the public in a way that's powerful enough to overcome the NHA's and CelestaCare's slick Public Relation efforts."

"Bob mentioned something about using the new, giant, digital projection screen that you've designed for Devan in this process."

"Not a bad idea," Laura said, "but pretty risky. The security is very tight around there."

Later that night, Tom found a letter that had been slipped under his door. The envelope had no return address. Laura stood behind him as he read, her hands resting lightly on his shoulders.

Dear Tom,
There are many things I want to tell you and so little time. I suspect that as soon as my whereabouts become known, further communication with you will be impossible.

We had no way of knowing our work would turn out this way, but we must often learn to live with worlds that go in different directions than we would like. I believe we must all accept that all of our endeavors, whatever they might be, have as an integral part of them, a certain incompleteness. In that is a basic truth of life and the proof of it is death. Most dangerous are those who are lulled into the belief that they can deny this incompleteness with the certainty of prematurely derived 'scientific' answers and try, in varied ways, to force others to accept them.

Sometimes human beings cannot face the worst that may happen to them. We make up stories to soothe our unrest, believe in our science and our inventions instead of what we see, feel, and know in our hearts. We fall in love with our inventions, Tom, and forget to care for those in our midst.

I believe that you and I have always stood for the same basic values. Your friendship and your devotion have always been of great importance to me. I know that, in your heart, you too have always felt a mandate to maintain the place of humanity in caring for the sick.

I watched you in the conference. You stood up against them all and tried to fight courageously for our place and our convictions. I knew that you learned some of the conviction of your position from me, and I was a proud and honored man. Don't be discouraged. It will take time, but someday, somewhere, once again the human interaction will take its rightful place in medicine. There can be no true healers without it.

I am an old man and I have had a serious head injury. Soon my condition will lead to a benevolent death by natural causes. I do not choose to seek treatment. I did not devote my life to the practice of medicine to turn myself over to a system that has no more of what is human than this one.

You have always been and will always be held in my highest esteem. I shall cherish our closeness until the end.

Goodbye, my dear friend and colleague,
Carl

Tom's eyes welled with tears. He folded the letter and laid it on his desk.

Less than an hour after Tom read the letter, Carl Hammerstone collapsed on the street in downtown Philadelphia.

When the NHA Ambulance dispatched to the scene arrived, Carl was still breathing. The pupils of his eyes were unequal in size, and there was a large, swollen area with a gaping cut on the side of his head. He was quickly carried inside the ambulance. After the rear doors of the van were closed, before the driver and his assistant could start an intravenous line, they noted that Carl had stopped breathing.

Looking down at Carl's arm, the driver saw that he wore no points bracelet. "Just as well he exited on his own," the driver said, matter-of-factly. "When we treat those with no bracelets, the paper work is pure hell."

As the ambulance drove away, the familiar message poured from its top mounted speakers:

You are watching the skilled, efficient operation of the Health Care Providers of the National Health Agency. Benefiting from the latest in technology, another person is receiving the best health care available. Thank you for any help you might have provided in this situation and thank you for your continued support of a system aimed at providing you, your family, and your neighbors with the very best health care possible.

Chapter 50

Two days later, Tom arrived home from work and found a note in his mailbox. "PETER HANSEN IS ON TO SOMETHING," the unsigned message said.

Minutes later, he placed a telephone call. He caught Hansen, his epidemiologist friend, still working in his office at Devan.

"Hello Peter, how's the microbe tracker?" Tom asked when Hansen answered the phone. "It's been a while. I saw you from a distance at the conference."

"Yes, it was a fiasco. I'm sorry. I had to stay out of it."

"What have you been up to?"

"Same old stuff."

"Still working on the epidemic?"

"Never ends. I have stacks of printouts to go through. You should see my office. It's piled so high with journals and papers, there's hardly room here for me."

"Anything new turning up about the epidemic?"

"Er, no, same as before. The virulence of these bacteria is unbelievable. I hope it never gets loose again. Thank God for Lilacicin."

"I guess that sooner or later, you'll figure out where it originated."

"Probably later, maybe," Peter said. "Still looks like a terrorist act to me, but it's been two years now. The FBI still has nothing. Time flies."

"Yes, it does."

"I can say that a few things might be beginning to fall into place," Hansen said.

That was it: the statement Tom had expected at some point in the conversation. The rest of Peter's comments were distractions. Tom breathed deeply and looked at the note written on the index card he held in his hand. He knew. All the telephone lines at Devan were monitored. He changed the subject.

"Remember the resident who was working with me when the epidemic began," Tom said. "You made rounds with us those first few weeks you were here."

"Sure. It was Bob Kaplan, right?"

"Yeah. I ran into him the other night at Flint's newsstand."

"He mentioned that he saw you."

"Oh, you've talked with Bob?" Tom asked.

"We've sort of gotten to be friends. I just recently had lunch with him. We had a long talk about what's happened over the past few years. Bob's always been a little too rebellious; needs to watch his step." Peter chuckled.

"I agree. You know about the Healers?"

"Tragic. I was sorry to hear about Carl Hammerstone. Never got to know him as well as I would have liked to."

"Yes. He was a fine man. Wonderful teacher and friend. I'll miss him, that's for sure. Well, Peter, just wanted to check in with you and say hello."

"Tom, it's been a long time. We lost contact after you moved to Starr. We ought to get together," Peter interjected.

"I'd love it. Name a time."

"What about early tomorrow morning? We can have a chat about old times, battling the epidemic."

"Where?"

"My office is probably best," Peter said. "But it's a mess."

"I've seen it before. I believe I can handle it."

"Eight?"

"Fine. I'll be there. Have some coffee made."

Tom placed the phone back on the receiver and reviewed the conversation. He guessed that Bob and Peter had lunched together that very day. The message on the index card had to be another one of Bob Kaplan's tip-offs. Peter Hansen must have told Kaplan something and he wanted Tom to know.

The next morning at Devan, Tom entered the epidemiology section of the Medicine department shortly before eight. He smiled when he saw the giant magnifying glass painted on Peter Hansen's office door. What could be a more fitting logo for a man known as the Sherlock Holmes of bacterial infections? Tom remembered the days of the epidemic: spending long hours together in Peter's office, trying to make sense of the spread of the deadly illness, the two of them, collaborating on developing an agenda for the Epidemic Task Force conference at Devan.

In the reception area, the expression on the secretary's face immediately told Tom that something was wrong.

"When I arrived this morning, I saw that Manager Hansen had your name on his book for eight. I tried to call you at your office," she told Tom. "No one answered. I didn't want to bother you at home. Manager Hansen became very ill in the night. He's been admitted to a tenth floor automated unit."

"Admitted? Is he okay?"

"Fair. They're still doing the diagnostics. High fever, stiff neck; he's stuporous."

"Then it's serious. Peter is a close friend. He's a fine person."

"I know. And highly respected around here. Vice Chancellor Cunningham arranged for him to be in a VIP single room."

"Do you suppose they'll let me visit?"

"I doubt it, but I'll call and check."

She called and made the request. Tom listened, sensing that her effort was perfunctory. Seconds later she told him that the manager in charge had refused.

"I'll call the floor myself. I'm going to see him," Tom said.

"Manager, you know the rules. Manager Hansen is very ill. They won't even let his family visit at this point."

"I'm sure, but I'm a doctor and I want to call that control station myself. Now what's the room number?"

"Ten...er...ten fifty-seven," she said.

"I need a telephone."

"Of course, here," she said, handing him the receiver across the desk. "I'll push the number in. But you're going to get the same answer."

"No, I want some privacy. I'll use Manager Hansen's office."

"Oh no, Manger...er...er...Doctor. Use this phone. Manager Hansen is awfully sensitive about anyone being in his office when he's not there."

"Peter Hansen wouldn't mind my using his office phone and that's what I'm going to do." He walked toward the door and opened it.

The secretary rose halfway from her seat, but once the door was opened she sat back down.

With the door to the office open, Tom stopped suddenly at the threshold and looked around the room. Peter's office was in perfect order. The wall maps that usually hung in disarray were hanging perfectly straight. The colored pins marking case distribution had been removed. The stacks of articles and computer printouts that usually covered Peter's research table were gone. The monitor screen on his computer was dark. Peter never turned his computer and monitor off. It was a quirk peculiar to him. He thought it bad luck to do so.

Tom looked back over his shoulder at the secretary. She gripped at the top of her blouse near her neck.

"Er...we've cleaned up the room since you were here last. It's not like it usually is," she stammered. "I don't blame you for being surprised. It doesn't look like Manager Hansen does it? We've been working on it for several days. About to get it straight. He's turning over a new leaf. Said he was getting too disorganized to accomplish anything." She forced a smile.

Tom did not answer. He passed through the door and closed it behind him. Sitting down at the desk, he picked up the phone and punched in the tenth floor control station number. He noticed that the other telephone line immediately lit up. He had not heard the phone buzz. The secretary was making an outgoing call. He guessed she was alerting someone about his being there. Tom waited for an answer to his own dialing.

He pulled out the top desk drawer on the right. Empty. Then the second drawer. The same. The top drawer on the left. Cleaned out.

Too many times he had watched Peter Hansen riffle through those drawers frantically looking for some lost data sheet in the disorganized piles of unfiled papers.

The control station answered. Tom identified himself and asked permission to visit. "Oh no, Manager Sullivan," the voice at the other end of the line said. "No visitors at this point. We can't even allow video visitation. Manager Hansen is in a critical condition. He's delirious and the informatics diagnostic process is in progress."

Tom slammed down the phone and walked toward the hall. He glared at Peter's secretary as he passed her desk.

"Manager Sullivan. Please wait. I have an updated report on Manager Hansen for you," the secretary shouted at him as he rushed by.

"I'll see for myself," the determined Sullivan shot back.

Minutes later, he got off the elevator on the tenth floor. In the VIP section, two brawny NHA Agents stood outside the entrance to Hansen's room. When they saw Tom approaching they stepped in front of the door.

"I want to visit Manager Hansen."

One of the agents looked over Tom's ID badge. "Sorry, Manager, no one's allowed in Manager Hansen's room. Anyway, he's pretty much out of it. Wouldn't even know who you are."

Over the shoulder of the agent, Tom could see through the small observation window into the room. He could see Peter Hansen lying in the bed.

Tom spoke louder. "I said I want to see Manager Hansen. I am a manager myself." One of the agents put his finger to his lips. "Shhhhh! Quiet down, Manager. Quiet down. Have you lost your mind?"

Tom moved toward the door.

The other agent grabbed him roughly by the shoulder. "We said no admission."

A series of garbled words floated out of the VIP room.

"What was that?" Tom asked and signaled for the two men to be silent.

The agent loosened his grip on Tom's shoulder and the three of them listened intently.

"Hansen's disease…Hansen's disease…Hansen's disease…Hansen's disease," a slurred voice screamed out.

"The man's delirious, Manager," the agent said. "Every so often he yells out like that. Keeps muttering about a disease with his name. He's out of it."

"Maybe he wants something," Tom said.

"He's on the central line, Manager. He has everything he needs."

"He'll be okay," the other agent reassured Tom. "Just let the Devan managers take care of him. You can talk with him when he's better in a day or two."

Tom stood his ground. "You need to hear me. I intend to see Manager Hansen today. Let me talk to the manager in charge."

They argued. Finally, one of them went to find one of the managers assigned to the case. When they returned with the young man, Tom explained that he and Peter worked together. Hansen was a close friend.

"Okay, you can go in for a second, but a short second. You'll see for yourself. Manager Hansen is in some kind of delirium. He's out of it. Diagnostics are still working."

The two agents watchfully accompanied Tom to Peter's bedside.

Peter Hansen lay in the bed with his eyes closed. His lips were parched and his face expressionless. His right hand curled around the tubing of the central line.

"Peter. It's Tom Sullivan. Can you hear me? Can you hear me?"

"See, it's like I said. The man's out of it," an agent said. "Look, he's even choking off his central line. Dangerous business for a man that sick. He'll need restraints." The agent freed the plastic tubing from Peter's limp hand.

Peter Hansen groaned. Then he mumbled the same string of words again. "Hansen's disease…Hansen's disease…Hansen's disease…"

"Is that all he says?" Tom asked the agents from the investigative division as they walked out of the room.

"That's it. The man makes no sense I tell you."

Tom rode down the elevator. Probably a sham admission, he reasoned. The coil of central line in his hand. Could it be that Peter was choking the line off to stop the flow of sedatives?

"Hansen's disease…Hansen's disease." What the hell was Peter trying to say? "Aha," he said out loud when the answer hit him.

Tom drove to his home instead of to Starr. Rushing into his study, he grabbed his National Directory of Infectious Disease Managers off his shelf, looked up a number, and scribbled it down on a scratch pad. He picked up the telephone and punched in the long distance number. The line began to ring.

Tom knew that Peter Hansen had come to Devan from the Centers for Disease Control in Atlanta. Before being on the staff at the CDC, he had done research in Baton Rouge, Louisiana, on leprosy, an illness also known as Hansen's disease. The fact that he and this disease coincidentally bore the same name was perhaps one of the reasons he had chosen infectious diseases and epidemiology as directions for his medical career.

The clinician-researcher with whom Peter had worked had now moved back to Carville, Louisiana, where the Leprosarium was originally located prior to being relocated to Baton Rouge. Manager Richard Dupont had now retired, but was writing a book about his life's work with Hansen's disease.

"Is this Manager Dupont?"

"Yes," the voice on the other end of the line replied.

"This is Tom Sullivan, in Middleside, Pennsylvania. I'm Medical Director at Starr Memorial Hospital here. I used to be full time faculty at Devan. I'm a close friend of Peter Hansen's. I'm in infectious disease."

"I see. What can I do for you?" Dupont asked.

"You authored a number of papers with Peter Hansen didn't you?"

"Yes."

"He's in the hospital in an automated unit on a central line."

"Oh no, what's wrong with him?"

"They're saying that he's had a subarachnoid hemorrhage. The diagnosis may be bogus."

"I certainly hope he's better soon."

"I was supposed to meet with him this morning, but when I arrived at the hospital, he had been admitted. His office was immaculate. Charts hanging straight, papers neatly stacked, computer shut down."

"That doesn't sound like Peter's office."

"Someone had cleaned it out. Was Peter on to something about the epidemic?"

Richard Dupont cleared his throat. "I'm sorry, I don't think I understand," he said.

"I went to visit him on the ward. They had him in a VIP single room. NHA Agents were guarding him closely. They watched my every move. Hovered over me the whole time I was there."

"Did Peter say anything to you when you visited him?" Dupont inquired.

"He was delirious."

"Did he say anything that made any sense, Manager Sullivan?"

"The only thing he said was "Hansen's disease." He said it over and over, a dozen times. That's why I called you. I thought there was a chance that he was trying to tell me something. I figured the perseverated 'Hansen's disease' might be a disguised reference to leprosy and some kind of code. He might have been trying to steer me toward thinking of his work in Louisiana. I know that you were Peter's research associate. He spoke of you often, and I know that you're still one of his closest friends. He might have wanted me to contact you."

"Listen, Manger Sullivan. Are you on a secure phone?"

"I think so, but I can't be sure."

"Then find one you're absolutely sure of, and call me back as soon as you can."

Chapter 51

Near a row of ivy covered, red brick buildings, Tom and Laura sat on a bench and watched the graduates and their families move down the path toward the graduation exercises on the Green. The warm, spring day glowed with sunshine; the lilac shrubs were in full bloom. The sweet fragrance of their blossoms, swept along by the soft spring breeze, filled the air.

Bannock's bronze statue of Paul Devan stood on the sunbathed, grassy knoll near where they sat. Close to Devan's feet, two small boys played the game of *"POINTS"* while their mothers sat on a bench talking. One of the children lay on the ground playing the role of the consumer while the other knelt down next to him, pretending to be his manager. Tom and Laura listened as they played.

"I'm putting in a central line," one child said. He carefully fastened a length of plastic tubing to the other child's neck with a strip of the lilac-colored plastic tape. The tubing ran to a toy replica of an automated treatment console. "How many points do you have? Show me your bracelet. Come on! Hold it out here!"

The other child extended his arm. He wore a small bracelet that simulated the real points bracelet he wore on his left wrist.

The manager-child aimed the toy point scanner toward the bracelet.

"Ha! — only two hundred points!" he said to the consumer-child, reading the digital print-out that appeared on the console. And you need a heart transplant. That won't do it. You're gonna need six thousand points for this operation."

"Maybe the NHA will give me more points," the patient-child said.

"We'll see," the manager-child said. He pushed a switch on the miniature console. The digital readout began to scramble and soon a number came up on the display. "Boy are you lucky. It says that you're deserving. You must be saying your prayers. The NHA gave you extra points. Maybe you'll be given eternal life."

Both children wore Theotechnicist t-shirts. Overlaying a purple, cross-like "T" projecting up from a computer monitor, the words, "GOD," "TECHNOLOGY," and "ETERNITY," were laid out across the shirt's front in bright, lilac glo-color letters. The back of the shirt bore another motto: "CELESTACARE — FOR ALL YOUR HEALTH NEEDS — NOW AND FOREVER."

Laura gazed up toward the sky through the branches of the ancient oak trees. Tom looked up also. Beyond the outstretched limbs he could see faint puffs of white clouds moving slowly against the clear blue sky.

"What now?" Laura asked.

"When this is over, we'll have to leave," Tom said.

"Will you let me go with you?" Laura asked.

"I would be honored. Maybe you can teach me something about computers," Tom said.

The children shouting nearby interrupted their exchange.

"No points. You're out of points. You're going to exit!" one boy screamed. "No more treatment for you."

"No I'm not," the other said desperately. "I'm not gonna exit."

"Oh yes you will. You're out of points and you're exiting. Game's over, and I win."

They stood up and began pushing one another. The child with the tubing attached to his neck began to cry. Their mothers ran toward them. "Stop it! Behave yourselves! It's only a game!" one of the parents shouted.

"Only a game," Laura repeated knowingly to Tom.

"Who knows," Tom said, "if all goes well, maybe I'll be teaching in another medical school. I'll train doctors to care for people again. I'll teach a kind of medicine that isn't so certain it has all the answers." He smiled. "Maybe I'll even start a medical school. Can you imagine a school named the Sullivan University School of Medicine?"

Laura looked at him admiringly. "You know, you might just do that."

"Of course I'll need a Director of Biomedical Informatics," he said and smiled.

Laura's expression showed her satisfaction, "I think I'll have to get to know you better first," she said.

"Are you sure you're up for this little routine today?" Tom asked.

"I'm sure," she answered. "You, Bob, and I have turned out to be quite a combination. If this doesn't do the job, nothing will."

People continued to stream along the walkway toward the Green. Tom looked up and saw Bob Kaplan walking toward them.

"Happy Graduation Day," Kaplan said when he reached them. He glanced at Laura, beamed, and then looked back at Tom.

"Today's program may just turn out to be another one of those giant leaps," Bob said.

"Another giant leap backward?" Tom asked.

"Not a chance," Kaplan said. "Forward, ever forward."

Kaplan glanced toward the Green. "You can see the monster all the way from here." He pointed off into the distance through the trees toward the huge, gray, steel and concrete slab structure of the screen that towered over a wide expanse of grass.

"Yes," Laura said, "It's one of CelestaCare's most expensive projects. It's a state-of-the-art structure. The display allows for slide and digital video presentations at any time of day — even in bright sunlight. They say they'll use it for consumer education."

"Can you imagine what NHA propaganda will look like projected two hundred feet wide and one hundred feet tall?" Kaplan queried. "It's opera on the grandest scale. It's opera with a massive digital backdrop, with an outstanding cast here for the opening. It even stars Alexander Wade." Bob handed Tom a plastic compact disk jewel box. "Here's the CD I promised you. Enjoy it. It's a beautiful recording."

Tom read the title. "Thanks," he said. "Fauré's *Requiem* is one of my favorites. Will you hold on to this for me Laura?"

She took the disk and put it in her purse.

Kaplan turned to leave, then stopped. "Oh Tom, the word is that Cunningham thinks that you'll keep trying to put forth your explanation of the marasmus syndrome. He's not happy with you."

"If only Strasberg hadn't died. What a fine man he was," Tom said.

"Leo Strasberg's death was a fortuitous happening for CelestaCare and the NHA. They ruled it a T-effect exit. But we know about those kinds of things now," Kaplan said.

"We should all be careful," Tom said.

Kaplan looked downward. "Yeah, poor Peter Hansen. He got it too."

"I'll miss them," Tom commented sadly.

"Bob, don't take any chances," Laura said.

"For the moment, I'm in the clear. They think I'm this zany guy who makes bizarre sociopolitical videos of charming women for kicks, a harmless fellow, possibly gone mad." He put his fingers in the corners of his mouth and contorted his face into a "mask of comedy."

"Still, be careful," Laura said.

"Sure you two won't join me on my walk?"

"No, we need some time to plan our exit from this opera," Tom said winking at him. "It may be nearing the curtain."

"Okay you two, but dark tombs, firing squads, stabbings, and deaths from tuberculosis are off limits. Okay?"

"It's a deal," Laura said, amused.

Bob tipped his fingers off his forehead, then turned and walked away.

The crowd grew larger: more faculty, more parents, more wives and husbands, more lilac academic gowns. Laura and Tom watched as Kaplan blended in their ranks and joined the promenade.

Chapter 52

When Tom and Laura arrived at the Green, they paused at its edge, and looked out across the hundred rows of lilac-colored cloth-draped chairs set up on the grass in front of the raised stage. Behind the stage, the giant display screen rose toward the sky. They walked toward the projection center alongside the rows.

"I'll sit here and wait," Tom said, taking an end aisle seat halfway down.

"Fine," Laura said. "I'll check out the projection center."

A few moments later, Laura reached a small, grass clearing in front of the stage. She stopped briefly and eyed the concrete projection center area underneath the ledge of the stage. Tucked away on the side of the building was the entrance to the bunker-like structure. She approached the door and pushed the call button to gain entrance.

"Yes?" a voice answered from inside the projection center.

"It's Dr. Laura Clark."

For a moment there was silence. Laura knew she was being studied through the narrow, glass portal in the door.

Soon, the electronic lock clicked. "Come on in, Dr. Clark," the operator said, swinging open the heavy, steel door. "It's kind of you to offer to be with me during the first run of the equipment. I'm a little anxious since the program is being televised and beamed across the nation."

"I wouldn't miss it, Burt. A lot of work went into this project. I feel good to have had a part in designing it."

"You should be proud of your work," the man said.

"I am," Laura said. "Health care consumers must be educated."

The man smiled. Over the pocket of his lilac-colored knit shirt was a CelestaCare emblem. Below it, "Burton Willoughby, M.D." was embroidered with dark purple thread. The initials "M.D." had come to be the abbreviation for "Media Director."

Laura walked back to the thick, metal door and looked through the narrow slit of glass window.

"Can't see much through that," the operator said. "But the outside cameras give you a view of any part of the festivities you're interested in."

Ten monitors topped the console, displaying scenes from ten cameras aimed at the stage and the audience outside on the Green. Willoughby demonstrated the zoom control to show Laura how they could view a wide field or move in for a close-up view.

"Have you seen the documentary?" Willoughby asked.

"No."

"It's spectacular. Director Wade refers to the moon walk in his introduction, you know. In fact, there's even a short clip of the famous 'first step' scene right after his first few sentences. I understand that Ms. Weeks used the clip because of the blast-off to Mars that's scheduled for next month."

"That's a perfect choice," Laura said. "The audience will get a real kick out of that."

She studied the monitors. Outside, the crowd was gathering and the seats rapidly filling with people attending the graduation exercises. People poured through the pathways interspersed between the rows of antique, lilac trees that circled the Green. Before Laura entered the control booth, she had smelled the unusually fragrant odor that characterized the Devan campus at this time of year.

Even inside the control booth, the perfume of the flowers was pungent. It reminded Laura of what was said to be Devan's original reason for planting the lilac shrubs. Perhaps they thought the fragrance could even mask the smell of Destrudo, she speculated, reflecting on the NHA's choice of lilac as its official flower and color. She watched as Burton Willoughby fine-tuned the controls on the projection console. "How long?" she asked.

He glanced over at the count-down clock, then back at the monitors. "Procession begins in six minutes sharp."

The students and dignitaries congregated for the processional at the rear of the audience. The parents and families took their seats.

"There's the man," Willoughby said, pointing at the third monitor.

On the monitor Laura saw that Alexander Wade had taken his place at the front of the procession and next to him was Ray Cunningham. Fisher, Clark, and several other dignitaries were also in line waiting to come forward.

"Isn't that Oliver Sellers standing on Wade's left?" Laura asked.

"The one and only," Willoughby said. "He made a special visit to Devan for the graduation exercises. Look at the staff he's carrying. It looks like a St Anthony's Cross. Amazing!"

"Yes, but I've been told that the symbol is simply a 'T' for Theotechnicist," Laura commented.

"Hmmm," Willoughby murmured. "I guess that's a possibility."

The count-down clock ran to zero. The synthesizer began playing "God Bless America." Stu Sizemore, dressed in a lilac-colored tuxedo, bow tie, and cummerbund, came to the microphone on stage and spoke. He even wore a sprig of lilac plume in his lapel. "Welcome everyone, to the Devan University Health Care Manager graduation exercises — celebrating over one hundred and fifty years of unsurpassed, perfected excellence."

The crowd rose, eyes turned toward the rear, and the procession began. Wade, Cunningham, and Sellers came down the aisle first and took their places next to each other on the stage. Wade's bodyguard, Victor Brandt, surveyed the crowd from behind the NHA Director. The parade of faculty and students came down the side aisles and proceeded up the stairs to the stage taking their places in the rows of chairs in front of the backdrop of Devan flags arranged behind them.

When the music stopped, Sizemore sat down first, followed by the students and faculty.

Cunningham walked toward the podium, briefly surveyed the crowd, then spoke. "Esteemed visitors, family, faculty, and soon to be managers. Today, we are blessed to have a very famous manager with us. He is the beloved father of Theotechnicism and he will offer our opening prayer. I give you Manager Oliver Sellers and his lovely wife, Elizabeth."

The crowd cheered and whistled. Oliver and Elizabeth Sellers came forward and asked that the audience bow their heads.

Sellers prayed:

> We thank you God for giving me your holy revelation in the magnetic resonance imaging machine. We thank you for giving us the National Health Agency to do your work. We thank you for the fragrance of these lovely lilacs that adorn the Devan campus and surround us this day. We thank you for the founder of this university, your worker Paul Devan, for surely he would have been a supporter of the Theotechnicist movement and its blessed work. We thank you for our health care system, for those that run it, and for the holy work it does. God bless every one of these new managers and show them the way to conduct their deserving consumers to the life eternal. God bless the deserving. Amen.

Elizabeth Sellers stood next to him during the prayer, holding a copy of the Theotechnicist bible in her right hand.

After the prayer, the crowd settled back into their seats and Cunningham returned to the podium. The class leaders were introduced and the commencement day awards presented. Cunningham made special note of Carl Hammerstone's death.

"We are pleased at this time to be able to honor one of Devan's most outstanding faculty members," he said. "This esteemed colleague exited recently under the most unfortunate circumstances. We now honor his memory and dedicate today's exercises to him. He was a person who gave immeasurably to health care and to Devan and we will all miss him."

Tom was seated fifty rows back from the stage. He glanced toward Bob Kaplan who was sitting on an aisle about ten rows away. Bob was shaking his head. Tom's face flushed.

Cunningham then introduced Alexander Wade. He announced that Devan University was to confer an honorary degree upon him on this special day, and Wade came forward.

With Wade standing beside him, the Vice Chancellor read the text accompanying the kudos:

Alexander P. Wade, graduate of Devan Health Care Center, leader in matters of health care, administrator, and most eminent manager, you have brought to the people of this country the highest standard of health care ever known to civilized man. Out of the ashes of our antiquated system of medicine, you have caused a phoenix to rise. You have created a system that protects and mandates the highest forms of equitable health care for every citizen of this nation. In awarding this degree, Devan University School of Health Care recognizes your humanitarian contributions to the well-being of humankind. I am certain that the founder of this great health care center, Paul Devan, smiles down upon us from his place in the eternal life. We award you the Honorary Degree of Doctorate of Health Care Finance.

Cunningham placed the regal, purple velvet hood over Wade's head and arranged it on his shoulders. The hooding brought explosive applause and the people in the audience rose to their feet to give the Director a standing ovation.

Wade accepted his degree and followed his acceptance with a brief statement to the graduates.

"The government is entirely behind you in your efforts," he said. "We have, at last, built an economically sound health care system. Today, on this new, giant screen behind me, you will see the story of its creation."

The Director then conferred the degrees of Heath Care Manager on the new managers, while proud parents, spouses, and significant others looked on. After he read their names and handed them their diplomas, Cunningham placed the lilac-colored hood of the Health Care Manager's Degree over each graduate's head. The audience applauded after each new manager received his or her certificate. Some parents wore broad smiles while others blotted their eyes with tissues, tearfully experiencing the happiness of the day.

When the last student had received his degree, Wade sat down. The pride-filled graduates shuffled noisily as they congratulated one another. Murmurs of exhilaration rippled through the crowd. Brimming with joyful expectancy, the audience waited for the finale.

Chapter 53

Inside the control station, Burton Willoughby prepared the console to run the NHA documentary. He glanced at the clock counting down the seconds to the show's beginning. Stu Sizemore stood at the right side of the stage and Raymond Cunningham stood across the way on the left.

Cunningham heralded the beginning: "And now, the moment you have all been waiting for — on our spectacular, new, reality-view screen, in vivid color, the awe-inspiring story of the creation of the National Health Agency."

The audience cheered and broke into wild applause.

Across the wide stage, Sizemore picked up the remarks to give the credits. "Filmed and produced under the direction of Ms. Carole Weeks, Chief of Public Relations of the National Health Agency, Devan University is pleased to present, on its new, computer-driven, giant, digital video display, this spectacular cinematic review." He turned toward Cunningham.

"Let the telling of the story of the creation begin!" Cunningham loudly ordered.

Burton Willoughby watched Cunningham carefully to time the beginning of the film with the introduction. Holding the earphones tightly against his ears, he listened, watched the monitor, and precisely on cue, threw the switch that flashed the huge, three dimensional image of the NHA, plumes-of-lilac logo on the screen.

A collective "*ooooooh*" came up from the audience, like those from crowds watching spectacular fireworks on the Fourth of July.

"It's running. *Wheeeew*," Willoughby said with relief. He pushed his chair back from the console, looked up at the monitor, and folded his hands. "Gorgeous, isn't it, Doctor. You should be very proud of your work."

The credits rose up over a still shot of the NHA logo. Among them was the notation of Laura Clark's development of the computer driven display and a statement of Devan's appreciation of CelestaCare's gift of the giant digital display apparatus to the health care center.

"Look at the size of that image. Isn't that terrific?" Willoughby asked as he glanced toward Laura to see her reaction. She was staring straight at him.

Willoughby waited for an answer, but heard none. He looked at the computer scientist more closely. His smile melted as if he knew something was wrong.

"Well, what do you think Dr. Clark? What do you think?"

Laura, a blank stare in her eyes, was slowly rotating her face clockwise. Her tongue protruded slightly from her mouth, her eyes seemed to wander, and she breathed heavily, making snorting sounds.

"What's wrong?" the operator asked with growing concern.

"I'mmmmm foone," Laura slurred. She began smacking her lips, then her head fell forward as if she had suddenly fallen asleep.

Willoughby watched in terror when suddenly Laura's head jerked back violently and her eyes rolled upward. She clenched her jaw, her neck muscles tightened, and she bared her teeth. Her hands began to shake. She began making vociferous grunting noises.

Startled, the frightened operator pushed his chair back with such great force that it toppled and slid across the floor. "Oh my God!" Willoughby shouted.

Laura's shaking hands curled up at the wrist and her arms extended like straight iron rods. Then, her arms began jerking randomly, then stretched and folded in a more regular rhythm. Suddenly, a massive jerk of her body threw her from her chair and she began to thrash about on the floor.

Willoughby stood paralyzed with fear. Momentarily, he dropped to his knees, loosened Laura's blouse and belt and shook her by the shoulders. Her bizarre movements continued. In her groin area a large wet spot appeared on her dress.

"Geez, an epileptic seizure!" Willoughby said as he prepared to run for help. He glanced at the console to make sure that the NHA program was moving along, and then rushed toward the door. He threw the bar up, then pulled the switch on the automatic latch. The exit lock whirred, and then leaning back to use his weight, he pulled the door open.

Once outside the door, Willoughby dashed toward a security guard standing off to the side of the doorway. Frantically motioning to the guard he pointed toward the entrance to the bunker. "It's CelestaCare's computer expert, Laura Clark. She's had a seizure. Help me, quick," he said, trying not to disrupt the ongoing program.

Together they ran back toward the bunker door.

Inside the bunker, Laura's simulated seizure was over. Tom Sullivan's brief course in faking a seizure was a success. After Willoughby ran through the doorway, she had "seized" a moment longer for effect, then opened her eyes and looked around to be sure that the operator had gone. Seeing Willoughby outside at a distance, she jumped to her feet and rushed toward the heavy, steel door. She pushed with all her strength, but the heavy door barely moved. Laura's quick glance at the hinges showed them to be new, un-oiled, and caked with rust. "Damn," she uttered.

Willoughby and the security guard were now coming within a few yards of the open door when Tom Sullivan jumped to his feet and charged down the aisle. Using the hundred-plus feet of aisle to gain momentum, he moved with all the speed, force, and accuracy of the track star he had been. Then, at precisely the moment the security guard arrived at the bunker entrance, Sullivan drove his shoulder into the guard's side jolting him back away from the door.

Ray Cunningham's and Alex Wade's heads were turned and tilted upward, their eyes looking up at the image on the massive display. But the bodyguard, Brandt, watched Tom's bolt down the aisle and saw him disappear around the side of the building.

"Security check," Brandt ordered into the microphone of his two-way radio. "What the hell is that man doing running down the aisle?" He strained to keep himself from dashing to the side of the stage to peer around the side of the building.

The force of Tom Sullivan's blow threw the guard several feet from the door. When he witnessed the charge, a stunned Burton Willoughby halted and began to back away.

Quickly regaining his balance, Sullivan slipped into the bunker and threw his weight against the door. It slammed shut with a loud clang. He threw the lock switch and pulled the cross bar down into its notch.

The guard stumbled to his feet and regained his composure. He stood outside the door. "Open up. I said open up," he barked loudly. Inside Laura and Tom heard his shoulder bumping against the door with futile thumps and thuds. The heavy, bolted door held fast.

Seconds later, three FBI agents wielding automatic weapons appeared at the doorway to the bunker. They quieted the people sitting nearby, then one of them spoke to Willoughby and the guard. "Shhhh," he said. "For now, let the show go on. We'll get them. There's nowhere they can go but out this door."

Brandt strained to listen to the sounds of the altercation coming over his two-way radio, then to the FBI agent responding to his question. "Reply, security check. Risk contained," the agent reported to Brandt. "Sullivan and Clark under guard. No imminent danger."

Inside, Tom was leaning against the door catching his breath.

Laura spoke. "Are you okay?"

"Fine," Sullivan said, massaging his bruised shoulder.

"Guess we've got ourselves safely locked in here for the moment, right?"

"Guess so," he said.

"Let's run Kaplan's disk. It's time for the requiem for the NHA."

"Fantastic idea!" Sullivan said.

Laura rushed back to the console, reached into her purse, and took out the Fauré's *Requiem* compact disk case that Bob had given Tom. She opened the case, removed a digital video disk, and placed it in the secondary drive. Feeling safe, she stood back calmly, watched the monitors, and waited.

The NHA disk ran on. A breathtakingly mammoth view of an American flag waving in the wind filled the screen. The audience cheered.

The picture then faded into a full face frame of Alexander Wade, then cut away to a scene of Wade behind his desk in the Agency

Office. Soon Wade's sound track narration of the story of the creation of the NHA began:

> Two years ago, we would not have guessed that we would be able to come this far with our plans. Two years ago, American health care was in shambles. Now, we are able to provide services for all Americans. We have a Universal Health Plan in place. Like those men who walked on the moon, and those who will walk on Mars, we have indeed made a giant leap forward.

The audience applauded. The scene from the first moon landing appeared on the screen. Lumbering along on the dusty surface of the far away natural satellite of Earth, the astronaut was taking one giant step forward for man. Laura located the reverse switch and pushed it to the 'on' position.

"Here goes," she said.

Tom watched the monitors.

Immediately, on the giant screen, the moon walker began to walk backwards. The crowd roared with laughter. Laura and Tom exchanged a smile. It was the "giant step backwards" that Kaplan always made reference to. This little touch was for him.

Laura found the switch for the drive that ran the NHA disk. She quickly turned the drive off and simultaneously turned on the one to play Kaplan's disk.

Suddenly the deafening booms of massive explosions reverberated over the speakers.

Cunningham jumped to his feet. "What the hell is going on?" he cried out, putting his hands over his ears to block out the thunderous bass sounds that pounded his eardrums.

"It's Tom Sullivan and Laura Clark. They've taken over the projection booth," Brandt told Wade and Cunningham. "But don't worry. The FBI has them trapped in there."

A picture of the hydrogen bomb explosion mushroomed on the screen with the title, "THE DESTRUDO DIRECTION – BRINGING DEATH TO HEALTH CARE," as an overlay. When the scene changed to a picture of hundreds of dead bodies laid out for burial after the nuclear bombing of Hiroshima, the enigmatic title remained on the screen.

"The what?" people in the audience asked those sitting next to them. "What did that say?" "What's Destrudo?"

Almost immediately, another caption rolled across the picture of the rows of bodies. This one read, "THE NEW HEALTH CARE: THE DELIBERATE DELIVERY OF DESTRUCTION AND DEATH."

A loud pistol shot replaced the hydrogen bomb explosion, when the horrifying picture of the summary execution of a Vietnamese soldier in the streets of Saigon filled the screen. The immense size of the image made the horrified wince of the dying man and the spattering of blood even more terrifying. The audience was stunned.

Kaplan's narration of his video boomed over the speakers, covering the Green with the truth. "Throughout history there have been times when Destrudo, the force of destruction, takes over. When this happens, life comes to this..."

Scenes from the Nazi concentration camps in World War II flashed on the giant screen. Corpse-like, wasted victims. Pictures of the ovens, smoke curling up from the chimneys above them. "Here, millions died," Kaplan said. Next on the screen, the audience saw Russian tanks rumbling into Parliament Square in Budapest in 1956. The tanks and soldiers fired indiscriminately into the crowds of unarmed people. "Many were killed that day," Kaplan said. "But when the revolution was over, thousands of people were dead.

Then the display filled with a picture of the faithful followers of Reverend Jim Jones in Guyana after he convinced them to drink a fruit drink laced with a fatal poison. "Nine hundred and fourteen dead." That scene was followed by pictures of columns of tanks roaring down toward protesting citizens in Tiananmen Square in Beijing. "Hundreds, perhaps thousands, died in the pandemonium," the voice of Bob Kaplan said. A shot of the wreckage of terrorist downed Pan Am Flight 103 in Lockerbie, Scotland flashed on the giant, liquid, crystal surface. "Two hundred and seventy dead." Scenes of the Oklahoma City bombing disaster followed. A Federal Court building in shambles. "One hundred and sixty-eight dead."

Scenes of other atrocities and horrors followed: Bosnia, rape and death in the name of ethnic cleansing; the Columbine High School shootings; suicide bombings in the Middle East; and, finally, hijacked planes crashing into the World Trade Center and the toppling of the two skyscrapers — near three thousand dead.

"This is Destrudo, the force of Destructiveness," the voice of Kaplan said.

The scene changed to a news clip showing the removal of bodies from the automated unit accident at Ritter Park Hospital in Houston. On the sound track, Bob Kaplan's voice picked up the narration. "Only a few people died in Houston. Only a few people, the NHA said. Only seventy-eight. And after all, they were all over seventy years old, so how could you hold a little mistake like that against the National Health Agency or CelestaCare? It was only a side effect — just a little T-effect problem. And only seventy-eight people died."

From inside the projection booth, Laura zoomed in with an outside camera to take a closer look at Cunningham and Wade. When Wade momentarily turned his head back from looking up at the crystal screen to look at the audience, she could see that even his expression was pained. The ever composed Director was quickly becoming undone.

Chapter 54

On the screen, the audience saw weeping, grief-torn survivors watching the removal of the bodies of their loved ones from CelestaCare Ritter Park Hospital in Houston. The towering screen with its surrounding sound system powerfully conveyed the painful horror of the moment. The stirring notes of *Mars, the Bringer of War* from Holst's *The Planets* lent background music for the wails of sorrow and cries of disbelief coming from the mourners.

There was a sequence from an old newsreel from the 1940s. It showed a stooped, weary man standing on a street corner in Washington with the nation's Capitol in the background. "This man says the Nazis are committing mass murder and no one will believe him," the newscaster was saying. From the newsreel archives, Kaplan had resurrected an old film of Leo Strasberg's father struggling, without success, to convince the nation of the magnitude of Nazi atrocities. "It's no use," the elder Strasberg finally acknowledged to the filmmaker interviewing him on the street. "Sick pretense forbids recognition of the truth."

Kaplan's narration continued, "People pretended that there were no concentration camps. It was massive deception. We must never let deception of that magnitude occur again. No government, no ideology or religion, no use of media or technology should ever blind us to the reality of Destrudo."

A scene from the acute marasmus syndrome conference in the historic amphitheater at Devan flashed on the screen. It was the sequence Kaplan himself had filmed. Wade was speaking to Carole

Weeks shortly after his arrival in the hall. Kaplan's eavesdropping microphone captured their dialogue. "This is it, Ms. Weeks," Wade told her calmly, "your moment of triumph. You are living proof that the media can convince people of anything. If you can't negate Hammerstone's findings and convince them that the marasmus syndrome is unrelated to the automated systems, nobody can." The woman in the lilac-colored dress in the film clip nodded in agreement.

Carole Weeks, sitting in the sixth row at the graduation, had come to see her own production on the giant screen. She sat up and leaned forward. On her face was a faint appreciative smile.

On the giant display, Cunningham made the pronouncement that the marasmus syndrome was unrelated to the machines. "Yes, it has become clear that we are dealing with a brain chemical rearrangement of the most vicious variety — completely unrelated to our lifesaving automated system of care," he said in another scene Kaplan had recorded at the conference.

A shot of a child, alone and isolated in an automated unit cubicle, followed. Still, silent, emaciated, gaunt-faced, and hollow-eyed, he was slowly dying from system-related starvation. The camera zoomed in on the plastic central line coming from his neck. Busy health care workers hurried up and down the hallway, ignoring the little boy as he lay suffering alone.

The scenes of the child with the wasting syndrome were immediately followed by a sequence of an interview with Carl Hammerstone. His hand was on the shoulder of another child who had recovered from the syndrome after being removed from the sterile atmosphere of the hospital. Hammerstone spoke of the importance of human contact in the healing process. He told how contact with caring people had overcome the death-like barren treatment conditions.

Then, a still picture of Mary Adkins with the caption, "Victim of the Acute Marasmus Syndrome" flashed across the vast screen. First there was the photograph of her on the beach in her bikini, and then the picture of her that had been taken shortly before her death. In the second picture, her ninety-three pound wasted body and the hollow stare of her eyes showed a sickening contrast with her condition at the beach. She looked to be a victim of prolonged starvation.

Next, in a sequence that lasted less than a minute and a half, Leo Strasberg spoke. A close-up of the aging Strasberg, shot from an angle that showed his most powerful features, filled the immense screen with his authoritarian presence. The attentive audience watched the close-up of the old man's eyes as they beamed the full power of his sincerity, his wisdom, and his humanitarian concern. He held a picture of the emaciated Mary Adkins in his hand, and eloquently explained his formulation of the cause of acute marasmus, using words that seemed to spring out from the screen with clarity:

The syndrome stems from isolation, from separation, from interpersonal loss, from grief. It is as if the child that is a part of each of us is left alone and abandoned. There is renewal of the recent epidemic's threat of death, a resurgence of primitive fear and insecurity related to the threat of harm. Then, being seen as less than human, we grow lifeless and die, fulfilling the destiny that has been chosen by some unknown destructive adversary. A world too long void of people drives us to surrender and give up our last breath.

I have no doubt that this woman's wasting was due to her isolation. She was abandoned in the deadly, machine-like atmosphere of the hospital. The technology removed caring people from her side. She lost her sense of life through the enforced loss of relationships. She was a casualty of the force of Destrudo.

People must care for people, for a true caring process affirms us as alive. When those who care for the ill cease to treat them as living human beings, you may be sure that death will soon come. When the face of the other is no longer attended, death will ensue. This is the Destrudo Direction, the path of death.

Carole Weeks watched the production with great interest. Without question, Kaplan had studied her techniques in depth. She knew that he was using methods that he had learned from her to attack what she herself had done. Kaplan, the filmmaker, had been successful in finding the right combination of symbols — the core scenes that would connect each sequence with the unconscious knowledge of those acts of horror within each person in the audience. He had ferreted out archetypal symbols of the destructiveness of humankind, symbols that would reverberate through the souls of all those who watched his film clips projected on the huge screen.

Suddenly another sequence exploded on the giant display surface: one shot after another, rapidly flashing on the screen. Dozens of pictures of gaunt faces and wasted bodies, a full three minutes of gruesome images of people lying in the automated care cubicles, stricken with the wasting of the acute marasmus syndrome.

Scattered gasps of shock sounded over the Green as the audience viewed the sequence. Many in the crowd could not watch and covered their eyes.

"*This* is the power of Destrudo!" Kaplan's voice boomed over the sounds of the audience.

Kaplan closely watched the people sitting near him. He studied their pained faces. The intensity of their reactions demonstrated the success of his work. People leaned forward in their chairs, their hands placed over their mouths with gasps of horror. He saw others with frightened eyes and contorted faces. In almost everyone's expression, he could feel enraged antipathy and disgust toward what they had seen.

Kaplan leaned back. He was content that the showing of the film was his finest hour, the culmination of his creative effort. He was confident that his arrow had hit its mark. The work of art on the screen was the summation of his rebellion against injustice and his devotion to the persistence of ethics in medicine. The film stood as a monument of his admiration for physicians like Tom Sullivan, Carl Hammerstone, and Leo Strasberg. He breathed a deep sigh of satisfaction and felt pride in knowing that he had done as he had promised Doctor Strasberg he would do.

The secret of the T-effect exits came next in the video. Kaplan showed how people seemed to be getting well and were then murdered by those in charge of the system. Using the same mannequin setting Laura had used, Kaplan brilliantly demonstrated how the fake cardiac arrest could deceptively be layered over the actual clinical happenings for a given patient. Then he ran a composite picture of some forty persons who had been murdered in the system. Each, in some way, was identified as being involved in activities opposing the NHA or the Theotechnicist movement. Tom noted that pictures of Katie, Peter Hansen, and Leo Strasberg were included in the group of people targeted for murder by the NHA.

There was more, and when it began the crowd became quiet and still. In the documentary's final sequence, Kaplan revealed the truth about what had happened to Ross Mandell. Narrating the video he himself had made when Mandell was in the hospital, he showed how the Senator had been murdered while the monitors ran a cover-up program.

The night of the Senator's death, Kaplan had violated regulations and gone toward Mandell's single VIP room to speak with him only to find NHA agents removing his murdered corpse. While Kaplan video recorded the macabre scene from a dark, shadowed corner down the hospital corridor with his Shinakawa camera, a Mandell look-alike entered the hospital room, climbed into the Senator's bed and was hooked to the central line. The NHA videographers were preparing to produce the fake death scene that was to become Ken Clark's most famous "death video."

"Holy shit," Wade said to Cunningham. "This film has punch, real punch. How the hell are we going to handle this?"

Cunningham turned to Brandt. "Get those people out of the bunker. And get Kaplan too. All three of them. I want them arrested right now."

"You want them carried out in front of all these people? You'll make heroes out of them," Brandt told him.

"Heroes or not, I want them under arrest and out. I'm in charge at this university. Now get with it!"

Uncharacteristically unnerved and stunned, Wade contributed his go-ahead nod, and Brandt complied with the order.

Brandt was down the stairs and outside the control station door in a flash. "Arrest those people," he said to the FBI agents. "By order of the Director of the NHA."

"Relax," one of the agents said. "we'll take care of them."

Brandt tried to open the thick, steel door himself. It wouldn't budge. Looking in through the slit of a window, he could see Laura at the controls.

Tom realized that someone was trying to force the door open. He looked out through the glass slit and his eyes met Brandt's.

"Open the damned door. There's no way you can get away," Brandt yelled. "Open this damned door. Your show is over!"

"Sure," Tom said calmly. He flipped the lock switch and shoved the large bolt of the door upward.

"Okay, we'll take it from here," the FBI agent said, flashing his badge and identification to Brandt. Another agent brought Kaplan over to join Laura and Tom. Brandt stepped back.

"This is treason you know," the agent in charge told the three.

Brandt smiled. "Damned right," he said. "What about the cuffs?"

"Later," the agent in charge said. "We don't need to provoke this crowd."

As the three walked though the crowd with the armed agents behind them, Kaplan held his clasped hands victoriously above his head. The crowd cheered. Members of the media rushed toward the filmmaker with their microphones and cameras.

"No comments from these people," one of the agents said. "We need to protect their rights."

"It's free speech, man, first amendment," Kaplan said and turned toward the reporters.

"It's all in the film, the whole story," Kaplan said. The reporters were recording his every word on camera. "Watch it closely and you'll see. It's been one giant leap backwards for medicine, but we hope we can turn it back the other way."

Carole Weeks pushed her way through the crowd of reporters and stepped in front of Kaplan. She was breathless. "Your work, Robert Kaplan, your work was…," she paused and gave him a two thumbs up sign, "fantastic!"

"Thanks, Ms. Weeks. That's a real compliment coming from you," he said shaking her hand. "You're a real artist."

Carole Weeks blushed.

"That's enough," the FBI agent in charge said. "Move on."

"I think so," Kaplan said quietly. "I think so. Yes, I think that'll do it."

The agents led Laura, Tom, and Bob off to a security van and shoved them inside. After the FBI agents climbed inside, the lilac-colored van pulled away.

Chapter 55

"Okay, where's your car parked, Manager?" the FBI agent asked Tom.

"Four blocks away. Down this street three blocks, then take a left," Tom told him.

When they arrived at Tom's Cherokee, the agent in charge turned and spoke. "Manager Sullivan, you people had better get out of Middleside as soon as you can. It'll take us a while to round up the suspects and complete our investigation."

Laura was bewildered. "Wait a minute. We're not under arrest?"

The agent shook his head.

"We had better do what they say, Laura," Tom told her. "I'll fill you in as we go."

"Tom, why are they letting us go?"

"They know we're the good guys," Tom replied.

"I don't understand."

"Trust me," Tom told her. "You'll need to pack some clothes to bring with you. We're leaving today. Now."

"Now?" she asked.

Tom turned to Bob Kaplan. "What about you, Bob; are you coming with us?" he asked.

"No, I'll hide out in Middleside, wait for this all to unfold, let it cool down a bit, then make my way back into the scene. We'll be in touch. Maybe someday I can be on the faculty of that medical school you're always talking about starting."

"A full professor with tenure," Tom said, shaking Bob's hand.

Minutes later, Tom parked his car in front of Laura's house.

"I don't understand what's happening," she said.

"Not yet, Laura. It's a complicated story. Go ahead and get your things. Please trust me."

She paused for a moment in thought, then reached for the door release. "I won't be long," she said as she got out of the car. "Are you coming in?"

"No, I want to wait here."

She went inside.

A few minutes later, Ken Clark pulled into the driveway in his black Mercedes. Tom watched as he got out of the car and headed toward the house. He stopped, almost too casually, to pick up the just delivered afternoon newspaper. He looked toward Tom's car, then directly at the manager, and, treating him as if he were invisible, turned and walked into the house.

"Laura, Laura," Ken called out, tossing the unopened newspaper on the couch.

She did not answer.

He walked into the bedroom. She was laying a few dresses and outfits in a travel bag and filling a small duffel.

"You're leaving, aren't you Laura?"

"That's right."

"I know you had to do what you did today and I know you're not going to believe this, but I wish you wouldn't go."

She stopped her packing and looked up. She thought she detected something new in Ken's statement, perhaps human feeling. It made her think of long ago, when she truly thought he had feelings for the well-being of others and had chosen him as a mate.

"Yes, I want you to stay," he continued, "to help undo the damage that was done today. You people have stirred up some real serious trouble. But I believe I can get you clemency. We'll have to find a way to discredit Kaplan's film. It won't be easy, but I believe we can do it."

"Damage control? That's why you want me to stay? You still believe I would work on that crap that you're so busy selling."

"Why not?" he asked. "Alex Wade wants me in Washington. He says I have far too much talent to waste here. I won't be in

Middleside, but you could go on working with the computer programs, refining them, making them better and better."

"Oh, sure!"

"You have a duty to God and your country you know." He fingered the Theotechnicist "T" hanging around his neck. "Theotechnicism is the only hope for humankind. Eternal life for the deserving. Alexander Wade is a prophet."

"You're over the edge," Laura said. She turned from him and began packing again.

"I have plans for a new computer program, one that we can play on the room monitors to provide a kind of entertainment that will substitute for the presence of people. We can create an artificial interpersonal environment. Can you imagine? Software that simulates caring people. Perhaps some kind of animation that's interactive like an old style doctor or nurse. That would certainly be cheaper than people. And Taylor Blaine says it might even prevent acute marasmus. He's with us all the way. Digital Video Care we could call it. Now that's a challenge for you, isn't it?"

Laura shook her head in disbelief as she listened.

"There's no reason for it not to work. It would be very cost-effective. You could stay and do the programs. You are still the best, you know. You have the most innovative ideas, Laura. Why this is really your system, your baby."

She stopped packing and looked at him. He had grown older in the past year. He seemed shorter, more stooped over, and his voice was smaller. He was another time in her life, a time that had passed. "I'm leaving now, Ken. I've heard enough and had enough. You'll have to build your health care utopia by yourself, without me."

"Why are you so angry?" he asked.

"It's really sad, and you don't even know it," she said, glaring at him. "That's the saddest part. If you could keep this mayhem going, someday, someone in your screwed-up system will decide that you should be on the central line. Someone will decide that it's time for you to exit, T-effect style. Maybe you'll run out of points or maybe they won't like your particular brand of Theotechnicism. Maybe they won't like your smile or the way you look at someone. They'll get a reading for extending your point allowance and it won't compute.

You'd be one more piece of flesh in the way. They'll run right over you."

"We must have faith in the technology. Oliver Sellers has been told that it will insure the future of humankind. We must have faith."

She picked up her duffle and the travel bag. "Goodbye, Ken. Stay well. I'm off to another place and I really don't care if I ever see you again."

His expression did not change. He said nothing.

She felt him watching her as she walked through the door and out to Tom's car. She chose not to look back. For a fleeting moment, she wondered what he might be feeling in response to what she had said, and then she concluded that it was just as well that she didn't know. He probably had no feelings at all.

Laura opened the back door of the car. She threw in her travel bag and duffle, then got in the front seat and pulled the door shut.

She looked over at Tom, breathed a sigh, and smiled broadly.

"Tell him goodbye?"

"Long ago. I did that a long time ago. I'm ready to get out of here," she said, putting on her seatbelt.

"Then let's go," he said and started the car. "I have one stop to make. It won't take me long."

"Where's that?" Laura asked.

"Flint's. Flint's Books and Magazines. I want to pick up an afternoon paper."

"Ken just brought ours in. It was on the couch."

"Had he read it?"

"No, it wasn't opened. Why?"

"Ken's surprises are far from over."

As they drove off, a police car, with it's red and blue lights blinking, came down the street toward the Clark house.

Tom was in and out of Flint's in less than a minute. Before he got back in the car, he stood tall and looked nostalgically for a few moments at the old building and then across the street at the Devan Campus. In the distance, he could see a section of the new, giant screen rising above the buildings and trees. He breathed in deeply and smelled the lilacs. What a wonderful fragrance, he thought. Then he opened the door, got into the car, and handed the newspaper to Laura.

She looked at the headlines. Her eyes widened. "Good Lord! What is this, Tom Sullivan? Have you been working behind my back?"

"Had to. If our plans fell through, I didn't want you implicated. Showing Kaplan's video was bad enough, but accusations like this — that's another ball game." He started the car and drove off.

"How long has this news been out?" Laura asked.

"The newspapers just hit the stands. The media specials probably came on radio and television about the same time. Well, what does it say? Read it. I haven't seen it in print."

The headlines read, "HEALTH CARE CONSPIRACY UN-COVERED."

"Thank God! It's over," Tom said.

Laura read on:

Devan University Health Care Center's eminent epidemiologist, Manager Peter Hansen recently died of a so-called 'T-effect exit' at Devan Hospital. Before he died, however, he sent his files with the results of his studies on the patterns of spread of the deadly epidemic of two years ago to a close friend and colleague in infectious disease, Manager Richard Dupont of Carville, Louisiana. Manager Hansen's studies confirmed his early suspicions that the epidemic was spread intentionally. The bacteria, Hansen conclusively proved, was the same microbe maintained in pure cultures at the U.S. Army storage center for use in bacterial warfare. Rendered highly resistant to antibiotics by the introduction of a genetic particle of DNA known as a plastid, the bacteria was responsible for causing what was at first an untreatable disease.

Over two million people died prior to Dr. Laura Clark's discovery of the lifesaving antibiotic, Lilacicin. It appears that the bacteria were distributed by a messenger flying in various disguises to large cities around the country under the guise of delivering organs for transplantation to CelestaCare hospitals.

"Tom, this is unbelievable."

"It's big time Destrudo. The horrible truth is that Ken, Wade, and Cunningham have worked together for a long time. They're responsible for the deaths of millions of people," Tom said. "Ken and Wade procured the bacteria through Ken's old army connections and Ken worked out the final plan to spread the disease. They did it to propel their plan forward. The cornerstones in their plan were crashing the health care industry finances and instituting PointCure. Wade has always been a self-righteous, closeted, religious fanatic and Sellers' theology was a perfect fit with his health-care-for-the-deserving project. You were interested in better health care, but Wade immediately saw your automated care delivery system as an ideal matrix to play out his scheme. Ken had you do the videos of death scenes to see if they could be used to build in an effective, convincing disposal system for the opposition. Acute marasmus was a surprise. But they were determined to keep the automated units going, regardless."

"And still are. When we were at my house, Ken was still talking about improving the automated systems. He talked about a program to simulate interpersonal relationships. Bob's film had no impact on him. It was simply something to discredit."

"Ken will be in federal custody soon. There were about fifty people involved in the original plan. Even Oliver Sellers was linked. Every one of them will go to prison or worse."

"I wish I could feel sorry for Ken, but I can't," she said, laying the newspaper in her lap.

"He's a sick man," Tom said, "but a very dangerous one."

"How long have you known about all this?" Laura asked.

"Only three days. Peter Hansen talked with Bob and Bob tipped me off. I set up a time to talk with Peter. Peter was ill when we were scheduled to meet, but managed to give me a clue. Then I called his friend in Louisiana. It's a very long story. I'll tell you everything..."

She interrupted. "No wait, this is all happening too fast. Slow down."

"Then, when you're ready, I'll fill in the details."

"Just one question. Who was the unknown messenger that spread the bacteria?" Laura asked. "The person would have had to work closely with Ken. Does anyone know who it was?"

"Peter told Richard Dupont that it was Jeanne Donnely, the very person assigned to keep tabs on me and report on my activities. It took Peter a long time to track her movement, but she was identified in at least ten cities in a period of two or three days before the epidemic. She was trained in the military to handle these bacterial cultures, and if necessary, to release them. To make the epidemic begin on schedule, she used a set of timed-release capsules filled with the bacteria.

CelestaCare even knew that one of the Lilacicin-like antibiotics you designed long before the epidemic began would protect against the bacteria if you took it early enough. But they kept that under wraps too, except to protect themselves. And Jeanne carried the timed-release pods of bacteria and deposited them in hidden places all over the country. She carried them in small, cooler boxes like donor kidneys and hearts."

Laura shook her head. "But why? Why would anyone want to kill so many innocent people?"

"Destrudo, Laura. Like Strasberg said. They wanted power and money and they wanted to use medicine to get it. Carl was right. The plan was well thought out."

"How did you time this so well? First Kaplan's film, the agents, and then the news release."

"I contacted the Attorney General's office and the FBI and gave them the information from Richard Dupont. Dupont had all of Peter Hansen's findings in safe keeping and sent copies to Washington immediately. I told them about our other discoveries. They had also uncovered information that proved it was no accident that CelestaCare got the contract from Wade to install the computerized units across the country. They suspect that Wade is the person who devised the plan to eliminate Mandell. They even believe that the President was targeted as their next high-level T-effect exit.

I gave them our plan to occupy the projection booth and show Kaplan's DVD, and they said they would get us out of there in one piece. They let me time the news release. I faxed the information to Katie's father. It was easier for a small-town, Oklahoma newspaper editor to hold on to it until the authorities could organize and it was time for the release. He put it on the wire the minute the graduation exercises began."

Laura's expression was one of disbelief.

"I think it's time for us to go," Tom said, pulling away from the curb.

"My head is swimming with all the information, but I'll make it," Laura said.

"It has been a long day," Tom said.

Driving toward the interstate, they passed Devan Hospital and then the CelestaCare complex. Cutting near the edge of warehouse row, they saw that the area was still closed off with white and black, crosshatched barricades and yellow, plastic streamers imprinted with the words, "KEEP OUT — CRIME SCENE."

Soldiers with M-16s on their shoulders still stood guard in front of the fire gutted old warehouse building.

Twenty minutes later they were on the outer loop of the interstate, heading west into the afternoon sun. On the right of the interstate, across a field, Laura saw an old drooping, wire mesh fence, part of the enclosure that once surrounded an abandoned waste disposal area used during the epidemic. Beyond the fence, grasses and vines were growing over the piles of remaining rubble and the natural process of reforestation was beginning. Slowly nature's life forces were healing the sores that had infected the hillsides and valleys on the outskirts of Philadelphia.

Laura looked out at the field with its new growth. Funny, she thought, how things come back to you from the past when you need them to explain your world. She remembered her college botany. There was an order to the natural reforestation. First would come the tall, thin grasses and the saw briars with their wide, slick, green leaves. After that, berry canes would grow. Then there would be the cedars, the conifers, and later the hardwoods. Someday there would be a strong, new forest there. It was the way nature worked, she thought: cycling, renewing, recreating, and starting over again.

She felt intimately involved with what she saw. She looked over at Tom. He looked at her for a brief moment and she pointed toward the huge, yellow signs that said: "KEEP OUT — CONTAMINATED SOIL — INFECTIOUS WASTE." The paint on the signs was beginning to peel.

"Someday those signs will come down," she said. "The earth will be pure and clean again. In time, it will all be different; in time, the earth will be renewed and healed."

Tom smiled, nodded in agreement, gently took her hand in his, and looked ahead down the road.

AUTHOR'S NOTE

The reader will note that Tom Sullivan's insights into the acute marasmus syndrome are moved along by the knowledge, influence, and guidance of his medical school professors, physician Carl Hammerstone and physician-psychiatrist Leo Strasberg. In the novel *POINTS,* Tom observes that patients with the acute marasmus syndrome manifest extreme emotional symptoms and physiological responses: severe grief, withdrawal, depression, wasting and even death. These occur in response to their separation and isolation, and in reaction to the interpersonal distancing of their caregivers. In being avoided, abandoned, dehumanized, and starved for human contact and nurturing, patients treated in the CelestaCare automated units internalize the feeling of being interpersonally or socially dead. They deteriorate physically and become susceptible to overwhelming disease.

While the course and descriptions of the emotional and physical states described in *POINTS* are fictional, these happenings are related to a number of similar phenomena which may be found in the medical literature. I wish to acknowledge and credit those relevant concepts and observations found in the works of the authors that follow and to suggest that interested readers look to this body of scientific literature for further detail.

Bowlby J. Processes of mourning. *International Journal of Psychoanalysis* 1961;42:317-340., Bowlby J. The Adolph Meyer Lecture, childhood mourning and its implication for psychiatry. *The American Journal of Psychiatry* 1961;118:481-498., Bowlby J. Pathological mourning and childhood mourning. *Journal American Psychoanalytic Association* 1963;11:500-541., Cannon WB. "Voodoo" death. *Psychosomatic Medicine* 1957;19:182-190., Engel GL, Reichsman F. Spontaneous and experimentally induced depressions in an infant with a gastric fistula, a contribution to the problem of depression. *Journal of the American Psychoanalytic Association* 1956;4:428-451., Engel GL. A life setting conductive to illness, the giving-up – given-up complex. *Bulletin of the Menniger Clinic* 1968;32:355-365., Kastenbaum R: Psychological death, In: *Death and Dying: Current Issues In The Treatment of The Dying Patient.* Pearson L, ed. Cleveland: The Press of Case Western Reserve University, 1969:1-27., Lindemann E. Symptomatology and management of acute grief. *American Journal of Psychiatry* 1944;101:141-148., Spitz R. Anaclitic depression, an inquiry into the genesis of psychiatric conditions in early childhood, II. *The Psychoanalytic Study of the Child* 1946;2:313-342; Sudnow, D: Dying in a public hospital, In: *The Dying Patient*. Brim OG, Freeman HE, Levine S, and Scotch NA, eds. New York: Russell Sage Foundation, 1970:191-208.

I am deeply grateful for the influence all of these authors have had on my own appreciation of the importance of the relational world in the practice of medicine. My book, Barton D, ed. *Dying and Death, A Clinical Guide for Caregivers*, Baltimore: The Williams and Wilkins Company, 1977., may give the reader additional insights into this area.

David Barton

ABOUT THE AUTHOR

David Barton, M.D., is a psychiatrist in private practice in Nashville, Tennessee. He also holds an appointment as a Clinical Professor of Psychiatry at the Vanderbilt University School of Medicine. Dr. Barton was one of the early physicians teaching and working in the area of adaptation to life-threatening illnesses, dying and death. His writings include a book and a number of scientific publications on these subjects. He was a founder of one of the first hospices in this country, Alive Hospice in Nashville. This is his first novel.

Printed in the United States
33292LVS00010B/24

9 781418 440770